The Hall of the Revered lies below
the Spires of the Forge.

Enter the door above the tangled valley.

Look neither left nor right. The riches there are
not for you.

Hold to the path that leads to the Hall and find
what waits in the shade of . . .

THE GRIEVING TREE

The
DRAGON BELOW

Book One
The Binding Stone

Book Two
The Grieving Tree

Book Three
The Killing Song
January 2007

THE GRIEVING TREE

The
DRAGON BELOW
BOOK II

DON BASSINGTHWAITE

THE GRIEVING TREE

The Dragon Below · Book 2

©2006 Wizards of the Coast, Inc.

Cover art by Michael Komarck
Map by Rob Lazzaretti
First Printing: March 2006
Library of Congress Catalog Card Number: 2005928121

9 8 7 6 5 4 3 2 1

ISBN-10: 0-7869-3985-0
ISBN-13: 978-0-7869-3985-5
620- 95467740-001-EN

U.S., CANADA,
ASIA, PACIFIC, & LATIN AMERICA
Wizards of the Coast, Inc.
P.O. Box 707
Renton, WA 98057-0707
+1-800-324-6496

EUROPEAN HEADQUARTERS
Hasbro UK Ltd
Caswell Way
Newport, Gwent NP9 0YH
GREAT BRITAIN
Save this address for your records.

Visit our web site at www.wizards.com

With thanks to Mark for encouragement and to Ole for patience above and beyond the call of duty.

The events of *The Binding Stone*

On the western edge of the Eldeen Reaches, Geth and Adolan rescued Dandra, and brought her to the tiny hamlet of Bull Hollow at the same time as Toller d'Deneith and Singe arrived in the lonely community. Singe and Geth had served together during the Last War in a Blademarks company called the Frostbrand, a company destroyed nine years before, during an infamous massacre at the Karrnathi town of Narath. Once friends, they were now bitter enemies—Geth had been hiding from his past in Bull Hollow while Singe had been hunting for him at every opportunity.

They were forced to put aside their differences, however, when Bull Hollow was attacked by Dandra's pursuers: savage hunters of the Bonetree Clan, followers of the Cult of the Dragon Below, accompanied by four-armed aberrations called dolgrims. In the attack, Bull Hollow was devastated. Toller was slain by Hruucan, a vile dolgaunt who almost killed Singe as well before the wizard drove him off with a blast of magical flame. Adolan was cut down by a Bonetree hunter as he defended Dandra.

Geth, Singe, and Dandra made a break for the wilderness, using Dandra as a lure to draw the Bonetree hunters and the dolgrims away from Bull Hollow so the survivors might have a chance to flee.

In the aftermath of their escape, Dandra revealed why the hunters and the dolgrims pursued her. Although she appeared to be a kalashtar, she was in fact, the spirit of a psicrystal—an intelligent tool created by kalashtar psionic powers—inhabiting her creator's body. The true kalashtar, Tetkashtai, was now trapped in the psi-crystal, their spirits exchanged as part of a terrible experiment by Dah'mir, a charismatic priest of the Dragon Below and the leader of the Bonetree clan. The only survivors of a group of three kalashtar trapped by Dah'mir, Dandra and Tetkashtai had survived because Dandra had found the strength to claim Tetkashtai's crystal during an unguarded moment. Working together to use their psionic powers, Dandra and Tetkashtai had been able to escape and flee.

Knowing that the Bonetree hunters would not give up their pursuit and determined to avenge the deaths of Adolan and Toller, Geth, Singe, and Dandra decided to confront Dah'mir. Pushing hard, they reached the ancient port town of Yrlag in search of passage for the long trip around the coast to Zarash'ak in the Shadow Marches. An elemental galleon of House Lyrandar, *Lightning on Water*, provided speedy transport, but a few days into the voyage, they discovered that Ashi, one of the Bonetree hunters, had managed to catch up to them and board the galleon as well. They captured her, but found that she was in contact with Dah'mir and that the priest now knew their plans. Dandra, however, determined that the crystal headband Ashi had used to contact Dah'mir actually belonged to Medalashana, one of the other kalashtar who had been abducted along with Tetkashtai.

Upon reaching Zarash'ak, the captain of *Lightning on Water*, Vennet d'Lyrandar, revealed himself to be a follower of the Dragon Below as well. Seeking power, he betrayed them and freed Ashi. Geth, Singe, and Dandra were able to escape, but Vennet used another passenger, a half-orc merchant named Natrac, to bait a trap. Unwilling to abandon Natrac, the three attempted to rescue him. Thanks to the unexpected aid of an orc druid, they were almost successful—until Dah'mir arrived, mesmerizing Dandra with his very presence and apparently killing Geth with a spell of disease. Captured by Ashi and wracked by the mental powers of Medalashana—now mad and renamed Medala by Dah'mir—Singe could only watch helplessly as Dah'mir rewarded Vennet and promised to call upon his services again, then commanded his other servants to make preparations for a return to Bonetree territory.

Unknown to both Singe and Dah'mir, though, Geth had

survived. After several days of fevered delirium, he woke in the village of the Fat Tusk orc tribe, rescued along with Natrac by Orshok, the druid who had aided them in the fight against Vennet. To his amazement, Geth discovered that Orshok and his aged teacher Batul were Gatekeepers, the same sect of druids, enemies of the Dragon Below, to which Adolan had belonged. Geth begged for their help to rescue Singe and Dandra, but Batul was reluctant to place the Fat Tusk tribe in conflict with Dah'mir and the dangerous Bonetree clan. To secure the orcs' aid, Geth and Natrac faced the task of proving themselves by passing through Jhegesh Dol, a ghostly fortress from the long-ago Daelkyr War. They survived and emerged from Jhegesh Dol carrying two long-lost artifacts: a Gatekeeper amulet and a sword forged by hobgoblins of the Dhakaani Empire during the ancient War.

With a raiding party of orcs, including Batul and Orshok at his back, Geth raced to intercept Dah'mir, but the priest and his captives reached the heart of Bonetree territory, a great earthen mound, ahead of them. During the journey, Singe discovered that Dah'mir was much older than he appeared and that his experiments with kalashtar were intended to create a new line of servants for the powers of the Dragon Below. Upon reaching the Bonetree mound, he was also confronted by Hruucan, the dolgaunt he had injured in Bull Hollow. Hruucan demanded the chance for a rematch duel with Singe, and Dah'mir granted his request. Singe had, however, struck up a friendship with Ashi, discovering that she actually carried the blood of House Deneith and that she had a deep sense of honor that was unsettled by Dah'mir's activities and the worship of the Dragon Below. As he prepared to fight Hruucan, he appealed to her honor, begging her to use the distraction of the duel to try to rescue Dandra.

Dandra, meanwhile, had been taken into the Bonetree mound and woken by Dah'mir. In the shadow of the device that had exchanged her and Tetkashtai—a construction of brass and crystal with a huge Khyber dragonshard at its heart—Dah'mir's illithid servants and Medala used telepathy to lay bare Dandra's secrets. Dandra learned Medala's secrets as well, though. She had escaped from her crystal prison by using her strength of will to return to her body and murder the spirit of her psicrystal, an act that drove her mad and put her in Dah'mir's power. The third kalashtar, Virikhad, had not had that strength of will and had remained trapped in his psicrystal as his body died.

Dah'mir wanted to conduct further experiments on both Dandra and Tetkashtai, but was furious to find that Tetkashtai's crystal was actually in Geth's possession. Dandra's connection to the crystal showed that Geth wasn't actually dead, however. Already alerted to the orc raiding party by strange black herons that served him, Dah'mir reasoned that Geth was making an attempt to rescue his friends. Leaving Dandra trapped, he and Medala departed to prepare an ambush.

While Singe dueled Hruucan—and was given a severe beating by the dolgaunt's speed and skill—Geth and the orcs attacked the mound, falling into Dah'mir's ambush. The confusion gave Singe the chance he needed to launch a last attack against Hruucan, however. Grappling the dolgaunt so he could not flee and protected by his own magic ring, the wizard cast a fiery spell that immolated Hruucan. Geth and his allies fought clear of their attackers and rallied around Singe, only to find themselves surrounded once more. Dah'mir used the full weight of his dominating presence against Geth, demanding that the shifter give him Tetkashtai's crystal, but Geth resisted with the aid of a collar of black stones, a Gatekeeper artifact that had once belonged to Adolan. Enraged by Geth's resistance and by magical attacks from Batul and Singe, Dah'mir transformed, revealing his true identity as a dragon!

As orc raiders and Bonetree hunters fled, dolgrims turned on enemies and allies alike with new ferocity. Dah'mir took to the air, attacking fleeing raiders with gouts of acidic spit. Knowing they had no individual weapons or spells capable of harming a dragon, Batul proposed a desperate plan to Geth. The Daelkyr War had been won by the combined might of Gatekeeper magic and Dhakaani weapons like the sword Geth had claimed from Jhegesh Dol. The two of them might be able to sacrifice themselves to beat back Dah'mir long enough for the others to escape. Geth agreed, but before they could put the plan into action, Medala attacked them all with her formidable psionic powers.

Dandra, however, had been freed from Dah'mir's laboratory by Ashi. Unable to access her own powers fully without Tetkashtai's aid and threatened by the devastating fascination Dah'mir wielded over kalashtar, she was forced into a desperate plan. Acting swiftly, she caught Medala by surprise and put Virikhad's psicrystal into her hand. The imprisoned and thoroughly insane spirit was unleashed on Medala and she was destroyed in a burst of silvery light. Freed from Medala's influence, Batul and Geth made their move. Batul invoked nature's own fury in a punishing storm that kept Dah'mir off balance while Geth closed to attack him. Dah'mir took wing, but Geth clung to him and was able to spot a point in his chest where a Khyber dragonshard was embedded in his scales. Swinging his Dhakaani sword, he struck, piercing Dah'mir's chest and shattering the shard.

Although the blow was not deep, Dah'mir writhed and fell out of the sky. His black herons rose to meet him and as the dragon and the shifter fell through the flock, Dah'mir somehow vanished, leaving Geth to fall alone. He splashed into a river from which his friends were later able to pull him, but neither he nor Batul could offer any explanation for how a single blow could injure a dragon so badly.

Elsewhere, however, Vennet d'Lyrandar woke to the panicked fear of his crew and found a black heron in his cabin. A heron that spoke with Dah'mir's voice.

CHAPTER

I

Karth raced down the narrow hallway below the deck of *Lightning on Water* and slid to a stop outside the captain's cabin. He pounded a fist against the door. "Captain! *Captain!*"

Vennet d'Lyrandar's response had the edge of someone just roused from sleep to an alarm. "What is it, Karth?"

The sailor choked, trying to spit out his message. "Birds, captain!" he said. "Dozens of them!"

The words were nothing compared to the sight that waited above deck—an entire flock of eerie black herons dropping out of the dawn-pale sky to take up roost all over the ship—but Karth heard Vennet spit out an exclamation and begin to stir. He sagged against the wall with relief. The captain would know what to do.

The sudden yelp of surprise that came from inside the cabin sent fear stabbing through Karth's guts. Already on edge, he didn't stop to think—he just reacted, lowering his shoulder and slamming his weight against the cabin door. "Captain!" the sailor shouted. "I'm—"

He was a big man and the cabin door had been built for privacy, not security. The force of his impact flung it wide and sent a hail of splinters flying through the cabin.

"—coming."

Two pairs of eyes looked at him. One pair belonged to Vennet and were wide with shock. The captain crouched atop his bed, still in his smallclothes, his bare chest heaving in surprise.

The other pair were bright acid-green and belonged to the tall black heron that stood in the shadows of the cabin. Thin bars of light fell through the shutters of the cabin's windows, striping the bird's feathers. Its eyes betrayed no surprise at all. Like the other herons that had burst out of the dawn to alight on the ship, it seemed utterly without fear. Even Karth's sudden and loud appearance didn't seem to have startled it.

If anything, it looked annoyed. It cocked its head at him and its eyes glittered.

"Leave us," it said. Its voice was as rich and smooth as oil.

Karth's guts clenched again. "Lords of the Host!" he whispered. He swallowed and glanced at the captain.

"Do it, Karth," said Vennet. The captain slid out of his bed, his expression softening from shock to amazement. He rose to his feet and stretched out an arm to gesture for Karth to leave. The dawn light flashed on the complex pattern of the dragonmark that covered the back of his neck and shoulders. Karth saw him glance at the heron before he added, "And tell the crew not to harm any of the birds."

"That," agreed the heron, "would be wise."

Instinct and long service more than anything else sent Karth backing out of the cabin. He couldn't quite manage to get an "Aye, captain" out of his mouth, though Vennet scarcely seemed to notice. As Karth stepped out through the doorway, he reached back inside, seized what was left of the door, and pulled it closed. The latch was broken. He settled the door against the frame and started to turn away.

But not before his gaze fell through one of the cracks that had opened in the wood.

Karth froze, staring like a butler at a keyhole. Inside the cabin, the heron stalked out of the shadows and as it moved, it changed. It grew taller and broader, its legs thicker, its neck shorter. Its wings became arms, its beak a face. The bird became a man with pale skin, black hair, and eyes the same acid-green as the heron's. What had been feathers blurred and merged, becoming robes of fine black leather. Crystals were set down each sleeve, half a dozen polished dragonshards that glowed a soft red against the black leather. Or rather, five shards that glowed red and one that was dim and scorched, as if it had burned from the inside out.

At the center of the man's chest, his robes were torn. The raw, bloody flesh of a deep wound showed through, though the man moved as if it caused him no pain at all.

Vennet fell to his knees before him. "Dah'mir," he said. "My lord, command me."

Karth jerked away from the broken door. Something wasn't right. He darted silently down the narrow corridor and back up onto the deck.

The crew of *Lightning on Water* stood clustered together, all of them staring at the herons that clung to the ship's rails and any other horizontal surface. With a chill, Karth realized for the first time that all of the birds had the same acid-green eyes. He tried to slip around the clustered crew, but someone noticed. "Karth! Is the captain coming?"

"What did he say?" called someone else.

"Does he know what's going on?"

"He's coming! He's coming!" Karth fought past the other sailors, then turned back. "He says not to hurt the birds."

"Can't anyway," said one of the men in a nervous voice. "Whenever you try, they just fly up out of the way, then settle back down, bold as halflings!"

A chill shivered along Karth's back. "Well, stop trying!"

He hastened to the stern of the ship. Mounted on huge beams behind the ship, the great elemental ring that drove the galleon roiled like storm clouds. Just enough wind escaped the ring to keep *Lightning on Water* moving and on course. Vennet's junior officer, Marolis d'Lyrandar, stood at the ship's wheel, his hands clenched on it. Like Vennet, he was a half-elf and carried the Mark of Storm that enabled him to command the ship while the captain slept. Though it had only been a short while since the herons had appeared—the sun had barely cleared the horizon—Marolis's face showed the strain of crisis. He glanced at Karth. "Where's Vennet?"

"He's—" Karth found his words sticking in his throat.

The three passengers that had taken passage with them on this run—a trip from Sharn in Breland to Trolanport in Zilargo, a departure from *Lightning on Water*'s usual routes along the south-western coast of the continent of Khorvaire—had joined Marolis rather than clustering with the common sailors. One of them, a pompous little gnome woman, spoke up. "Speak up, sailor! What did the captain say when you told him what was happening?"

"He—he said that he'd be out shortly, mistress Feita," said Karth.

"Shortly?" demanded one of the other passengers, a young Brelish man named Tomollan. "Shortly?" His voice rose and cracked.

Marolis turned to look at him. "There's no need to panic, master," he said tautly.

"Indeed." The third passenger was Cira, a beautiful woman and apparently a seasoned traveler to judge by the way she was keeping her head. She folded her hands. "If there was reason to worry, Tomollan, the captain wouldn't be so casually taking his time. If it makes you feel better, though, stay close to me. I have some skill in magic that could be—"

Marolis let out a hiss of relief. "There's the captain!"

Karth spun around. Vennet had emerged onto the deck. He wore his shirt open, hastily donned, but he had buckled on his sword belt and his cutlass hung at his hip. He strode past the gathered sailors without a word, making his way quickly toward the stern.

"He . . . uh, he seems to be in a hurry now," said Tomollan.

"Who's that?" asked Feita. "Boldrei's blessing, he's wounded!"

Dah'mir had followed the captain up from below. Where Vennet was hastening along the deck, however, the green-eyed man was strolling, nodding and smiling to the crew. All over the ship, the herons turned their heads to follow his casual progress. Strangely, the clustered sailors were dispersing in his wake, calmly returning to their duties.

"Captain d'Lyrandar!" Tomollan said as Vennet mounted the aft deck. "What's going on?"

Vennet ignored him. "Marolis, come about."

The junior officer stared at him. "Captain?"

"Come about, Marolis!"

Feita looked ready to spit venom. "Captain d'Lyrandar, what's happening here? Are we going back to Sharn? We're due in Trolanport tomorrow!"

Cira stepped forward. Her eyes were narrow and suspicious. "Captain, is something wrong? If my magic—"

"Ah, yes," Vennet said. "Your magic."

He took a fast step back. His right hand darted to his cutlass and he drew and swung it in one powerful motion. Cira was wearing a white gown. The cutlass slashed the pale fabric with red.

"It could be a problem," said Vennet.

Cira fell with a startled expression on her face. Karth and Marolis both stared in shock. Tomollan fumbled for a knife but Vennet's cutlass flashed and the young man reeled back, screaming and clutching his arm. Vennet followed and silenced him with another blow.

For all her pompousness, Feita reacted with the quick reflexes of her race, darting away from the captain's weapon and trying to get around him, maybe back to the safety of her cabin. Karth started to step forward, to try and restrain Vennet, but the half-elf raised his cutlass in silent threat. His eyes narrowed and he thrust his free hand toward Feita. Where his shirt hung loose across his back, Karth saw his dragonmark shimmer.

Wind summoned by the Mark of Storm howled from Vennet's outstretched hand to pummel Feita. The gnome staggered, stumbled—then was caught up by the powerful gust and tumbled, shrieking, over the ship's rail. Her shrieks ended in a splash.

The nearest herons turned to watch with glittering eyes.

"Lords of the Host! Man overboard!" Karth rushed past Vennet and leaped to the rail. Feita was struggling in the water. Even moving slowly, *Lightning on Water* was already passing her. He spun around to stare at Vennet and his bloody cutlass.

A hand fell on his shoulder. He looked up to meet a green-eyed gaze.

"Be at ease," said Dah'mir.

Up close, Karth could see that the smile on the man's face was strained, as if he held back tremendous pain. Even before the words were out of his mouth, though, it seemed to Karth that he could feel Dah'mir's presence pushing at him, overwhelming his will. He tried to struggle, tried to remember that he had just seen his captain kill two people and send a third to her death, but there was a charisma about Dah'mir. The strange man was right. There was nothing to worry about.

He watched Marolis fight and lose the same battle. Vennet repeated his order to bring the ship around and this time Marolis nodded. "Aye, captain," he said, spinning the wheel.

Dah'mir patted Karth's shoulder. "Why don't you dispose of those?" he said with a nod at Cira's and Tomollan's bodies. His voice was tired, but still powerful. "Then give the deck a good scrub."

"Aye, lord," Karth said above the rising howl of wind. Overhead, the ship's elemental ring began to churn furiously.

"Coming about," called Marolis. "Coming about and turning back to Sharn!"

"No," said Vennet. He bent and wiped his cutlass clean on Tomollan's tunic. "Not Sharn."

His world ended in fire. His last sensations were of the human wizard Singe clinging to him, then of a pinprick of heat as the wizard cast a final spell. He'd seen that spell before. He tried to leap away, but Singe's weight dragged at him, holding him in place for the scant moments it took for the pinprick to explode into an inferno. Flame seared the delicate buds of his skin, burning away every sensation but pain. It ate his chest tendrils and fleshy head growths. The powerful tentacles that sprang from his shoulders flailed in the fiery air—flailed, blistered, charred and finally went numb as they crumbled into ash. He screamed and fire filled his lungs, scorching him from the inside out.

The rage that consumed him was even hotter. As he burned, he tried to strike out at his killer, to take Singe with him into death but the fire finished him too quickly. He fell in silent agony, still raging at the wizard as he died and the world faded around him—

—until a flickering appeared in the stillness. His pain-maddened mind seized on it, tore at it, and the flickering vanished, snuffed out by his attention.

New strength shivered through his arms, though. New awareness woke in him. New . . . life.

Hruucan rolled over. His skin cracked and flaked away as he moved but he could *feel* again. Shifting currents of air touched his burned skin and showed him the world once more. It was night—Hruucan could sense it on the air. He could hear, too. He could hear voices.

Only a few paces away, two humans argued. Both of them held spears. One held a stick that smelled of oily smoke. An extinguished torch. The human with the torch shook it at the other. *"Toch tabeka tocha'ari! An ano totocha'ario!"*

They spoke the language of Dah'mir's humans, the Bonetree clan. Hruucan rose silently to his feet and drifted forward. He could sense other forms around him: the corpses of fallen orcs and humans, the broken chitinous hulks of dead chuul, the sprawled forms of slaughtered dolgrims. They stank with a day's decay, the passage of the corrupting sun. He still stood on the battlefield in the shadow of the Bonetree mound, he realized, though the fight was long since over. The Bonetree clan had slunk back to the abandoned field to pick over the bodies of the dead, now cold.

But the humans were warm, the heat of their lives pulsing inside them.

One of the humans sniffed at the air and made an expression of disgust. *"Do hiffi eche?"* He turned around. His face dropped in sudden fear. *"Khyberit gentis!"*

Hruucan lunged in a sifting burst of ash. He would have lashed out with his shoulder tentacles, but even through the haze of pain he knew they were no longer there. Instead, he struck the human who had cried out with the heel of his hand, pummeling him just under the ribs. The man went down with a weak gasp. Hruucan whirled on the other human, grabbing him before he could bring his spear to bear and wrapping him in blackened arms. He could feel the heat in the man, feel it rushing and beating . . .

The heat seemed to reawaken the buds of his skin. A shiver swept over him as they burst through the blackened crust and burrowed into the human's flesh. The human cried out in agony.

Usually the buds sucked out the moisture of any living creature the dolgaunt cared to embrace. Now they seemed to dig even deeper. Hruucan let out a grating moan as the buds burrowed into the human's very essence and sucked out his life.

The man's flesh began to smoke, then to smolder. Then it burst into flame. He died in Hruucan's arms and the dolgaunt felt stronger for it. Hruucan let the dead man fall and turned to the other human. He was still on the ground, trying shove himself away. His eyes were wide.

Hruucan's skin still flaked and crumbled as he took a step

forward, but beneath the ash was raw flesh. Flames licked his chest, but caused him no pain. In fact, they were very much like the chest tendrils that had been burned away before.

He flexed. They writhed.

He smiled and leaped for the human, wrenching him up from the ground. Skin buds and fiery tendrils tore the life out of him as well and set his corpse ablaze. When Hruucan shoved him away, some of the fire clung to him in long, writhing whips that sprang from his shoulders, drifting in the air. His tentacles given new form.

The night was sharp around him. His senses had been completely restored. More than restored: he could sense the ramshackle camp of the Bonetree clan well beyond the battlefield. Warm forms moved among the half-perceived shapes of the huts. More human lives to feed the furnace of his body.

But there was something else he could feel, too. Something far, far in the distance, pulling at him like a hook in torn flesh. Another being. Familiar. Hated.

Singe.

He turned to face the wizard's distant presence. His tentacles flared white hot and lashed the air. Singe's face danced before him and he moved after it, stepping up to the brow of an embankment and sliding down the other side, utterly lost in his anger—until hissing steam exploded around his feet. Pain burst within him and he leaped back.

Water rippled before him. The wide river lay between him and Singe. He could feel the wizard, but he could not follow.

"No!" he roared. *"No!"*

There were startled shouts from the direction of the Bonetree camp, the sound of hunters coming to investigate what might be moving—and burning—on the empty battlefield.

Blind with fury at the denial of his vengeance, Hruucan whirled around and raced to meet them.

The night filled with screams and smoke.

Batul raised his head sharply, looking away into the night.

Dandra froze, but her mind snapped out, summoning up psionic power. The droning chorus of whitefire hummed on the air, ready to be flung at any danger. Around the small campfire that was all they had dared to build, the others reacted as well. Ashi's sword and Singe's rapier made bright flashes in the shadows while the heavy blade of Geth's strange, ancient Dhakaani sword, forged from the twilight-purple metal byeshk, flickered almost like a shadow itself. Orshok snatched for the crooked length of his hunda stick, Krepis his axe. Natrac spun around, the mounted knife that fit over the stump of his right wrist a perpetual weapon. All of them held their positions, waiting with nervous energy for whatever might be out in the darkness.

"Batul?" Dandra asked.

"I heard something," said the old orc druid. His gaze—one eye good, the other filmed white and sometimes capable of seeing more than his good eye—remained fixed in the distance, a moment longer then he shook his head. "No," he said. "It was nothing."

His words were thin and weary. The others eased themselves back down, releasing their weapons but keeping them close. Ashi prowled the perimeter of their feeble camp before settling down as well. Dandra let the chorus of her power fade away. It wasn't easy—Tetkashtai clung to it like a child clutching a toy amulet.

No! she whined. The yellow-green light of her presence flashed and swirled in Dandra's mind's eye. *We need to be ready!*

Dandra looked down at the psicrystal that hung—once again—against her chest, and sent a soothing thought to her. *We're together again,* she reminded her. *We can summon the whitefire back when we need to. Let it go.*

Tetkashtai released her hold on the power reluctantly, then gasped and clawed for it again as Geth spoke up. "He's out there," he said. "Somewhere, Dah'mir's out there, and he's wounded and he's angry."

Dandra shot him an angry glare, but the shifter wasn't even looking at her. He was staring into the fire. Its light made his animal eyes shine in the darkness. Krepis grunted and said something in Orc. Natrac translated. "The only thing harder than killing a wild boar is not killing one."

Geth looked confused. Beside him, Singe groaned and lay back on the ground, covering his eyes with one arm. "It means," the Aundairian wizard said, "that if you're going to try killing something as dangerous as a dragon, you better make sure you do it right or you're in even worse trouble."

The shifter growled, sounding more like his usual self, and bared sharp teeth. "Well, when Dah'mir finds us, *you* try to kill him."

Dandra wanted to smile at the men's sniping, but she couldn't find it in herself. The day had been a long flight, hours spent racing along the river in an attempt to put as much distance between them and the territory of the Bonetree clan as possible. Her arms ached. All of them except Batul and Natrac had taken turns at paddling. There had been no time to rest—they'd told each other their stories when they weren't breathless from paddling—and little enough time to even think

And now that there was time to think, she had doubts.

She turned her attention back to her chosen task: cleaning Geth's great gauntlet. The armored sleeve had been forged from black, magewrought steel by a master artificer. It was weapon and armor both, with three low, hooked blades protruding from the back of the hand and flat spikes across the knuckles and along the ridge of the forearm. It was crude in comparison to her own weapon—a fast, delicate spear tipped with a glittering head of crysteel—but even she could appreciate the brutal effectiveness of its design and construction. With part of her mind focused on the careful effort of cleaning each spike and plate, and another part engaged in soothing Tetkashtai's trembling, terrified presence, conscious thought slowed to a dull, nagging . . .

In her memories, Dandra saw Dah'mir's handsome face again and heard her own question to him. *Why?*

Why had he done all of this?

It was a question he hadn't answered—maybe because he didn't need to.

She squeezed her eyes shut tight and clenched Geth's gauntlet between her fingers.

There was movement beside her. She opened her eyes to see Batul looking at her, his good eye flashing in the firelight. He leaned a little closer and asked, "Something bothers you?"

Her feelings gnawed at her. She hesitated, then looked up at the orc's wrinkled face. "We should go back to the Bonetree mound."

The words brought everyone's attention to her. Singe sat up as sharply as if he had been kicked. "Twelve moons, are you crazy?"

Dandra flushed and turned back to Geth's gauntlet, but Batul reached over and laid one gnarled gray-green hand on hers. "Dandra, if this is in your head, you should tell us more. Why should we go back?"

The kalashtar clenched her teeth. "Because this isn't over," she said. "Dah'mir isn't dead and we know that he's not going to just leave us alone. He's going to come back for revenge." She took a vicious swipe at Geth's gauntlet with the rag—a strip torn from the shifter's shirt—that she had been using to clean it. "He's going to come back for me."

"But you broke the dragonshard at the heart of the device he used on you, Medala, and Virikhad," said Geth. "Whatever plans he had are ruined."

"You didn't hear him, Geth. When he discovered how I'd escaped his device—how a *psicrystal* had resisted him—it was like he'd discovered the missing piece of a puzzle. I was an experiment to him, a problem to be solved." Dandra let go of the rag and returned Batul's grasp. "He wanted to drive us mad. Medala was his success. Virikhad was his failure. I was something unexpected. But now that Medala and Virikhad are gone and his device is broken, Tetkashtai and I are all that Dah'mir has left. And we still don't know why he did this to us! We need to go back to the mound. We need to find out if there's anything there that could tell us *why*."

Her voice shook. She forced her mouth closed. For a moment, all of them were silent. Inside her head, Tetkashtai's agitation had given way to a cowering fear. The presence was less than a spark. *Go back?* she said. *Back there? Back to the mound? Again?*

Then Singe spoke up. "Dah'mir told Ashi and I that Medala was the first of a new line of servants to the powers of the Dragon Below."

"A new line of what?" asked Natrac. "Mad kalashtar? That doesn't make any sense."

Dandra shook her head. "Dah'mir is insane, but he's still dangerous. Light of il-Yannah, what if he'd succeeded in turning Virikhad and Tetkashtai as well as Medalashana? How far would he have gone? How many other kalashtar could he have broken with his device?"

"His lair is in the middle of the Shadow Marches, Dandra," said Singe. "There aren't many kalashtar around here—look how much trouble he had to go through to lure you to him the first time."

"We were test subjects. That much I know. Dah'mir told me that his work needed refining. His intent was to do more." She wiped her free hand across her face. "I broke the binding stone, but Dah'mir might be able to start again with another dragonshard. We need to go—"

"Dandra." Batul squeezed her hand. She turned to look into his eye. "Dandra, we can't go back. It's already too late."

Dandra's expression tightened. "Prophecy, Batul?" she asked.

The druid shook his head. "No," he said, "just common sense. Look at us, Dandra." He nodded to their group, huddled around the fire, and she looked.

Geth's shining eyes had dark circles beneath them. Singe propped himself up as if he might topple over. Natrac was worn down. Ashi sagged. Krepis and Orshok looked half-asleep. Even Batul's shoulders were slack and rounded. Dandra blinked as understanding caught up to her. Baul nodded.

"We're exhausted," the old orc said. "We need to rest and regroup. It was luck and very little else that enabled us to bring down Dah'mir after he revealed himself as a dragon. The orcs who came with us on the raid are either dead or fled and already making their way home. I saw survivors among Dah'mir's creatures flee back into the mound when he vanished after Geth wounded him. Some of the Bonetree hunters still live, too. And Dah'mir—maybe he's inside the mound, too. Maybe he retreated there as well to lick his wounds. Geth's right—we don't know where he is." He squeezed her hand again. "We can't go back. Not now."

Dandra stared at him. He was right. For all the doubt that seethed in her, their exhaustion—*her* exhaustion—was inescapable. She clenched her fingers around Geth's gauntlet. "I can't just wait for Dah'mir to make me his prisoner again!" she said. "I have to do something, even if we can't go back to the Bonetree mound. There must be some way to figure out what Dah'mir has been planning!"

"Maybe," said Ashi, "there is."

Dandra looked at her. "What?" she asked. "How?"

The hunter stared into the fire for a moment before she answered. "There is a story told among the Bonetree," she said. "In the days of our ancestors, not long after Dah'mir came out of the east and gathered the clan together, he dispatched a group of hunters back into the east. When he came to us—" she bit her lip and corrected herself— "to the Bonetree, he'd left certain treasures behind in what the story calls *che Haranait Koa*, the Hall of the Revered. With the clan established, the hunters were sent to gather those treasures and bring them back to the ancestor mound."

She glanced up at Dandra. "The story tells that one of the greatest treasures they brought back was a great, blue-black dragonshard. Dah'mir made the hunter who placed it in his hands the first huntmaster of the Bonetree. The shard was enormous, 'the size of a crouching child' according to the story." She held up her hands to show the size.

Dandra drew a sharp breath as she realized what Ashi was describing. "The shard from the heart of Dah'mir's device," she said.

Ashi nodded.

Dandra sat back. "Il-Yannah! If the shard is real, then the story might be, too. If we can't get back to the Bonetree mound, the place Dah'mir came from before might give us some answers."

"Hold on!" Singe said. He looked across the fire at her. "We're talking about a story—a story about some place Dah'mir *might* have been two hundred years ago."

"The story is true," Ashi told him stiffly. "How else would generations of storytellers have known about the shard? The Bonetree didn't go inside the mound."

Batul nodded in agreement. "Stories can hold much truth, Singe. The lore of the Gatekeepers tells little about Dah'mir, but it does tell that the Servant of Madness came to the Shadow Marches out of the east like a blight on the dawn."

"We'd still be chasing a story two hundred years old on a hunch." Singe looked to Geth for support, but shifter just shook his head.

"You're asking the wrong person." He patted the heavy, jagged blade of his Dhakaani sword. "I walked through a phantom fortress that's been a story for thousands of years."

"When I told you that Dah'mir had led the Bonetree for ten generations, you doubted me," said Ashi. "That story was the truth."

Singe grimaced and held up his hands in surrender. "Twelve moons! Maybe it wouldn't hurt to look into it."

New hope leaped in Dandra's heart even as Tetkashtai shrank back further in her terror. "Where does the story say we can find the Hall of the Revered, Ashi?"

"*Che Haranait Koa shenio otoio ches Ponhansit Itanchi,*" the hunter said, the phrase rolling off her tongue like a formula. "The Hall of the Revered lies below the Spires of the Forge."

"And where are the Spires of the Forge?" asked Singe.

Ashi opened her mouth, then froze and closed it again. She shook her head, the beads woven into her thick gold hair clacking softly with the motion. Singe cursed. "That's not much help!"

"The Bonetree remembered the trials the hunters faced in their journey, not the route they took!" Ashi said between clenched teeth. "The story tells only Dah'mir's instructions to the hunters: The Hall of the Revered lies below the Spires of the Forge. Enter the door above the tangled valley. Look neither left nor right. The riches there are not for you. Hold to the path that leads to the Hall and find what waits in the shade of the Grieving Tree."

They all just stared at her. "Rat," Geth grunted. "It's like a riddle. I hate riddles."

"It's a start," said Dandra firmly. She tried to think of something that might narrow their search. "Does the story say how long the hunters' journey took? Did they cross open water at all? Did they cross mountains?"

Ashi shook her head again. "No, no water, no mountains. They walked. The story says they were gone for a season."

"Half a season there and half a season back," said Batul. "The Bonetree mound lies in the heart of the Marches. Travel half a season east and you're in the west of Droaam."

Geth's eyebrows rose. "Grandmother Wolf. Dah'mir came to the Shadow Marches from the barrens?"

"It's possible," Singe said. "Go any further east and you would run into civilized lands." He sat back, scratching the patch of beard that clung to his chin. "A place called the Spires of the Forge somewhere in the west of Droaam."

Dandra looked at Batul. "Does Gatekeeper lore mention these Spires?"

The old druid shook his head. "No. But Gatekeepers of old had little concern for things outside the Marches."

"We'd need to know where we were going," said Geth. "We don't want to just wander around in Droaam. That's dangerous territory."

Ashi grunted. "And the Shadow Marches aren't, shifter?"

"We have you, Batul, Krepis, and Orshok to guide us here," Geth growled back. "We'd need to find a guide who knows the land in Droaam, someone who might have heard of the Spires of the Forge."

"A guide—or a historian," said Singe. In spite of his earlier objections to the idea of seeking out the Hall of the Revered, Dandra recognized a gleam of curiosity in Singe's eyes. "The story is two hundred years old."

"Historian or guide, we'll find someone in Zarash'ak," said Natrac. "House Tharashk's prospectors and bounty hunters often spend time in Droaam—and if they can't help us, I know someone with an interest in history, who might be able to."

"An 'interest' in history?" Singe asked doubtfully. "Natrac, the City of Stilts isn't exactly well-known as a center of learning."

Natrac gave him a dark look. "You underestimate Zarash'ak. It's worth the try though, isn't it? We're going to be there anyway."

There was a brief silence as faces around the campfire blinked at him. Natrac looked at them all and asked cautiously, "We are going back to Zarash'ak, aren't we?"

"I don't know," said Dandra. In the rush of their escape, she hadn't even thought about it. Her only concern had been getting away from the Bonetree mound and Dah'mir. The great river eventually flowed all the way to Zarash'ak though—all they had to do was follow it downstream. She looked to Batul once more. The old druid spread his hands.

"You're all welcome with the Fat Tusk tribe," he said, "if that's what you want. But Fat Tusk's territory lies to the west and you won't learn anything about the Hall of the Revered or the Spires of the Forge there."

"Zarash'ak it is," said Singe. He raised an eyebrow. "What about you, Batul? If we're following Dah'mir's trail, I wouldn't mind having a Gatekeeper with us."

The old druid shook his head. "Fat Tusk needs me," he said. "Come back when you've done what needs doing and tell me the story."

Across the fire, Orshok shifted. "I'll go, teacher." Batul turned his head to regard his younger student and Dandra saw Orshok swallow before spitting out a rush of words. "When you sent me to Zarash'ak to watch for the Servant of Madness, I saw a world I'd never seen in the marshes. When we fought the Bonetree clan and the creatures of Khyber, I felt an energy I'd never felt before. When we faced Dah'mir, I felt—"

Batul held up his hand. "Enough, Orshok. I understand. My place wasn't always with Fat Tusk." He gave him a thin smile. "If Geth, Singe, and Dandra will have you, you can go."

"We'll have him," said Geth. "I'll watch over him."

One hairy hand strayed to the collar of polished black stones that he wore around his neck, and Dandra knew that he was thinking of the last Gatekeeper to wear it: his friend Adolan, who had died protecting her from the Bonetree hunters in the Eldeen hamlet of Bull Hollow. That night seemed so long ago now—and the decision that she, Geth, and Singe had made to find Dah'mir afterwards so simple and naïve.

Suddenly she wondered what consequences were going to come of the decision they had just made. Within her, Tetkashtai shuddered in dread.

"Dandra," said Natrac, "you look like something is still bothering you."

She forced herself to push aside her new doubts. It felt good to know that they were once again doing *something* and not just fleeing blindly from the dragon's power. Whatever happened, it was better than doing nothing. "I haven't had the best experiences when I've visited Zarash'ak before," she said. It might not have been what she was really thinking, but it wasn't a lie, either.

Natrac shook his head. "This time," he reassured her, "will be different. You'll stay at my house. I'll show you the best side of the City of Stilts while you're there." He rose to his feet and executed a grand, flourishing bow.

The sight of the half-orc—dressed in ragged, blood-stained clothes and standing in the middle of a wild, dangerous swamp—bending low like some pompous dandy was too much for even her exhausted mind to resist. Dandra's lips twitched and curved, and, for the first time in what felt like weeks, she laughed.

Chapter

2

Looking out over the rooftops of Zarash'ak under the bright light of morning a little more than a week later, Dandra had to concede that Natrac was right. So far, this visit to the City of Stilts was different from her previous experiences. The first time she'd been to the city—as a psicrystal—Tetkashtai, Virikhad, and Medala had fallen to Dah'mir's waiting power within an hour of their arrival. The second time, she and Singe hadn't even made it off Vennet d'Lyrandar's ship before the treacherous half-elf had attacked them in an attempt to capture her for Dah'mir.

This time, they'd simply paddled up to one of Zarash'ak's public water landings the previous day and walked away from their boats without even looking back—Batul and Krepis had left them several days before, striking west for Fat Tusk territory on a swiftly built raft. Once he'd set foot on the raised wooden streets of Zarash'ak, Natrac had become a changed man, resuming the role of the confident, brash merchant they'd first met on *Lightning on Water* and shedding the aura of grim survivor he'd taken on in the swamps. "By Kol Korran's golden bath," he had sworn, looking around with satisfaction, "I am never leaving Zarash'ak again!"

He'd escorted them through the city as if they were visiting dignitaries, pointing out the sights and parting crowds with shouted commands. His house, a tall structure in a well-cared for section of the city, looked like it was shut up when they arrived, but more shouts and a fist pounding on the door had brought an old, gray-haired servant to the door. The man had almost fallen down at the sight of Natrac—and then recoiled at the sight of the stump of Natrac's right wrist. "Dol Arrah, master—the rumors were true!" he'd gasped.

"It depends what those rumors were, Urthen," Natrac had said, throwing his good arm around the servant's shoulders and drawing him inside. "Now come to your senses. We have guests to look after!"

Like Natrac, Urthen had seemed to undergo a transformation as he'd opened up windows, set rooms to airing after his master's absence, and rushed to accommodate five unexpected guests. He'd apologized extravagantly for a hasty dinner of rough food—chickens spread with a spicy sour paste and crushed flat to make grilling them easier—fetched from a nearby tavern, lukewarm baths with hard soap, and beds improvised from cushions, but after so long traveling, Dandra felt as though she was surrounded by luxury.

Waking in the morning without the dawn sun shining in her face was even better, and when she had finally risen, it was almost as if she'd woken in a palace. Urthen had taken her clothes away while she'd slept and had them laundered overnight; they'd been returned smelling of herbs and flowers. She'd sought out the old man in the kitchen to thank him and had been directed up several long flights of stairs to a wooden platform built across the flat roof of the house. Under a canopy of white canvas, he'd served her a breakfast of cool mint tea, fruit, and fresh golden *ashi* bread smeared with honey.

Maybe, Dandra thought as she sat back and stared out over the railing around the platform, there was something to be said for Zarash'ak.

"Twelve moons, you look like the lady of a great house."

"I feel like the lady of a great house." Dandra turned and smiled at Singe as he stepped out onto the platform. The wizard's clothes had been laundered as well, and his freshly washed blond hair shone as bright as the rooftops of Zarash'ak.

In her mind, Tetkashtai made a noise of annoyance. *Stop that!* she said in waspish tone.

Dandra held back a grimace. The presence had slowly shed her persistent state of fear during their journey downriver.

Unfortunately, much of that fear had transformed into stinging bitterness. She hadn't quite forgiven Dandra for breaking the great shard and ruining Dah'mir's device, her only hope for regaining her body. Dandra had tried to make her understand that Dah'mir would never have reversed what he had done to them—that in fact he might not have been able to—but Tetkashtai had settled into a deep resentment.

For the sake of peace within her own mind, Dandra turned her thoughts away from Singe as he sat down. Urthen came hurrying up from inside the house with another tray laden with bread and tea. "How was your breakfast, Mistress Dandra? I wasn't certain what kalashtar preferred."

"It was very good, Urthen," she assured him.

It was coarse, said Tetkashtai. She spun out a memory of her favorite breakfast: taslek broth taken with an egg swirled into it.

That sounds so bland, Dandra said.

It wasn't bland, Tetkashtai replied. *It was subtle.*

Dandra fought her instinct to crinkle her nose for fear of offending Natrac's servant.

The others joined them slowly, all looking well-rested and—except for Ashi—well-scrubbed. The Bonetree hunter had splashed water over herself and her clothes, but no more. Natrac arrived last to the table. The half-orc wore robes of fine fabric with full sleeves that fell to cover his missing hand. "Urthen," he said as the old man poured cold tea for him, "there's a wright in Drum Lane who's supposed to be particularly talented at making artificial limbs. I think I'd like to call on him tomorrow."

"I'll make the arrangements, master." Urthen handed Natrac a note that had been folded and sealed with a dollop of yellow wax. "A response to the message you sent last night."

Across the table, Singe raised an eyebrow. "Is this from your would-be historian, Natrac?"

Natrac had been coy about the contact he thought might be able to help them. He'd kept his or her identity a secret, but had hinted that it would be someone likely to impress them—or at least to impress Singe. Dandra was certain the half-orc wanted to prove to him that Zarash'ak was more than just a collection of buildings built on stilts above a swamp. It seemed that he was determined to draw the suspense out until the last minute. His only answer to Singe's question was a cryptic smile as he struggled to open the folded note with one hand, a smile that turned into a growl as the paper defied his efforts. He raised his right arm, shook the knife mounted over his wrist clear of his sleeve, and slit the paper neatly.

Dandra caught a glimpse of careful, clean handwriting before Natrac held the note up and away from the rest of them. His smile returned and he folded the note once more, tucking it into his robe. "Urthen, we'll be out for dinner. You know where." He winked at his servant.

The old man smiled back and bent his head. "Master." He picked up his tray and moved away.

"You're still not going to tell us?" asked Dandra.

"You'll find out." Natrac sipped his tea. "We shouldn't waste the day though. Shall we find out what House Tharashk can tell us about the Spires of the Forge?"

Dandra and Singe nodded, but Geth growled and tore into a thick piece of bread. "Not for me," he said. "You do what you need to do—I'm not going to be stuck inside talking all day." He looked to Orshok and Ashi. "Do you still want to see the sights of Zarash'ak?"

"Dagga!" said Orshok eagerly.

Ashi shrugged, but gave a little nod.

Natrac set his tea down and spread his hands wide. "If you're sure," he said. "It probably would make things easier if there weren't six of us looming over someone, but . . ."

"I'm sure," Geth said flatly.

"If you insist." The half-orc reached for bread. "We'll be spending most of our time near the herb market. Why don't you meet us there around mid-afternoon? The market is easy to find. There's a shrine to Arawai and Kol Korran in the heart of it. Look for us there."

"Done." Geth took another bite of his bread and gave Dandra and Singe the grin of someone who had just escaped from an onerous task.

"That was easier than I thought it would be," Singe muttered as he stepped out from Natrac's house and onto the street a short while later.

"Let someone think an idea is their own," said Natrac with satisfaction, "and they're more likely to follow it."

Dandra felt the slightest twinge of guilt as she followed the two men out into the morning sun. "I'm still not sure I like tricking Geth and Ashi," she said—then held up a hand as Singe looked back at her and raised an eyebrow. "I know," she added. "It's for the best."

While the human and half-orc members of House Tharashk often spent much of their time in the wilderness, Tharashk was still one of the great dragonmarked houses. Its most talented members carried the Mark of Finding. Getting answers from them was going to take respect, diplomacy, and a certain amount of charm. Geth and Ashi, on the other hand, had a tendency to act before they thought. Even Dandra could see that their absence was likely to make their search smoother—and that simply telling them that they should find something else to do wasn't likely to work. Instead they'd enlisted Orshok in their scheme of persuading the rough pair that the search would be tedious and time-consuming.

The druid had taken to the lie eagerly. Dandra was fairly certain that he had no desire himself to be engaged in talk when he could be exploring Zarash'ak, but she still felt as though she was somehow corrupting the young orc.

Natrac reached out and patted her shoulder as they walked. "Don't worry, Dandra, they won't get into trouble. Zarash'ak isn't as dangerous as all that."

She gave him a level look. "You told us to carry our weapons." She shifted her spear in its harness across her back.

The half-orc smiled. "You're less likely to get trouble if you look like you can give trouble back. That's just common sense." He drew her after him. "Come on—we've got a lot of the city to see ourselves."

Dandra had spent the first part of her existence in Sharn, but as Natrac led them deeper into Zarash'ak, she began to think that even the vertical neighborhoods of the City of Towers were nothing compared to the tangled streets of the City of Stilts.

Built up from individual stilted platforms and raised walkways, Zarash'ak was a confusing sprawl of a city. The wooden streets turned and crossed seemingly at random. New sights appeared without warning around corners, between buildings, and across bridges.

She smelled the great herb market, however, before she saw it. Zarash'ak was a city of pungent, marshy odors, but gradually Dandra became aware of a new scent on the air. The smell was complex: strong and wet, resinous and sharp. It teased at her nose with soft perfumes and bit at it with harsh, peppery notes. She breathed deep, drawing it all in. "Is that the market?" she asked Natrac.

He nodded then led them around a corner.

A wide wooden plaza opened up before them, crowded with people of many races and alive with noise. Human merchants called out from stalls, declaring the freshness and potency of their products. Half-orc and orc farmers and gatherers sat among big baskets, trying to attract the attention of the traders who would buy their crops in bulk. Porters raced among the crowds, sacks and bales balanced atop their shoulders. Buyers strolled the paths of the market, shouting back at merchants and farmers and porters alike. At the center of the market, a round structure painted green and gold rose above the stalls—the shrine Natrac had mentioned, Dandra guessed.

The astounding odor she had smelled before lay over everything, the mingled scent of innumerable herbs. "Amazing!" she whispered.

What? Tetkashtai demanded. What is it?

The presence could see and hear, but she had no sense of smell, only memories of it. *The market smells wonderful*, Dandra told her. She tried her best to communicate the odor, but Tetkashtai just scowled.

A true kalashtar would find such an unsophisticated stink revolting.

Dandra had to work to keep her anger from showing on her face. *I like it.*

Of course you do, Tetkashtai said.

Natrac led them across one side of the market. Both Dandra and Singe stared at the plant life displayed in the stalls they passed. Dandra had imagined the market would sell only leafy herbs, but instead all conceivable fragments of a seemingly infinite number of plants were on sale. Leaves of all shapes and sizes. Twigs. Stalks. Bark. Chips and slivers of wood. Flowers. Seeds. Roots. Fresh. Dried. Each stall was enveloped in its own particular scent as well: some peppery, some sweet, some acidic, some utterly foul.

"Where do all of these come from?" asked Singe above the noise.

"Some of the common ones are grown in villages around the city," said Natrac, "but a lot are wild. Locals gather them, pool them, and send someone into Zarash'ak to sell. A few come from really deep in the Marches or are particularly rare." He pointed to a merchant who was shaving slices off a big, hard stalk as if it were some kind of woody cheese. "That's rotto stem. A piece that big probably earned whoever found it enough money to live off for two months."

"What's it used for?"

"You cook it in wine, then make a face cream out of it. It takes away wrinkles."

"Truly?"

Natrac gave him a suffering glance. "No," he said, "people pay a small fortune just for the pleasure of putting hot mush on their face."

Dandra looked around them. "Do you think the people who bring the herbs in from the deep Marches will be the best ones to ask about the Spires of the Forge?"

"Not just them," said Natrac. "Anyone who spends time in the wilds tends to congregate around here—especially members of House Tharashk. Dragonshard prospectors, herb scouts, and bounty hunters all have the same concerns when they're in the wild and they like to share information."

He stopped in front of one of the buildings that faced onto the market. It looked strange to Dandra's eyes—part tavern, part tea room. Through a window, she could see a mix of rough humans and half-orcs sipping gingerly from steaming mugs. "What kind of place is this?"

"It's a *gaeth'ad* house. You don't find them much outside of the Shadow Marches. Just think of it as a tavern." Natrac stepped up to the door. "Wait here. I may not be long."

He went inside. Dandra glanced at Singe. "What's *gaeth'ad?*"

"The herbs from the Shadow Marches can do more than take away wrinkles," the Aundairian told her. *"Gaeth'ad* is herb tea with a kick. A skilled *gaeth'ad* master can brew a custom tea that will make you feel however you want to. House Jorasco has hired masters to brew sedatives, but mostly *gaeth'ad* needs to be really fresh to be potent."

Natrac's business inside the house took almost no time at all. "We're in luck," he said as he emerged. "There's a Tharashk bounty hunter in the city at the moment who's supposed to know western Droaam. He favors one of the other *gaeth'ad* houses, but the person I spoke to thinks he might be there now. I'm told he's the best available."

"That sounds like a good start," said Singe. "Let's find him."

The *gaeth'ad* house that Natrac led them to had a crooked hunda stick like Orshok's hung over the door to serve as a sign. Unlike the previous house, its windows were covered in slat shutters that allowed air to circulate but gave those within a greater degree of privacy. Dandra paused for a moment inside the door to let her eyes adjust. The interior of the house was a dim, quiet room broken up by screens made of coarse paper. The screens made it hard to judge how many people might have been in the place—perhaps half of the tables that she could see were occupied, though she couldn't always see whether their occupants drank their tea alone or in the company of someone else. The atmosphere was thick, humid even for Zarash'ak, and laced with a sweet-acrid smell.

Natrac walked up to the bar, a long polished counter that stood in front of jar-lined shelves more suitable to an apothecary's shop, and spoke in Orc to a young half-orc on the other side. A few coins changed hands, disappearing into her sleeves, and she nodded. She pointed deeper into the maze of screens. Natrac turned back to Singe and Dandra.

"He's here," he said. "Follow me."

Behind a screen at the very back of the house, a high-pitched voice was speaking softly in a harsh language Dandra didn't understand. Every few minutes, a deeper voice would add something in the same language. Natrac paused just beyond the screen and cleared his throat. The high-pitched voice broke off and

Dandra was certain that she heard the soft whisper of a dagger being drawn.

"Yes?" called the deeper voice.

"I'm looking for Chain d'Tharashk," said Natrac.

"Come through," said the deep voice. "All three of you."

Dandra felt a trace of unease. She held up the three fingers to Singe and mouthed silently, how did he know?

The wizard looked unimpressed. He lifted a foot and pointed to it. Chain had heard their footsteps, Dandra realized.

"Old trick," Singe murmured as Natrac disappeared around the screen. Singe gestured for Dandra to follow the half-orc, then fell in behind her.

The man who sat at the table on the other side of the screen was large. No, Dandra thought, "large" didn't do him justice. Standing up, he would be taller than Natrac, maybe as tall as Ashi. His muscles were nearly as thick as Geth's, bulging out from beneath a stained, sleeveless leather shirt. Nearly obscured by hair on his left forearm, a small dragonmark twisted and turned in a slash of color. The thick stubble on the man's face matched the length of the stubble on his shaved head. Beneath heavy eyebrows, his eyes were dark and alert. "You've found me," he said. "I'm Chain."

His voice matched the rest of him—dark, heavy, and threatening. Any doubts Dandra had about leaving Geth and Ashi behind vanished immediately. Chain was a walking challenge. She didn't think either the shifter or the hunter could have even spoken to him without starting a fight.

There were two chairs before the table. Natrac took one and Singe gestured for Dandra to take the other. She seated herself, shifting her spear out of the way. There was a fourth chair, but it was occupied by the source—or so Dandra assumed—of the high-pitched voice she had heard before. A goblin crouched in the chair, his slight frame tensing as Dandra touched the shaft of her spear. Reddish eyes in a flat face the color of dirty parchment watched each of them closely. One of the small creature's hands was hidden by an enormous account book. Dandra guessed that it was holding the dagger she had heard drawn. She made a show of moving her hand away from her spear and he relaxed. Slightly.

Chain sat back, his chair creaking under his weight, and looked them over with such intensity that Dandra felt as though he was committing their appearances to memory.

As soon as Natrac had finished introducing himself and them, Chain asked, "So what do you want?"

Singe was just visible out of the corner of Dandra's eye. She saw his face tighten. "Blunt, aren't you?"

"People don't hire me for my charm. You want charm, hire an elf." The big man reached out and picked up a mug of *gaeth'ad*. "You want the best, hire me."

Chain's manners grated across Dandra's nerves worse than Tetkashtai's bitterness. "We didn't say we wanted to hire you," she said.

"Then you're wasting my time." Chain turned his head and nodded to the goblin. The little creature look back to the account book and began babbling in his harsh language as he ran thin fingers down a column of close-written text.

Natrac winced at the dismissal and shot Dandra a glare. She felt her stomach flinch—and Tetkashtai's silent derision—at her misstep.

Natrac leaned forward. "*Poli*, Chain—my friend tends to talk before she thinks. We do want to hire you. We're told you know the western barrens of Droaam better than anyone."

"I know all of Droaam," Chain said. The goblin paused as soon as his boss spoke, one finger still pressed against the account book.

"I'm sure of it," Natrac agreed quickly. "But the west is really all that—"

"Just get to the point. Who do you want found?"

Natrac coughed. "Not who. What. We're looking for a place."

Chain's eyes narrowed and he looked them over again as he drank from his mug. The goblin pursed his lips and spoke a few words. Chain nodded, his face darkening. He sat forward and slammed the mug down on the desk. "You're treasure hunters."

"What?" asked Dandra. "What makes you think we're treasure hunters?"

"By the look of you, you've seen a lot of traveling very recently, but if you're looking for some place in Droaam, you're not finished yet. And you're an unlikely mix—a well-dressed half-orc who's been through rough times, a kalashtar, and an Aundairian who, unless I'm wrong, has served with the Blademarks."

Dandra saw Singe stiffen.

Chain snorted. "Don't look surprised. You sweat Deneith discipline." The bounty hunter leaned back and crossed his arms. "Treasure hunting and war are the only things that bring together a mix like that and as far as I know, the war is still over."

"Fine," said Singe. "Call us treasure hunters. Does it make a difference?"

"Rates go up. I help you, I get a cut of whatever you find."

Singe raised his head and gave Chain a hard look. "That's mercenary."

"You've worked for Deneith. You should know all about that." Chain rubbed a rough hand across his chin. "What's on the schedule, Preesh?"

The goblin flipped ahead in the account book, checked a column, and said in words Dandra understood, "You're clear."

Chain leaned across the desk. "Tell me more."

Natrac glanced at Singe and Dandra, then looked back to Chain. "Have you ever heard of a place called the Spires of the Forge?"

Chain rapped his fingers against the tabletop. "Ten silver," he said.

"What?"

"Ten silver," Chain repeated. "Sovereigns, trade bits, matching weights—I don't care. You've just asked me a question. You want an answer, it's ten silver."

"You said to tell you more," Dandra protested.

"Tell, not ask."

"Ten sovereigns is a steep price for a simple answer," said Singe. "Either you've heard of the place or you haven't."

Chain picked up his mug and took another drink. "You're taking up my time," he said. "A man needs to eat and Preesh doesn't work cheap. Ten silver could clear this all up right away."

Singe grumbled under his breath and looked to Natrac. The half-orc reached into a pouch and produced ten silver sovereigns, pushing them across the table to Chain. "There," he said. "Now—have you heard of the Spires of the Forge?"

The big man scooped up the coins. "No."

Dandra stared at him. "No?" she said in shock.

Chain shrugged. "Never heard of them." He raised his heavy eyebrows. "They were what you were looking for?"

"Yes!"

"Then we've just saved ourselves a lot of trouble." He drank again.

Dandra rose to her feet, fury and the close air of the *gaeth'ad* house making her head pound. "You just took our money!"

"You paid for an answer. I gave it to you," the big man said. "Don't blame me if it's not the answer you wanted to hear." He remained seated but the goblin had tensed again.

Singe put a hand on her shoulder. "Easy," he said. "He's right."

She could tell from the sound of his voice that he wasn't happy either. She glared at Chain. "What about the Hall of the Revered? Have you heard of that or is it going to cost us another ten sovereigns?"

Chain's shoulders tightened, making his muscles bulge. "I'll throw it in for free," he said. "No. I've never heard of the Spires of the Forge *or* the Hall of the Revered."

"Thank you," said Natrac. The half-orc rose quickly. "We'll be on our way, then. Maybe someone else—"

Chain moved with a speed that shocked even Dandra, surging up out of his chair to lean across the table and snap in Natrac's face. "You try," he said. "You just try. But here's another free answer: if I haven't heard of a place in Droaam, then it doesn't exist. You ask any other bounty hunter, prospector, or scout and they're not going to be able to help you either. You've already come to the best. If I can't help you, nobody can!" Natrac flinched back. Chain flung up an arm, pointing back out of the *gaeth'ad* house. "Get out."

"I—" Natrac started to say, but Singe grabbed the half-orc with his other arm and hauled both him and Dandra away. Dandra caught a last glimpse of Chain as the big bounty hunter slammed himself back down into his chair. Curious faces peered at them as they hastened out of the house and back into the herb market.

"Twelve bloody moons!" cursed Singe. "What a—"

"What a *dahr!*" said Dandra through clenched teeth. She looked at Natrac. "Do you think he was lying?"

He shook his head. "That was business, Dandra. He had no reason to lie."

"What about trying other people? Do you think it was just his ego talking when he said no one else would know anything?"

"It doesn't look like he would admit to having rivals, does it?" said Natrac. He shrugged. "There's no harm in trying to find other sources, but Chain *was* supposed to be the best in the city right now. If he doesn't know, maybe House Tharashk isn't the answer."

"We were only gambling that Tharashk would have the answers we need, Dandra," Singe pointed out. "There's still Natrac's historian."

Dandra took a deep breath, trying to cool her rage at Chain's grating manners, and lifted her chin. "But we're gambling on that, too, aren't we?" she said with determination. "I'm not going to give up on Tharashk that easily. I don't think Chain knows as much as he thinks he does."

"We've got time to ask around." Singe squinted up at the sun, still high in the sky. "We're not supposed to meet Geth and Ashi for a long while yet." He chuckled and shook his head. "Twelve moons, we might as well have had them with us all along!"

Dandra glanced at him. "I don't think that would have helped."

"No, but I would have enjoyed watching them beat down Chain. That would have been worth ten sovereigns." He smiled wistfully.

"Do you really think we fooled them?" asked Ashi.

"Probably," said Geth as they moved through the crowds on one of Zarash'ak's broader streets. The sun was high; the day was hot. He, the hunter, and Orshok had lingered at Natrac's house well after the others had gone. Geth had luxuriated in the shade of the canopy on Natrac's rooftop, napping on a stomach full of bread and honey and grateful for the first day in weeks that there was no need to paddle a boat or hike across country. He twisted as he walked, loosening muscles that had been knotted for too long and added, "Singe likes to think he's clever."

"He *is* clever," Orshok pointed out.

Geth gave the young orc a glare but bared his teeth in a grin, too. "When you've known Singe for as long as I have, you get used to him. You can tell when he's up to something. I would have known he was trying to get rid of us even you hadn't said anything, Orshok."

The druid looked vaguely disappointed. "You would have?"

"A clever man is most vulnerable when he's trying to be clever. Someone wise told me that."

"Who?" asked Orshok suspiciously.

"Robrand d'Deneith, the man who recruited me and Singe into the Frostbrand company of the Blademarks when we were your age. One of the greatest commanders to ever lead a Blademarks company." Geth let out a little snarl of satisfaction. "He had Singe figured out. The old man could keep him in knots if he wanted to."

Ashi's face darkened. "So we fooled Singe by doing exactly what he wanted us to do?" She looked down at Geth. "How is that outwitting him?"

"Because we chose to do this ourselves." He stretched his arms out in the bright sunlight. His ancient Dhakaani sword was a weight at his side, but he'd left his great gauntlet behind. There was no need for it and the day was too pleasant to worry about armor. "I like House Tharashk—they tend to be more honest than other dragonmarked houses—but I don't want to spend all day going from tavern to tavern talking to them."

"That was Singe's argument, too," said Orshok. "We're doing what he wanted for exactly the reason he said we should."

Geth opened his mouth to reply, then closed it again. He gave Orshok another glare. This time the orc smiled. So did Ashi. Geth glowered. "Come on," he grumbled, "Let's see what we can see."

They followed the crowds, less out of any random choice than out of another principle handed down by Robrand d'Deneith: where there were people, there would be something interesting. Geth's old commander's wisdom didn't fail them. They wandered through a market where merchants from beyond the Shadow Marches offered the finest items from across Khorvaire. They passed a theater where criers called out the coming evening's bill, while mummers on the other side of the street gave a show for thrown coins. At a shrine dedicated to the Sovereign Host, they stopped and went inside so that Orshok and Ashi could marvel at a faith unfamiliar to both of them. Geth stood by the door, nodding to the priests tending the shrine, as the druid and the hunter stared at the shining images of the nine gods.

Orshok gave him a solemn look as they left the shrine. "When the daelkyr came from Xoriat to invade Eberron during the Daelkyr War, the Gatekeepers fought them. We sealed the gates to Xoriat and bound the surviving daelkyr in Khyber. What did the Sovereign Host do?"

"I don't—" Geth ground his teeth together. "Ask Singe. He's the clever one. Who's hungry?"

The streets of Zarash'ak were dotted with vendors selling cheap food that people bought and carried with them, eating as they walked. Geth had seen the process when they had been in Zarash'ak before: he led Ashi and Orshok to one stall where they bought thick rounds of *ashi* bread, then on to another to buy roast vegetables or spicy grilled meat to stuff inside. The meat was snake—Orshok insisted on checking stalls until he found some that he declared fresh enough to eat. The orc tending the grill gave them a hearty grin and extra slatherings of the hot and sour sauce that spiced the meat.

The sauce numbed Geth's mouth and brought tears to Orshok's eyes, but Ashi just ate her meal in solemn silence as they wandered. Geth recognized this area of Zarash'ak—they were heading toward the deep water docks where ships coming up from the ocean found berths. If they wanted news of the world beyond the Shadow Marches, this would be a good place to find it. His eyes were on Ashi, however. Her body was tense, her posture guarded. Geth frowned over his food, "Is something wrong?" he asked her.

The tall woman's face twisted. She answered with blunt honesty. "I don't like cities."

Geth look around them as he took another bite of food. For all that Zarash'ak was an isolated island of civilization, it was also the only city of any size in the Shadow Marches—in the whole southwest of the continent of Khorvaire, in fact—and attracted an astounding diversity of inhabitants and visitors. The crowd on the street was made up mostly of humans, orcs, and half-orcs, but there were also elves and halflings and bandy-legged goblins. He could even spot another shifter on occasion, striding confidently among the other races. Their trio of orc, shifter, and human savage wasn't at all out of place.

"It's the crowd, isn't it?" Geth said. "So many people in one place?"

Ashi nodded tightly. "Having so many strangers around me—so many outclanners . . ."

She bit off her words, but Geth understood. Shifters were descended from the mingled bloodlines of humans and shapechanging lycanthropes. Their lycanthropic heritage gave them useful gifts, but also a predator's instincts. Crowds weren't that much different from herds and herds were either prey or a threat. It had taken him time and effort to ease the edge of being around strangers. Ashi was a hunter. She had the same instincts. He grunted. "You'll get used to it," he told her. He looked at Orshok. "What about you?"

The orc wrinkled his thick nose. "I like Zarash'ak," he said. "I miss Fat Tusk, though."

"At least you're welcome to go back to it," said Ashi.

"Do you miss the Bonetree?" Geth asked her. "Do you regret turning against your clan?"

"Do you miss your people?" she snapped at him in return.

Geth's gut knotted as Adolan's face flickered before him: his friend had died under a Bonetree hunter's axe. His lips twitched back, baring his teeth reflexively, and he growled at Ashi. The hunter jerked back and her hand went instantly to her sword—then fell away as a flush crept up her face.

"I'm . . . sorry," she said. "Blood in my mouth, it was not a good thing to ask." She hung her head. "I miss friends among the Bonetree. If they were dead, I wouldn't miss them as much."

Other faces joined Adolan's in Geth's memory, the faces of people he—and Singe—had served with in the Frostbrand. People he'd last seen in the northern Karrnathi town of Narath. People who were dead because of him. He clenched his jaw tight. "I understand," he said through his teeth.

Ashi's hand dropped back to her sword, though this time only to rest on it. The weapon had belong to her grandfather, absorbed into the Bonetree clan after being found wounded in the marches. Singe had identified the weapon as an honor blade of the Sentinel Marshals of House Deneith. That Ashi carried the blood of Deneith was one of the surprises they had discovered among the Bonetree. "Singe says that I'll have a new clan in House Deneith," she said. "Do you think that they'll take me in?"

"Ashi," Geth said, "I think House Deneith is going to be as surprised to learn about you as you were to learn about it."

The crowd thinned around them as the street they had followed opened onto the docks. Orshok's eyes went wide at the sight of the sailing ships gently rising and falling with the water. *"Kuv!"* he said in awe.

"You didn't see these last time you were in Zarash'ak?" Geth asked, turning to saunter along the docks.

"No." Orshok shook his head. "I stayed where Batul directed me to go, watching for the Servant of Madness. I didn't see much of the city." The druid stared at the ocean-going vessels they passed. "I'd heard they were big, but I did really imagine . . ." He looked ahead of them and his eyes grew even wider. "Look at that! What kind of ship needs no sails?"

"A Lyrandar elemental galleon," mumbled Geth as he stuffed the last of his bread and meat into his mouth. He looked up to follow Orshok's gaze—and the food in his mouth seemed to turn dry and tasteless.

Only three berths along, *Lightning on Water* nestled against the wood of the dock, the great elemental ring that drove it glinting like blue glass in the sun. A much smaller boat—a river craft—was tied up beside it and the galleon's crew were busy loading it with supplies as though for a voyage. The hair on Geth's forearms and on the back of his neck rose. Black herons rode the breeze around and above the Lyrandar galleon, perching boldly on its rails, among the rigging of nearby ships, and atop the piles of the docks.

Dah'mir's herons. Vennet d'Lyrandar's ship.

Beside the laboring crew stood two figures. One wore a dove-gray coat and had long blond hair that fell in a tail down his back. The other wore robes of fine black leather.

Their attention was on the crew, but as Geth stared Vennet and Dah'mir started to turn, walking toward them.

Barely thinking, he grabbed Orshok and Ashi and shoved them into the shelter of a narrow alley between two buildings. Orshok's gray-green face was flushed dark.

"That was . . ." he croaked in frightened disbelief.

"I know," Geth told him. "Be quiet!"

Ashi gripped the hilt of her sword. "Geth, we could end this! There's three of us and two of them."

"But one of them is a dragon!" he hissed at her. "Fighting Dah'mir would be suicide. Now be quiet and get back!"

Neither Vennet or Dah'mir had seen them and there was light at the alley's far end—he hadn't just hidden them in a dead-end. Geth thanked Grandfather Rat for a moment of good fortune. If they tried to make a break for it though, their movement was certain to draw the men's attention. The floor of the alley was covered in foul litter. Geth ignored it—he dropped to his belly and lay flat. Behind him, he heard Orshok and Dandra press back as well.

The black stones of Adolan's collar went cold around his throat. A moment later, Dah'mir and Vennet passed by the mouth of the alley.

Geth could barely bring himself to look up, but he did and caught a brief glimpse of the two men. Vennet looked the same as he had the last time Geth had seen him, though there was a hint of tension in his face. Dah'mir, on the other hand . . . When they had seen him before, the dragon's human shape had been always been elegant, graceful, and perfect. Inhumanly perfect. Now, however, he moved stiffly and there was a draw on his features. He looked tired. He looked like he was in pain.

The two men were talking. Geth strained his ears to catch their words.

"—will find enough fresh water to sustain the crew while we're gone." Vennet was saying. "Two weeks? You're certain."

"At most," answered Dah'mir, and the sound of his oil-smooth voice sent shudders along Geth's spine. "By the way, you might not want to pick your best men to accompany us, captain. The journey can be dangerous—"

His words cut off sharply. "Lord?" asked Vennet. "What is it?"

Geth's heart felt like it had stopped beating. The light from the mouth of the alley vanished as Dah'mir stepped back, his nostrils flared as if he smelled something bad.

For an instant, time seemed to stop as Geth and Dah'mir stared at each other, and Geth's attention focused on a single detail: the blue-black Khyber dragonshard that had glittered on the chest of Dah'mir's leather robes before was gone, shattered by Geth's sword, its place marked by a wet stain and a crudely mended tear in the leather.

Then Dah'mir's acid-green eyes flared. His lips peeled back, "You!"

A predator's instincts might have been focused on hunting and fighting—but predators knew when to flee, too.

Geth thrust himself away from Dah'mir, twisting to his feet as he moved. "Run!" he roared at Ashi and Orshok. *"Run!"*

CHAPTER

3

Orshok needed no encouragement. He sprinted down the alley faster than Geth would have thought possible. Ashi, however, stood frozen for a moment, torn between flight and the desire to fight. Geth didn't give her the chance to think about it—he just ran straight at her. The alley was too narrow for them to pass each other. "Go, Ashi!" he screamed as he charged at her. "Move!"

She spun around and ran. Geth put his head down and focused on moving his legs as fast as he could. With each pounding stride, he expected to hear the dragon's deafening roar and to feel hot, acidic venom spatter against his back. Trapped in the alley, they were all three an easy target. He'd seen the dragon's acid melt orcs and dolgrims alike on the battlefield at the Bonetree mound, flesh and bone dissolving into a hideous slop. Any time now, he thought to himself with mounting horror, any time now.

He heard Vennet shout for his crew, ordering them into pursuit. He heard a strange sharp whistle. He didn't hear a dragon's roar. He didn't feel acid drench him.

He burst out of the end of the alley and onto a quiet laneway. Orshok grabbed his arm, whirling him to a stop. "Which way?" gasped the orc.

Geth twisted around, looking back down the alley. Vennet stood at the far end, his cutlass raised, waving to someone—probably his crew—back on the docks. Beyond him, Geth could see Dah'mir, still in human form, standing and glaring. The shifter gulped and leaped away. He looked both ways along the laneway, then thrust a hand in the direction that seemed to lead back to a busier part of the city. "This way!" he said. "Grandfather Rat, if we can get into a crowd before Vennet's men are through the alley, we might lose them!"

"Men aren't the only thing we need to worry about!" Ashi pointed upward.

Black herons were rising into the sky above.

"Rat!" Geth cursed again. Bonetree hunters had once used the birds to track Dandra from the air. With Dah'mir to command them, he didn't doubt that they'd perform the same task for Vennet's crew, guiding the sailors right to them. He clenched his teeth. "We still don't want to be caught in the open! Come on!"

They'd almost made it out of the laneway and into the busier street at its end when shouts erupted behind them. Geth looked over his shoulder and saw a knot of sailors pouring out of the alley. "They've seen us!" he called to Ashi and Orshok—then they were all plunging into the crowd on the street.

For a panic-stricken moment, the shifter feared he had lost the druid and the hunter, only to find them right beside him. He struck out for the middle of the street, moving as quickly as he dared. Full out flight through the crowd would only draw attention to them, and getting through the milling throng quickly seemed unlikely at best. He looked behind them. The sailors were standing at the side of the street, looking around with a blank stare. Overhead, the herons spun in wide, lazy circles, as if still trying to pick out their targets. Geth drew a slow breath. Maybe they had a chance.

Vennet's voice rang out above the noise of the street. "There! There they are!"

Geth spun back around. Vennet and fully half of his crew were ahead of them. The half-elf must have known a shortcut through the twisting alleys—and he and his crew didn't need to worry about being stealthy. The sailors came hurtling through the crowd like stampeding cattle, ignoring the cries of the people they shoved aside.

The shifter twisted to look back the way they had come—and saw the other sailors closing, too, drawn by Vennet's shouts.

A crooked sidestreet opened nearby. It was empty. "Down there!" he told Orshok and Ashi. He pushed them past the people who stood like confused cattle, staring at Vennet and his men, and down the street. He followed—but not before snatching a long bolt of colorful fabric away from a woman standing on the corner. Her shouts followed him around the first sharp bend in the street.

"Ashi!" he called. "Stop and help me! Orshok, run slow—you're our bait!"

He saw the young orc swallow, but keep going. Ashi stopped and whirled around. Geth grabbed her and pulled her into the shelter of the bend. He thrust the free end of the bolt of fabric into her hands. "Hold tight to this."

Shouts echoed along the street. The first group of Vennet's men had come after them. Geth and Ashi pressed back. Geth drew a deep breath, reached inside himself—and shifted.

Instincts, reflexes, and animal features weren't the only legacy to shifters from their lycanthropic ancestors. Although they couldn't take the true beast forms of their ancestors, shifters could take on bestial aspects. Some could grow claws or fangs. Some could put on incredible speed or enhance their senses. Geth's shifting ability wasn't so flamboyant or deadly, but he had always thought it was even more useful.

As the shifting swept through him, his skin toughened. His hair bristled and seemed to grow thick. A sensation of invulnerability pounded in his veins.

When Vennet's men came pounding around the bend in the alley, their eyes fixed on Orshok, Geth roared and leaped out behind them. Startled, the men froze for just an instant. That was long enough for Geth. He darted forward, jumping around the men, the bolt of fabric unraveling behind him in an unlikely banner. Ashi realized what he was doing and ran around the other way to meet him, drawing the noose of fabric tight. Vennet's men found themselves abruptly clustered together, pinned by the colorful cloth before they could draw their blades. Geth and Ashi turned almost in unison and threw themselves against the trapped men, laying them down with a flurry of hard, fast punches and kicks.

One sailor managed to squirm free and pull out a knife as the fabric noose fell slack. He lunged at Geth. The shifter swatted his attack aside, but the knife still connected. The blade slashed his arm—and left no more than a score in his shifting-toughened skin. Geth growled and smashed his elbow across the sailor's face. The knife might have done no lasting damage, but it still *hurt*.

The man dropped like a stone, the last to go down—and just in time. Vennet's voice swept down the street. People were staring down from windows above. A short distance along the street, Orshok was waiting, hopping from one foot to the other, ready to run again. Geth let go of the fabric and grabbed Ashi. "Come on. Half a dozen down is only a start."

Ashi's eyes were bright as they sprinted after Orshok, whipping around another bend in the street. "It was too easy," she hissed between her teeth. "They moved slow. Did you see their eyes?"

Geth scowled. "I wasn't looking at their eyes!"

As soon as the words were out of his mouth, though, he could see in his memory exactly what Ashi meant. The sailors' reactions had been slow, almost as if they had been drinking. Their eyes had been focused, but also strangely distant—as if a part of each man's mind had been under the control of someone else. Another growl escaped him. "Dah'mir's influence!"

"Where do you think he is?" asked Orshok. "Word of Vvaraak, why hasn't *he* come after us?"

"Maybe he doesn't want to take to the sky over a crowded city," said Ashi.

Or, Geth thought, maybe he couldn't. The dragon's stiff movements, the haggard look of pain on his human face . . . maybe Dah'mir couldn't fly. Tiger's blood, he wondered, how badly did I injure him?

He kept the thought to himself. If Dah'mir was somewhere behind them, they couldn't led their guard down. Vennet and his men were still following, their shouts echoing along the twists of the street—once they lost them, they could worry about Dah'mir. Geth glanced down each of the alleys that split off from the street, but without exception, they were all even narrower than the street itself—and now was not the time to risk blundering into a dead-end.

Assuming that the twisting street wasn't itself a dead-end.

As they skidded around a final corner, though, the buildings that had hemmed them in fell away. The crooked street opened up, merging with other streets to make a plaza along the side of a broad canal. To their left and ahead, wide streets ran off through the city. To their right, a bridge leaped across the canal. The plaza was busy—ordinary people going about their day's errands, merchants strolling and talking, porters plodding under massive loads of goods. A strange smell like a hundred crushed plants mingled together made Geth's nose twitch.

"That's the herb market!" Orshok panted. The orc was running heavily, out of breath. "It's close—on the other side of the canal. Singe and Dandra will be there. They can help us!"

A chill rolled along Geth's back. "No!" he said, slowing in the middle of the plaza. "We can't lead Vennet to them. Dandra's vulnerable to Dah'mir's power."

"What do we do then?" asked Ashi. She swung around to face him—and her eyes focused on something high and behind him. Her mouth opened to shout a warning, but Geth was already spinning—

—as five black herons with acid-green eyes came swooping out of the sky, practically on top of them. He flung up one arm to shield his face and flailed wildly with his other, trying to bat the birds away. He smelled a greasy, coppery stink as one of the birds struck. Pain raked along his arm. As the birds flapped back up into the air, he glanced at his arm. The heron's sharp talons had drawn blood even through his tough hide!

He spun around. The birds were beating for altitude again, coming around. People across the plaza were shouting and turning to look. Ashi was helping Orshok to his feet. There were long slashes in the druid's sleeves and bloody scratches on his forehead. Geth jumped to his side, teeth bared. "I'm really starting to hate those damn herons!"

There was anger in Orshok's eyes. "Then let's give them something to worry about besides us!" He thrust his hands—his hunda stick clenched in one, the fingers of the other spread wide—toward the sky and spat a prayer.

Nature stirred and answered his call. In the sky above the wheeling herons, the afternoon light seemed to fold and part. With a chorus of brittle shrieks, four eagles burst out of the air and hit the herons in a flurry of feathers and talons. One of the herons fell to the wooden plaza almost immediately, its neck broken. The others scattered, pursued by the eagles.

The display of magic drew even more attention to them, however—some of it distinctly unwelcome.

"Geth!" shouted Vennet. "Ashi, you treacherous bitch!

Geth turned to see the half-elf standing in the mouth of the crooked street they had just left, his dim-eyed crew spreading out around their captain. He recognized many of them, including a formerly friendly, steadfast sailor named Karth. If Karth had been turned to hunting them down, Geth knew, something had definitely taken control of Vennet's men.

He also knew that they couldn't just keep running. He crouched down, a snarl tearing itself from his throat and reached for his sword. Ashi was at his side, her hand on her weapon as well. The bystanders closest to them pulled back swiftly.

Then Orshok's voice rippled through the air in another desperate prayer. The afternoon light vanished in the roiling cloud of thick mist that took shape all around them.

"Grandmother Wolf!" Geth's curse was lost in the shouts of alarm from the people around. The shifter reached out and grabbed the dim shape that was Ashi and pulled her with him toward Orshok. The young orc loomed out of the mist like a ghost.

Geth grabbed him, too. "Move! This isn't going to stop Vennet!"

"He can't see us."

"He can't see us *yet*," Geth told him. The fear of the crowd gave him a desperate idea. The body of the heron killed by Orshok's eagles lay nearby. Pushing Ashi and Orshok toward the right side of the plaza, he scooped up the dead bird and hurled it off through the mist in the opposite direction. There was dull thud and a startled shout as it hit someone.

An instant later, the mist across that side of the plaza vanished in a howling rush of wind as Vennet, drawn by the sudden cry, unleashed the power of his dragonmark.

The blast of wind drew out more cries from the startled people in the plaza. Abruptly, the shifter, the hunter, and the druid weren't the only ones running away from Vennet. Geth kept a tight grip on Orshok and Ashi, keeping them ahead of him as bodies packed around them in the remaining mist. "Stay low!" he said. "Keep moving with the crowd!"

He heard splashes nearby as people fell off the edge of the plaza in their haste to flee, but up ahead the shouting crowd actually seemed to be condensing. He guided the others that way, pushing his way through the noisy crush to take a place just in front of a wide-eyed porter jogging along with a tall basket strapped to his back. Two merchants squeezed him on the left, a ragged beggar on the right. The mist lightened as they approached the edge of the cloud, then thinned and vanished as they broke clear.

They were in the middle of the bridge over the canal, just part of a frightened throng fleeing magic and the threat of violence in the plaza.

Geth felt Orshok stiffen. "Geth, this is the way to the herb market!"

"I know," said the shifter. "Brace yourselves and keep moving." He glanced at the men around him, then leaned toward the closer of the two merchants. "Sorry for this," he said.

The man barely had time to give him a curious look before Geth hooked a foot around his leg and swept it out from under him. The merchant flailed and went down, clutching at his companion and pulling him off balance as well. Geth kept moving even as the porter staggered to avoid the fallen men, knocking another person to the ground and leaving his tall load swaying. The porter tried to right himself—and failed. His basket tipped and fat green melons flew out, bouncing on the bridge and tripping still more people. Those who could see what had happened tried to slow down and dodge around the fallen people, but the press of the crowd didn't let up. New shouts of confusion and fear rang out.

Geth caught Ashi and Orshok and pushed them on through the milling mob and off the bridge, then, as the street opened into the edge of a vast market, out of the crowd and into the shadow of a merchant's stall. Safe for a moment, he took a deep breath. "Did it work?" he gasped.

Ashi peered cautiously back the way they had come. "*Rond betch*, what a mess! Vennet's not going to get through that fast!"

"Where is he?" asked Geth.

"The mist is lifting." She paused, then added, "He's still on the plaza, looking like he's trying to decide what to do."

"Herons?"

Ashi's eyes turned to the sky. "None close."

Geth sagged back. He released his hold on the shifting and its rush of invincibility bled out of him. The sting of the scratches inflicted by the heron's talons faded, eased by the fading power. Geth let his breath out in a grateful hiss and looked at Ashi and Orshok. The hunter was still tense, her hand hovering close to her sword. The druid was drenched in sweat and trembling, his fingers gripping his hunda stick. Geth nodded to both of them. "Easy," he said. "I think we're safe—"

"Geth! Twelve bloody moons, what have you done?"

Geth leaped up like a rabbit, lunging for Singe where the wizard stood in the street and dragging him under cover with a hand over his mouth. Dandra and Natrac were with him—Ashi swept both of them into hiding as well.

Geth eased his hand away from Singe's face. "What are you doing here?"

Singe's eyes went from wide to narrow. "We *were* coming to see what all the commotion was. Did you have something to do with this? What's going on?"

"Vennet and Dah'mir are in Zarash'ak," Geth told him with a growl.

Dandra tensed. "What? How?"

"Dah'mir's in human form—he was with Vennet at the docks. We just got away." Geth jerked his head toward the bridge. "Vennet's still in the plaza over there. He might still figure out where we've gone. Dah'mir's herons are hunting for us from the sky. We need to find some place to hide—the sooner the better."

"Lords of the Host," cursed Natrac. He stepped back out into the street, looked quickly in the direction of the bridge, then gestured for the others to follow him. "This way. Quickly!"

The half-orc ducked across the street and, brushing aside a hanging curtain, squeezed between two stalls. Geth sent Orshok and Ashi after him, then Dandra and Singe. Dandra's face was pale with fear, her jaw set with determination. Singe's hand hovered near his sword. They crossed quickly, heads down, Singe walking to shield Dandra's red-brown skin and distinctive clothes from anyone who might be watching. Once they had disappeared behind the curtain, Geth stepped cautiously into the street and glanced back at the bridge.

Ashi's description of the aftermath of their passage as a mess was accurate. People were still milling about on the bridge. A few were down. More people were gathering to see what had happened. Geth felt a twinge of guilt and hoped that his desperate play hadn't left anyone badly injured.

He couldn't, however see Vennet or any of his crew, and that was all he could have asked for. He eased himself through the knots of people who had stopped to gossip, then, as soon as he was under the cover of the stalls on the other side of the street, dove through the curtain and after the others.

The stalls had been set up across the mouth of a narrow passage—probably deliberately. One of the stallkeepers was vanishing back into his tiny place of business with clinking coins in his hand. A moment later, the curtain ruffled as crates were shoved across its street side. Anyone passing would be unlikely to guess at the passage beyond.

"How did you know this was here?" Geth asked Natrac.

"It's a pickpocket's bolthole," said the half-orc. "Spend time in Zarash'ak's markets and you start to recognize them—and to keep a hand on your purse. Pickpockets like to stick close to them."

Geth's hand twitched toward his belt, but Natrac shook his head. "Any pickpockets will have gone straight to the crowd on the bridge."

He led them a little further down the passage. Geth couldn't have called it an alley—it was just barely big enough to squeeze down sideways. After a short distance, however, it opened up into a tiny, stifling hot courtyard no larger than a small room and with walls rising high enough around them that it felt like being at the bottom of the hole. Laundry had been hung on lines overhead, obscuring any view of—or from—the sky. Two other passages no wider than the first let out from the courtyard in different directions. Natrac lowered himself onto a crude bench someone had knocked together. "We should be safe here for now."

Singe turned to Geth, Ashi, and Orshok. "What happened?"

Geth related everything they had seen and heard on the docks and since. The story left Dandra looking troubled. "Dah'mir and Vennet?" she asked. "I don't like the sound of that."

"Vennet's a toad," said Singe, biting at his words. "You should have seen him with Dah'mir after he helped capture us. He was on his knees faster than a Thrane before an altar. After the battle at the mound, maybe Dah'mir thought he needed a new ally."

"How could he have gotten to Zarash'ak before us?"

"Powerful magic, probably," Singe answered with a shrug. "We saw him vanish, didn't we? He's a dragon. He could have done almost anything."

"Do you think Vennet knows that?" asked Orshok.

The question left all of them silent for a moment before Geth growled an answer. "Do you think he would care?"

"Vennet's greedy and power-mad, but I don't think he's stupid." Singe sat down on the bench beside Natrac. "Why do you think they'd be going back up river?"

"They're going back to the Bonetree mound," Ashi said grimly. "Dah'mir told Vennet two weeks—the journey to Bonetree territory takes two weeks."

"Dah'mir could fly there faster in his dragon form, couldn't he?"

Geth bared his teeth. "I think he's still injured." He traced the stain and mended tear that had marked Dah'mir's robes on his own chest. "It would explain why he didn't chase us himself—and why he'd be traveling with Vennet. Maybe Vennet is more than just a convenient ally."

Ashi's eyes opened wide, flashing in the gloom, and she stretched her hands. "If Dah'mir's weak, we should attack! We have the element of surprise!"

Singe looked up sharply. "He's still a dragon, Ashi! We're guessing that he may not be able to fly, but that doesn't make him helpless. He's dominating Vennet's entire crew and he still has magic." The wizard's lips pressed together into a thin line. "I'd want to know more about just how weak he was before I took him on."

Dandra paced back and forth across the courtyard, her fine-featured face troubled. After a moment, she said, "Dah'mir will have guessed that we're all here together. I don't think we can stay in Zarash'ak."

"You think he would delay his journey up river to hunt for us?" asked Orshok.

"What's waiting for him at the Bonetree mound? Nothing."

Dandra turned, stopping her pacing for a moment. "If he leaves Zarash'ak, he risks losing us."

Geth squeezed his fists together, but nodded. "I wouldn't walk away from us," he said. "So where do we go? Have you found out anything about the Spires of the Forge?"

Dandra, Singe, and Natrac exchanged a glance, then Dandra shook her head. "House Tharashk told us nothing. We've tried a bounty hunter and two dragonshard prospectors. None of them have heard of the Spires of the Forge—the bounty hunter claimed they didn't exist."

"They exist," said Ashi firmly.

"That doesn't do us any good if we can't find them," said Singe. He tapped his fingertips together. "There's still Natrac's historian, but I don't think going out to dinner is such a great idea. Natrac, if we can make it back to your house unseen, do you think your historian could come to us?"

Natrac's face tightened. "Going back to my house might not be a good idea. Vennet knows where I live. I invited him to dinner once."

Geth growled. "You *what?*"

"We were on good terms at the time," the half-orc snapped. "I didn't know he was going to end up cutting off my hand!"

"He doesn't know you're still with us," Ashi pointed out.

"No, but if Dah'mir has told him that a half-orc with one hand fought with Geth and Singe at the Bonetree mound, he'll probably put it together."

"Does Vennet know your historian?" Dandra asked.

They all looked at her. She spread her hands. "If Vennet doesn't know your historian, we'd be safe there."

Natrac looked doubtful. "I don't want to expose her to danger."

Her. A woman. It was the first time the half-orc had given away any information at all about his historian. In another situation, Geth might have teased him or tried to drag out more, but this was no time for jokes. "If we can get there without being spotted, she won't be in any danger," he said. "Besides, we need her information, don't we? The sooner we get it, the sooner we can get out of Zarash'ak."

"The hard part will be going anywhere without being seen," said Ashi. "We might be able to avoid Vennet, but the herons can see anything in the streets."

Natrac exhaled slowly. "I know a way," he said. "We should wait here a while, give Vennet a chance to move on, then we'll go." He looked up, his eyes dark. "But if anyone gets hurt . . ."

"No one will get hurt, Natrac," Geth said. He thumped his fist against his chest. "I promise. We'll be like ghosts. No one will even know we're there."

Dah'mir was waiting by the river boat, sitting on a water cask as if it were a throne, when Vennet finally returned to the docks with his crew. Dah'mir's green eyes flashed. "You didn't catch them," he said.

"No," Vennet told him. "They got away." He hesitated, then added. "Ashi was with Geth, lord."

"I saw her," said Dah'mir. "It doesn't please me."

Vennet's crew moved around them, silently loading the last of the supplies into the river boat, resuming the tasks they had abandoned to take up the chase. The strength of Dah'mir's control over them was, Vennet had to admit, astounding. Even during the chase, not one of the men had roused. It would take only one of the men escaping and passing on word of what had taken place on *Lightning on Water* for House Lyrandar to begin an investigation. There would be rumors enough soon—his passengers and cargo should have been delivered to Trolanport days ago.

"Be at ease, captain," said Dah'mir. The green-eyed man must have guessed what was in his head—Vennet had wondered before at his uncanny knowledge, though Dah'mir insisted there was nothing magical about it, only practice in reading faces. "When I have regained my strength, the Dragon Below will see to all things. You will have the power and wealth you desire and your secret will be safe."

Vennet pressed his lips together. "I'm risking everything for you, lord."

"And your risk will be rewarded, captain. You have my word."

The priest's promise soothed the worshipper of Khyber within him. The first time he'd heard of Dah'mir—through Singe, then through Ashi—he'd seen the potential in allying himself with the priest. Betraying Singe, Geth, and Dandra had been little enough and he had profited from it. Dah'mir had rewarded him with two large and valuable dragonshards, a blue-black Khyber shard and a golden Siberys shard, now hidden in a strongbox beneath the floor of his cabin. The shards had been, Dah'mir claimed, a beacon to him after he had been wounded in the battle at the Bonetree mound. The priest had used powerful magic to fling himself and his birds through a plane of shadow, traveling hundred of miles from the battlefield to *Lightning on Water* in only hours.

But Vennet had been a scion of House Lyrandar long before he'd joined the cult of the Dragon Below. As awed and honored as Vennet had been to wake and find Dah'mir in his cabin and in need of his aid, the training of Lyrandar had left him skeptical. The priest wasn't telling him everything. There was something about the battle at the Bonetree mound that he had left out. Vennet believed his tale of the orc raiders and the Gatekeepers, of Ashi's betrayal, of Medala's destruction at Dandra's hand, of the dolgaunt Hruucan's fiery death at Singe's—of Dah'mir's own injury by the strange ancient sword wielded by Geth. The wound that scarred the priest's chest still showed no sign of healing even a week later.

That Dah'mir had panicked at his wounding and fled to distant safety where his attackers couldn't follow—Vennet could believe that, too. He'd watched Dah'mir's frustration as the strength drained out of him. The priest tried to hide it, but Vennet knew that every command he issued to the crew made him weaker. He'd seen him attempt magic and watched his spells falter. The key to regaining his strength lay in returning to the Bonetree mound, the heart of his power. That was what he needed Vennet for.

There was something else though, Vennet knew. Suspicion crept in at the back of his mind, lifting the hairs on the back of his neck. He prayed to Khyber that he'd made the right decision in siding with the priest.

There was one thing about Dah'mir that he had worked out for himself, however. "Lord," he pointed out, "if Geth is in Zarash'ak, Dandra probably is, too."

Dah'mir's mouth twisted in anger, the expression darkening his face like a cloud across the sun. He cut Vennet off with a snap. "I had guessed that myself, captain! Zarash'ak has too many hiding places, though. We can spare no more time. I *must* return to the Bonetree mound. That is my only concern. I want to leave as soon as the boat is ready."

For the first time, Vennet heard an edge of desperation in the priest's voice. He bent his head, holding back a sly, self-satisfied smile. "I know, lord. I anticipated it. But just because we can't stay to look for her and her companions doesn't mean that someone else can't search them out and hold them until we return. I took the initiative of contacting someone and offering him the job." Vennet gestured for the heavily-muscled man who had been standing back in the shadows to join them. "I know his reputation. He's said to be one of the best bounty hunters available."

"I am the best," the man growled as he came forward. He met Dah'mir's eyes boldly. "I'll get you your people."

"Lord," said Vennet, "meet Chain d'Tharashk."

CHAPTER

4

They left the courtyard the same way they had entered. At the end of the narrow passage, Natrac muttered a few words in Orc to the merchants whose stalls hid the entrance to the bolthole, and the crates that blocked the curtain were shifted. Singe pushed past the curtain gratefully—after the stifling heat of the enclosed courtyard, Zarash'ak's open streets felt cool as a spring morning. The ring that he wore, an inheritance from his grandfather, protected him from fire, but it did nothing to shield him from simple heat. At that moment, there was nothing he wanted more than a dunking in cool water. A swim, a bath, even a pump that he could stick his head under . . .

A horse trough, he thought, I'd take a horse trough.

They didn't have time for even that dubious luxury. The crowds on the streets were thinning with the end of the day. They'd hidden in the courtyard for as long as they'd dared but there was still a good chance that Vennet, his crew, or especially Dah'mir's herons might still be abroad, and the thinning crowds left them that much less cover. As soon as they had all emerged—sticky and sweating—from the bolthole, they set off down the street at a brisk pace. They moved in two groups, trying their best to blend in, all of them alert.

Natrac took the lead, Singe and Geth at his side. They hadn't gone far before Geth growled under his breath. "You're taking us back to the bridge."

The half-orc nodded but didn't slow down. Singe looked up at the sky. There were no herons visible above the street, but the arc of sky overhead was relatively narrow, constrained by the buildings on either side. Once they were on the bridge—and in the plaza beyond—they would be exposed.

"Natrac," Singe said, "the idea was to get under cover. The bridge and plaza—"

"We're not crossing the bridge," said Natrac.

"Running alongside the canal doesn't seem much better," Geth pointed out.

"We're not doing that either." Natrac's voice was on edge. "We're going down into the webs."

Singe shot a glance at him. Natrac's face was set as tight as his voice, as though he was preparing himself for something unpleasant. Before he could ask him more, though, Natrac held up his right arm, gesturing for them to stop. The bridge on which Geth, Ashi, and Orshok had escaped from Vennet was just ahead, the casual flow of people around it giving no hint of the panicked, tangled mob that had flooded across earlier. Singe scanned the bridge, the plaza, and the sky for signs of observers or an ambush.

The silhouette of a heron moved across a sky red with twilight. "Is that one of Dah'mir's?" Singe asked.

Geth squinted, then shook his head. "I can't tell."

"We only need to get across the street." Natrac pointed ahead. "There are stairs leading down to the canal just to the left of the bridge. That's where we're going."

Singe twisted around and looked for Dandra and the others. They were less than a dozen paces away, pressed back against a wall. Singe caught Dandra's eye and gestured to the stairs Natrac had indicated. She nodded. He turned back to Natrac. "Let's go."

Darting across the street and down the stairs for no other reason than the distant presence of a bird actually felt vaguely ridiculous. A half dozen similar—but much more deadly—situations that he had experienced over his years as a mercenary flitted through Singe's mind. Running for cover on a battlefield in Cyre as arrows fell. Infiltrating an enemy camp. Leaping aside as a hostile wizard hurled bolts of lightning at him. Retreating through the shadows of Narath as the soldiers of Aundair, countrymen he had left behind when he joined the Blademarks of House Deneith, flooded the streets . . .

Dodging around strolling shoppers might have felt ridiculous, but his heart was still racing as he paused on the stairs to be sure that Ashi, Orshok, and Dandra made it into hiding as well. Dandra came last, shepherding the others before her even though, he knew, she could easily have outpaced them both. He fell in beside her as they hurried down the long flight of steps toward the canal below. "You saw the heron?"

She nodded. "Do you think it saw us?"

"I hope not." Singe gave her a closer look. There was a particular set to Dandra's chin and the line of her jaw that Singe had come to recognize as an expression of her unstoppable determination. It was an expression that she wore only when she was up against formidable resistance—most particularly internal resistance. His eyes flicked to the yellow-green crystal hanging around her neck, then away. "Is Tetkashtai bothering you?" he asked.

"Does it show?"

"If you know what to look for."

Dandra grimaced, but nodded again. "She's terrified at even being in the same city as Dah'mir," she said. "All she wants to do is get away from him."

"I can't say I entirely blame her. Even if Geth's right and he's weak, I don't like knowing he's this close." He twitched his shoulders. "It puts me on edge."

"You might be on edge," Dandra said tightly, "but I know you'll step back. Every time Tetkashtai gets this way, she comes closer to falling over."

Her eyes flickered as some inner dialogue passed between her and the presence. Singe raised an eyebrow as her face tightened a little more. Tetkashtai could hear what Dandra heard. "What does she say?" the wizard asked.

"You don't want to know."

Singe bit back the curiosity that her answer roused in him. The very first time that Dandra had touched his mind in the mental link that kalashtar called the *kesh*, she had shown him Tetkashtai as she saw her: a formless aura of yellow-green light, at the same time both part of her and something separate. That was as close as he could come to experiencing the union that Dandra had with the presence—and he knew that it was as close as he *should* come, too. Dandra was the only one who could stand up to Tetkashtai. Geth had tried drawing on the presence's power once and almost ended up a prisoner in his own body. Singe knew better than to try.

Even though it cut him to see Dandra struggling alone with such a shadow across her fiery, determined personality.

At the bottom of the stairs, the wooden island of a landing spread out. Only one edge of it faced onto the canal—the rest of it extended back beneath the platform of the street above. Skiffs skirted the landing, making deliveries and ferrying passengers along the canal, but when a boatman called out to Natrac, offering his services, the half-orc just dismissed him with a wave and a scowl. Instead, he led them away from the stairs and further into the gloom below the city. The massive pillars and stilts that supported Zarash'ak rose above them like naked trees. The last hints of the fresh smell of the herb market were cut off, replaced by the stink of the silty water that moved sluggishly past their feet.

On the opposite side of the landing from the stairs, one end of a tangle of planks and rope had been secured to spikes driven into the wood. The other rose up at a sharp angle toward the shadows overhead, creating a trembling construction that was half ramp and half rope bridge. Singe lifted his head, following the lines of rope.

Hidden in the darkness of the underside of Zarash'ak, long spans of suspended walkways bounced, shifted, and swayed in a complex network like the weavings of some enormous spider.

"The webs?" Singe asked.

Natrac nodded.

"Grandmother Wolf!" said Geth, his eyes wide and shining in the dim light. "They're incredible. Who built them?"

"Goblins," Natrac said. "Clever little vermin. There aren't that many of them in the city and they like their own space. The webs are still mostly their territory but there are other groups in Zarash'ak who use them, too. I don't think even Vennet would try looking for us down here." He stepped cautiously onto the angled bridge. The ropes creaked at his weight but held. "Be careful," he said over his shoulder and began to climb.

One by one, they followed after him. To his surprise, Singe found that the bridge was actually very well constructed. It bounced and swayed as they moved along it, but only within a narrow range of motion. Under the lighter weight of goblins, the bridge might not have even shifted at all. It had been built with more than goblins in mind, though—there were two ropes on either side of the foot bed, one low for small travelers, the other higher for human hands and arms. The overhead walkways, once they reached them, were similarly well-built, though cramped. Two humans would have been forced to squeeze together if they wanted to pass on the walkway and the rough, age-darkened wooden patchwork that was the underside of Zarash'ak hung just a few feet above Singe's head. Only the dim vista of slow water and massive pillars broke the oppression, a spectacular sight in its own way.

For a moment, Singe was reminded of the fantastic bridges and skyways that leaped between the towers of Sharn—except that the bridges of Sharn smelled a lot better than the shadowed webs. Singe wrinkled his nose as a ripe stink welled up from below and enveloped them. "Twelve moons," he said, taking shallow breaths through his mouth. "Does the smell just keep getting worse?"

"There are dead spots in the flow around the stilts," said Natrac. "Anything that gets caught in one just floats until it rots."

"How far do we have to go?"

"Around to the other side of the city." The half-orc made a face, thrusting his tusks out. "The problem is that paths through the webs don't run under everything and they don't always take the most direct route."

"Then keep moving," Ashi said. "The sooner we reach our destination, the better."

As long as he could keep track of which of the patches of twilight that penetrated the darkness below Zarash'ak marked the canal where they had entered the webs, Singe felt like he knew where they were. As soon as he lost that point of reference, though—and all it took was glancing away at the wrong moment—he felt instantly disoriented. The paths of the webs were strange. The ropes and cables that supported the walkways and bridges weren't perpendicular like the walls of buildings. They ran at odd angles. They crossed and knotted and merged. The walkways rose and dipped, flowing around the strange upside-down architecture of Zarash'ak's underside: the hanging cellars of buildings. the enormous beams that lay beneath the streets, the huge bulges like barrels the size of ships' hulls that Natrac said were cisterns.

"Constructed by House Cannith when the city was still growing," he explained. "They collect Zarash'ak's drinking water. Those of us who can afford it have our own, but those who can't have to fetch water from the public cisterns."

Their group wasn't alone on the webs. As they moved beneath other parts of the city, goblins appeared out of the gloom, darting past them on the narrow walkways without a moment's hesitation or a second glance. On broader ledges constructed around the massive stilts or on platforms hung from beams above, more goblins—and other folk—gathered. On one crowded multi-level collection of platforms, apparently the webs' version of a tavern, Singe spotted humans and half-orcs, along with a knot of hobgoblins. The goblins' larger kinfolk were taller and bulkier than a human man, with small yellow eyes, orange-brown hair, tufted ears, and flattened faces. Singe was just as happy that they didn't see more of them.

"There weren't many goblins in the streets above," he said. "Do they all live down here?"

"*Dagga.*" Natrac's eyes searched the gloom and he pointed. "Do you see that?"

As night fell across the city above, the shadows of the webs deepened. Singe could barely see through the gathering darkness, but he could make out irregular shapes clinging like giant spider nests to several pillars. "What are they?"

"Goblin homes. Rope and board, woven together."

"What do the goblins do when the river rises?"

"Most of them climb to safety and the water washes through the webs. Once it recedes, the goblins come back, dry things out, and repair anything that needs repairing." Natrac slapped at a thick rope, making it quiver in a way that brought a stiff grimace out of Ashi. "The webs have survived the worst that Zarash'ak can throw at them. Not even fire has much effect on them—it just smolders and smells bad."

Geth was peering over the edge of the walkway on which they stood, a more substantial construction than most. He cocked his head suddenly. "Natrac, what's that?"

Singe followed his gaze. Down below, the water seemed to have given way to foul, dark mud and yet another strange shape, this one large and blocky. He actually stared at it for several moments before he realized that it was a crumbling stone building, half-sunk in the mud and leaning at a crazy angle.

Natrac smiled. "When the Five Nations and the dragonmarked houses first started paying attention to the Shadow Marches," he said, "they tried erecting the same kinds of buildings they knew at home on some of the islands in the river. Supposedly they were so full of brilliant plans for dealing with floodwaters that they didn't bother talking to the local clans and tribes." He nodded toward the leaning ruins. "Their buildings started sinking before the river had even flooded. Even after the locals suggested building on stilts, some people kept trying. Zarash'ak is built over clever ideas." He turned away. "We're close to where we need to be. Let's find a way back up to the streets."

"Guides?" called a high, slippery voice. "You need guides?"

Singe spun sharply, his hand going to his rapier. The lone goblin who stood on the walkway before them twitched large ears—one missing a good half of its length, bitten off to judge by the ragged scar that was left—and blinked reddish eyes. "Easy!" he said. "Big folk get nervous too easy in the webs." He smiled, showing crooked, needle-like teeth. "You need guides to get you back topside?"

"You move quietly for a guide," said Singe. He examined the goblin. The little creature carried a long knife on either side of his belt. "You're well-armed for one, too."

The goblin shrugged. "Not always a guide."

Singe raised an eyebrow. "Well whatever you are, I don't think we need one right now."

"Wait." Natrac touched Singe's arm and whispered, "We could use directions. It will get us out of here quicker."

"You trust him?" asked Geth from Singe's other side.

"I wouldn't follow him across the street, but there are six of us and we're expecting an ambush. We'll be fine." Natrac raised his voice. "Five copper crowns if you direct us to the nearest exit—no tricks. We can find our own way."

"Ban." The goblin shrugged again and pointed along a walkway that intersected the one they stood on. "Turn left, then right. Look for the straight ladder."

"Thank you." Natrac's hand reached into a pouch and he stepped forward to give the goblin his reward.

Singe looked down the way that the goblin had pointed. He couldn't see much in the gloom, but the walkway looked open and clear, with no possible hiding places. Maybe the goblin had given them honest directions.

Maybe not. Singe dipped his fingers into his money pouch and brought out a copper coin. He clenched the coin tight and murmured a word of magic into his fist—then stepped forward and flung the coin as far as he could along the walkway.

Released from the concealment of his fingers, the coin flashed with magical light. It was no brighter than a torch, but in the dimness of the webs, it was dazzling. Singe shaded his eyes and followed the coin's arc as the others gasped in surprise.

Screeches of dismay erupted from the shadows and startled goblins dropped like spiders out of their hiding places among the great beams overhead, tumbling down to the walkway and scurrying away from the unexpected magic.

Natrac bellowed like an angry bull. His hand opened, scattering copper crowns across the walkway, and clamped around the goblin's scrawny neck, wrenching him off his feet. The goblin kicked and struggled, but Natrac simply held him away. He raised the knife on his right wrist. "Now," he said, "which way do we really go?"

His eyes bulging, the goblin pointed in another direction. Natrac growled and started to set him down.

"Maybe not yet," said Singe. Down the other walkway, goblins were edging back into the light of the glowing coin, their fear fading fast as they realized that the magic was nothing that would hurt them. A few were turning bright eyes back to the group of bigfolk that had intruded on their territory. Natrac glanced at the goblin in his grip.

"If you think they care enough to see you stay safe, you'd better tell them to stay back." He lowered the goblin to the ground and eased his grasp on his throat. The goblin drew a rasping breath and shouted something frightened in its harsh language. The other goblins paused and pulled back.

"Good," said Natrac. "Now let's find that exit." Keeping a firm grip on the goblin's shoulder, he steered the little creature along the walkway. Singe and Geth took the rear of the group, keeping their eyes on the goblins behind them.

The way back to the upper streets of Zarash'ak, a flight of steep stairs that rose up to the edge of a narrow courtyard, was actually remarkably close but not particularly easy to spot. The goblin gang, Singe thought, probably did good business ambushing those looking for it. Natrac dragged the goblin along with them up the stairs, then released him once they were all in the courtyard above. The goblin disappeared back into the webs with a series of barking curses that Singe could only imagine were promises of vengeance if they were ever caught in the webs again.

Natrac ignored him and looked around. "This way," he said.

They had emerged from the webs in a part of the city unlike the others Singe had seen. The buildings were older and the orc influence on them—and the people—more obvious. The street rang with loud music, rough laughter, and the guttural Orc language. The odors of food and drink drifted on the evening breeze: *gaeth'ad*, ale, and the spicy grilled meats of the Shadow Marches. At an open window above their heads, an old woman with the heavy build and pronounced jaw of a half-orc sat, slowly chewing something and staring at them as they passed. Many of the people on the night-dark street gave them at least a curious glance. Singe had the feeling that travellers seldom came to this part of Zarash'ak.

Natrac stopped them before a large, ramshackle house, most of its many windows wide open to the evening. A good deal of shouting and banging was coming from inside, as if a horde of children had been turned loose within. Singe glanced at Natrac curiously. "What is this place? An orphanage?"

"Not exactly." The half-orc strode forward. The door of the house was decorated with an iron door knocker in the shape of an egg. Natrac lifted the hammer and rapped it against the striking plate vigorously.

The sounds of a scuffle broke out on the other side of the door, broken up by an angry voice and a wail of protest. A moment later, the door opened. The half-orc boy who stood on the other side was as tall and heavy as a human adult, but his face still had the greasy complexion of an adolescent. Behind him, two young girls—orc tusks thrusting up from their lower jaws, identical except that one of them had a hand pressed over her ear—stood and stared at the visitors.

"Kuk?" asked the boy.

"Bava osh?" Natrac asked in return. The boy looked him over, then nodded.

"Dag." He turned away from the door and bellowed out, *"Nena!"*

From somewhere inside the house, a woman's voice shouted back in harried frustration. Singe couldn't quite catch what she was saying, but he could imagine the meaning well enough—I'm busy! Who is it? The two half-orc girls exchanged silent, sly looks as the boy and the unseen woman shouted back and forth. Finally footsteps came rapping toward the door in a brisk march and the woman's exasperated words grew clearer. *"Diad, choshk sum bra—"*

The woman who stepped around a corner and into sight of the door was human. Generously built and well-endowed, she had thick, dark hair held back from her face with a colorful scarf and wore a fine, matching dress. She was older, middle-aged, perhaps of an age with Natrac. She held an infant, but she took one look at Natrac and thrust the baby on the older boy, then leaped forward to wrap her arms around him. "Natrac! When I got your message yesterday . . . Lords of the Host, I thought you were dead!"

"Bava! Careful!" Natrac twisted to hold the knife on his right arm away from her. She glanced down and let out an outraged gasp.

"I'd heard you'd been kidnapped—"

"Dagga," said Natrac grimly, but he squeezed the woman tight with his left arm, burying his face in her hair. Singe caught a faint murmur as he whispered something to her. Behind them, the young girls and the older boy looked on in surprise. After a moment, Natrac and the woman separated.

Quick as a spear thrust, the woman caught him across the face with a resounding slap. *"Shekot!* You're late for dinner! The food's almost ruined!"

Natrac rocked back a step with the force of the angry blow, then twisted around to the woman's side and put his arm across her shoulders to avoid another. A spot of blood showed at the corner of his lip, but he smiled at Singe and the others.

"This is Bava Bibahronaz," he said proudly. "An old friend. Bava, these are some new friends."

He introduced them all and if Bava was surprised at having an Aundairian, a savage of the Shadow Marches, a kalashtar, a shifter, and an orc all turn up unexpectedly on her doorstep, she didn't show it. "Welcome," she told them, then looked to Natrac and added fiercely, "I don't know whether to slap you again or hug you. What's going on?"

Natrac sighed. "That's a night's story. Bava, we need your help—"

Bava reached up and pressed a thick-fingered hand across Natrac's lips. "Natrac, every time I see you, you need my help!" She turned her head sharply and called to the half-orc boy, "Diad, take care of Noori. Mine, Ose, clear your brothers and sisters out of the dining room. Our guests are here—finally."

"Bava, it's not our fault!"

Diad slouched away, the baby cradled with surprising gentleness in his arm. The little girls darted off. Singe could hear them shouting as they ran—throughout the house, the voices of children died away for a moment, then resumed in an excited buzz. Bava paid them no attention, but just shook her head at Natrac's protests. She stepped away from him and hooked her arms around Geth's and Orshok's arms, pulling them through the door. "You look like men who enjoy a good meal," she said. "I'm surprised you'd let Natrac dawdle when dinner's waiting." She glanced back over her shoulder to call to the Singe and the others. "Come on! Come inside!"

Natrac stared after Bava with a look of mingled frustration and fascination on his face. Singe and Dandra glanced at each other, then Dandra asked delicately, "Natrac, how is it you know Bava?"

The half-orc bared his tusks at her and stomped off into the house. Singe, Dandra, and Ashi followed him through the door—Singe pulled it closed behind them. Inside, the house was cool and dim. The walls and floor were worn with age and the abuse inflicted by many active children. From a flight of stairs that rose up to the house's second floor, a series of young faces peered down. Their features varied widely, but all of them were young half-orcs. Ashi stared back at them and growled fiercely. The children darted back.

Dandra stared around at the house as they followed the sounds of Natrac's footsteps and Bava's laughter. "This isn't quite what I expected from a historian. Even a would-be historian."

"Me neither," Singe agreed. He frowned. "I feel like I should know Bava's name. I've heard it somewhere before."

"It's a clan name of the Shadow Marches," said Ashi. "*Bibahronaz*—the Howling Rabbit clan. I think they're from the southwest."

"That's not where I would have heard it. The Bonetree is the only Marcher clan I know." Singe searched his memory for the reason Bava's name seemed familiar. "I feel like I've known it for a long time."

The hall ended in a dining room with a huge battered table and mismatched chairs. Mine, Ose, and two other half-orc girls waited in a corner, staring at their guests. Natrac, seeming a little less surly now, had taken a chair and Bava was seating Geth and Orshok on either side of what was presumably her place at the head of the table. Singe's gaze, however, was drawn to a large painting that hung on a long wall of the dining room. In strong colors and bold strokes, it depicted a feast: humans, orcs, and half-orcs in both savage and civilized clothing, all sharing a table set amid the abundant wild plant life of the Shadow Marches. The style, especially the depictions of the plants of the Marches, was distinct and instantly recognizable. He dropped into the nearest chair, still staring at the painting.

"You're Bava Bahron," he said in awe.

"Bibahronaz," Bava corrected him. "No one ever got it right."

"I had a lecturer at Wynarn University who called you the greatest artist ever to come out of the Shadow Marches." Bava waved the comment away, but Singe pressed her. "I've seen some of your paintings. They're beautiful. Wynarn has your *Golden Asp* and the Royal Collection of Aundair has your *Union of Tharashk*. I remember staring at *Wild Grapes in Ruins* for hours."

"One of my first works," said Bava with a nod. "Not my best, but I liked it." She cocked her head. "I'm curious: where did you see it? It's been in the private collection of an Aundairian family named Bayard for twenty years."

A nasty smile flashed across Geth's face. Singe held back a

grimace and kept his voice level. "Casual friends," he said. "I saw it as a boy."

"You see?" said Natrac. "I told you that you underestimated Zarash'ak. With people like Bava, the City of Stilts can stand as high as Fairhaven or—"

Bava smacked him in the back of the head as she walked behind the table. "Hush!" she said with a smile. She gathered Mine, Ose, and the other two girls, sweeping them before her through a door at the other end of the room.

Dandra leaned across the table to Natrac. "How many children are there in this house?" she asked, a trace of amazement in her voice.

"Usually around a dozen."

"Are they all hers?" the shifter asked bluntly.

"No," said Bava with a chuckle, stepping back through the door. There was a platter of meat in each hand and she held the door open with a foot so that the little girls could follow her through, each of them carrying a bowl or a few plates. Through the open door, Singe caught a glimpse of a large kitchen—and the same faces he had seen peering down from the stairs before. Bava let the door swing shut after the girls and turned to the table herself. "Not all of them, anyway. Mothers don't always want half-orc children, even in Zarash'ak. I give them a place where they are wanted."

"There's an orc legend of the *Ghaash'nena*, a spirit that protects lost children," said Natrac. "Bava is the *Ghaash'nena* of Zarash'ak."

The elbow of the guardian spirit dipped as she passed and clipped him sharply on the ear. As Natrac cursed and rubbed his abused head, she smiled down at him. "Maybe instead of repeating silly stories, you could make yourself useful," she said. "You know where the wine is. Bring some out."

Natrac held up his knife-hand. "One hand," he reminded her.

"I'll help," said Ose eagerly.

"Me, too!" Mine added.

Natrac hung his head in mock resignation and pushed away from the table, following the two chattering girls back into the kitchen. Geth laughed and grinned at Bava. "How long have you known Natrac?" he asked.

"Almost too long to remember," the large woman said. "It will have been twenty years soon."

"Impossible," Singe said. "You couldn't have been born then."

Bava wagged a finger at him. "Don't flirt with me, Aundairian," she said. "You're too skinny." But a smile spread across her face and as she turned back to setting plates out on the table, she added, "We met in Sharn. I'd been there for five years, but I found out later that Natrac had only been in the city for two."

"You left your clan's territory for a city?" asked Ashi.

The large woman looked up at her. "If you're from the deep marshes, *sheid*, it must sound like a terrible thing, but I'd visited Zarash'ak many times. I knew that if I wanted to do more than paint huts and draw tattoos, I had to leave the Marches. So I went to Sharn. It was a hard decision. I think Natrac had an easier time of it when he left Graywall. Not that he had much choice in the matter—"

"Graywall in Droaam?" Singe said. "Natrac isn't from Zarash'ak?"

"You didn't know?" Bava's face turned red. "Host. I should have thought . . ." She clenched her teeth. "I shouldn't have said anything. Don't tell Natrac."

"What? Why?"

"Because I promised I wouldn't tell anyone." She set down the last plate and reached for a bowl of leafy green vegetables.

Geth, however, sat forward. "Can you answer one thing, though?" he asked. "What did Natrac do before he came to Zarash'ak? Was he a gladiator?"

Bava hesitated then shook her head. "Not as such. Now no more!" She turned away just as Natrac, Mine, and Ose returned with wine. Singe glanced at Geth curiously, but the shifter's eyes were on Natrac. The half-orc's were on Bava. Singe exchanged a look with Dandra, who only shrugged in confusion.

Bava got everyone seated with wine and food in front of them, then chased out the little girls, shut the door that led into the hall, and seated herself. "Now," she said with the same strong confidence she had before Singe had asked her about Natrac's past, "tell me what's going on."

She listened with a careful intensity to their story, interrupting only to ask a few probing questions that brought out anything they tried to skim over. As the tale unfolded, their food grew cold and their wine remained untouched. Diad wandered into the room and took a seat at the table—Bava gestured him out immediately, her face hard and rapt with attention. When they had finished, she reached for her wine and drained the glass, then passed the bottle around the table and made sure everyone had some.

"You don't mind that we came here, do you?" Natrac asked, his voice urgent. "If I'd known that Dah'mir and Vennet were in Zarash'ak, I would never have contacted you in the first place. Kol Korran's wager, I wouldn't even have stopped in the city."

Bava let go of Orshok's hand—at some point during their story, she had slipped her hand into the young orc's grasp—and reached out to pat Natrac's. "Don't think of that, Natrac. You know I'm always here." She shook her head. "And I thought the *Ghaash'nena* was only supposed to watch over children."

"Can you help us?" asked Dandra. "Do you know anything about the Hall of the Revered or the Spires of the Forge?"

"In spite of what Natrac might think," the large woman said, "I'm not a historian. But I think I do know why he brought you to me." She stood. "Come upstairs."

When she opened the door to the hall, Diad jumped up from where he had been crouched on the floor. Bava gave him a cross look. "How much did you hear?"

The young man's flushed face and tongue-tied expression said everything. Bava frowned. "Don't tell anyone *anything*," she said. She nodded back into the dining room. "Clear the table and don't let me catch you eavesdropping again!"

The half-orc boy rolled his eyes but Bava gave him an impatient grunt and he trudged past them into the dining room.

Natrac leaned toward Bava as they stepped out into the hall and Singe heard him murmur, "Is he too much trouble?"

"He's running with groups he shouldn't, but what boy doesn't?"

"If there's anything I can do—" Natrac started to say, but Bava shook her head.

"You're there when he needs it," she said. "That's enough."

Bava led them back to the stairs Singe had noticed before. The house had grown quiet as they ate and talked. Most of the children the wizard had seen and heard earlier were already asleep. As they climbed the stairs up to the house's second floor and then to its third, he could hear the soft snoring of children mixed with the whispers of those few who were still awake. From the third floor, they climbed yet another flight of stairs, this one even narrower. Bava pushed open a door at the top and they stepped into a broad open space that smelled of oil paint. A slow breeze whispering through tall windows with carved screens stirred the air; the same windows allowed the light of the risen moons to fall in silvery patterns across the floor. Stretched canvases were pale, flat blocks in the moonlight. Sketches on paper, tacked onto one wall, rustled like sleepy birds. A half-completed painting stood fixed to an easel, the colors drained from its surface by the moonlight to leave only swirls of light and dark. Bava opened the shade on an ever-bright lantern and colors leaped back into the work. "My studio," she said, ushering them into the chamber.

A large cabinet with long, flat drawers stood against one wall. Bava went to it and slid open a drawer. Singe peered over her shoulder—and raised his eyebrows in amazement. The drawer held maps, laid out flat. The one on top showed a section of northern Aundair; another, as Bava flipped through them, Cyre before its destruction in the Mourning.

"I collect them," said Bava, without waiting for the question. "Maps were what first introduced me to art."

"What good's a map of Cyre?" asked Geth. "Cyre's gone."

"Maps are memories. They show you the way things were on a larger scale than any painting." Bava found what she was looking for and slid a large piece of stiff, heavy leather from the drawer, turning gracefully to lay it out on a table. "You might as well ask what good an old map of Droaam is."

Dandra gasped and stepped forward as Bava moved back out of the way. "You have a map of Droaam two hundred years ago?" They all gathered around the table, looking down at a big stained parchment that had been mounted to the stiff leather for support.

"Closer to three hundred actually," Bava said, "and technically it was still western Breland then, but I think it will be good for what you need."

Singe gazed down at the old map with awed respect. The

parchment looked like it might be brittle, but the inks upon it were still bright and clear. The map was a work of art, the text written in an elegant script, the features of the landscape drawn with a careful hand. Illuminations marked major landmarks and decorated the map's margins. The whimsical figure of a fleeing traveler marked the route through the Graywall Mountains toward Sharn. A hideous cockatrice stood guard over the fabled ruins of Cazhaak Draal, the Stonelands; a banner held by a statue with an expression of horror on its petrified face warned would-be travelers to turn back. Dozens of other banners highlighted other areas of danger or interest.

"Twelve bloody moons!" he said. "This is perfect!" He whirled and wrapped his arms around Bava, planting a kiss on her cheek.

"Easy!" she cautioned him. "You haven't found what you need yet."

"But we will." He bent over the map, studying it. "Batul said that a season's journey east of the Bonetree territory would put someone in the western half of Droaam." He held his arm above the map, bisecting it, and began scanning all of the banners, illuminations, and labels to the left. Dandra and Natrac clustered close as well. The others just stayed out of their way. Geth tried to look over the map from the side until Singe snarled for him to get out of their light. The shifter gave up and wandered away to peer through the windows at the moonlit roof tops of Zarash'ak.

It didn't take long for Natrac to curse. "I don't see anything."

"Don't say that," said Dandra tightly without looking up.

Singe held his tongue, but there was already an unpleasant doubt gnawing at him. He went back and examined labels a second time, peering at the map until his eyes stung and his head ached. There was nowhere marked as the Spires of the Forge. Or the Hall of the Revered. He put an arm around Dandra's shoulders. "Dandra . . ."

The kalashtar sighed. "I know." She turned away from the map. "Nothing. Il-Yannah, I don't believe it!"

Bava stood up from where she was sitting with Orshok and held out her hands. "I'm sorry," she said. Dandra accepted her embrace of consolation.

Singe raked fingers through his hair. "Maybe the Spires of

the Forge aren't in Droaam," he said. He looked to Ashi. "Could the story be wrong? Could the hunters Dah'mir sent to the Halls of the Revered have been gone longer than a season? Could they have gone in another direction?"

The hunter shook her head. "The Bonetree preserved its stories carefully."

"Maybe the Spires of the Forge," Geth said suddenly, "aren't what we think they are."

They all looked at the shifter. Geth still stood at the windows, looking out over the city. He gestured with a thick, hairy hand. "Come here. Look outside. What do you see?"

Singe went to stand beside him and look out through the carved screens over the window. "I don't see anything."

"Here." Bava pulled on the screens over a pair of windows and they swung open, revealing doors and a small balcony surrounded by a wooden railing. Singe stepped outside into the moonlight. Bava's house wasn't much taller than many of the buildings around it and the view wasn't particularly spectacular. The most Singe could see was a forest of chimneys thrusting up from the roofs around.

He looked back to Geth. "What? I still don't see anything."

The shifter wore a grin that exposed all of his sharp teeth. "Think about the Bonetree camp. They lived in huts. They didn't have chimneys. How do you describe chimneys to someone who has never seen one?"

"I know what a chimney is!" protested Ashi.

"But maybe your ancestors didn't!" Singe ran back to the map and whooped. "Here!" He held his finger above a banner far in the south of the territory on the map and read the notation on it, *"Taruuzh Kraat.* Ancient ruins supposed to be the remains of chimneys of a Dhakaani stronghold below."

"I know the word *kraat,"* said Geth. "It's Goblin for a smithy." He moved to Singe's side and peered at the map. "Grandmother Wolf! 'The Hall of the Revered lies below the Spires of the Forge.' Do you think it could be this Dhakaani stronghold?"

"How can it be below ground, though?" asked Orshok. "According to the story, Dah'mir also told the hunters to look in the shade of the Grieving Tree. A tree can't grow underground."

"A tree can't grieve either. It could be a metaphor, the same way the Spires of the Forge could actually be chimneys." Singe looked to Bava—and to Dandra, still held in the large woman's arms, her face wide with hope. "Bava," he said, "do you have a contemporary map of Droaam? I want to see what's in this spot now."

Bava turned Dandra loose, glanced at the ancient map, then hurried to the map cabinet. Dandra stood before Singe and Geth. "You think this might be it?"

"I can't be certain," the wizard said carefully. "We might have to make the trip there to be sure, but I have a good feeling about this."

"You might want to change that feeling," said Bava. She laid another map, newer and emblazoned with the crest of House Tharashk, on the table and pointed to the location the ancient map labeled as Taruuzh Kraat. The new map marked the site as Tzaryan Keep.

Singe frowned. "What's wrong? Taruuzh—Tzaryan. It could be a development of the same name."

Bava shook her head. "No. Tzaryan Keep is the stronghold of one of Droaam's warlords, Tzaryan Rrac."

"That's bad?" asked Dandra.

"It's not good," said Bava. "He's an ogre mage—as big and powerful as an ogre but with magical powers, too. And Tzaryan Rrac's smart. They say he's an alchemist and a scholar and that he's trying to civilize himself. He's adopted a personal insignia like a human lord." She tapped her finger on a four-pointed blue star drawn on the map beside name of the Keep. "He's even hired an old general who served one of the Five Nations during the Last War to train the ogres who serve him as troops."

"I've heard that, too," agreed Natrac.

Singe looked from the half-orc to Bava and back.

"Not to be rude," he said, "but how do you know all this?"

Natrac cleared his throat. "A few months ago, Tzaryan caught some dragonshard prospectors from House Tharashk poaching in his territory and sent them back to Zarash'ak—minus their hands. But Tharashk wants to stay on the good side of the powers of Droaam, so instead of protesting, they sent an envoy to Tzaryan with gifts and goods. It was a big spectacle, the talk of Zarash'ak."

"Did the envoy come back?"

"Yes," said Bava. "Apparently, Tzaryan likes receiving visitors—at least when they come openly and with big gifts. According to the envoy, he holds court like a lord and debates like a sage. After the envoy returned, Tharashk had nothing but praise for Tzaryan."

"But did they send anyone else to visit him?" asked Geth pointedly. Bava shook her head. The shifter grunted.

"Light of il-Yannah." Dandra leaned against the table, staring down at the two maps. "We think we know where we need to go—but we can't get there."

"No," said Singe. "I think we can."

Dandra, Geth, and the others all looked at him. He gave them back a smile. "We go the same way House Tharashk did. We pay Tzaryan Rrac a visit."

CHAPTER

5

"**G**randfather Rat," said Geth. He stared at Singe and only one thought came to his mind. "That's insane. That's so insane that even a madman wouldn't try it."

"Why not?" Singe asked. He stepped back from the table and paced around Bava's studio, hands pressed together in front of his face as he thought. "If House Tharashk could do it, why can't we?"

"Because they're a dragonmarked house! They have resources. They've got a name." Geth flung out his arms and bared his teeth. "What have we got besides a story and a dragon hunting us?"

Singe stopped his pacing and turned to Ashi. "Does the Bonetree story mention an ogre mage at the Spires of the Forge?" The hunter shook her head. Singe spread his hands wide. "So presumably Tzaryan Rrac came to the area after Dah'mir left. He might not know Dah'mir was ever there. We just need a reason to visit the ruins."

"It doesn't sound like Tzaryan is particularly fond of treasure hunters," Geth growled. "Remember what he did to the Tharashk prospectors?" He held out one hand and chopped at his wrist with the other.

Natrac shifted uncomfortably. "Could you please not do that?" he asked.

Geth winced. "Sorry." He looked back at Singe. "You see what I mean?"

Singe shrugged. "We don't go as treasure hunters. We go as

researchers, interested in the history of the ruins. Tzaryan fancies himself a civilized scholar, so that's how we approach him." He stood up straight. "I didn't attend Wynarn and come away with nothing."

Geth looked around at their group. Ashi, Orshok, himself . . . a savage, an orc, and a shifter. He snorted and rolled his eyes. "He's not going to believe that we're all scholars!"

"My bright young assistant," said Singe, reaching out an arm to Dandra. "And our brute bodyguards." He swept his other arm past the rest of them. Geth bared his teeth. Singe tilted his head and smiled. "Droaam's a dangerous place. A scholar who wants to study Dhakaani ruins needs muscle to back him up."

Geth started to snort again, but stopped himself and looked at the wizard again. He'd known him too long to picture him easily as anything other than a rapier-wielding, spell-flinging mercenary—but if any of them could play the part of a scholar, it was Singe.

Grandmother Wolf knows he's good enough at making me feel stupid, the shifter thought. "Say we do it. We don't actually know anything about Taruuzh Kraat. Tzaryan probably does. What if he challenges you on something?"

"Then I yield to his superior knowledge and he feels smug. I've never met a scholar who doesn't enjoy feeling he knows more than someone else."

"Except Tzaryan's not a dusty lecturer with an audience of students," said Natrac. "He's a Droaamish warlord with ogre soldiers waiting to mangle people for him."

Singe glanced at Dandra, then at Ashi. "Well?"

Dandra drew a deep breath and let it out slowly—then nodded. "It's risky, but it sounds good."

Ashi nodded as well. "It sounds a lot easier than trying to fight our way in. I think we should try."

Geth turned to Orshok. "What about you?"

Surprise spread across the young orc's face. "You're asking me?"

"You're coming, aren't you?"

Orshok grinned, then nodded vigorously—though Geth doubted that he would have done anything else. He looked at Ashi. The hunter gave him a hungry smile and said, "I've never had the chance to fight an ogre before."

Geth crinkled his nose. "I'm glad there's a bright side for you." He looked down at the maps on the table, the old and the modern. "So how do we get there? I don't think we want to stay in Zarash'ak any longer than we need to."

"You go by sea." Natrac tapped the modern map, pointing to the coast of Droaam. "A town called Vralkek. It's not much, but it's the only real port in Droaam. It's not too far from Tzaryan Keep, either." He measured out the distance with his fingers. "A little less than a week overland, I think."

"Then tomorrow we try and find ourselves passage to Vralkek," said Singe.

Bava insisted that they stay the night in her house. Geth had to admit that the offer was more than agreeable—especially when Bava produced more wine to celebrate their discovery, the first bit of good luck they'd had all day. While they talked and drank in her studio, Bava got out a pen and ink and made copies of both her maps for them.

Eventually—the wine finished and the ink on Bava's maps dry—they found space on the floors below and went to sleep. Or at least the others went to sleep. Geth lay awake, their narrow escape from Vennet playing out again and again in his mind. Sleep didn't come. After a time, he rose again and headed back upstairs to Bava's studio. He didn't bother to uncover Bava's ever-bright lantern. He opened the tall doors that led onto the little balcony and stepped outside to look out over the night-shrouded City of Stilts. Night in Zarash'ak was different from nights in the swamps—or in the forests of the Eldeen Reaches. Lights broke the shadows, spilling out from taverns and bobbing along in the hands of torch boys, but to shifter eyes that could see in the dark, the extra light made little difference.

What he noticed was the noise. In the swamps and in the Eldeen, nights had been silent, broken occasionally by an animal's call. In Zarash'ak the noise was constant, even at a late hour. Dogs barking, voices arguing, the slam of doors, the clatter of footsteps. Laughter, singing. A distant scream.

Footsteps climbing the stairs to the studio. Geth glanced over his shoulder as Singe opened the door and started at his first glimpse of the figure on the balcony. One hand darted for his rapier, the other thrust out in the mystic gesture of a spell.

"It's me," Geth called softly.

The wizard relaxed, hands dropping, and made his way across the darkened studio with human night-blind clumsiness. "Don't tell me you can't sleep," he said, voice pitched low. "I have Dandra believing you can sleep anytime, anywhere."

"Someone needed to stand guard." Geth turned back to face the night.

"Vennet and Dah'mir aren't going to find us here."

"Old habits stick," he growled. "What are you doing up?"

Singe stepped up to lean on the balcony beside him. "I couldn't sleep."

Geth grunted. For a few moments, they stood in silence, then Singe asked, "What do you think it is that Natrac doesn't want to talk about?"

"I don't know."

"What made you think he used to be a gladiator?"

Geth stared into the dark and narrowed his eyes. "Just before the attack on the Bonetree mound, while we were waiting for Batul's orcs to move into position, we could hear Hruucan beating the light out of you—"

Singe grimaced. "I *was* fighting back," he said.

"From the sound of it, you weren't doing a very good job," said Geth. "Natrac read the noise of the crowd like a gambler reads a game of cross. He said it was the sort of thing you picked up in an arena and I asked if he'd been a gladiator."

"What did he say?"

"He didn't give me a straight answer. I guess everybody has their secrets." He turned his face to look up at the discs and crescents of the moons in the sky.

Singe didn't say anything. Geth glanced back at him. The wizard was staring down into the street below, but it didn't seem as if he was looking at anything in particular. One hand moved on the balcony railing, palm rubbing the smooth wood. "Singe?" Geth asked.

The wizard spoke without looking at him. "I remember something else that was said at the Bonetree mound." Geth's guts felt hollow. He didn't answer. Singe raised his head. "You said we would talk about Narath."

"I remember." His words came back to him. *Singe, about Narath—if we get out of this, we'll talk. No more running.*

The promise brought back memories of the battle at the Bonetree mound, of the crush of dolgrims and Bonetree hunters, of the shock of Dah'mir's transformation and the acrid stink of the dragon's corrosive venom. But it also carried all of the memories of an older battle, of black ash and red blood staining the snow of northern Karrnath.

He'd told Adolan about the massacre years ago. But Adolan hadn't been in Narath.

Geth gripped the rail. "Singe, I—" He clenched his teeth, grinding them together. "I'm not ready."

Singe's silence was cold. He stepped back, his face hard and angry. "You're not ready? *You're* not ready?"

"Later," said Geth. "Another time—"

"Later?" Singe spat back at him. "It's been nine years, Geth. How much later do you need? I hunted you for four years after Narath. I only gave up because you vanished—if I'd known where you were I would have called in every favor anyone ever owed me and brought an entire Blademarks company down on your hairy backside. If the Bonetree hunters hadn't attacked, I would have hamstrung you that night I found you in Bull Hollow and carried you back to Karrlakton to face the lords of House Deneith. The Frostbrand company died in Narath, Geth. Robrand d'Deneith might as well have died there."

Geth turned away. Singe grabbed his shoulder. The shifter spun around and thrust his hand back. "I don't want to talk about it!"

"Bloody moons, maybe I do!" Singe's face was blotched with red. "The Aundairians that attacked Narath shouldn't have been able to get past the waterfront—but they did. Treykin was on the barricades. When it was all over, Robrand and I found him. He was still alive—barely. My people had left him trying to hold his intestines in his body with his hands."

The sound of Treykin's braying laugh stung Geth's ears. "Robrand said that once we joined the Blademarks, our people were the other members of the company."

Singe's anger hissed between his teeth. "Don't quote the old man's words back to me. I tried to help Treykin and he spat at me. He wouldn't let an Aundairian give him the mercy that Aundairians had denied him—but before he died, he told Robrand the barricades had been overrun from behind and forced open. The attacking troops had found a way into the town. There weren't many ways through the walls of Narath. Robrand and I only had to check two of them before we found out how the Aundairians got into Narath."

Geth hunched back, the hair on his forearms and on the back of his neck bristling. "Don't," he growled.

Singe didn't stop. "A sewer," he said. "A dung gate that three men could have held. *Should* have held. We found signs of a struggle—but we found the bodies of only two of the three men assigned to that gate. There were tracks in the snow, though. Someone had fled."

Geth clenched his fists—and his jaw. He said nothing. Singe gave him a look of disgust, then added, "Robrand went to Karrlakton in person to report the Frostbrand's failure to protect Narath. The old man was a true commander. He carried the blame. He told the lords of Deneith that the massacre of Narath was his responsibility. The lords accepted that—and took everything away from him. Most of Deneith won't even say his name now. They don't want to recognize that he even existed." He took a slow, deep breath. "I want answers, Geth. I want to know what happened."

The hollow in Geth's guts had grown, swelling into a pit and engulfing him entirely. He was numb. Narath surrounded him. Wounds he had thought long healed felt like they had been ripped open again. His tongue seemed swollen in his mouth. There were no words in his throat.

He shook his head, mute.

Singe's mouth twisted. He turned and stalked back into Bava's studio. A moment later, Geth heard his feet on the stairs.

The shifter crouched down, resting his cheek on the bars of the railing and staring out between them.

Dandra woke to the whispering of children.

It was tempting to go back to sleep. She probably could have done it even over the murmur of the children's activity. Tetkashtai, though, was fully alert. Her yellow-green glow shimmered in Dandra's mind, prodding her. *Dandra! Dandra, wake up! Listen to them!*

There was an edge of panic to the presence's mental voice, but then there almost always was. Still, Dandra opened her eyes. The room in which she, Natrac, and Orshok had found space to stretch out was suffused with a pale gray light. Through an open window she could see a gentle, enveloping morning mist.

Natrac was still asleep. Orshok's blankets were empty, though there was no sign of the druid. Bava's children, all of them it seemed, were clustered together at one end of the room, a couple peering cautiously out of the window. Dandra could just catch their words. She blinked the haze of sleep form her eyes and tried to focus on what they were saying.

". . . should wake *Nena*."

"She doesn't want to be woken unless it's important!"

"I don't like this!"

"Quiet!" One of the figures at the window was Diad. He raised his head over the sill, then ducked back and turned around. His eyes were wide and his heavy jaw was thrust forward. "They're still there."

A flash of unease set Dandra's heart beating faster. She sat up. "Who's still there?"

The children turned like a flock of birds, moving in unison to face her as she rose from her blankets. One of the smallest whimpered and ducked behind another. Ose and Mine, the twins, came forward, though. "Goblins," said Mine in a low, serious voice.

Ose added, "They're watching the house."

Dandra glanced at Diad and the young man nodded. Dandra picked up her spear and crept forward to join him at the window. "Show me," she said.

Diad looked outside again, then gestured—below the level of the sill—to the right. "There's a cistern," he said. "There are two of them hiding behind it. I think I recgonize them. They're from a gang called the Biters."

Cautiously, Dandra lifted her head until she could just see outside. Through the mist, she could see the shape of the cistern and the broad, round head of a goblin on the other side of it.

One of the goblin's ears had been bitten off halfway along its its length. Dandra slid back down.

"There are more," said Diad. "They're hiding—I don't think they know we've seen them. Most are watching the front door, but there are some at the back door as well."

"How many?"

"We've counted twelve. There could be more."

"It's every goblin in Zarash'ak!" Ose said.

"No, it's not," her sister corrected her. "They wouldn't all fit on our street!"

Dandra gestured for them to be quiet. "Diad," she said. "Wake your mother." She looked at the other children. "The rest of you stay away from the windows."

She woke Natrac, then went looking for the others. Roused by a hunter's instincts, Ashi was already awake and alert. Singe stirred reluctantly at Dandra's touch—his eyes were shadowed by dark circles as if he hadn't slept well—but he sat up sharply at news that the house being watched. "Vennet's crew?" he asked as he kicked off tangled blankets.

Dandra shook her head. "The goblin gang from the webs. They must have tracked us down." She helped him to his feet and led him and Ashi back to the room with the children. "Diad's waking Bava. I'm still looking for Geth and Orshok."

"I'm here." Orshok appeared in the door of the room, still in the act of pulling his shirt over his head. Bava pushed past him to sweep down on her children with her arms spread protectively. The artist wore a loose gown that flapped and billowed around her. Both she and Orshok had an unmistakable flush on their cheeks. Natrac's eyebrows rose. Orshok's gray-green face darkened in a blush.

Bava fussed over her children, gathering them together and admonishing them to stay quiet. Only when she seemed satisfied that nothing had happened to them did she turn back to Dandra and the others. "What's going on?"

Dandra repeated what she had told Singe, but Bava frowned. "That can't be right."

"Why not?" asked Natrac. Bava looked at him sideways.

"You've lived here as long as I have, Natrac. Have you ever heard of a goblin gang coming out of the webs looking for revenge?"

The half-orc's forehead pinched together and and he thrust out his tusks. "You're right. It's happened sometimes when they're fighting with a rival gang, but—"

"I've heard another reason they come up," interrupted Diad. Everyone turned to look at him. He flushed and his mouth closed sharply, but Singe gestured for him to continue. The young man took a deep breath, then said, "They say the Biters are for hire. Pay the right price and they'll do anything."

"For hire?" Dandra's gut felt like it was filled with stones. "Light of il-Yannah. Dah'mir and Vennet."

Ashi frowned. "You think Vennet hired goblins? Why not send his sailors? Or hire half-orcs?"

"Don't underestimate goblins, Ashi," Singe said. "They may be small, but they're nasty and there's usually a lot of them." Singe clenched his fist. "Twelve moons, even if Vennet did hire them though, how did they find us?"

Natrac paled. "Urthen knew we were coming to Bava's for dinner last night. Boldrei's hearth, do you think they might have—?"

"It's possible," said Singe grimly. "We could just be making assumptions, though. We need to find out what's going on."

"We need to find Geth," Dandra said. "Il-Yannah, where is he?"

A look of anger flashed across Singe's face. "Is his sword still here?" he asked.

"Yes," Ashi told him. "It's with his blankets."

"Then he's probably upstairs," Singe growled. He turned and stormed for the stairs that led to the studio.

Dandra stared for a moment, then darted after him. "Singe, what is it?"

"Geth and I had a little discussion during the night." The wizard's voice was tight.

Dandra let out a hiss of frustration. "I thought that whatever you two had against each other had passed!"

"It hasn't."

They reached the stairs with the others not far behind. Singe started climbing. Dandra grabbed his arm and turned him around before the others could catch up to them. "What happened at Narath?" she demanded.

"Ask Geth sometime. See if he'll tell you." He pulled his arm away and kept climbing, flinging open the door at the top of the stairs.

Dandra caught a fleeting glimpse of Geth sleeping curled up in a corner, but no more than that—the opening door wrenched the shifter out of slumber. He uncoiled in an explosion of muscle and hair, leaping up and landing in a crouch, arms raised and crossed, ready to block or to strike.

Singe didn't even hesitate before striding into the room. The wizard and the shifter locked gazes. Dandra saw Geth's lips pull back from his teeth in a snarl of anger—and maybe even fear. She moved forward quickly, putting herself between the two men. "Geth, we have a problem."

His lips seemed to peel back even further. "Whatever Singe told you—"

"No," Dandra said. "A real problem." She told him about the goblins without waiting for him to relax—though strangely, he seemed less tense once she had, as if grateful for an enemy to fight. Orshok had brought his sword up from downstairs. Geth crept up to the edge of the balcony and peered over, into the fog. He grunted, then slid back and returned to take the weapon and buckle it on.

"They've got us too well covered," he said. "If we try to pinpoint where they all are, they're going to spot us and they'll know we've seen them."

"What do you think they're waiting for?" asked Bava. "Are they going to attack?" There was a fierceness in her voice, a rage that promised swift retribution for any threat to her children.

Singe shook his head. "If they were going to attack, they would have done it before dawn. I think they're waiting to try and take us when we leave."

"Goblins usually follow a strong leader," said Natrac. "Take the leader out and they fall apart." The half-orc had a deadly serious look on his face. Out of the corner of her eye, Dandra saw Geth and Singe share a glance—their first without overt hostility.

"Good idea," Geth said. "We still have the problem of spotting the leader, though."

The doors onto the studio's balcony stood open. Through them, Dandra could see the flat rooftop of the building across the street. "I can spot the leader," she said. She pointed through the doors. "The goblins are all watching Bava's house. If I'm over there, they won't be looking for me, but I'll have a clear view of them. I can use my powers to reach it and to call back to you."

Singe's eyes narrowed. "The long step and *kesh?*"

"It's a long way to reach back with *kesh*," she said. "Someone may need to stand close to the doors—it will make contact easier, but you'll risk exposing yourself to the goblins."

"I'll do it," said Singe. He glanced at the others. No one spoke against the idea. The wizard nodded to Dandra. "Be careful." He stepped back.

Dandra tightened her grip on her spear and took a deep breath, then reached out to Tetkashtai. *Help me*, she said.

She could have done this herself, but Tetkashtai's aid made it easier. The presence extended her light, wrapping herself around Dandra. She drew on the power of their union, bending it to her will, sliding it through the fabric of the world. She took a step forward and the air rippled around her.

When she put her foot down, she stood on the rooftop across the street. Just as at Natrac's house, a wooden platform had been laid down on the roof. Unlike Natrac's roof, however, no one had taken care of this platform for some time. Her sudden weight brought a sharp cracking out of the wood.

Dandra bit back a curse and dropped immediately to one knee, freezing in place and listening. A few harsh mumbles drifted up from the street below, but nothing more. She let out her breath and rose cautiously to a crouch. Picking her footing carefully, she crept closer to the edge of the roof. If this platform had ever had a railing to keep people from falling off, it was gone now. Dandra stretched out and looked over the edge.

The mist of early morning was slowly burning away as the sun climbed higher above the horizon. It wouldn't be long before it was gone entirely. It was already thinner at ground level than it had been. Dandra picked out the goblins hiding behind the cistern easily. Two more were hidden inside an abandoned barrel. Three stood in the shadows of a doorway. More crouched in an alley that ran between Bava's house and its neighbor. More still lurked on the far side of the house, peering around the corner onto the street.

All of the goblins had weapons at hand—knives, short swords, and spiked maces. And there were more of the creatures than there had been in the webs. The goblin with the torn ear had brought friends—but while he had been in charge in the webs, it didn't look to Dandra like he was the leader now. None of the other goblins were looking to him. Diad had said some goblins were watching the back of the house as well. It was possible that their real leader was back there, but she doubted it. It seemed more likely that he would be with the largest number of goblins. The leader had to be at the front of the house—she just couldn't spot him.

She looked across the street and into Bava's studio. Singe stood just inside the doors to the balcony, carefully out of sight of any goblins below. Dandra reached out to him with *kesh*, stretching her thoughts across the distance to brush at his mind. He opened himself to her. *Do you see the leader?* he asked.

No. Dandra wove an image of her view from the roof and sent it to him through the mental link.

Singe let out a silent grunt at the goblins' numbers and positions. *That doesn't look good.*

I have an idea, Dandra said. *We might be able to draw the leader out if you show yourself.*

The wizard's thoughts were skeptical. *That could be dangerous. We might be giving ourselves away.*

Then you'd better make it look casual.

Across the street, Singe looked up and gave her a grimace—but when he stepped out onto the balcony, yawning and stretching as if just rising, he didn't show any sign that he knew either she or the goblins were there. He stood still for a moment and scratched at his chest, then turned around and went back inside. The reaction among the goblins was immediate. Dandra watched a flurry of activity sweep through them as they readied weapons and sat up a little straighter. From the far side of the house, one goblin detached himself from the others and darted across the street. She had to lean out from the roof and crane her neck to watch, but she saw him run into an alley alongside the very building on which she perched—somewhere from which a leader could watch unseen and protected. *There we go,* she thought to Singe with satisfaction. She passed the glimpse of the running goblin along to him.

And felt surprise shoot through Singe's thoughts. *I recognize that goblin,* he said. *That was Preesh—the goblin that was with Chain yesterday!*

Chain? asked Dandra. She twisted her neck again to peer down at the mouth of the alley—

—just in time to see Preesh emerge from it with confusion on his round face, as if he had gone into the alley looking for someone but had not found them.

No one had come out of the alley since she'd been watching. At least not onto the street.

Dandra stiffened. *Singe!* she called as she pushed herself back from the edge of the roof. *The alley across the street—ask Bava if it goes anywhere.*

It took a moment for the wizard to reply. *She says it's a blind alley. It doesn't go anywhere, but there's an old ladder—*

The weathered wood of the rooftop platform creaked behind Dandra. Heavy footsteps pounded in a sudden rush. Dandra twisted, throwing herself blindly to the side, catching a glimpse of a polished black cudgel as it flashed down where her head had been. Tetkashtai shrieked in fear.

Chain grunted and spun to follow her.

—running up to the—

Singe's alarm blazed through the *kesh* as he saw what was happening. "Dandra!" he shouted, and his voice echoed both in her ears and in her mind.

She rolled to her feet with Singe shouting and Tetkashtai screaming in her head at the same time. It was too much to handle—she let go of the *kesh* and Singe vanished from her mind. Across the street, the wizard lunged back out onto the balcony, his eyes wide with shock.

"Itaa!" bellowed Chain as he surged forward, cudgel swinging.

Goblin shouts rolled up from the street below. Dandra saw Singe look down, then leap back into Bava's house. The cudgel lashed out again. Dandra stumbled and it whistled past her belly.

Chain spun around to deliver another blow. Dandra jumped back again—and stumbled as her right foot slipped off the edge of the wooden platform. She staggered and the edge of the roof swayed in front of her, promising a long drop down to a street swarming with goblins.

Chain's cudgel flashed down.

Dandra clenched her jaw and shifted her weight, pulling herself back from the edge. She pushed against the roof with her toes—and with her mind. Her feet left the uneven footing of the rooftop to skim the air. She slid back toward the expanse of the roof with the ease of thought, and Chain's cudgel missed her for a third time.

The big man's only reaction to her sudden display of power was a slight narrowing of his dark eyes. He shifted his grip on the cudgel, wielding it with both hands and beating at her with all the strength of his massive arms.

Dandra's spear whirled up. She gripped the shaft, holding it across her body to deflect Chain's punishing blows as she twisted and slid from side to side. The pale wood bent and shivered with each impact, but it didn't break. The unrelenting force of Chain's attack forced her back, then back again.

Burn him! said Tetkashtai. Visions of fiery white bolts and explosions of flame filled Dandra's mind.

We're on a wooden building, Dandra snapped back. *There are people inside! And he's too close!* The instant it would take for her to draw on whitefire—or any of her powers—would be all the time Chain needed to get a solid blow past her defense.

"Chain!" she gasped. "What are you doing? We tried to hire you."

"Tried." Chain's voice was a focused rasp. His cudgel hammered her spear again, the impact stinging her hands. "Didn't. Someone else knew the value of hiring the best, though!"

Dah'mir! Tetkashtai wailed, her fear tangling Dandra's thoughts.

Be quiet! Dandra moved back a little further. Chain followed her keeping her within his reach.

"What do you want?" she asked him.

"You," the big man said. He drew back his cudgel.

Dandra slid away again—

—and her back hit something hard and unyielding, one of the chimneys that had inspired Geth the night before. Chain had backed her up against it deliberately. A thin smile creased the man's face. His cudgel slammed forward.

Dandra released the force that kept her aloft, dropping instantly and crouching down even further. Chain's blow passed just over her head to smash into the chimney pot. Sharp clay shards and crumbling mortar flew everywhere. Chain wheezed as a cloud of soot exploded into his face. Dandra pushed herself out from under him, jerking the butt of her spear up between his legs as she moved. Chain twisted to take the blow on his thigh, but his wheeze still turned into a hiss and he hopped back a pace.

Dandra spun around the chimney, putting it between her and Chain. She could hear the harsh, excited shouts of the goblins in the street, the distant, frightened cries of Bava's children, the curses of the people in the building under her as the commotion outside finally roused them. A voice came floating up the ruined chimney. Dandra winced at the anger in it. "Sorry!" she called down.

"Bitch!" said Chain, his face blackened with soot. His cudgel whirled up. "You float, but you're not getting off this roof unless you can fly!"

All the rage that Dandra had felt for the man after meeting him yesterday came flooding back to her. She spread the fingers of one hand and thrust them at the chimney. A wave of *vayhatana* rippled from her hand, snatching up bricks and debris loosened by Chain's blow and blasting them at him. The bounty hunter cursed and spun around to shield his face. The chunks of brick that rained against his broad back made him stagger.

Dandra stepped onto the air and leaped over the remains of the chimney to fall on him as he turned back around. Her spear spun sharply and the butt cracked across his wrist. Chain yelped. His hand sprang open and his cudgel fell—but his other hand grabbed her arm. He dropped, rolling onto his back with a crash and dragging her with him. Caught off guard, Dandra flew over his head and slammed down hard onto the roof. She landed across the battered wooden platform. Planks splintered at the impact and pain arced through her back. The breath rushed out of her lungs. Her spear clattered down somewhere out of her reach.

Chain twisted around without rising and kicked out with both feet. Dandra rolled at the last moment, trying to absorb the impact, but the blow was still powerful enough to send her tumbling across the platform. She grabbed at the broken wood before she could slide right off. Right at the edge of the roof, fighting through the pain and Tetkashtai's terror, she forced herself up to her hands and knees as Chain strode forward.

On the street below, the goblins were clustered around Bava's door, pounding on it. A scattering of other people stood back on the mist-shrouded street, looking like they weren't certain if they should get involved. No one was looking up at the rooftop.

Dandra swung back to Chain. He wore a sneer on his unshaven face. "Who's the best?" he demanded. One hand reached down to grab her collar and drag her up. The other pulled back, curled into a fist.

The sudden roar that rose up from the street made both him and her look down to see Bava's door swing open and Geth charge through like a raging beast. The shifter waded right into the middle of the packed goblins, clearing the way for Singe, Ashi, and Orshok to follow. The others had their weapons out, but it was Geth who drove the goblins before him with howls and curses. The little creatures fought back, though, shrieking and pressing forward. Dandra saw Geth slap one out of the air as it tried to leap over its fellows. He reached to his belt and swept out his sword, raising the weapon above his head with another roar.

For a moment, all of the goblins seemed to freeze, their heads turning to stare at the jagged, heavy Dhakaani blade—then their shrieks turned into yelps and their press into a frenzy as they fought to flee. Chain's eyes went wide with angry surprise. He opened his mouth and drew breath to shout at the scattering goblins.

Dandra brought up her arms and drove both fists hard into the big man's belly just below his ribs. It was like punching a wall—Chain's muscles were solid—but the blow cut off his words. His shout became a strained grunt. His eyes turned back to her. "Bitch!" he hissed.

She shifted, jerking a knee toward his crotch in a feint. He twisted to protect himself—and Dandra spun a web of *vayhatana* around his cudgel, lying forgotten on the roof. She wrenched on the weapon and it leaped into the air. Heavy, polished black wood slammed into Chain's head with a satisfying thump. His eyes rolled back and he crumpled.

Dandra heaved on his body, pushing him away from the edge of the roof. She panted and wiped her mouth as she stared down at him. *"Dahr!"* she spat.

CHAPTER

6

A glance down into the street showed her the aftermath of the goblins' sudden flight. Geth stood with his sword still raised, looking up at it in dumbfounded amazement. Ashi actually seemed annoyed that the fight was over before it had begun. Bava was just coming out of her door, hurrying to talk to the neighbors who rushed in now that the goblins were gone. Up and down the street, windows were open and people were staring out into the fading tatters of mist. Everyone was looking at the scene in the street, though Dandra could hear some of the people in the building under her feet complaining about noises on the roof.

Singe was the only one looking up. "Dandra!" he shouted. "Dandra!"

She leaned over the edge slightly and waved. Relief surged on his face and he sprinted for the alley at the side of the building.

Dandra winced. They would be better off abandoning the roof, not putting more people on it. She looked at Chain, senseless at her feet. It was tempting to leave him, but if someone had hired him to track them down, they needed to find out more. They needed to get the bounty hunter away from here, though. She was reasonably certain that interrogating a member of House Tharashk in public wasn't a good idea.

Across the street, the doors on the balcony of Bava's studio still stood open. Dandra stole another glance at the scene below. Singe was still the only one who had bothered to look up. She didn't think that would last any longer than the morning mist.

She stretched out her thoughts, reaching for Geth with *kesh*.

Get back to Bava's studio, she ordered him. *Take Ashi. Hurry!*

The shifter started and glanced up, but Dandra didn't wait to see if he followed her instructions. She turned back to Chain's unconscious body. The air rippled as she wove an invisible net of *vayhatana* around him. Chain rose from the ground, arms dangling. Dandra clenched her teeth. *Tetkashtai, I could use your help with this.*

The presence was still churning in fear at the fight. Dandra directed a mental slap at her. *Tetkashtai!*

The presence shrank back. Dandra pulled her close, drawing on her more practiced control of their shared powers.

Chain's body turned and glided off the roof, drifting out over the street.

Dandra waited for someone below to exclaim at the sight, but no one did. Letting out a slow breath, she guided the big man through the misty air and across into Bava's studio. As soon as he was through the doors, she lowered him to the floor, then released her power with a gasp of exertion. Chain wouldn't stay unconscious for long, she knew—hopefully Geth and Ashi would be quick about getting up to the studio. Spinning around, she snatched up both her spear and Chain's cudgel, then hurried across the roof toward the gap of the alley. The ladder Bava had mentioned poked up above the roofline slightly. She peered down it.

Singe was about halfway up, climbing quickly. "Singe!" she called softly. He looked up at her. She pointed down to the ground. "Go back down!"

"What about Chain?"

"I've taken care of him. Get down. We have to get back to Bava's studio."

Singe gave her a quizzical look, but started back down the ladder. Dandra took another look at the alley floor and drew a deep breath, focusing her concentration—then hopped over the edge.

Chain had gotten one thing right: she couldn't fly. But she could float very well. The open edge of the roof had never been as much of a danger to her as the big man had thought.

The fabric of space whispered around her as she fell, easing her descent. Singe stared as she dropped past him and landed in an easy crouch. The wizard kicked off from the last few feet of the ladder and landed much more heavily. "I saw Chain hammering at you!" he said in amazement. "You could have gotten away from him whenever you wanted?"

"Light of il-Yannah—run away from that bully?" She smiled at him—a smile that brought an aching twinge from her bruised face. She hissed in pain.

Singe stared at her a moment longer, then wrapped his arms around her. She returned his embrace.

Tetkashtai seethed at their touch, outrage breaking through her fear. Dandra let Singe go reluctantly. "Back to the studio," she said. "We have someone to talk to."

In front of her door, Bava was talking to concerned neighbors, convincing them that the attack had been some kind of attempt at robbery by the goblin gang. Most of the neighbors seemed to accept the idea. Natrac had joined Bava to support her—the half-orc nodded at Dandra and Singe as they skirted the small crowd and slipped inside the house.

Bava's children were gathered on the second floor of the house under Orshok's watchful eye. "It's over," Dandra told him.

Orshok shook his head. "Bava told me she'd skin me if I left the children before she came back."

Singe laughed. "I'd believe her."

When they reached the studio, Chain was awake—and staring with angry eyes at the blades of Geth's and Ashi's swords. Both the hunter and the shifter looked more than ready to put sharp metal through him if he moved.

"Careful with him," Dandra told them. "He's the best."

The big man's wrists and ankles had been bound with shackles. Singe squatted down and examined the bonds. "Magewrought," he said. He looked up at Geth. "Where did you find those?"

"He was carrying them," said Geth. "We searched him before he woke up." He jerked his head at a small heap of gear on a table. "What did you do to him, Dandra?"

She described Chain's attack and their battle on the rooftop. Chain's face turned red with rage as she spoke until he looked ready to jump in with his own version of events. A flick of Ashi's sword kept him quiet, though. The Bonetree hunter nodded approval at Dandra's tale. "A good fight."

"If it hadn't been for Geth driving off the goblins, I don't think it would have been over so quickly," Dandra admitted. "How did you do that, Geth?"

The shifter shook his head. "I don't know. They just ran." He held out the Dhakaani sword. "It didn't feel like the sword did anything magical, but maybe it did. The only thing Batul could tell me about it is that the Dhakaani made it to fight daelkyr and their creations. Those were normal goblins—it shouldn't have done anything to them."

"I think there's more to that sword than meets the eye," said Singe. He poked through Chain's gear.

Dandra leaned over to look at the pile. It contained a short sword, several small knives, a flat case that Singe opened to reveal lock picks, gloves, a spindle of cord spun with some metallic fiber, a few small pouches that gave off a rank odor, a couple of greasy sticks, and a small dark glass bottle. She added the man's cudgel. Singe raised an eyebrow at the sight of it.

"A densewood cudgel, tanglefoot bags, smokesticks, irontwist cord—you're well-equipped, Chain," he said. He picked up the bottle, frowned at it and pulled out the stopper to sniff carefully at its contents. He blinked and snorted as he closed it again. "It smells like week-old tea. What is this?"

"*Gaeth'ad* essence," said Natrac as he, Bava, and Orshok come up the stairs into the studio. "Bounty hunters use it to keep their prisoners docile until they can get them locked up. They say it's especially good for keeping spellcasters restrained."

Singe's eyes narrowed as he set the bottle down. "Really? I think it's time we started asking some questions." He sat down in front of Chain. "I doubt you carry shackles and *gaeth'ad* essence around on a regular basis. Someone hired you to find us. Maybe to capture us. Who was it?"

Chain glared at him and said nothing. "I'll take a guess," Singe continued. "Vennet d'Lyrandar? Half-elf with long blond hair, gray coat with big silver buttons, dragonmark on the back of his neck, captain of an elemental galleon called *Lightning on Water?*" He tilted his head. "Maybe a man named Dah'mir? Tall, green eyes, wears a black leather robes with dragonshards set along the sleeves?"

Chain's eyes flickered, but he kept his mouth closed and his face remained hard. Singe pressed his lips together and looked up at Dandra. "I don't suppose you can do that thing Medala did and inflict pain on someone through their mind?

Dandra blinked. He knew she couldn't duplicate Medala's vicious power—just as she knew the wizard wouldn't want it inflicted on someone else. Medala had tormented him with waves of phantom pain too many times when he was a prisoner of the Bonetree. He was trying to intimidate Chain, she realized. She shook her head, acting along. "No. I could burn him, though." She reached for whitefire and the droning chorus of her fiery power throbbed on the air.

Chain's ears twitched at the sound and he swallowed—but his lips twisted into a self-assured smile. "Maybe you could," he said. "But you wouldn't. I know when I'm being played."

"Singe," said Bava coldly, "let me do this." The artist's face was pale with rage and for the first time, the accent of the Marches was strong in her voice. She went over to the heap of Chain's gear and selected two knives, examining their glittering edges as she pulled them from their sheaths. She turned around and looked down at Chain. "No one threatens my family."

She flipped one of the knives through her fingers with a frightening dexterity, then reached out to prod off the lid of a pigment jar. The knife dipped into the jar and emerged dusted with a green powder used for making paint. Bava wiped one side of the flat of the blade against her forehead, turning the paint into a savage smear, then stalked across the studio, knife held out.

If she was playing Chain, she was doing a very good job of it. Dandra looked to Singe and Geth, but the men were frozen, their eyes nearly as wide as Chain's. Ashi looked uncomfortable—the hunter was a fearless warrior, but Dandra knew she preferred offering her enemies a clean death. She didn't like torture. *"Cheo do doi, Bava?"* she asked.

"Doa at harano," Bava said.

At Dandra's side, Singe whispered a translation. "I do it for honor." His face was taut. "Twelve moons, I don't like this."

Ashi's face took on a grim cast. She stepped back out of Bava's way. The large woman moved close to Chain and brought the knife close to his forehead. The bounty hunter's hard expression trembled and his eyes crossed, trying to look up as Bava pressed the knife against his brow, marking him the same way she had marked herself.

Then she took hold of one of Chain's ears and stretched it away from his head. She settled the blade of the knife against the flesh where ear met scalp—

"Vennet d'Lyrandar," said Chain. His voice was steady but his body was tense. Dandra could tell it was taking all his willpower to maintain a cool demeanor.

Bava's knife didn't rise from his ear, but she didn't force it any lower, either. Chain's eyes darted briefly sideways and up to where Bava stood. "Vennet hired me to track and find you," he added quickly. "He introduced me to Dah'mir at the docks, but nothing more. As soon as Vennet approached me and described the people he wanted me to find, I recognized you. He didn't know I'd already met you. I thought it would be easy money, but he's *not* paying me to take torture."

"You could just be repeating names to keep us happy," Singe pointed out. "Answer another one: why would Vennet hire you when he could look for us himself?"

"He and Dah'mir were leaving Zarash'ak. After Vennet introduced me to Dah'mir, they both got in shallow-draft boat and put out into the river."

Dandra felt as if a weight had been lifted from her shoulders. Dah'mir had left Zarash'ak. She saw Singe glance at Geth, however. The shifter's eyes were narrow. "They left Zarash'ak?" he asked suspiciously. "Without looking for us?"

"That's what they hired me for," snapped Chain. His voice rose into a sharp yelp as Bava gave a tug on his ear.

"How did you find us here?" Dandra asked.

Chain lifted his manacled arms to point at Natrac. "He introduced himself when we met, didn't he? It was easy to find his house. An old servant there told me where to find you."

"Urthen!" Natrac curled his hand into a fist. "Dol Arrah turn away—Bava, save me an ear!"

"No," said Singe sharply. "No one's going to cut anything off. Bava, let him go."

Bava released the bounty hunter with an obvious reluctance, twisting his ear hard and smacking him on the back of the head as she let go. "Come near my family again and no one's going to save you," she spat at him.

Chain's face twisted. "You don't know who you've just made your enemy!"

"Neither do you." Bava flung down the knives. They stuck, quivering, in the floor on either side of Chain's knees. She turned away. Natrac went after her. After a moment, Singe leaned forward.

"I don't suppose you'll take more money to abandon the contract?" he asked.

Chain glared up at him, his face hard, and snarled something in Goblin.

"I didn't think so." Singe glanced at Geth and Dandra and flicked his head to the other side of the studio. They moved away from Chain, leaving Ashi and Orshok to watch him, and gathered around the table with the heap of the bounty hunter's gear.

"Do you think he's telling the truth?" Dandra asked. She couldn't keep the hope that Dah'mir was gone out of her mind. Tetkashtai was almost singing at the news.

"About Vennet hiring him, yes," the wizard murmured. "Maybe about Dah'mir leaving, too. The question is, what are we going to do with him? He's not going to give up."

Dandra grasped his meaning immediately. "If we leave him here, he's just going to come after us."

"We could kill him," said Geth. Dandra and Singe looked at him in unison. The shifter shrugged. "Or we could let Bava kill him."

"Nobody is killing anybody in cold blood." Singe ran a thumb through the whiskers on his chin. "We were lucky that Chain didn't tell Vennet and Dah'mir he'd just met us. He won't make that mistake again. If they meet him when they get back to Zarash'ak, you can bet he'll tell everything this time—and he knows we're looking for the Spires of the Forge."

Geth bared his teeth. "And if anyone knows exactly where that is, it's Dah'mir. Tiger's blood! We can't let him find that out. It's the only thing we've got on him right now!"

"We could take Chain with us," said Dandra. "Abandon him in Vralkek—or ship him on to Sharn."

"Bring someone who's hunting for us along for the journey?" Geth growled. "That's what we tried with Ashi on *Lightning on Water!*"

"It would have worked if Vennet hadn't been planning on betraying us all along." Dandra spread her hands. "That won't happen this time."

"It would be simpler to kill him."

"You said that about Ashi, too." Singe looked at Dandra. "It won't be easy finding a ship that's willing to smuggle a kidnapped member of House Tharashk."

Geth groaned. "We're going to do it?"

"I don't see another option," said Singe. "Although we'll need a way to keep Chain quiet until we get him away from Zarash'ak—I don't know any spells that would control him."

Dandra bit her lip. "None of my powers would either." She looked across the room. "Maybe Orshok—?"

"Grandfather Rat," Geth said. "Does it always have to be magic?" He reached down to Chain's gear and hefted the black cudgel, then turned and strode for the bounty hunter.

Dandra caught her breath. "Geth—"

Chain saw what was coming. He tried to twist out of the way, but the cudgel caught him across the back of his head. The bound man gasped and swayed, his eyes glazing over.

Dandra grimaced. "Geth, we can't just keep hitting him!"

"Easy." Geth held up his other hand—and the dark bottle of *gaeth'ad* essence. Dropping the cudgel, he grabbed Chain's head and forced it back, then pulled the plug on the bottle with his teeth and poured a measure of the contents into Chain's slack mouth. The man sputtered immediately, but Geth forced his jaw shut until he swallowed.

"Was that enough?" asked Orshok critically. "Or too much?"

"We'll just have to watch and see," said Geth, hopping off of Chain. The bounty hunter was choking and cursing them all. Ashi picked up the cudgel and moved to stand behind him. Chain stopped cursing. Geth replaced the stopper and tucked the bottle into a pouch. "We should try to get on a ship and out of Zarash'ak soon as possible, though."

"The sooner you get this *shekot* out of my house, the better," said Bava.

Dandra turned around. The artist and Natrac had returned. Bava glared at Chain with scarcely diminished anger. Dandra went to her. "Bava," she said, "I want to thank you for showing us your map and for your hospitality." She pressed her hands together and bent her head over them. "We've repaid you badly."

"Dandra, I would help you again." Bava's voice was strained. "But next time, no uninvited guests, please." She took Dandra's hands and kissed her on both cheeks. "Once the essence takes effect, you should go. It won't be long before the watch comes to investigate the fight."

Chain was already starting to look dazed. Dandra nodded. "We're taking him with us," she said. "It will be a long while before he's back in Zarash'ak."

Natrac drew a deep breath. "I'm coming with you, too," the half-orc said.

"What?" Geth turned to him. "When we got here, you said you'd never leave Zarash'ak again."

"The people I love here are getting hurt. Urthen. Bava." Natrac squeezed the large woman's hand. "For what? My house? It will wait. Vennet knows me. If he and Dah'mir are looking for you, they'll come for me first—just like Chain did. Like Dandra said after the battle at the mound, I have to do *something*." He thrust his tusks forward. "I still owe Vennet revenge. I'm not just going to wait for him to come to me."

He held out his fist. Geth grinned and bashed his own fist against it. *"Kuv dagga,"* he said.

They separated as they left Bava's house. Finding passage to Vralkek was a priority, but Natrac was anxious to check on Urthen, worried that Chain might have done something drastic to the old servant. He and Singe headed off to his house, with Orshok along as well to offer healing magic if it was needed, while Dandra, Geth, and Ashi—taking Diad to guide them—went down to the docks. The others would meet them there.

They took Chain with them, too. By the time the *gaeth'ad* essence had taken its full effect on him, the bounty hunter could do no more than stand and stagger along, but Natrac no more wanted him around his house than Bava did around hers. In the end, Dandra agreed to keep the drugged man with her. Between Ashi and Geth, supporting and guiding him was easy enough. and Bava supplied them with an enveloping cloak and a big conical straw hat to disguise him.

Unfortunately, guiding someone so obviously in disguise through the streets of Zarash'ak was suspicious in itself. A couple of stall-keepers stared at the big, shrouded figure draped across Ashi and Geth.

"Drunk," the shifter grunted at them.

"Early for it," one responded.

Geth bared his teeth in a smile. "He started last night."

Dandra touched Diad's shoulder. "Take us through quiet streets," she said. "I don't think it would be good to run into the city watch."

They made it down to the docks without incident. Dandra thanked Diad and sent him on his way, then surveyed the ships that lined the nearest stretch of dock. "Where do we start?" she asked.

"At the other end," said Ashi. She pointed. "There's Vennet's ship."

Lightning on Water was tied up a good sixty paces away along the busy docks, but Dandra still felt a chill at the sight of her. The sleek lines of the elemental galleon had, when she'd first seen the ship, spoke to her of speed. Now they reminded her of nothing so much as a serpent, ready to strike. The ship was still. No crew moved on the deck, though Dandra could see the dark forms of Dah'mir's herons perched along the rails like sentries.

"The boat they were loading yesterday is gone," Geth said. "There are fewer herons, too, I think. It looks our friend here was telling the truth." He nudged Chain, making the drugged man stumble.

Dandra stared at the ship, a surge of pity for the sailors knotting her heart. Vennet's crew had been good men. She'd seen nothing to suggest that they shared their captain's faith in the Cults of the Dragon Below and she knew what it was like to be trapped by Dah'mir's mind-numbing power. Her teeth clenched tight. "Do you think Dah'mir and Vennet took the whole crew upriver?"

"They couldn't have. Their boat wouldn't have held them all," said Ashi.

"And Dah'mir told Vennet not to bring his best men," added Geth. "It sounded like they were planning on leaving some of the crew behind." He cocked his head. "Why?"

"Because we should try and do something for them. They don't deserve to be Dah'mir's puppets."

Geth flinched. "Cousin Boar, Dandra!"

Tetkashtai echoed Geth's sentiments. *No!* she said. *We can't. How would you free them? You couldn't free yourself. And it could be a trap!*

Dandra answered them both at once. "I have to try."

An idea was already forming in her head. There was a stack of crates waiting on the dock not far from *Lightning on Water*. Dandra headed for them, forcing Geth and Ashi to follow or be left behind. Chain's staggering progress made stealth all but impossible, but Dandra watched the herons carefully. The birds didn't seem to pay any attention to what was taking place on the docks. She ducked into the shadow of the crates, then peered at the ship and at the herons again as the others wrestled Chain into hiding. The birds still hadn't moved.

A fragment of rope lay on the dock nearby. Dandra reached out with a whisper of *vayhatana* and sent the rope slithering back and forth like a snake. So long as it was on the dock, the herons ignored it—but the moment she sent it wriggling toward the ship's gangplank, the nearest birds turned in unison to watch it.

She released her power and the rope fell limp. Dah'mir's birds watched it for a moment more, then resumed their previous inscrutable poses.

"Ashi," Dandra asked, "how intelligent are the herons?"

"Like dogs. Dah'mir bred them that way. They'll take commands, search out specific people—the way they did when we tracked you into the Eldeen Reaches."

"Has Dah'mir ever turned the herons against the Bonetree hunters?"

Ashi tilted her head. "No," she said. "Even yesterday, they attacked Geth and Orshok, not me. They trust Bonetree hunters from the moment they're hatched. I think that's something else Dah'mir bred into them."

"Good. That's what I was hoping." Dandra raised her chin in determination. "Geth, take care of Chain. Ashi and I are going onto the ship."

Geth's breath hissed between his teeth. "At least wait for Singe to get here. Or let me go."

She shook her head. "You need to watch Chain—and my idea

works best with two people." She looked at Ashi. "If a Bonetree hunter approached the herons with a prisoner, what would happen?"

Ashi shrugged. "I don't know. Maybe nothing. I'd be more worried that Dah'mir or Vennet may have left orders for the crew."

"Trust to il-Yannah. Geth, if something goes wrong, we'll call." Dandra handed her spear to Ashi. "Let's make it look real. Take my arm as if you're restraining me."

They stepped out from behind the crates and crossed the docks. As they drew close to *Lightning on Water*, a number of the herons had turned their heads to stare directly at them. Dandra could feel the birds' cold green eyes—so much like Dah'mir's—on her. She tried to hang limp in Ashi's grip, a defeated prisoner.

They're not going to believe this, wailed Tetkashtai. *We don't even know that they understand what a prisoner is.*

Dandra's heart skipped. She hadn't entirely considered that. *As long as they still trust Ashi, we should be fine.*

You fool! We're going to be captured for certain!

At the bottom of the gangplank, Ashi paused. "Do we go on?" she asked softly.

"Yes." Dandra took the first step onto the gangplank, expecting the herons to spread their wings and take to the air at any moment. Her head was pounding in time to Tetkashtai's fear. She focused on putting one foot in front of the other, on climbing the gangplank. The temptation to look up was strong. She resisted it.

Then they were at the top of the gangplank and stepping onto the ship. And the birds hadn't moved.

Silence clung to *Lightning on Water*. The deck was empty except for one haggard crewman who crouched in the shade of the captain's cabin. He stared at them but moved no more than the herons had. Dandra eased herself from Ashi's grip and squatted in front of him. His eyes—empty and dull—followed her.

"Where is the rest of the crew?" she asked.

"Below," he said. His voice was hoarse.

"Did Vennet give you any orders before he left?"

"Obey Dah'mir."

"And what did Dah'mir tell you?"

"To take day watch until he returned."

Dandra's eyes narrowed. "What about the others?"

"They wait."

Ashi crouched down beside Dandra. "Can you release him?" she murmured.

"I'd rather try with someone I know." She rose. "Let's see if we can find Karth. He had a level head."

They found the stairs that led below. Ashi went first, moving slowly and allowing her eyes to adjust. She kept her hand on the hilt of her sword. Dandra followed cautiously, her spear reclaimed and ready.

There was little reason for fear, though. The remaining crew of *Lightning on Water* sat or crouched or lay in motionless silence. Except for the faint sounds of breathing and the few heads that turned to look at the two intruders into the gloom, Dandra would have thought she walked among dead men.

Karth sat against the curve of the ship's hull. Dandra remembered him as a big man, but he seemed strangely diminished. His eyes, though as dull as those of the man on deck, also held a haunted look in their depths. When Dandra spoke his name, he didn't respond. She said it again, a little louder, then took him by the shoulders and shook him. "Karth!" There was slight flicker in the man's eyes, but nothing more.

"Geth and I hit them when we fought yesterday and they didn't wake," Ashi said. "Can you reach inside his head?"

Medala could have touched Karth's mind easily—that had been the focus of her powers. All Dandra had, though, was the *kesh* and the idea of linking her mind with one so deeply under Dah'mir's influence was frightening. Just the thought of it made Tetkashtai shrink like an ember. Dandra's gut clenched.

She had to try.

The sailor on the deck had said he and the others were following orders left by Dah'mir and Vennet—powerful suggestions rather than direct domination. Maybe she could jolt Karth free. "Watch me," she told Ashi, "if I become like them, I've probably fallen to Dah'mir's power. Get me out of here and back to Singe."

"There's no way to protect yourself?"

"It would take more than I'm capable of. Powerful psionics. Maybe magic. But not even Medalashana was able to shield herself from Dah'mir on her own." Dandra gripped Ashi's hand for a moment. "Wish me luck."

Ashi returned her grasp silently, then let go. Dandra turned to Karth. *Tetkashtai—*

No!

Tetkashtai, help me! Dandra seized the presence and pulled her close, then looked directly into Karth's haunted eyes. *Karth,* she called silently, pushing her mind toward his. *Karth, can you hear me?*

The *kesh* trembled between them, sliding across Karth's thoughts without finding purchase, like walking on ice. Dandra could feel Dah'mir's touch, the cold grasp of his domination. Karth's mind was there, but locked away. He was struggling, though. She could sense it. Dah'mir's power had been stretched thin, but it was too much for a human mind to break through alone—even she touched it and shied away. There was a lingering madness in the dragon's presence that left her feeling unclean.

Beyond the barrier of his power, Karth shivered and seemed to fade, exhausted.

Dandra thrust out hard, wielding the *kesh* as she would her spear and pouring all of her will into one focused burst. *Karth!* she shouted.

The spear of her will stabbed deep into the cold barrier that held Karth prisoner—stabbed deep and pierced it. The *kesh* slipped through, drawing Karth to freedom. A hundred wild, desperate thoughts burst out of the man, flooding her. Dandra gasped and jerked back from him.

His hands reached out and caught her. "Dandra?" he gasped. "Dol Arrah bless you." He was trembling.

"Karth, are you hurt?" She felt **exhausted** and exhilarated at the same time. Inside her mind, Tetkashtai cowered.

"I—" He swallowed. "The captain? Dah'mir?"

"Gone," said Ashi.

Karth focused on her. "You . . . I chased you yesterday. You were with Geth. But the captain said you were . . ."

"Ashi is with us now, Karth." Dandra eased her arms out of the man's desperate grip, then pushed him gently back until he was sitting again. "Tell us what happened to you."

When she'd been in Dah'mir's power, the world had sped

by her in a blur. Karth, however, remembered everything. His story flooded out of him as if it had been waiting for release. Dandra listened in dismay as he told of the appearance of the herons on the ship, of his discovery of Dah'mir in Vennet's cabin and Dah'mir's transformation from heron to man. Her stomach knotted at Vennet's murder of his passengers so that the ship could be turned back to Zarash'ak. Through the days of the voyage, the crew had been held in thrall to Dah'mir's presence, seeing and hearing everything, but unable to act against his or Vennet's orders.

When Karth had finished, Ashi let out a hissing breath. "So now we know what happened to Dah'mir after the battle at the mound."

Dandra nodded and turned back to Karth. The big man was shaking and staring around at his listless, silent mates. "What did Dah'mir and Vennet expect all of you to do while they were away?" she asked him.

"There are supplies on board—food and water. Dah'mir told some of us to share them out every night."

"He expected you to survive for four weeks like that?" growled Ashi.

"Four?" Karth glanced up. "Two. They were heading toward something called the Bonetree mound in the depths of the Marches."

"The journey to the Bonetree mound takes two weeks. Back again is four, three at best," said Dandra. Karth shook his head.

"They expected the whole trip to take two weeks. The captain can use his dragonmark to call wind's favor and speed their trip."

Dandra exchanged a glance with Ashi, then cursed. "Il-Yannah! All the more reason not to wait before we leave Zarash'ak."

Karth seized her arm like a drowning man might seize a piece of floating wood. "Leave? No, you can't." He nodded toward the rest of the crew. "What about them?"

Dandra bit her lip. She had the strength to free one or maybe two others, but then she'd have to rest. Maybe Orshok's prayers could help free some of the others. It could be done—it had to be done, though Singe and Geth might not like it. "We'll make sure you're all freed," she promised, "but you probably shouldn't stay around Zarash'ak either."

"Believe me, we won't." He pointed at a half-elf watching them with dark and empty eyes from a corner. Dandra recognized Vennet's junior officer—during their voyage on *Lightning on Water*, he had taken over the ship at night, controlling her with his own dragonmark while Vennet slept. "Free Marolis and he can take command. There are provisions in the articles of House Lyrandar—if a crew believes the captain has turned away from the house, they can remove him from power and take the case before the trade ministers of Lyrandar. Lords of the Host have mercy on the men Vennet and Dah'mir took with them, but I don't think we can wait for their return. With what Marolis and I have seen, we have enough to go before the ministers now."

Dandra's eyebrows rose as sudden hope kindled inside her. "Karth, where would you find these ministers?"

"By the articles, we have to go straight to the nearest one or be declared mutineers. The nearest to Zarash'ak would be Dantian d'Lyrandar in Sharn."

Embers of hope turned into flames. "Sharn?" she asked. A wide smile spread across her face. She doubted if she could have held it back even if she had wanted to. "Karth, do you think you and Marolis could do us a favor?"

Karth spread his hands. "Dandra, you've freed us from a nightmare—for you, we'd do anything."

Even watching *Lightning on Water* for any signs of trouble, Geth saw nothing until one of the herons tumbled abruptly off the ship and into the water below with a knife sticking out of it. At almost the same moment, Ashi reared up behind another, shearing it in half with the bright blade of her sword before leaping for the next. Dandra was a swift and graceful blur near the stern of the ship as her darting spear transfixed yet another bird.

The startled herons reacted before he could. They flapped into the air with a flurry of greasy black feathers and a chorus of screeches. Ashi vaulted up and cut down a fourth bird as it took flight, but then they were out of reach of her sword.

But not of Dandra's powers. Geth saw her look up at the whirling flock and thrust out her hand. White flames erupted in a roaring gout to engulf another five of the remaining heron. Ashes and embers fell like hot rain.

In only moments, just three of Dah'mir's weird birds remained, two beating hard for the safety of the sky, one—its feathers smoking—tumbling down to the dock. Dandra's fingers tracked the climbing birds. Two bright, fiery bolts streaked up and caught them, blasting them out of the air.

The heron that had tumbled to the dock, however, righted itself and landed on its feet. Green eyes looked up to watch the destruction of the last of its flock. Geth saw the bird turn its head as if surveying the dock, then with an uncanny intelligence strut toward the nearest sheltering nook.

Chain wasn't going anywhere. Geth released his grasp on the bounty hunter, sprang out from behind the crates, and pounced on the heron. It screeched and struck at him with its beak—the shifter snarled and snatched back a bleeding hand, but got his other fist around the heron's skinny neck and squeezed. Long thin legs thrashed. Geth clenched his injured hand on the bird's neck as well and wrenched hard. Bones cracked. The bird went limp.

Across the dock, people were staring at Dandra's display of power. Geth rushed to *Lightning on Water*'s gangplank. "Ashi! Dandra!" he shouted. "What's going on?"

Dandra appeared at the ship's rail. Her eyes widened slightly at the heron in Geth's hand. He held it up and shook it at her. "What are you doing?"

"We've found our passage to Sharn!" Dandra called back. She slapped the rail.

"We're taking Vennet's own ship?" Geth bared his teeth in a grin. "Grandfather Rat, that's justice! Singe is going to soil himself."

He dashed back to the crates and to Chain. The bounty hunter had staggered and fallen without his support. He was sprawled in the shadow of the crates, limp as one of the dead herons, Bava's cloak a puddle around him. Geth wrapped his arms under Chain's and hauled him to his feet. There was a long bloody scratch on one of the big man's hands. A piece of wire that had bound a crate twisted out—Chain must have fallen against it as he crumpled. Geth snorted. "I hope Vennet didn't pay you in advance," he told the drugged man.

"I'm zhe besht . . ." slurred Chain. "Zhe besht! Don' fuhget it."

"Well, the best is going for a trip." Geth guided him to *Lightning on Water*. Ashi was waiting for him and between the two of them they wrestled Chain up the gangplank.

As he stepped onto the deck of the ship, Geth felt a flush of triumph sweep through him. It felt very good, he thought, to be one step up on Dah'mir.

CHAPTER

7

The sun was setting as the river boat rounded a final bend and Vennet saw the mound rising up against the orange sky. After days of following the river through marshes flatter than a calm ocean, its rounded height seemed nearly mountainous.

Seated at the center of the boat, Dah'mir pointed to shallows beneath a path cut in the rising riverbank. "Put in there."

The men Vennet had picked from his crew dipped their oars and made for the shallows, giving the boat just enough speed that she came gliding gently to a stop and kissed the bank like a lover. Two men hopped overboard and tied the boat to a worn post driven into the ground. Others began unloading their gear and supplies. Dah'mir gave a short whistle to the two herons that stood beside him in the boat and the birds flapped into the sky, joining the dozen or so other herons that had followed them from Zarash'ak. All of the birds whirled down to settle in along the riverbank.

Vennet scanned the bank above. It was empty. "Where's the Bonetree clan? I would have thought they'd come to investigate a boat tying up in their territory."

"The herons have seen them, captain," said Dah'mir, "and they've seen the herons. They know I've returned."

Vennet looked at the priest. "But they haven't come to greet you?"

Dah'mir didn't answer him. Vennet clenched his teeth. The journey up river had gone quickly, but more than ever the half-elf was certain that the green-eyed man was keeping something from him. They were so close to the mound and to his promised reward, though, that there was little he could do but trust him.

He rose, then helped Dah'mir to stand and disembark. The priest had grown steadily weaker over the days of the journey. Vennet had somehow come to expect that he would become stronger as they approached the Bonetree mound, but there had been no miraculous recovery so far. Only the day before, Dah'mir had been forced to call for aid in rising in the morning. His strong frame had become gaunt, his pale skin dry and drawn. The wound in his chest remained open. Vennet had seen it once or twice. He wasn't quite sure how any man could live with an injury like it.

Maybe the power of the Dragon Below sustained Dah'mir. Certainly his will and intelligence had never dimmed. Vennet had seen his eyes shining fever bright through the days and nights on the river. As he helped Dah'mir off the boat and up the steep path to the top of the riverbank, Vennet had the feeling that even if Dah'mir's body failed entirely, the priest would carry on. The image came to him of a withered corpse with burning acid-green eyes ruling the Bonetree clan like a lich-king. He shivered.

On his arm, Dah'mir stiffened. Vennet glanced at him. "What is it?"

"Something has burned here."

Vennet sniffed. Now that the priest had pointed it out, he could smell something on the cool evening air: a faint stench of old ashes. Dah'mir was right. Something had burned. As they came over the top of the bank, he saw what it was.

What must once have been the Bonetree camp or settlement had been put to the torch. The ribs of tent poles stood broken and black. The walls of huts were charred and crumbled. Here and there, new green shoots of grass poked out of the scorched earth, but otherwise all plant life had been seared away.

There were bodies scattered through the ruins, too. Vennet counted half a dozen at a glance. They'd been burned as thoroughly as the huts of the camp, hard black flesh clinging to dark sticks of bone. A couple had died fighting but others, including the small corpses of children, looked like they had fallen while fleeing. Strangely, there seemed to be no signs of injury on the bodies—no bones sliced by blades or smashed by clubs.

Dah'mir was staring as well, though with curiosity rather than shock or horror. "What happened here?" Vennet asked him.

The priest shook his head, then nodded toward the mound that rose—still covered in waves of green grass—beyond the burned camp. "Continue on," he said.

They passed through the camp. Their feet and the feet of the sailors following listlessly behind made no noise on the soft carpet of ash that covered the ground.

Closer to the mound lay the battlefield that Vennet had expected to find. The ground had been churned and scarred by fighting. More bodies lay scattered across it, ravaged by decay and scavengers, the stink of their rotting already dissipated. Vennet recognized humans and orcs, the four-armed skeletons of dolgrims, stranger skeletons that might have been dolgaunts, empty carapaces that must have been chuuls. The battle at the Bonetree mound had been fierce.

But over top of the battlefield lay burned patches—not so extensive as in the Bonetree camp, but more distinct because of it. Two burned corpses lay in one blackened patch, three in another closer to the camp. A pattern of charring lay across the whole battlefield, as if lamp oil had been drizzled at random then set alight. Dah'mir studied the marks as though reading some meaning in them. He nodded again, but this time not toward the mound. "That way," he said. "I need to speak with the Bonetree hunters."

Through the gloom of twilight, Vennet could see a handful of armed figures. They stood well beyond the last of the burned patches, keeping their distance. They didn't move as Vennet and Dah'mir approached, however. If they were keeping their distance from anything, Vennet realized, it was the burned land. Once he and Dah'mir were beyond the blackened grass as well, Vennet glanced at the priest and murmured, "Should I have the crew make camp, lord?"

In his heart he was almost hoping Dah'mir would say no, but the green-eyed man nodded, his eyes fixed on the Bonetree hunters. Vennet clenched his teeth and paused long enough to look over his shoulder at the men who followed. "Make camp," he called, then added, "Set a watch."

"That was unnecessary," Dah'mir said as the men shrugged off their equipment and began to pitch the same rude camp they had every night of the journey up river. "They have nothing to fear from the Bonetree."

"It's not the Bonetree I'm worried about," said Vennet. "Something feels wrong."

The waiting hunters—four of them, three men and a woman—still hadn't moved, though as Vennet drew closer to them he could see that they weren't standing like stoic statues either. Instead they twitched and fidgeted, their eyes darting back and forth across the twilight landscape. Their dark gazes lingered on Vennet and he knew they were studying him—the stranger who walked with their priest—just as he was studying them.

All of the hunters wore tattoos and strange piercings, but they also bore recent, serious burns. The man who stood at the fore of the group carried an angry red stripe across his chest that looked as if he had been struck with a flaming lash. "Revered!" he said. He dropped to his knees, the fingers of his free hand darting up to touch his forehead and his lips. Behind him, the other hunters repeated the gesture, though not smoothly. One of the men was trembling in fear, his eyes fixed on Dah'mir.

If the priest saw the man's fear, he paid it no attention. "Breff," he said to the hunter who had spoken. "Are you the master of my hunters now?"

Breff nodded tightly as if struggling to maintain his composure. "Master of few, Revered. We saw the herons, Revered. We knew you had returned. We—"

He bent his neck suddenly, turning his face away from Dah'mir. "Revered," he moaned, his composure crumbling, "what did we do to anger the Dragon Below? We don't understand. During the battle, the children of Khyber turned on us and now your fiery hand drives us from our homes and keeps us from the ancestor mound. Is it because we fled when you assumed the power of the Dragon Below? We saw Ashi leave after the battle with the outclanners—are we punished because of her betrayal? Tell us!"

Breff's plea made no sense at all to Vennet, but Dah'mir pressed his lips together in thought, then pulled himself away from Vennet's support to stand on his own before the kneeling hunters. "Breff, tell me what happened here."

"After the battle, we waited like cowards for night to fall again, gathering the survivors in the grasslands beyond the mound," said the hunter, "then we returned to our camp to pray for your return. Two of the hunters took a torch to survey the battlefield. I don't know what they found, but suddenly there were flames in the night and a terrible howl." The hunter looked up again. "We went to see what was happening and were met by your hand, his body in flames."

"My hand?" Dah'mir's eyes narrowed. "Hruucan?"

Breff nodded.

A memory stirred in Vennet—while they had been allies, Ashi had told him of the Bonetree's hunt for Dandra. Dah'mir had named the dolgaunt Hruucan as his Hand and put him in charge of the band of Bonetree hunters. "I thought Hruucan was dead," the half-elf said to Dah'mir uneasily. "You said Singe killed him."

"He walks, outclanner," said Breff. "After the camp burned, we fled from him. He didn't pursue us. When the flames died down, he seemed to be gone. We tried to return and restore the camp, but the Hand came back again, stealing flame from our cooking fires to turn against us. We moved our camp further away, but he still reached for us." He shivered. "The Bonetree is reduced, Revered. Many of our children and elders are gone. The survivors of the clan hide in the grasslands."

"So where is Hruucan now?" asked Vennet. "We crossed the battlefield and didn't see him."

Breff shook his head. "He is a scourge on the Bonetree. Perhaps he cares nothing for outclanners. Perhaps he lies quiet before the Revered."

"No," said Dah'mir. "I don't think so." His eyes flashed in the dusk. "A torch on the battlefield, stolen flame—Hruucan died in fire but we carried no fire across the battlefield."

Vennet stiffened and whirled. His crew's camp was growing. Wood gathered the night before and carried along had been laid beside a makeshift fire pit piled with tinder. One of the crew crouched beside the tinder, flint and steel at the ready. The camp was beyond the burned zone, but unease filled Vennet. "No fire!" he bellowed.

His warning came too late. The hands of the sailor beside the fire pit were already in motion, striking flint against steel with practiced ease. Sparks leaped into the tinder and the man gave them a gentle puff of air. Flames crackled and blossomed—then seemed to leap into the air, leaving only scorched tinder behind as they stretched like a gossamer thread back to the blackened battlefield.

On the battlefield, a burned corpse stirred. Vennet froze. Behind him, he heard one of the Bonetree whimper in fear. He glanced over his shoulder to see the hunters on their feet, their hands tight on their weapons.

"Revered, it's him!" said Breff.

The sailor at the firepit looked at the cold tinder in confusion and struck a new shower of sparks. More flames bloomed.

"Stop!" Vennet shouted. He started forward—but Dah'mir's fingers dug into his shoulder.

"Don't move!" the priest hissed.

The stirring corpse rose to its feet with a faint whisper like crumbling ashes. It shambled toward Vennet's crew, black skin cracking to reveal glowing embers beneath. The movement and the glow caught the attention of some of the sailors. Two drew short swords and moved forward. Someone called out to Vennet. "Captain! Danger on deck—"

Before Vennet could even think to respond, the corpse lunged forward with astounding speed. Claw-like hands grasped the nearest sailor in a horrid embrace. The man screamed in agony as he burst into flame. The other sailors flinched back—one or two retreated a pace. The burned corpse flung the dying sailor aside. Bright flames clung to it, tendrils of fire writhing around its chest and hanging like clumps of hair from its head, long burning tentacles weaving above its shoulders.

The tentacles of a dolgaunt reborn in fire.

The creature exploded in a fiery whirlwind of motion, its movements fluid and supple as if the sailor's death had given it new energy. Tentacles wove around another sailor. He burned. Fists and feet pummeled others, knocking them back with smoke rising from their clothes. More sailors fell, their bodies engulfed in devouring fire. More screams rose. Vennet wanted to order his men to fall back, but he felt paralyzed.

One of the Bonetree let out a wail and bolted. "Revered?" Breff asked.

Dah'mir made no reply. Vennet heard Breff hiss, then spit a

desperate order in the language of the hunters. Footsteps darted away and he and Dah'mir stood alone.

The last of the sailors fell. Flames rose around the burning dolgaunt. The creature's body was a horrible, shifting mass of flaking ash, raw new flesh, and smoldering embers. Only the empty black pits where eyes should have been remained constant. They turned on Vennet and the dolgaunt began to glide forward as smoothly as flame given life—or rather unlife. Heat and hatred seemed to flow from the dolgaunt in equal measure, and yet Vennet felt only a profound, unnatural chill in his spirit. He fumbled for his cutlass, though his gut told him it would be of little good against a creature that had already died once before.

"Hruucan!" called Dah'mir.

The fiery dolgaunt didn't stop his advance.

"Hruucan!" Dah'mir said again. He pulled himself around in front of Vennet. "Hruucan, stop!" The priest drew a breath and stood tall. He seemed almost to swell. The strength of his presence was a dark cloak around him. His voice was sudden thunder in the dusk. "By the power of the Dragon Below, I command it!"

Hruucan rocked backward as if struck—and stopped where he stood, his blazing tentacles lashing the air.

Dah'mir took a step forward. "Hruucan," he said, "do you know me?"

The thrashing of the dolgaunt's tentacles, of the fiery tendrils on his chest and head, quickened for a moment, then fell still. Hruucan bent his head. "Dah'mir," he said. His voice was deep and grating. "My master."

"Good," said Dah'mir with a nod. "Vennet, your arm—quickly."

The aura of his presence collapsed like the passing of a cloudburst, leaving the priest looking more exhausted than before. Vennet reached forward and caught him before he could fall. Hruucan's tentacles stirred.

"You're injured," he said.

Vennet's belly, still clenched tight, seemed to squeeze into a knot with the fear that Hruucan might take advantage of Dah'mir's weakness. The dolgaunt kept his distance though and Dah'mir only gave a weak, cold laugh. "And you're dead, my Hand."

"I died with hatred of Singe in my mind," said Hruucan, "and rose the same way. Fire renews me. Life is my fuel. When I take my revenge on Singe, perhaps I will join him in death."

"Did you kill my Bonetree hunters?" Dah'mir asked as if scolding a child.

Hruucan showed no sign of remorse. "Their lives sustained me," he said. He turned and swept a hand across the smoldering bodies of Vennet's crew. "These will sustain me for a time as well."

To hear the priest and the undead dolgaunt speaking so casually sent a ripple of horror through Vennet. A sort of mad courage rose out of the fear that gripped him. "They were my crew!" he snapped at Hruucan. He looked to Dah'mir, leaning on his arm. "How are we supposed to get back to Zarash'ak and *Lightning on Water* without them?"

"Be at ease, captain," Dah'mir said. "When I have my strength back, you won't need a crew. I will see you back to your ship wherever she may be."

Shock and anger ran up Vennet's spine. "What do you mean by that?" he asked.

Dah'mir's voice was weary. "The dragonshards that led me to sanctuary on your ship are still onboard her, aren't they, captain? I can still sense their beacon call. Perhaps your crew have stronger wills that I expected, but whatever the cause of it, your ship has been on the move for several days." He lifted a hand and pointed into the darkness. "That way. I expect whoever controls her is making for Sharn."

Vennet stared at him. "My ship has been stolen? *My ship has been stolen and you didn't tell me?*" His voice rose. "If my crew reaches Sharn with *Lightning on Water*, I'll be exposed! What good will the power and wealth you promised me be then? How could you not tell me this was happening?" He tried to thrust Dah'mir away from him.

The priest's fingers sank into his flesh like talons. Acid-green eyes glared at Vennet, cold and furious. "The disposition of your ship is of no concern to me, *Vennet*." Dah'mir spat his name rather than his title for the first time. "She is where she is and we are where we are—and where we are is what matters. The restoration of my strength is all that concerns me now. It should be the all that concerns you as well." His fingers dug deep. "You will receive your reward—I have promised it—but do not assume that I owe you anything else."

There was something in Dah'mir's eyes beyond mere fury, something strange and alien that made Vennet's guts quiver with fear, but the half-elf had anger between his teeth as well. "But you do, *Dah'mir*. My bounty hunter will have found Dandra, Geth, and Singe in Zarash'ak."

"Singe is with your ship," said Hruucan.

Both Vennet and Dah'mir turned to stare at the dolgaunt. "How do you know?" hissed Dah'mir.

"I feel him like a wound." Hruucan's tentacles lashed the air. "The river has prevented me from pursuing him, but I still feel his presence. When I was awake last, I felt him there—" He pointed almost directly south. Toward Zarash'ak, Vennet realized. "—but now I feel him there." He swung around to point southeast.

The same direction Dah'mir had pointed.

Hruucan faced both priest and captain. "It takes little imagination to guess that the movements of Singe and your ship are connected."

"Storm at dawn," Vennet cursed.

A thin smile curled Dah'mir's lips. "Your bounty hunter failed, Vennet."

Vennet growled. "You'll find Dandra where you find Singe, Dah'mir. I think we both have an interest in *Lightning on Water* now."

Dah'mir's smile faltered. His face hardened. "Take me into the mound," he said.

Vennet's rage carried him past the burning bodies of his crew, across the battlefield, and up to the looming bulk of the Bonetree mound. It carried him through the tunnel mouth that opened in the mound's side, a dark scar under the light of the rising moons. It carried him down the first twenty paces of the tunnel that pushed into the earth beneath.

Then—as the tunnel turned twice in quick succession and all hint of moonlight, night air, and the outside world was cut off—it faltered.

Perhaps Dah'mir felt the tension in him. The priest chuckled softly. "Are you frightened, Vennet?"

The half-elf stiffened. "No."

Hruucan just laughed.

The rippling flames of the dolgaunt's tentacles and the ember-glow of his burned body were their only illumination in the tunnels. By their shifting light, Vennet could see that the tunnel floor had been worn smooth from use. They passed the mouths of chambers and other tunnels, but Dah'mir kept them moving along the most well-worn route—although at one chamber entrance he stopped. "In here," he said. "I need to see something."

Vennet guided him into the chamber. Hruucan followed and the light of his body splashed across a towering device of brass tubes, wires, and crystals. Vennet recognized it from Dandra's tale of her capture and torture at Dah'mir's hands—it was the device that the priest had used to separate his kalashtar subject's minds from their bodies, exchanging them with the spirits of their psicrystals. He recognized the tables to which Dandra said the kalashtar had been bound. One of them still held the remains, somehow preserved by the stale atmosphere within the mound, of a kalashtar man. His skull looked like it had been ripped apart.

On the floor before the device of brass and crystal was a blue-black Khyber shard, the biggest dragonshard Vennet had ever seen. For a moment, he forgot his fear in a rush of greed. The shard was the size of small child. Sold at market it would be worth a considerable fortune.

Dandra had described just such a shard as the heart of Dah'mir's device. Vennet looked up at the device again: there was a hole torn through the tubes and wires that matched the size of the shard. The great blue-black crystal rested atop a network of cracks in the flagstone of the chamber floor. It had, Vennet guessed, been hurled to the ground hard enough to shatter the stones. He looked more closely at the shard itself.

A deep crack ran through the shard's center. It had been ruined.

Dah'mir's grasp was tight on his arm. Vennet looked down at him and felt his fear come rushing back. The priest's face was pale with controlled rage. Vennet wouldn't want to be whoever had broken the shard.

"I've seen enough," said Dah'mir after a long while. "Go back to the tunnel. Our destination lies deeper."

As they penetrated further, the frequency with which other tunnels and chambers appeared increased. The floor became not just worn, but slippery-smooth. The silence of the upper tunnels that Vennet had taken for granted was broken. There were harsh whispers in the depths and scrapes of furtive movement in the darkness. Some of the whispers sound threatening.

"Dolgrims," murmured Dah'mir. "Act calm. They'll attack if they sense fear."

The tunnel opened into a chamber wider than the reach of Hruucan's light, but both he and Dah'mir moved across it with confidence. Vennet might have been supporting Dah'mir but he would have been lost without the priest's guidance. The darkness of the chamber seemed unending. At some point, the whispers of the dolgrims faded away as well. Vennet felt unease rising up his throat like vomit. Just when it seemed that he would be sick, though, Hruucan's flickering light fell on a wall of rock pierced by a narrow passage.

"Here," said Dah'mir. "Go carefully."

Vennet didn't need the warning. The floors and walls of the passage were rough, not worn smooth. The tunnel was seldom traveled. He edged forward, leading Dah'mir. Hruucan stayed back—the passage was so restricted that it trapped the heat given off by his body. Vennet could feel hot air circulating around him, like standing too close to a roaring fire.

The passage ended in a dark crack. Vennet stepped out of the glow of Hruucan's tentacles and into a seeming void. His foot struck a loose rock—it clattered away into the darkness, raising a cacophony of distant echoes.

"I told you to be careful," Dah'mir said. He raised his voice and called out an arcane word. Arcs of dim blue radiance streaked through the chamber, veins of crystal embedded in the walls woken to light by the magic. Vennet caught his breath.

A cavern soared around them, opening above and below. They stood on a broad ledge about halfway up from the cavern floor. More ledges stepped down like gigantic benches on the cavern's other walls. The floor of the cavern was broken and uneven, but about twenty-five paces across. At floor level in the opposite wall was another broad tunnel. Stones ringed the tunnel mouth in a rough arch--stones etched with symbols and interspersed with the shining blue-black of Khyber shards.

"Storm at dawn," breathed Vennet.

"So close," wheezed Dah'mir. "So close." He gestured sharply. "Help me down!"

Vennet glanced over the side of the ledge. The rock face looked as though it had been worked like clay to form a series of irregular steps down to the cavern floor. He went first, choosing his footing carefully and helping Dah'mir down each step. The priest moved with the care of a frail man. "The shifter will pay for this," he murmured with each cautious movement. "He will pay."

Hruucan leaped down with a careless grace to join them as they crossed the floor. Vennet stared up at the stone ring built around the tunnel. The stones clearly didn't come from within the cavern—they were a mix of colors, sizes, and textures. Many had the smooth curves of river stones, others the broken sharpness of quarried rock. Up close, he could see that they were held in place with a dark but glittering mortar.

"What is it?" Vennet asked.

"A seal," said the priest. "A seal devised by Gatekeepers to restrain forces they feared." He pulled away from Vennet and eased himself to the ground, kneeling before the tunnel.

"A Gatekeeper seal?" Vennet's tortured gut felt ready to rise once more. His heart was pounding in his chest. When he'd been tutored in the classrooms of House Lyrandar, the ancient myths of the Gatekeepers had been curiosities. When he'd been taught the lies of the Sovereign Host, the Gatekeepers hadn't been mentioned at all. Only when he'd found faith in the Dragon Below had he learned more of them—enemies of the powers of Khyber, creators of the seals that had for millennia restrained the great lords of the dark, the alien daelkyr. He swallowed. "You're going to break it?"

"No," Dah'mir said. "But I don't need to."

He sat back on his heels, his leather robes pooling around him, the red Eberron shards set in his sleeves flashing in the dim light as he raised his arms above his head. A chant began to ripple from his lips. Vennet didn't recognize the words. They were like nothing he had ever heard before, neither a true language nor the syllables of magic. They hurt his ears and sent horror stabbing through him. They soaked into his head like wine into a white cloth. When a second voice took up the chant, he cringed and looked to Hruucan.

The dolgaunt, however, stood silent. It took a moment for Vennet to realize that the second voice was his own, that his lips and tongue were moving in time to Dah'mir's. That he had settled down to kneel on the rocky floor as well.

He thrust himself to his feet and stumbled backward, but the words of the priest's chant stayed with him, forcing themselves out of his mouth. He tried clamping his hands over his mouth. It only muffled the words. The chant rose to a peak.

Within the ring of the Gatekeeper seal, the air shimmered and grew bright. The tunnel beyond seemed to contract, rushing toward him—

And Vennet peered through an enormous lens into a great chamber, the throne room of a wealthy lord. Of a prince!

Except that the courtiers who turned to look back through the window were tall and spindly beneath their fine robes. They had broad, hairless heads with slick, pulsing skin and dead white eyes—and dangling, writhing tentacles where there should have been a nose and jaw. Mind flayers.

There were other strange creatures as well. Dolgaunts stood as guards and dolgrims crawled on the floor like dogs. A mind flayer carried a small creature like an eyeless monkey on its shoulder. A beautiful elf-like woman turned to reveal thick fleshy tendrils growing among her hair and down her back.

At the center of the grand chamber, on a throne carved from glittering black stone, sat a human man of astounding beauty. The robes that spilled off him exposed pale, muscular arms and a broad chest. His hair was black as night and fine as silk; his skin was as pale and smooth as marble. His eyes were solid acid-green, the same color as Dah'mir's but without pupil or iris. His ears, his nose, his brow, the line of his jaw—all were so perfect that it took Vennet a long moment to realize that he had no mouth, only smooth skin between nose and chin.

"Storm at dawn," whispered Vennet. A fragment from the rites of the Cult of the Dragon Below came back to him. *They are perfect in their power. They are without flaw save those flaws they choose. Their triumph is delayed but not denied —they will hold Eberron as they held Xoriat. They are the great lords of the dark and nothing is beyond their will.*

Dah'mir touched his fingers to his forehead and his lips, then bent low, prostrating himself. "Master," he said, his voice thick with adoration.

The voice that answered the priest crashed through the cavern like thunder. It slammed into Vennet and sent him staggering. The half-elf screamed at the sound of it. He clapped his hands over his ears, but it did no good. The only sound he blocked was his own scream. The voice of the great lord of the dark, of the daelkyr, was in his mind.

Vennet had stood at the helm of *Lightning on Water* to guide the ship through storms, the rain lashing him, the roar of the gale and the howl of the ship's great elemental ring blending together until he could hear nothing else. The daelkyr's voice was like that except that the thunder was broken by the rise and fall of words. Words that Vennet could recognize but not grasp—words far larger and older than him. Words that seemed older than Eberron itself. They ate into him like bitterly cold acid, numbing and searing at the same time. He stumbled and fell, cracking his knees against the rough stone of the cavern floor.

Dah'mir seemed to understand the daelkyr's voice, though. As the thunder stopped and Vennet reeled at a moment of respite, the priest shook his head and turned his eyes downward. "No, master," he said. "Your new servants aren't ready. There have been complications. Medala is dead—"

The daelkyr spoke again. Vennet reeled. Across the cavern, he saw Hruucan, standing as motionless as a soldier on parade, shift his weight and brace himself. Even Dah'mir went pale.

"The kalashtar who escaped, master. She found allies. I captured her and returned her to the mound, but her allies recruited Gatekeepers. There was a battle—"

In the great throne room beyond the lens, there was a soundless stir as mind flayers looked at each other. The daelkyr sat forward, his voice a whip crack on the air.

"Dead, master," Dah'mir said. "All of them—killed by the kalashtar's allies." His hands fumbled with his leather robes. "I was wounded, too. It was a chance blow, a desperate strike, but the blade was Dhakaani and powerful."

He parted his robes. Vennet was behind him and couldn't see the wound he exposed, but he heard the sucking sound of leather peeled away from raw, bloody flesh.

Contempt emanated from the daelkyr. Vennet fell over and wept as the silent words of disgust that rolled from the great lord peeled back the layers of his mind. Hruucan staggered and went to his knees.

Dah'mir fell prostrate one more. "Master, I know! I am weak! Without the shard, my strength is gone, your gifts fade." A shudder shook him. "There is more, master," he added with the despair of someone forced to deliver ill tidings. "The great stone has been broken."

The daelkyr said nothing. The only sound in the cavern was Vennet's own weeping. He couldn't tear his eyes from the daelkyr and his priest, however. He saw Dah'mir hesitate, then look up. "It's not the end, master. I believe I can create another stone, one suited to our needs and not a flawed cast-off. One closer to the true stones. My studies, my experiments—I can draw on them." Dah'mir took a ragged breath. "It will take time."

The thunder of the daelkyr's voice rolled again. This time, though, it seemed to Vennet that he could actually understand something of the green-eyed lord's silent speech. As his thoughts fell apart, the ancient words became distinct. They burned in his tortured mind, melting sanity like wax. *We have time.*

Dah'mir lifted himself from the floor and wrenched his robes wide once more. "Then heal me, master! Heal me, I beg you!"

The daelkyr sat back, his eyes narrowed—then held out a hand. A mind flayer, taller than its fellows and with long tentacles that made Vennet think of an old man's trailing beard, stepped forward and placed a blue-black dragonshard in the daelkyr's hand. The great lord stroked the shard for a moment, then casually pitched it forward toward the shimmering lens.

For a moment, the bright air within the ring of the Gatekeeper seal rippled and churned like water as the shard plunged through it. The dark crystal fell free. Dah'mir, rose to his feet, stretched out a hand, and snatched it from the air. His eyes were wide and shining.

"Vennet!" he called. His voice cracked. "Come here! If you want your reward, help me now!"

Vennet would gladly have given up the wildest of his dreams for power and glory just to have fled the cavern. His limbs and his will, however, seemed to belong to someone else. Trembling, he rose and moved forward. The eyes of the daelkyr and all of his strange and horrible courtiers were on him as he stepped around to stand in front of Dah'mir. The wound in the priest's chest lay bare, a jagged rip in his flesh. Broken ribs showed in its red depths. It oozed dark blood and thin clear liquid like the seepage from a blister. There was no sign of festering or rot. It could have been inflicted only moments rather than weeks before.

Dah'mir held out the dragonshard. Still staring at the wound, Vennet took it without looking—then gasped as his hand closed around its cool surface. Power thrummed beneath his fingertips, like grasping a rope under too much strain and ready to snap. He looked down at the shard. It was the size and shape of a thick spike, longer than a finger, tapering from a narrow point to a flat-topped bulb three fingers wide. The swirls that patterned its heart seemed almost to shift as he watched.

Before him, Dah'mir tugged his robes wide and pushed out his chest. "Close the wound, Vennet!" he commanded. "Close the wound with my master's shard and restore my strength!"

Blood pounded in Vennet's ears. He flipped the shard around in his hand and drove the narrow end deep in Dah'mir's wounded chest. Warm, ragged flesh licked his fingers. He snatched them away. Dah'mir staggered back a pace and stared down at the blue-black stone in his chest.

Then he flung back his head and roared.

The flesh of his chest writhed and knit together around the shard, leaving its flat top glittering against his pale skin. The writhing of the priest's flesh didn't stop there, however. His skin thickened, the metallic luster of copper spreading across his chest, up to his throat, and down to his belly. The black leather of his robes became scaly and thick, merging with his body—which grew and kept growing. Arms and legs twisted. Hands grew massive talons. Dah'mir stretched and immense copper-sheened wings burst from his sides, a tail from the length of his back. His chin became sharp and pointed, his face a muzzle. Horns thrust back against his head. His wild eyes opened into great shining orbs of acid green.

The dragon reared back and a second roar shook the cavern. *"I am restored! Thank you, my master! Glory to Khyber, the fallen and shunned!"*

Vennet curled back, thrusting himself away from the awesome majesty of the wyrm. The presence that Dah'mir had worn as a man seemed magnified. Conflicting urges tore at Vennet: flee from the monster or fall down and bow before Dah'mir's power. He screamed, vomiting his fear, and cowered. His saber was in his hand, held like a shield. His dragonmark burned across his back. On the other side of the cavern, Hruucan laughed at him, his fiery tentacles lashing.

The echoes of roar and laughter spoke to him. *He's a dragon! You've pledged yourself to a dragon!*

"I know," Vennet croaked.

Not many people live to see both a dragon and a daelkyr.

"Then I'm dead."

Not yet.

Dah'mir settled back to crouch on four legs, his wings folded against his scaly sides. "I will not fail you, master. A new line of servants will bow before you." He dipped his body, lowering his horned head to the ground, then sat back. His wings fluttered around him and his body writhed once more, this time folding in on itself, becoming smaller, becoming human-sized once more—

—then, strangely, even smaller. Scales becomes greasy black feathers and Dah'mir stood in the center of the cavern as a heron, just as he had in Vennet's cabin. Except this time, he was the one who looked startled. He swelled back into a dragon, then shrank into a heron once more.

"My human form!" he screeched. He twisted and spread his feathered wings. "Master, what happened to my human form?"

The laughter of the unnatural creatures of the daelkyr's court reached through the eerie lens as a faint hissing, but Vennet could read the mocking expression on their faces. The daelkyr sat forward on his throne. His voice throbbed in Vennet's mind. It didn't seem so terrible now, as if the ancient words had burned away his pain and fear. He still cringed though at the cold anger of the daelkyr's tone. *Failure is punished.*

Dah'mir flinched. "Master?"

Bring me my servants and your human shape will be restored.

"But master, how? How can I do your work? I cannot walk among humans! I have no hands!"

Use the hands of others. Let them walk for you. The daelkyr's expression dimmed. He sat back. *Bring me my servants.*

Vennet saw Dah'mir tremble. His heron-head dipped. "I understand."

The lens within the great Gatekeeper seal shimmered and the vision of the daelkyr's weird court snapped and collapsed. Dah'mir turned on spindly legs to look first at Hruucan, then at Vennet.

The half-elf slid his saber back into its scabbard and held out his hands. "Dah'mir," he said. "My master."

The long, dark walk up from the cavern and out of the mound seemed faster the second time. Maybe it was because the whispers of the dolgrims had fallen silent. Maybe it was because Vennet felt none of the fear he had before. He felt strangely giddy, in fact, and only Dah'mir's rage kept him quiet.

Anger was an aura around the heron. He flew where he could, leaving Vennet and Hruucan to follow in his wake, and walking where he couldn't, forcing them to match his waddling pace. He said nothing.

Dawn had broken when they emerged from the mound. Vennet blinked at the radiance. Hruucan bared his teeth at the light that fell on him, but without eyes, he didn't flinch. Dah'mir leaped into the air as soon as he could, beating his wings to gain height—then transforming into his dragon form in mid-air. He settled back to the ground of the battlefield before the mound and his shining eyes looking down on Hruucan and Vennet.

"Your desires come to the fore, Vennet," he said, his voice a rumble. "We're going after your ship. I need Dandra and Tetkashtai. I will begin my research with them." His talons gouged grooves in the ground. "You will be the first rider I've born willingly in my life. Feel honored."

"I will," Vennet said. "I do."

"Wait!" hissed Hruucan. His tentacles whipped through the air. "You can't leave me. If Singe is on that ship . . ."

"I wouldn't leave you behind," said Dah'mir. His eyes narrowed as he considered the fiery dolgaunt's tentacles. "Fire revives you, but can you extinguish yourself?"

Hruucan's tentacles stiffened. "No."

"Then let me." Without warning, the dragon reared and his tremendous leathery wings hammered on the air. Vennet twisted away and covered his face to protect himself against the sudden blast of wind and dust stirred up. Grit choked the air, worse than salt spray in a storm.

Look to Hruucan, the rushing wind whispered in his ears. Vennet turned.

The dolgaunt was staggering against the air and dust, his flames guttering like candles, simultaneously blown away and smothered. His tentacles streamed out and vanished. The red embers beneath his skin flared bright, then turned black.

Hruucan fell to the ground, a charred corpse.

Dah'mir folded his wings. The dust in the air began to settle. Without even being asked, Vennet went to Hruucan's body. His skin was hot, crisp, and fragile, like burned paper. The half-elf stripped a tunic off the rotting body of an orc who had died with an axe in his skull. The fabric was stiff and stank of decay. There were maggots clinging to it but he shook them off and wrapped the tunic carefully around the bundle that was Hruucan. "To keep him from crumbling as you fly," he told Dah'mir.

The dragon nodded and bent down so that Vennet could climb onto his back. "Sit at the base of my neck," he said. "Hold tight."

Vennet barely had time to settle himself and wedge his hands among the thick scales that ran down Dah'mir's back before the dragon coiled and leaped into the air. His wings snapped out, beat down and caught the wind. They climbed. Dah'mir let out a strange whistle and the herons that had traveled with them from Zarash'ak burst from the riverbank below to soar up and meet them. They had to fly fast—even barely beating his wings, Dah'mir was still climbing. The Shadow Marches spread out below Vennet and he laughed.

Like flying in an airship, the passing wind howled.

"Better!" Vennet shouted back.

Far ahead, clouds piled up in a thick bank. Dah'mir soared toward them and after what seemed like only a few moments, they plunged into the thick mists. The sunlight vanished, leaving everything damp, cool, and dim.

"Prepare yourself!" Dah'mir roared. Peering past his neck, Vennet saw him stretch out a foreleg and heard him snarl a word of magic.

One of the red Eberron shards embedded in the scales of his leg flared suddenly and seemed to burn. Darkness flared around them, as if the world had been turned inside out and what had been bright was made black.

"I have flown through a plane of shadow to reach you," Dah'mir had said when he first appeared on *Lightning on Water*.

Vennet could see nothing but dim forms as they whisked through the weird dark skies, but the shadow winds were as talkative as the winds of Eberron. *What about the reward Dah'mir promised you?* they asked. *What about wealth and power?*

Vennet laughed, the speed of their passage snatching his breath from between his teeth. "I have my reward!" he said.

CHAPTER

8

Chain looked up as Singe climbed down the ladder-like steps of the aft hold of *Lightning on Water*. "Look at you," said the bounty hunter. "Dressed up like you're trying to impress someone."

In the glow of the everbright lantern that lit the hold, Singe tugged on the hem of the vest he had bought during their last few hours in Zarash'ak, part of a sturdy but stylish outfit well suited to the part of a traveling scholar. "I can tell it's working," he said. "This is the first time I've come down here and you haven't cursed me."

Chain's eyes narrowed. "We've stopped during daylight this time. We must be in Vralkek. You'll be leaving soon. The next time I see you I'll have a sword in my hand."

Singe cocked his head and gave Chain a long look, then drew his rapier.

"Back up," he ordered.

Chain shuffled backward as far as he could, pulling tight the chains that shackled him to a strong bolt embedded in the deck. Singe leaned cautiously close to examine the heavy padlock that held the chains. The first time Singe had come to inspect his bonds, Chain had tried to use the slack in the chain to attack him. The wizard had demonstrated to him that while he wasn't quite as fast Dandra, he was fast enough to avoid a clumsy attack. A stinging blow from the flat of his blade had left the bounty hunter sitting uncomfortably for two days.

Whatever worries, he might have had, however, Chain's bonds were just as they had been when they'd bound him almost a week ago. Bolt, lock, and chain were still solid. The same shackles had once held Ashi prisoner, and if the hunter's strength hadn't been enough to free her, Singe was certain Chain's wouldn't be either. He stepped back. Chain eased forward and squatted on the deck, glaring up at him. Singe clenched his teeth at the man's blunt rage. There was nothing else to say. They'd reassured Chain that Marolis and Karth would let him go at Sharn, and had apologized—though Chain didn't make it easy—that this had been necessary.

He stepped back toward the steep stairs, keeping his eyes on Chain. When he was safely out of reach, he sheathed his rapier and turned away.

"I'll be coming for you!" Chain called after him.

The others were waiting on deck. "How's our friend?" asked Geth.

"He says hello—oh, and that he'll be coming for us."

Geth snorted. "Let him." He closed his right fist in a clash of metal. The shifter had donned his great gauntlet. The black metal gave back a dull gleam in the early afternoon sunlight. He was also wearing a coat stitched with wide bands of heavy leather, a sort of light armor that had been another of Singe's purchases in Zarash'ak. The coat was less for protection and more for show: the color of the fabric underneath the leather bands was similar enough to Singe's new outfit to be suggestive of livery. Geth hated it. Singe thought it made him—and Orshok, Natrac, and Ashi, all of whom had similar clothing—look more professional and intimidating.

Dandra had another opinion. "Sometimes kalashtar who share the same lineage deliberately wear clothes in matching designs and colors," she'd said when Singe had first coaxed their companions to wear the new gear.

"And?" Singe had asked.

"It looks like they're trying too hard," Dandra had told him. She'd kept to her own distinctive clothing.

Karth came trotting along the deck. "We've hailed one of the local boats. She's alongside, waiting to take you ashore," he said. He offered Singe his hand. "Olladra's fortune," he said.

"Thank you," said Singe, returning his grip. They'd told Karth and Marolis most of their story—they owed the crew of *Lightning on Water* that much at the very least—though they'd left out the truth of Dah'mir's nature and of his experiments on kalashtar. Karth and Marolis would tell their own tale to the ministers of House Lyrandar. Singe, Dandra, and Geth had all agreed there were some things the great house didn't need to know.

The others said their good-byes as well, though Karth reserved his most heartfelt farewells for Dandra and Orshok—Dandra because she had freed him and Marolis, Orshok because his prayers had helped the rest of the crew overcome Dah'mir's power. As they made their way to where a ladder had been thrown over the ship's rail, other members of the crew clustered around the young druid, offering their thanks. Orshok flushed at the attention and scrambled quickly over the side and down to the waiting boat to escape it. Singe was the last one down the ladder. He waved to Marolis—the half-elf had stayed at the ship's wheel, holding the ship steady for their disembarking—then shook hands with Karth again.

"Good luck with the ministers of Lyrandar," he said. "Be careful of Chain. I think he might try something."

Karth grinned. "He's on a ship that's soon going to be leagues away from land again. What can he do? We're not going to let anything keep us from getting to Sharn."

Singe squeezed his hand. "Good man." He let go and clambered down the ladder.

The boat below was nothing more than an open top fishing craft that smelled strongly of last week's catch. Between him, the five others, and the four weathered half-orcs that were her crew, the boat was crowded. Singe crouched with Orshok and Natrac in the stern as the crew of the little boat pulled hard on the oars, taking them away from *Lightning on Water* and toward the rugged coast of Droaam. Orshok was still staring at the ship, watching her in fascination. When the fishing boat had pulled far enough away, Singe heard Marolis shout. A moment later, the great elemental ring that drove the ship churned as a gale blasted out of it. The sleek ship moved again, slowly at first but quickly picking up speed. As she headed back out to the open ocean, moving faster and faster, her hull rose up out of the water to reveal the two great running fins normally hidden below the water line. The narrow profile of the fins allowed the ship to cut through the waves with the greatest possible speed.

Orshok's eyes were wide. Singe slapped him on the shoulder. "Turn around, Orshok. Have a look at Vralkek."

"In a moment," the orc said distantly.

Natrac laughed. "Give him a chance, Singe. You only see things for the first time once."

The wizard shrugged, then turned to survey Vralkek for himself. Marolis had brought *Lightning on Water* as close in as he dared without knowing more about the port's harbor. It had been more than close enough. Compared to Zarash'ak, Vralkek was nothing, its waterfront largely empty. It had more in common with distant Yrlag, far away where the lonely western coast of the Shadow Marches met the southern fringe of the Eldeen Reaches. Yrlag had, so Geth had been told by Adolan, once been the westernmost outpost of the Dhakaani Empire and that heritage still showed in tremendous works of ancient engineering and crumbling ruins. Singe could see some of those same elements in Vralkek, but apparently more had befallen the port since Dhakaan's end than had befallen Yrlag. What ruins were visible were in worse condition. An old stone pier was nearly hidden beneath a tangle of rickety wood. What he had thought to be a partially submerged shoal was, he realized as they passed it and drew into the harbor proper, actually the broken and age-rounded remains of a mighty breakwall.

Orshok gasped sharply. Singe twisted around to look at him. "What is it?"

The druid's gaze were still on *Lightning on Water*, now well distant. He pointed with his hunda stick. "Something fell overboard."

Singe squinted at the ship. "Really?"

"I saw something," Orshok insisted. "Like someone falling over the side."

"Mirage," said Natrac. "Sometimes it's hard to judge the distance between things on the ocean. You probably saw something much closer, between us and the ship. Maybe a bird, maybe a dolphin breaking the surface, maybe just a wave."

Orshok looked doubtful. "I'm sure it was right beside the ship."

"What would it have been?" asked Singe. "Marolis would have stopped if one of the crew had fallen—and I can't imagine they would have." The shadow of Vralkek's docks fell over them and a moment later the structure cut off their last glimpse of *Lightning on Water*. "Forget about it," Singe told Orshok. "We're here."

He turned around again. The half-orcs at the boat's oars ignored the dock and pulled right up onto a beach that smelled almost as strongly of fish as their boat. Gulls swooped in, perhaps thinking that the boat's passengers were the catch of the day

Although Karth would already have paid the fishermen, Singe gave them an extra silver sovereign each. "What's a good inn?" he asked. "And where can I find guides to take us into the interior?"

The answer to both questions was a place called the Barrel, though Singe doled out a few crowns more as they passed through the town to confirm it. He was exceedingly careful about showing his money, though. Vralkek was that kind of town. He could feel it as soon as they climbed up from the beach and stepped into the muddy streets.

It wasn't just an air of desperation and crime that gave Vralkek a sense of danger. Singe could feel eyes on him. Eyes appraising him as prey—financially and literally.

Dandra took a step closer to him as they walked. He felt her mind brush against his in the *kesh*. Her thoughts carried echoes of unease. *Singe* . . . she said.

I know, he responded.

There was a reason Droaam was called the nation of monsters and that reason walked the streets of Vralkek. Orcs and half-orcs stood on corners, laughing coarsely. Goblins skulked in the shadows. Gnolls—rangy creatures with the bodies of lean humans and heads like hyenas—strutted along as though they carried the authority of town guards. In a smithy, a muscular minotaur pounded red-hot iron. Along a roofline, a trio of harpies cackled, flapped ragged wings, and watched the world below. A band of hobgoblins stood clustered around the door of one building as if to repel anyone who might try to enter. A series of loud thumps and a low moan drifted out as Singe and the others passed.

The hobgoblins watched them go by. Furry, wolf-like ears twitched and turned, tracking them. Singe's hand dropped to the hilt of his rapier. He did see humans as they walked, but they were few and generally looked either half-feral or broken and hollow. The broken ones had the marks of slaves. Singe wouldn't have trusted the feral ones to bury a corpse.

"I don't like this place," he murmured so that the others besides Dandra could hear him. Geth gave him a sharp-toothed grin.

"Bothers you, does it?" the shifter asked. "Being in a place where humans are the ones who stand out?" He swaggered like the gnolls, seemingly at home among the monsters, though Singe noticed his eyes roamed the streetscape with the alertness of an animal in strange territory.

"Well, it bothers me," said Natrac. "This is why I've always avoided Droaam before."

Singe glanced at the half-orc. He walked with his knife-hand visible and stayed close to the others, but the grimness that had vanished with their return to Zarash'ak had reappeared. The persona of the blustering merchant seemed stretched over it, like a dwarf wearing a mask and calling himself an elf.

He's protesting too much, said Dandra through the *kesh*. *Remember what Bava said.*

I agree, Singe said. *What's he hiding?*

Even Orshok, who probably could have blended in with the other orcs in the town, looked uncomfortable. Only Ashi seemed completely at ease, maybe even energized by the atmosphere in Vralkek. She moved with a confident stride, her back straight, her eyes bright, a hunter among hunters.

She was also drawing as much attention as all of them put together. "Ashi—" he started to say in soft warning.

He didn't have a chance to finish. From among a cluster of gnolls beside the street, a massive figure rose up out of a crouch. Its limbs were thick with muscle, its arms nearly as long as its legs. Its head was heavy and hideous, with matted, greasy hair. Its lower jaw was thrust forward, exposing misshapen teeth as big as Singe's thumbs. From where he stood, the wizard caught a whiff of the foul stench of its unwashed hide. An ogre. A male.

Upright, the creature was easily half again as tall as Ashi. He stepped directly into her path and leered down at her. "Human girl acts tough." The ogre pinched his lower lip with two filthy fingers in imitation of Ashi's piercings. "Gots little tusks. Tough *and* pretty."

For one anxious moment, Singe was afraid Ashi was going to draw her sword. That was the last thing they needed. A naked blade could provoke a street fight. He could see that Geth was thinking the same thing—the shifter stiffened and turned sharply toward Ashi.

But the Bonetree hunter just stood and looked up at the ogre, her face and eyes hard. She said nothing. The laughter that had risen among the gnolls died out and after a moment, the grin on the ogre's face sagged and faltered. A sneer replaced it. The ogre beat his hands against his chest. "You wants?" it growled. "Thinks you can beat?"

"I know I could," Ashi said. Her voice was low and confident. The fingers of her sword hand clenched and spread. "You think you can beat me?"

The street around them had grown quiet as the mingled creatures on it turned their attention to the confrontation. The gnolls who were with the ogre muttered among themselves, but stayed back. Geth threw a glance to Singe and twitched his head toward Ashi. Singe knew what he was asking—should he step in? The wizard shook his head. Ashi had started this. She needed to resolve it on her own or the creatures of Vralkek would be on them like leeches on a wound.

The silence between the hunter and the ogre stretched out. Big greasy drops of sweat formed on the monster's forehead. Ashi's brow dropped. Her face grew dark—

The ogre broke. "Girl is pretty," he said finally. "Just sayings girl is pretty. Don't sees human girls so pretty and tough." He raised his heavy head and glared around the street. "Just sayings!"

He stepped back out of Ashi's way and the hunter nodded her head. Singe noticed, however, that she remained alert as she moved past the monster and rejoined him and the others. Noise returned to the street. His heart racing, Singe hustled them all onward.

"That was impressive, Ashi!" said Dandra under her breath.

Ashi grunted. "Are all ogres such cowards?"

"No," said Singe with a wince. "Usually they're just angry." He glanced at Ashi. "Please don't do that again."

"I could have beaten him."

"Yes, but he had a lot of friends—and just because Droaam is country of monsters doesn't mean they don't have laws. I don't think we want to get in trouble here."

The taproom of the Barrel was a very different place from the *gaeth'ad* house where they had met Chain. Both house and taproom were dark, but that was where any resemblance ended.

The Barrel was alive with sound, the crowd of its patrons talking, shouting, and laughing, filling the air with the sound of strange languages—Singe picked out Orc and Goblin immediately, but could only guess that the booming tongue that occasionally rolled above other speech was Giant. The place was a rush of smells: musky and pungent bodies, stale ale, sizzling meat, even an undertone of blood. Dandra flinched at the odor.

"Not the Zarash'ak herb market, is it?" Singe asked her as they made their way toward the bar. She shook her head.

Somewhat to his surprise, no one had taken much notice when their group opened the outer door—the Barrel had separate entrances to the taproom and to the upstairs inn where they had taken rooms for what would hopefully be a short stay in Vralkek. Maybe, Singe thought, human-dominated groups weren't such an unusual sight in the town after all. Maybe the patrons of the Barrel just didn't care that much. Either way, so long as no undue attention came their way, he was happy.

"Ashi," said Natrac, "I think you have some admirers." He nodded toward a knot of goblins who were muttering among themselves and glancing frequently at the hunter. Ashi crinkled her nose and ignored them.

"It's a good thing we don't need to keep a low profile," Singe muttered. He looked at Ashi. "Don't worry. A reputation for strength probably isn't a bad thing to have around here."

He moved up to the bar. A female gnoll with one eye stood behind it. "Six," said Singe, slapping down a handful of copper coins. He caught the gnoll's eye. "We're looking for a guide. The innkeeper upstairs said you could help us."

The gnoll's voice was high and barking. "He said you'd be coming down." She gestured to an empty table, then turned to draw their ale. "Space to talk. Settle yourselves. I'll send people over. Where do you need to go?"

"Tzaryan Keep."

Thin lips around the gnoll's dog-like muzzle pulled back. "Dangerous."

"I know."

"Sit," she said, handing him the first two mugs. "I'll bring the rest."

Three chairs had been provided around the table. Geth moved to sit down in one, but Singe nudged him with an elbow. "Stand," he said. "A chair for me, a chair for Dandra, a chair for the guide."

"What?" asked the shifter.

"You're a guard. You stand behind me and watch my back."

Geth glowered at him. "It makes a tempting target."

"Just watch it—don't stick anything in it." He gave one of the mugs to Geth then clacked the other against it. "Here's to better luck than we had with Chain."

When the gnoll barkeep brought the rest of their ale, she brought something else as well—a half-orc in worn and travel stained clothes. "Ryl," she said by way of introduction, then departed.

The half-orc settled into the empty chair. Singe looked him over. Ryl seemed well-traveled and, at least by the standard of the Barrel, not particularly desperate. "So," he asked him after a moment, "you could take us to Tzaryan Keep?"

"I could," the half-orc said. "Easy traveling—dangerous passage. I've got a question for you, though. Is Tzaryan Rrac expecting you?"

"Not as such," Singe told him. They'd worked out their plan during the voyage fro Zarash'ak. "But I'm sure he'll be willing to talk to me. I want his permission to study the Dhakaani ruins near Tzaryan Keep."

Ryl thrust out his jaw. "I can take you to within sight of the keep. I won't go any further if Tzaryan's not expecting you."

"Fair enough." There was another gnoll standing nearby, obviously waiting his chance to talk to them. Singe nodded to Ryl. "Stay in the Barrel. We'll let you know when we've made a decision."

The half-orc rose and made way for the gnoll. "I'm Kagishi," the hyena-headed creature said. His voice was a whine. "I'll work cheap."

His clothing was frayed and heavily patched. The fur that covered his lean body was thin and mangy. An unstrung bow of Brelish make was slung across his back—along with a quiver that was completely empty of arrows. Singe felt Dandra take his hand underneath the table and give it a little squeeze of warning. He gave no reaction, but raised an eyebrow to Kagishi. "You know Tzaryan Keep? The ruins there?"

"Does Tzaryan Rrac know you're coming?" Kagishi asked like Ryl's echo.

"No."

Kagishi flinched. "That will cost you extra."

"You said you'd work cheap," said Natrac.

The gnoll looked uncomfortable. "There's cheap and there's stupid."

The reactions of Ryl and Kagishi were echoed by the next two guides to seek them out. A black-haired shifter who Geth took an immediate dislike to and a whip-like human both hesitated as soon as they learned that Singe's party would be approaching the keep unexpected. The human offered to arrange for a runner to precede them and alert Tzaryan Rrac to their approach—a sensible and tempting offer. The shifter told them the same story of the House Tharashk dragonshard prospectors that they had heard from Bava and suggested that what they needed was more protection. By coincidence, he knew a number of others who would be willing to accompany them.

Geth bared his teeth and growled at him before he could even finish the suggestion. "Boar's whiskers! Do you think we were born moonstruck?" He stepped around from behind the table, shifting as he moved—his thick body seemed to grow even thicker, his hair denser. "Get out of here!"

Their would-be guide bared sharp teeth as well. His hands flexed and what had been heavy nails grew suddenly into long, sharp claws. The two shifters glared at each other for a moment, the hair on their bodies bristling, then the black-haired shifter stepped back and swiftly vanished among a crowd that had barely even glanced at the confrontation.

Geth growled again, this time in satisfaction, and turned back to their table. He dropped into the third chair and looked at Geth and Dandra. "I assume he's out of the running," he said.

Singe nodded. "I think we've talked to enough now." He twisted around so that he could see all of the others. "What do you think of—"

"There's one more," said Orshok. He gestured. Singe turned back around.

On the edge of the crowd stood a goblin. The short creature was looking up at them nervously. "Yes?" Singe asked him.

"You need guide Tzaryan Keep?"

The goblin's voice was thin and harshly accented. Singe considered him. He hadn't thought of a goblin as a guide, especially in Droaam where it seemed that most of the population could and did swallow goblins whole. This goblin, however, carried a multitude of scars. He was clearly a survivor. Singe flicked his fingers at Geth—the shifter vacated his chair with a groan—and waved the goblin forward. "Who are you?"

"Moza." The goblin hopped up into the empty chair, standing rather than sitting in it. Being at eye level with the larger people around the table seemed to take away some of his nervousness. "You need guide?" he asked again.

Singe nodded. "Yes," he said, "we need a guide to Tzaryan Keep." He skipped right to the information the other guides had asked for. "And no, Tzaryan Rrac doesn't know we're coming but we're not trying to sneak into his keep. We're walking right up to his door."

"I hear," Moza said. "What you want with Dhakaani ruins?"

Singe sat back, a little surprised. None of the other prospective guides had even blinked at his mention of the ruins—and certainly none had asked about the ruins before he'd even mentioned them. "How do you know about that?"

The goblin seemed strangely taken aback at the question. His nervousness returned, his eyes darting around the taproom briefly then coming back to Singe. He tugged on his ear. "I hear."

He sounded barely convinced by his own answer. Singe frowned. "What do you care if I'm interested in the ruins?"

The goblin flinched a second time. He started to look around again.

Ashi bent sharply to whisper in Singe's ear. "On your left—there's a hobgoblin woman in the crowd. She's giving him cues." The wizard turned his head.

If he hadn't been looking for her, he probably would have missed the hobgoblin woman completely. She had slipped herself in beside a group of gnolls, their height hiding hers, their brownish fur making her yellowish skin and orange-brown hair stand out a little less. Black leather armor studded with darkened rivets blended into the shadows of the taproom.

Her furry ears stood high and were turned toward their table. She was gesturing to Moza, her mouth shaping exaggerated words.

Between one heartbeat and the next, however, dark eyes met Singe's gaze. The hobgoblin froze for an instant, then dropped down, vanishing among the crowd.

Singe leaped to his feet, taking a fast step in the hobgoblin's direction as Ashi lunged across the table to grab for Moza. The goblin squealed and slipped away from her grasping fingers, slithering down out of the chair. Dandra and Natrac flinched. "What are you doing?" Natrac asked in a yelp.

"There was a hobgoblin," growled Geth. "I saw her."

"That was a set-up!" spat Singe. "Someone is—"

Before he could say anything more or take another step, the door of the taproom opened—and for the first time, the patrons of the Barrel grew silent and still.

The sun was beginning to set outside and in from the fiery brightness stepped two . . . four . . . six ogres. Unlike the ogre that had accosted Ashi in the street, however, these were clean and well-groomed. Singe couldn't have said that they looked any more intelligent, but they moved with a purpose and discipline that was distinctly unusual in an ogre.

All of them carried massive maces and wore stiff jerkins of heavy hide. Emblazoned on the jerkins was the insignia of a four-pointed blue star. Tzaryan Rrac's insignia.

"Twelve bloody moons," Singe cursed under his breath. "What are they doing here?" He eased back to the table. The others did the same, those who were standing crouching down a bit to make themselves less conspicuous.

Through the open door, Singe could see the silhouettes of at least two more ogres standing guard outside. The ogres inside the Barrel scanned the silent room. The gnoll barkeep hurried up to the largest of the monsters. The ogres that flanked him raised their weapons at her approach but lowered them again at a glance from their leader. He and the gnoll exchanged words.

Her hand rose and pointed straight to Singe and the others. The ogre leader nodded and made his way across the room. The Barrel's patrons pressed back out of his path.

"Tiger!" hissed Geth. "What do we do?"

Singe swallowed. "Act calm," he said. He sat up straight in his chair and the ogre leader leaned across the table. Even cleaned up, the monster's breath reeked of decayed meat.

"Are you Timin Shay? he asked.

Timin Shay had been a childhood friend killed in a cart accident as a young man. Singe had taken to using the name as an alias long ago. He'd given it to the innkeeper of the Barrel. "Yes," he said. "I am. What's this about?"

"You're looking for a guide to Tzaryan Keep?"

The ogre pronounced each of its words with care, as if taught to speak the language properly. Singe nodded. A hint of relief, as if he was pleased that he had found the right human, flickered in the ogre's eyes. He stood straight. "I serve Tzaryan Rrac. By order of the general, you are invited to travel with us as we return to Tzaryan Keep."

Singe blinked in surprise, then looked left and right to Dandra and Geth. The kalashtar and the shifter both wore started expressions as well. He looked back to the ogre. The general . . . Bava and Natrac had said that Tzaryan Rrac had hired a veteran general of the Last War to train his troops. Judging by the utter change in the ogres standing before them, his training was extremely effective. Singe licked his lips, trying to think of what to do.

"What's your general's name?" he asked.

"He is the General," the ogre said.

Singe clenched his teeth. "Fair enough," he said. "How does the General know I'm looking for a guide to Tzaryan Keep?"

The ogre looked as if he was trying to find an answer to an unexpected question in an unfamiliar language. "The General hears about your looking," he said awkwardly.

"The General hears quickly," said Dandra. "What is he doing in Vralkek anyway?"

The ogre's face tensed in frustration. "The General brought us to Vralkek to test our discipline."

Singe heard someone else's voice behind the ogre's word; he had probably learned the response by rote after listening to orders from his commander over and over again. The presence of Tzaryan's troops in Vralkek was an annoying coincidence, but it was plausible. Placing troops into an urban setting to test their discipline was a common enough training practice. Robrand d'Deneith had done the same thing to him and Geth when they were being trained in the Frostbrand. He glanced at the shifter again.

Geth narrowed his eyes and shook his head. Don't accept.

Singe looked Dandra. She shrugged. Maybe.

His gut told him that the General's invitation, if unexpected, was a boon to them. In the company of ogre troops, they would be safe from virtually any danger they might encounter. There would be no doubt that Tzaryan Rrac would know they were coming. They would probably even be escorted right to the ogre mage if they asked for it.

On the other hand, his head told him to be wary. The thought of traveling with this unknown general, among ogre troops, directly into the presence of someone they were, after all, trying to deceive, seemed too dangerous. It was far too simple and far too convenient. They were putting themselves directly into Tzaryan Rrac's power.

He bent his head toward the ogre. "Thank the General for his invitation, but we prefer to travel on our own.

The ogre looked completely confused. His sloping forehead rippled into furrows deep as a plowed field. "By *order* of the general, you are invited to travel with us as we return to Tzaryan Keep," he repeated, this time with greater force—and a different emphasis. He gestured and the ogres with him moved to stand beside the table.

"Singe," growled Geth quietly, "I don't think this is exactly an invitation."

"Figured that out, did you?" Singe asked. Six of them, six ogres, he thought—they were evenly matched, at least until the troops outside the Barrel came in. They were also surrounded and in a very cramped space. Even if they could fight their way free, though, they would have earned themselves an enemy close to Tzaryan Rrac.

He looked up at the ogre leader and smiled. "I misunderstood," he said. "Of course, we'd be honored to accept the General's protection in our travels. Would it be possible for me to meet him to offer my thanks in person?"

The ogre looked relieved but his answer to the request was blunt. "No," he said. "But she can." His eyes settled on Dandra—then wavered to Ashi. For a moment, he looked confused again, then he thrust a finger at Dandra. "Her," he said decisively. "The General asks her to ride with him on the journey."

Singe stiffened. "What? No!"

Dandra, however, was already rising. "I'd be honored," she said—even as the *kesh* brushed Singe's mind. *Don't worry*, she told him silently, *I'll be fine.*

You'll be a hostage! Singe warned her.

I escaped Dah'mir and the Bonetree clan. I can escape this General if I need to. An image of her using the long step to vanish from one place and appear in another flickered through the *kesh*.

If anyone was going to be a hostage, Singe had to admit that Dandra made a good choice. *Be careful*, he told her.

The ogre leader stepped up to wrap one meaty fist around Dandra's arm, then gestured for his troops. "Take them to their rooms."

Ashi started to open her mouth, but Singe quickly put an elbow into her side. Her protest didn't go unnoticed, however. The ogre leader glared at her, then looked down at Singe. "You should sleep. We leave early in the morning."

"Of course," said Singe. He shot a glance at Geth. The shifter moved to take a position beside Ashi, keeping her calm, as Singe led the way past the ogres and toward the taproom's door. The others followed him, each of them shadowed by an ogre. Outside—the noise in the taproom rising once again in excited gossip—they were turned toward the stairs leading up to the Barrel's rooms. Singe glanced over his shoulder and exchanged a glance with Dandra as the ogre leader led her off in another direction.

"Lords of the Host!" cursed Natrac. "I don't know if this is good or bad!"

"I think," said Singe, "it might actually be good."

Geth growled. "If this is good, I hope things don't get any better."

Darkness vanished in a burst of fiery light and Vennet blinked against the radiance of the setting sun on open ocean. Far below, a ship—his ship—crawled against the plain of water. "Hold fast!" bellowed Dah'mir. The dragon's head and neck bent, his wings followed—and his body plunged down through the air at a terrible angle.

Vennet shouted with delirious excitement. Acceleration and the rushing air pressed at him, threatening to tear him from Dah'mir's back or Hruucan's bundled body from his arms. The sudden brightness and the speed forced his eyes shut, but he could hear just fine. The wind screamed around him. *There's the ship! They're on it! Find them! Kill them!*

Dah'mir pulled up out of his dive only a ship's height above the water. Waves rushed past as they bore down upon *Lightning on Water*. "Be ready to jump when I hover!" he said.

"Aye, master!" Vennet braced himself. The ship rushed up to meet them. Dah'mir's wings arced and scooped, beating hard just as they passed over the deck. Flat wood and screaming sailors were only a few paces below.

"Now!"

Vennet thrust himself free of the dragon's scaly body and leaped for the deck.

Time had barely seemed to pass while Dah'mir plunged through Shadow, but some small part of Vennet realized even as he jumped that if it had been morning when they left the Bonetree mound and the sun was now setting, then he had spent hours clinging desperately to the dragon's back. His limbs were cramped and stiff. His fingers were clenched into claws. Movement was awkward.

He hit the deck with a crash that sent agony flaring through an ankle.

He tried his best to protect the bundle that was Hruucan, but even so he felt the dolgaunt's inert body crumble a little bit more under the impact.

"C-captain?" A familiar face bent over him, pale with horror. Karth, Vennet realized it was Karth. Steadfast, solid—

"Traitor!" he shouted and lashed out with a backhand blow that sent Karth reeling back. Vennet dropped Hruucan and forced himself to his feet, trying to get his bearings.

He stood on the aft deck. Below on the main deck, the crew that he had left in Zarash'ak raced back and forth, driven mad with fear at the sight of the dragon that circled the ship. The ship continued to surge forward through the water, though. Even Dah'mir was hard pressed to match her speed. Vennet spun around.

Only Marolis seemed to have resisted the terror of the dragon's appearance. He clutched the ship's wheel, his knuckles white, his face even whiter as he stared at his captain.

Above him, the great air elemental bound into the ship howled a song of wordless power.

Vennet leaped toward his junior officer. "Stop this ship!"

Marolis didn't speak, but just shook his head. He spun the wheel sharply, bringing the ship hard over and sending the deck canting at a dangerous angle. Terrified sailors lost their footing and slid across the wood. Hruucan tumbled and rolled, crashing into a hatch. Vennet had seen far worse in storms. He leaned against the sloping deck and ripped his cutlass from his scabbard.

"Stop!" he roared. "Stop!" He wrapped both hands around the hilt of the cutlass and swung it in a powerful arc. The weapon chopped into the angle of Marolis's neck, cleaving flesh and jumping as it hit bone, stopping only when the blade became wedged in the ruin of the man's chest. Marolis sagged, his dead weight dragging on the wheel, rolling the ship in the other direction. Vennet cursed and kicked his body away. He grasped the wheel and held it steady, then narrowed his eyes and called on the power of his dragonmark.

Heat flared across his shoulder and the back of his neck. Vennet channeled the magic of the mark into the wheel, feeling it skip and strike among the chips of dragonshards that had been used in the wheel's making. Through the wheel, he sent a stern order to the bound elemental. *Full stop!*

The howl of wind ceased instantly, the churning circle of mist condensing back into a solid ring. *Lightning on Water* slowed, momentum carrying her on through the water.

Moments later, Dah'mir's herons caught up to the ship.

The birds had kept up with them in their passage through Shadow, but Dah'mir's final burst of speed had left them behind. Now they fell on *Lightning on Water* like locusts on a field of grain. Beaks pierced and snapped at the flesh of screaming sailors. Claws raked. Ripped out of their fear, the sailors tried to fight back, but their attacks were clumsy. The greasy black feathers of the herons became sodden with blood.

Dah'mir circled around and hovered briefly above the deck, great wings beating a gale. "Find them, Vennet! Find Dandra! Find Geth! Find them all!"

"Master!" Vennet wrenched his cutlass from Marolis's body and leaped down to the main deck. He raced through a whirlwind of screeching bird and wailing men, sliding on slippery wood, and dropped down through the hatch that led to the passenger cabins. One by one, he flung the doors open—meeting no resistance.

He clenched his teeth and pushed through the door—once shattered by Karth—of his sleeping cabin. It was empty as well. He drew a ragged breath, a dark suspicion dawning on him. "No," he said to himself. "No. No! No!"

He tore into the hidden compartment in his floor and ripped open his strongbox, scattering coins, gems, and tradestrips of precious metal. Bloody hands emerged with a packet wrapped in pale fabric. Squeezing a fist around it, he raced back up onto the deck.

"Master!" he screamed at Dah'mir. "They're not here! They're not here!" He flung the packet to the deck. Pale silk, now stained, unfolded. Two large, sparkling dragonshards—one blue-black, one gold—bounced across the blood-slick deck. "We followed your shards, not them!"

In the air above, Dah'mir's eyes narrowed. "Impossible! Check the holds!"

Vennet darted to the forward hold first, pausing at the bottom of the steep stairs to scan the shadows, then slowly pushing forward. The hold was packed with cargo that had once been destined for Trolanport. He listened closely, ignoring the creaks of a moving ship, the sloshing of water, the last groans and whimpers of his dying crew. He could hear and see nothing. Vennet mounted the stairs and stalked grimly toward the stern and the aft hold. Dah'mir said nothing as he circled. The black herons had retreated to the rails of the ship, leaving only torn bodies behind.

The moment he descended the stairs, Vennet heard a muffled sobbing. An everbright lantern had been hung near the stairs. Vennet lowered the shade. The sobbing stopped, stifled, as light flooded the hold, but he knew where it had come from. He slid forward silently, cutlass ready.

Chains lay on the floor. Someone had been held prisoner—and recently. There were fresh, bright scratches on the open lock and a piece of bent wire, the kind sometimes used to bind crates, still stuck out of the keyhole. Whoever had been held prisoner had escaped. Vennet clenched his teeth. He wasn't going to find the people he wanted here, he realized, but he might find answers.

The sobbing had come from behind some crates. Vennet slid up to them, paused, then stepped around sharply.

A length of wood swung at him. He leaped back and sliced with his cutlass. He felt it bite flesh. The wood fell to the floor.

Karth stared at him. The sailor's face was wet with tears. He clutched at his arm and blood seeped between his fingers.

Vennet held his cutlass steady. "Where are they, Karth?"

The sailor's mouth opened and closed, but no sound came out. Vennet cursed. He reached out and grabbed Karth's shirt, hauling him out of his hiding place and dragging him to the center of the hold. He flung him down beside the chains. "Who was held prisoner here?" he demanded.

"A bounty hunter," Karth choked. "A bounty hunter named Chain."

Vennet ground his teeth together so hard they hurt—then twisted around and slammed the hilt of his cutlass across Karth's face. The man staggered, stunned. Vennet grabbed him and hauled him close, swiftly wrapping the length of chain tight around his wrists. He strung the chain through the bolt in the floor and, just as Karth realized what was going on and started to struggle, hooked the lock through the chains and squeezed it shut. The bent wire that had picked the lock before he flicked far away into a corner of the hold, then watched as Karth tried to wrench himself free of the chains.

"What was Chain doing a prisoner in my hold?" Vennet asked him. "Where is he now?"

"I don't know! I came down here to hide from you and he was gone!" said Karth. He was starting to sob again. Blood from his wounded arm was running down to turn the chains red. "Dandra captured him in Zarash'ak,"

"Well then, where's Dandra?" Vennet shouted. "Where's Geth? Where's Singe? Where's Ashi? Where are they?" He swung his cutlass, cutting deep into the deck only a span from Karth's legs. "Tell me or by Khyber's glory, I will start cutting pieces off you just like I did Natrac!"

"*Vralkek!*" Karth wailed. "We let them off in Vralkek. They're traveling to Tzaryan Keep."

"Thank you." Vennet wrenched his cutlass out of the deck and turned for the stairs. Karth sobbed in fear behind him—sobs that rose into a frightened shout as Vennet climbed up onto the deck.

"Captain? Captain, I told you where they are. Set me free." Chains rattled as Karth climbed to his feet. "Captain, set me free!"

Dah'mir was waiting on the deck in his heron form. "Well?"

"Vralkek," Vennet said. "Headed to Tzaryan Keep." His face twisted. "Storm at dawn, they must have left the ship while we were in Shadow."

"Tzaryan Keep," repeated Dah'mir. "How did they—?" The heron's expression was inscrutable, but his eyes seemed to flash in the dying light and when he spoke again, his voiced seethed. "Ashi. The tales of the Bonetree. Vennet, find Hruucan. We'll be leaving shortly." He flapped his wings and hopped into the middle of the largest stretch of clear deck the ship had to offer, then transformed. *Lightning on Water* groaned under the sudden weight of a dragon, but Dah'mir looked unconcerned.

Vennet found Hruucan's body wedged among barrels and ropes, the stinking tunic half unwrapped from his charred form. He wrapped it up again, ashes sifting out with every movement. Vennet hoped that the dolgaunt wouldn't notice when he woke again. He hurried to Dah'mir and climbed back up to the base of his neck.

"Master," he said, "will we be able to catch them before they reach Tzaryan Keep?"

"We don't need to chase them anymore," said Dah'mir. "I know what they're trying to do."

With a leap that left *Lightning on Water* bobbing in the water like a toy, the dragon took to the air again, his herons following in his wake. They circled the drifting ship once, then broke to the northwest and began to climb into the gathering night.

For a long time after, it seemed to Vennet that he could still hear Karth screaming.

CHAPTER

9

Tzaryan Rrac's ogre troops marched Dandra across town to another inn that looked as if it had, in better times, been a place with aspirations. Singe had told her that until it had been weakened in the Last War, Breland had claimed dominion over the barrens. The inn was a fading remnant of Brelish civilization, clinging to a dream of luxury while ogres stood guard outside its door and painted plaster flaked away from the inside walls. Dandra saw no other guests—and no staff either—as the ogres hustled her through the common room and up a flight of stairs that creaked threateningly under the creatures' weight. On the upper floor, the leader of the ogres opened a door and gestured for her to enter. She looked inside cautiously. The room was sparsely furnished, but otherwise empty.

"Where's the General?" she asked.

"You wait here," the ogre said. "The General will send for you."

He pushed her through the door—it was like being nudged by a horse—then pulled it closed behind her. Dandra waited for the sound of a lock or a bolt, but there was nothing except the heavy footsteps of the ogres moving away. For a moment, she considered looking back out into the hall to see if a guard had been left behind, but there didn't seem to be any point. She had no intention of escape.

The room's single window faced west and the light of the setting sun painted the walls red. Dandra went over to the window and looked out over Vralkek. The Barrel was nowhere in sight. She tried reaching out to Singe with the *kesh*, but the wizard was too far away. She sighed, wrinkling her nose, and looked beyond the town. Far to the west, back in the Shadow Marches, Dah'mir and Vennet would have reached the Bonetree mound.

Dandra leaned against the window frame and wondered what the dragon's next move would be. He'd look for them, she was certain of it, but they'd broken their trail. Dah'mir wasn't going to have an easy time finding them again.

But he will find us, whispered Tetkashtai. The presence's light was dim in Dandra's mind. *He'll use magic. He'll hire another Tharashk bounty hunter. He'll—*

Dandra's lips pressed tight in frustration. Tetkashtai's frantic terror had ebbed into a hopeless depression that was almost as frustrating and just as infectious. At times, Dandra found herself fighting to keep from falling into the same pessimism. *Khorvaire is a big place*, she reminded Tetkashtai. *As far as Dah'mir knows, we could be anywhere. Maybe he will find us eventually—but it will take him time and by then we'll have uncovered his secrets.*

We might have uncovered his secrets, the presence pointed out. *We don't even know if we'll find anything—if we find these Spires of the Forge at all. And even if we do find all the answers you're looking for, what are you going to do with them?*

Dandra lifted her chin. *Whatever I have to.*

Tetkashtai's light flickered with a little of her old fire. *You're a fool*, she said with disdain.

Maybe I am, but at least I'm doing something. Would you rather end up like Medala or Virikhad? Dandra spun out a memory of her last, fleeting mental contact with Tetkashtai's one-time friends: Medala harsh and raging, Virikhad desperate and consuming, both of them driven utterly mad at Dah'mir's hands.

Tetkashtai countered with another memory. In her mind's eye, Dandra saw the flash of silver-white light that had destroyed Medala's body as the two kalashtar, forced together by Dandra's hand, struggled for control of it. *No*, said Tetkashtai dryly, *I'd rather not. You will do whatever you have to, won't you?*

Shame and anger flushed Dandra's face. Tetkashtai gave her a mental sneer—and rage flared in Dandra. She reached up to the cord that held the psicrystal around her neck and tore it off, flinging the crystal across the room.

Tetkashtai vanished from her mind. Dandra closed her eyes and drew a breath between her teeth, grateful for a moment's respite from the presence's taunting, terrified influence. Tetkashtai's absence left her feeling hollow, like a part of her was missing, but she also felt in control of herself for the first time.

The feeling didn't last long. She'd barely had time to sit down on the edge of the room's bed when there was a pounding on the door. The ogre leader shoved it open. "The General will see you,"

She nodded and stood again, then hesitated. "Just a moment," she told him. She darted across the room and retrieved her crystal. As she settled the cord around her neck once more, Tetkashtai blossomed inside her, shaking and frail. *Dandra . . . she whined in fear.*

Dandra thrust her away. *Keep your thoughts to yourself for a while, Tetkashtai.* She turned back to the ogre. "I'm ready. Take me to the General."

The ogre seemed vaguely in awe of the confidence in her voice. He ushered her back out into the hall and along to a grand door at its end where two more ogres wearing the blue star of Tzaryan Keep stood guard. They stood to attention at their leader's approach. He seemed to take no notice of them, though, instead reaching easily over Dandra's head and tapping at the doors with a delicacy that made the wood shake. "General," he called.

A harsh voice answered. "Send her in, Chuut."

The ogre opened the door. Dandra stepped inside.

The General had claimed the largest room in the inn for his use. It was as sparsely furnished as Dandra's own, though at one time it must have been grand. Two worn chairs sat beside a large fireplace. One was empty. The other was occupied by a man who stood as she entered. He wore simple clothing: high boots, sturdy brown trousers, a light coat over a good shirt. There was a plain sword at his belt and he wore no ornamentation except for a blue star badge pinned to his coat.

He also, however, wore scarves wrapped around his head and over his face. All that Dandra could see of the man himself were dark, old eyes that peered between the shrouding scarves—and those eyes were narrowed in suspicion, wrinkles deep around them. "The kalashtar," he said.

Dandra's belly felt light and fluttering, but she forced herself to remain calm. Pressing her hands together, she bent over them in greeting. "You're observant, General."

"I don't like kalashtar," said the man. "They get inside your head. I told Chuut to bring me the *other* woman." He let out a long, slow breath. "Well, you're here now."

He sat down again, a little awkwardly. Dandra saw that his right leg and arm were stiff. When he gestured for her to take the other seat, she noticed as well that his right hand—hidden, like his left, in a fine black glove—was clenched into a claw. She forced her eyes away from it as she sat down, but couldn't help wondering what had happened to the man that he should take up service under a Droaamish warlord.

When she looked up, she met his eyes again. They were hard, daring her to say something about his concealed infirmities. Dandra sat still and held her tongue. After a moment, the General's gaze dimmed. He eased back in his chair.

"You have me at a disadvantage, kalashtar," he said. "You know more about me than I know about you. That should be corrected. What's your name and what do you and Master Timin want at Tzaryan Keep?"

Singe had suggested that Dandra choose a false name just as he had. She hadn't thought that she'd need one, but now she was glad that he had insisted. "My name is Kirvakri," she told the General. "Timin and I are traveling to Tzaryan Keep to ask Tzaryan Rrac's permission to study the Dhakaani ruins in his territory."

"You know that Tzaryan Rrac is no common lord?" The General sounded vaguely amused.

Dandra allowed herself a fleeting smile. "We had heard something to that effect."

"What's your interest in the ruins?"

Once again, Dandra was glad for Singe's coaching. The story that the wizard had concocted was close enough to the truth that it rolled easily off her tongue. "Master Timin holds a position in Queen's College at the University of Wynarn. His area of specialization is history and legend. Recently, we discovered that the clan one of our guards came from tells a tale about an ancient quest to ruins in Droaam. We believe the tale refers to Taruuzh Kraat, the ruins near Tzaryan Keep. Timin wants to confirm the legend."

"And you?" the General asked. His voice might have been harsh, but his questions were quick and astute.

She spread her hands. "I'm Timin's assistant and student. I go where he goes."

The General's eyes gleamed. "He seems young to have inspired such a dedicated student."

"He's gifted."

"And wealthy? You arrived in Vralkek on a Lyrandar elemental galleon."

Dandra shrugged casually. "We've been in the Shadow Marches, speaking with our guard's clan. When we left Zarash'ak, the captain of the galleon owed us a favor."

The General sat back and considered her, then after a moment added, "Tzaryan Rrac doesn't like treasure hunters."

In coming up with the tale that they would present to the warlord, Singe had learned from the conclusion Chain had drawn about their group: such an eclectic mix of peoples and backgrounds was undeniably odd. Even claiming Geth, Ashi, Natrac, and Orshok as their guards left Singe and Dandra suspect. Rather than simply deny the assumption, Singe had incorporated it into the story. "Robrand d'Deneith," he had told them, "used to say that a distraction is better than an outright lie. If someone thinks they know something secret about you, they'll ignore everything else and focus on that."

Dandra did her best to look outraged. "We're not treasure hunters!" she said to the General in a tone of injured pride—a tone that rang entirely false, confirming more than her words denied. Dandra thought she saw a smile tug against the scarf covering the General's face.

"Of course you're not," he said politely. "I'm just warning you. Tzaryan will likely want to speak to you and Master Timin—he enjoys the company of scholars—and if he discovers that you've come to loot his ruins . . ."

"Timin is looking forward to speaking with him as well," Dandra replied. "Tzaryan's reputation for learning precedes him."

The General snorted. "I'm sure his reputation for other things has preceded him as well. If you're smart, you'll pay closer attention to those." He rose, gripping the arm of his chair for support. "You've answered my questions," he said. "Return to your room and sleep. I'll give you a moment in the morning to speak with Master Timin—you might want to pass on my warning—but you'll ride with me."

"Your hostage," said Dandra as she stood up.

"To put it simply, yes," the General admitted. "Chuut will show you back to your room."

He held out his left hand. Dandra shook it clumsily, thought she couldn't quite manage to keep her eyes from flicking to the man's clenched and twisted right hand. The General's face tightened and he released his grip sharply. Dandra held back a wince at having offended him. "Good night, General," she said and turned to go.

She was reaching for the door when he said abruptly, "House Jorasco."

Dandra blinked and looked back at him. "General?"

He held out his right arm. "House Jorasco did this. And this." The General lifted his other hand to touch the scarves around his head and face. "You'll forgive me for covering myself."

Words froze on Dandra's tongue. "House Jorasco carries the Mark of Healing," she said after a moment.

"Healing and harming aren't so different, especially in the fire of war," said the General. "Consider that the next time you meet a halfling." He sat down again. "Good night, Kirvakri."

"House Jorasco?" Geth grunted as he heaved a saddle onto the back of one of the horses the General had provided for them, then looked back to Dandra. "That doesn't make any sense."

"I know," she said. "His right arm and leg, his right hand, his face. What could healers have done to him to leave him like that?"

Geth looked over his shoulder at the ranks of ogres—thirty of the big, smelly monsters—that were forming in Vralkek's street. The morning was still cold and misty. Few of the town's inhabitants seemed interested in rising so early to watch Tzaryan Rrac's troops move out. The General's ogre lieutenant, Chuut, stood close by, the reins of Dandra's horse in his hand, his gaze shifting between the General's "guests" on the journey and the other ogres. The General himself had yet to make an appearance. Geth wanted to lay eyes on this tormented soldier himself.

Singe scratched at his beard, his eyes narrow as he mulled over Dandra's tale of her discussion with the General. "There have been rumors," he said. "A dark shadow to Jorasco . . ." He shook his head. "It might be that he was injured and Jorasco could only do so much. He might just blame them for whatever scars he's left with. It's not important." The wizard glanced at Chuut, then lowered his voice. *"Kesh,"* he said.

Concentration passed over Dandra's face and a moment later, Geth felt her thoughts touch his—and those of the others as well. *Hurry*, Dandra said. *I can't hold all of us in the kesh for long.*

Do you think the General believed our story? asked Singe.

Completely, Dandra told him.

Natrac thrust out his tusks as he fussed with his gear, trying to disguise his part in the silent conversation. *We really are only a hair away from being treasure hunters*, he said. *What are we going to do if Tzaryan doesn't give us permission to investigate the ruins?*

Let's worry about that if it happens. Singe bent to his own saddle. *Do you think you'll be all right?* he asked Dandra.

If there's any problem, I'll call you or take the long step back to you. I'll be fine. Dandra reached out and laid a hand on Singe's shoulder for a moment, then the brief connection of the *kesh* faded from Geth's mind as she turned to Chuut. "I'm done," she said aloud. He handed her the reins of her horse and waited while she mounted.

Geth looked up at her. "See if you can get the General talking. I'm curious to know where he served during the Last War."

Dandra nodded and gave them all a smile, then turned and moved toward the head of the column of ogres with Chuut striding beside her. Singe glanced at Geth. "Does it matter?" he asked.

"I want to know what happened to him," Geth said defensively.

They finished saddling their horses and securing their gear. Although there were five of them, he and Singe ended up doing most of the work. Natrac's severed hand limited him, while Orshok and Ashi simply had no idea what to do. Neither hunter nor druid had ever ridden before. "Just once," Geth muttered as he held a stirrup for Orshok, "I would like to start a journey with everyone knowing at least how to sit in a saddle!"

Once they were mounted, Chuut returned and led them to their place near the rear of the column. Geth bared his teeth at the thought of riding in the stinking dust of sweating ogres.

Singe must have been thinking something similar. "Can't we ride at the front?" he asked Chuut with a grimace.

The ogre shook his head. "The General says you ride here. Hold your position."

"Where is the General?" asked Geth.

"Taking his place now."

Chuut moved away back up the column. Geth twisted and looked after him. Sure enough, the shrouded figure of the General was turning his horse in place beside Dandra near the column's head. "Grandfather Rat's naked tail!" Geth cursed. "He moves like a ghost!"

The General's hand rose and fell. Chuut's voice—echoed by the voices of one or two other lead ogres—roared out an order. "Tzaryan company, forward!"

The column began to move with a well-coordinated precision that would have done credit to a Blademarks company. "I would have thought they'd use commands in their own language," said Natrac.

"It's all in the training," said Singe. "The General has probably taught them this way. It looks like the man knows what he's doing."

They passed through the still sleeping town to the slow rhythm of big, trudging feet, punctuated by the clatter of horses' hooves. Geth watched the decrepit buildings slip away in the gray mist. Vralkek looked strangely peaceful in the silence of morning and he could almost pretend it was just another town—aside from the two gnolls lying drunk against one wall or the corpse of a harpy sprawled in the street, arrows piercing its feathered body. And where other towns of similar size often had paupers' huts clustered on the outskirts, Vralkek had nothing but crumbling, half-burned remains.

As even the burned huts fell behind them, another order rolled back along the column and the ogres picked up their pace, speeding up to a move at a distance-eating march. Geth growled softly. "They won't be able to keep this up over rough ground."

"We're not marching over rough ground," said Singe, a hint of amazement in his voice. "Look down."

Geth glanced at the ground passing beneath his horse's hooves and realized with a start that it was as finely cobbled and leveled as a city street. There had been no change in the hard clatter of horseshoes on stone as they left Vralkek. "A road?" he asked. "But there was no road on either of Bava's maps!"

"This looks like recent construction," said Singe.

"Who builds roads to the middle of nowhere in Droaam?"

Orshok pointed to a tall stone marker that loomed at the side of the road. "I think that's your answer," he said.

The stone was inlaid with a four-pointed blue star. Singe whistled. "Twelve moons, I think maybe we can thank Tzaryan Rrac's interest in civilization for making our journey a little bit easier!"

With the flat, solid surface of the road under them, distance passed swiftly. By the time the sun was fully above the horizon and the morning's mist had burned away, they were far beyond Vralkek and riding through some of the most desolate country Geth had ever seen in his life. As far as he could see in every direction, the land was very nearly flat. In many areas, it looked treacherously boggy. In others, very low hills rose like flat shoals in the sea of bogs. The vegetation was coarse grass and thorny scrub. Scattered groves of thick, black trees stretched for the sky. Occasionally, he caught a glimpse of ruins, old and worn stones half sunk in the mire. The only signs of animal life were a few white birds that soared high on the wind.

In his time, he'd seen many kinds of desolation, in many different places. The Last War had scourged nearly every part of the Five Nations. Only the fringes of the continent, places like the vast forests of the Eldeen Reaches or the thick marshes of the Shadow Marches had remained untouched. To the best of his knowledge, Droaam had also seen little of the Last War, yet the barrens had the same feel as battlefields Geth recalled from Cyre and Karrnath—only much, much older, as if Droaam had been ruined by time rather than by war.

Orshok stared around them in awe, stunned to silence. Because he was bound to the land and nature, Geth guessed, the druid could probably sense things about the barrens that the rest of them couldn't. When the young orc finally spoke, it was in a whisper. "What happened here?"

Singe shrugged. "Who knows? Ten thousand years ago, this was part of the Empire of Dhakaan. Hobgoblins ruled here until the Daelkyr War. After Dhakaan fell, the barrens lay empty until humans came to Khorvaire. When the Five Nations joined to form the Kingdom of Galifar, Breland was already claiming them as its territory, but its claim was tenuous at best. There have been more attempts to colonize the barrens than anyone could keep track of. Some succeeded and held on—like Vralkek—until Breland abandoned the region during the Last War. Others failed quickly. Some just vanished." He looked out across the bogs and low hills and drew a deep breath. "Researchers from Wynarn have spent lifetimes trying to pull answers out of this land. Twelve moons, what I wouldn't give for some of their notebooks right now!"

"You can spend all the time here that you want," said Natrac with a shudder. He shrank down in his saddle. "That feeling has always made me nervous, like there's something watching and waiting for its chance to reach out of the past and grab for you. It's not just here—it's everywhere in Droaam."

Geth glanced at Singe and raised an eyebrow. Natrac had just contradicted himself. The wizard's eyes narrowed and he gave a slight nod. He'd noticed it as well. "Natrac," said Geth, "when we were walking through Vralkek for the first time, you said you'd always avoided Droaam before this."

The muscles of the half-orc's heavy jaw tightened. "I meant that I avoided it whenever I could."

"But if you can say that the feeling of something watching and waiting is everywhere in Droaam," said Singe casually, "that must mean you've traveled the country fairly extensively."

"Not that much really," Natrac said. His voice was strained. "Enough to know I don't like Droaam."

"What about Graywall?" Singe asked. "Have you ever been to Graywall?"

Natrac looked at the wizard sharply, his eyes bright and hard, then turned around and stared at the marching ogres ahead of them. "Bava," he said after a few moments. "Bava told you."

There was a darkness in his voice, a sort of anger that Geth had never heard from the half-orc before, even when they'd sworn to take vengeance on Vennet for what he'd done. Blustering merchant, grim warrior—abruptly Geth felt like he was seeing a glimpse of a third side of Natrac, something deep and raw. "She didn't tell us much," he said. "Only that you'd been born in Graywall and that she'd met you in Sharn. We tried to get her to tell us more but she wouldn't."

"She'd already told you too much," Natrac snarled at him. "Lords of the Host, she promised me—" He shut his mouth tight and rode in silence.

Geth and Singe exchanged glances, then Geth nudged his horse a little closer to the half-orc.

"Natrac," he said quietly. "We've all done things we don't want to talk about—"

"Like Narath?" asked Natrac.

Hot anger and cold dread mixed in Geth's gut. "Who told you—?" he began, then caught himself. Natrac stared at him with flat, cool eyes.

"Nobody told me," the half-orc said. "All I had to do was listen. I remember hearing about the Massacre at Narath. You—and Singe—would have been on the losing side. If you don't want to talk about something you did there, it must have been bad."

"It's nothing that's going to affect us now," Geth told him. "It's over. It's in the past."

"So is what I did. You don't need to worry about it." Natrac fixed his eyes on a distant grove of trees. "I was born in Graywall, yes. I left it for Sharn—and then I left Sharn for Zarash'ak and a new life. I was gone from Graywall long before Breland abandoned the barrens and I haven't returned to Droaam since. Does that answer your questions?"

"You said that you'd spent time in an arena, but you weren't a gladiator," said Geth. "Does that have anything to do with this?"

Natrac's eyes flickered, but his lips just pressed together until they were almost white around his protruding tusks. He said nothing more.

Geth let his horse drop back to where Singe rode. "What did he say?" the wizard asked.

"It's nothing we need to worry about," said Geth.

"Did I hear him mention Narath?"

"It's nothing we need to worry about," Geth repeated harshly. He shifted his mount away again, ignoring the flash of anger that crossed Singe's face.

They rode in uncomfortable silence through the rest of the morning. Around midday, orders rang out, calling a break. The column stopped and the ogres fell out of formation. They sprawled out across the road and onto the firm land on either side of it, gnawing at chunks of unidentifiable meat, resting, and relieving themselves. Geth and the others dismounted as well. In addition to horses, the General had provided water and trail rations suitable for human consumption. They stuck close together as they ate. Disciplined or not, some of Tzaryan's troops were looking at them with an unpleasant interest.

At the head of the column, a hastily erected pavilion gave shelter from the sun to the General and Dandra. Geth could catch glimpses of the pair through the shifting mass of ogres. Their manners toward each other seemed distant, yet polite. "I wonder how they're doing?" he said.

Singe stood up from where he had been sitting. "Why don't we go see?" he suggested. He looked to Orshok, Natrac, and Ashi. "Wait here."

Chuut, however, stepped out of the crowd and stopped them before they had taken ten paces. "The General says you're to hold position."

"We just want to pay our respects to our host," said Singe, but the ogre was unmoved. Up ahead, Geth saw Dandra glance at them, then lean a little closer to the General. The man seemed to listen to her, then shake his scarf-shrouded head. Dandra looked frustrated, but she turned back to him and Singe, smiled, and gave them a wave.

"I think she's fine," the shifter murmured to Singe. He took the wizard's arm and tugged him back to the others. Chuut followed them for a few paces, escorting them, then left them with a final warning to stay in their place within the column. Singe's eyes were still on the pavilion, however.

"Twelve bloody moons," he said. "Is the General going to talk to us at all during this journey?"

"Maybe he doesn't want too many of us around him at one time?" suggested Ashi. "He might be afraid we would try to overpower him."

"Maybe," said Singe, but to Geth's ears he sounded doubtful.

In the afternoon, the land began to rise until they were riding through rolling hills sparsely covered in tangled trees. The woods were thickets compared to the great forests of the Eldeen, where the growth was sometimes so dense it was impossible to see more than a few feet beyond the edges of a narrow path, but somehow Geth found the open woodlands more unnerving. They had the same feeling of ancient desolation as the lowland bogs, intensified by the shifting shadows among the branches and trunks. The woods were silent as well, probably because the noise of the ogres' passage along the road hushed any birds or animals nearby, but Geth couldn't quite shake the feeling that the woods were always quiet, holding the secrets of ages behind tight-sealed lips. When they came around the side of a hill and the sweeping vista of a valley opened before them, he spotted the rounded longhouse and huts of an orc camp on its far side—but couldn't have guessed at how old the camp was. Nothing moved around the huts and no smoke rose from the longhouse. Its inhabitants might have been in hiding or they might have left a few days previously, or they might have abandoned the camp months or even years before. He asked Orshok what he thought, but by the time the druid had turned to look, the camp had been hidden by leaves once more.

"Like there's something watching and waiting for its chance to reach out of the past and grab for you," Natrac had said. Geth understood exactly what the half-orc meant. He flexed his right arm, listening to the soft creak of his great gauntlet. The armored sleeve was no use against imagined mysteries, but its weight was comforting.

Out of the corner of his eye, he caught Ashi twisting around and staring at the road behind them. He leaned over to her. "What is it?"

"We're being followed."

Geth raised a shaggy eyebrow. It was tempting to suggest that the feeling was in the hunter's mind, an effect of the eerie atmosphere, but he'd been around Ashi for weeks now. Her instincts were solid. He glanced over his shoulder as well. The road behind them was empty. "Where?"

Ashi shook her head. "Nowhere in particular. Sometimes in the woods, sometimes right on the edge of the road. A dark figure. Human-shaped, big as a large man. On foot."

"If they're on foot, they can't have been following us very long. Who in their right mind would follow a column of ogres—"

He was turning back to Ashi when the figure appeared for just an instant, darting through the woods from one tree to another on the north side of the road about sixty paces back from the end of the column. Geth got only the most fleeting glimpse of it, but as Ashi had said, it was human in shape and big as a large man. The clothing it wore was dark and close-fitted, probably leather. Its head seemed curiously smooth and rounded. He didn't get a good look at its face, but there was something vaguely familiar about the figure, though he couldn't place it.

"Rat!" Geth hissed. He scanned the faces of the few ogres that marched behind them at the very rear of the column, but there was no indication that they had seen anything. Their big ugly faces were slack, eyes glazed with the monotony of a long march. Geth gestured for Singe to join him.

The wizard, as well as Natrac and Orshok, listened to him and Ashi describe what they had seen. His eyes narrowed. "Following the column—or following us?"

"Geth," asked Orshok, "when you say the figure had a smooth head could it have been shaved bald?"

"I suppose so," said the shifter. "But I don't see—"

"It's Chain," Orshok said tightly.

Geth—as well as the others—stared at him. "Chain's in the hold of *Lightning on Water* on his way to Sharn," Geth said after a moment.

"What if he's not?" asked Orshok. The young orc's face was flushed. "I know I saw something fall off *Lightning on Water* yesterday. What if Chain escaped? Singe says he swore he'd be coming for us!"

Geth looked at Singe. The wizard shook his head. "It can't be him. I checked his chains before we left the ship."

"Chain or not, someone is back there," said Geth. "I don't like it." He pulled his horse around and out of the line of march, trotting up the column toward Chuut. He called the ogre's name and Chuut swung around. Rage crossed his face.

"The General said hold your position!"

"I know," Geth said. "But there's something you should know."

Chuut pulled a massive mace from his belt and raised it threateningly. "Return to your place."

Geth paused in the act of pointing to the woods behind the column. His eyes narrowed. "Chuut, we're being—" he began, but the ogre just stepped forward and bellowed in his face.

"I said you gets back to your spot *now!*"

His breath stank. Saliva spattered Geth's face—and anger surged in his belly. The last time anyone had yelled in his face like that, he had been a recruit to the Frostbrand company and a trainer had been drilling orders into him. If that was how Chuut was going to think, he needed a taste of real Blademarks command! Geth's lips peeled back, baring his teeth. He sat tall in his saddle and roared right back at the ogre. "Master Chuut, stand respect!"

The ogre's face went from rage to shock in an instant, but his body responded to the command even faster, taking two fast steps back and standing rigid, head up, weapon at his side. The nearest ogres stared in shock, stumbling as they tried to watch the confrontation and keep marching at the same time.

Swept up in his anger, Geth turned on them. "Tzaryan company, about and alert!"

The sudden order was more than the ogre troops could handle. Some stopped and turned out away from the column, hands on their weapons, ready for trouble. More tripped over their own feet. A few kept marching until they ran into—or stepped on—their comrades. In only moments, Tzaryan Rrac's troops were in complete disarray.

Geth rounded on Chuut once more. "Go to the General and tell him the column is being trailed by one enemy scout on the north side of the road. Bring back his reply." He leaned close and growled in Chuut's face. "I'll be waiting in my position."

Chuut trembled but didn't move. "Go!" Geth barked at him.

The ogre's head snapped down in acknowledgement and he raced off toward the front of the collapsed column. Geth dug his heels into his horse's side and trotted back to the others. Ashi, Natrac, and Orshok looked at him in amazement, but Singe wore a troubled expression.

"Don't look at me like that," Geth said. "I had to make him listen and I didn't feel like fighting him."

"It's not that," said Singe. His eyebrows drew down into a knot. "Those were Blademarks commands you used."

"I know." Geth bared his teeth again, this time in a smile. "Did you see those ogres jump?"

"Geth—*Blademarks* commands."

The shifter stared at him for a moment before the words sank in. Tzaryan Rrac's troops had been trained with Blademarks commands—by the General. "Oh," he said. "Oh, Boar's whiskers."

Ashi looked from him to Singe and back. "I don't understand."

"The General is selling House Deneith training to Tzaryan Rrac," Singe said grimly. "The Blademarks and House Deneith use their own commands in training. The commands aren't anything special, but if the General is using them, it means he's also using Deneith techniques to train Tzaryan's ogres."

"Maybe Tzaryan hired House Deneith," Natrac suggested.

Singe shook his head. "Then why is the General concealing his identity? I'm not even talking about the scarves—a member of House Deneith conducting legitimate business would use his name openly." He frowned. "And I'm reasonably certain the lords of Deneith wouldn't consent to training ogres. When they took on hobgoblin mercenaries during the Last War, the hobgoblins rebelled and carved Darguun out of Cyre."

A stirring among the ogres brought Geth's attention back to them—Tzaryan's troops were shifting into new positions as their leaders moved among them, quietly issuing new orders. Chuut was heading back along the column as well. Geth slapped Singe's arm and jerked his head toward the approaching ogre. Singe fell silent and turned to meet him.

Chuut carried a piece of folded paper. He stopped before Geth and Singe as if momentarily uncertain who was supposed to be in charge, then extended the parchment to Singe. "The General has orders," he said.

Singe took the parchment and unfolded it, quickly scanning the writing on it. His eyes narrowed. Geth stretched his neck and read over his shoulder.

Master Timin, send the shifter and the savage to locate our pursuer. Capture if possible. Tzaryan company will provide a distraction when you're ready. Move quickly.

"That sounds like a good plan," said Geth. He could see the General's intention immediately. If they were going to turn the tables on whoever was following the column, swift and stealthy action was needed. Ogres would crash through the woods like a herd of cattle, but the General had clearly recognized his and Ashi's wilderness experience. Geth swung a leg over his saddle and jumped down to the ground. "Ashi, we're going hunting."

Ashi's lips spread in a thin smile and she dismounted as well. Singe grabbed Geth's arm, though. "A good plan," he agreed, but held the paper down in front of Geth, "except that this is Dandra's writing."

"Maybe he had her write it for him." Geth held a hand up in imitation of the General's clenched fingers. "He probably can't do it very well himself."

"Then why is he carrying paper and ink at all? Something's not right."

Geth growled. The hours of riding through the haunted landscape of Droaam dragged on him. He wanted to be off after their stalking enemy. "Save your conspiracies, Singe. The General isn't the one sneaking through the woods behind us." He slipped free of the wizard's grasp and glanced at Ashi. The hunter slid the bright blade of her sword from its sheath. Geth turned back to Chuut. "We're ready."

The possibility of action clearly appealed to the ogre as well. His troubled face lit up and he spun to face the waiting troops. "Red squad, move!" he shouted, raising his mace and pointing back along the road. "Search south!"

About a third off the column split away and—with an enthusiastic roar—thundered back the way they had come, plunging off the road and into the woods with no attempt at stealth. A number of smaller trees came crashing down as ogres blundered into them. A blind and deaf man couldn't have missed the commotion.

Whoever had been following the column was guaranteed to be watching the ogres. Geth gestured for Ashi to take to the woods on the north of the road. Singe, however, drew a sharp breath. "Geth—"

The shifter shook his head. "Ashi and I will be fine. You look after yourselves. We'll worry about the General later."

He darted for the trees.

CHAPTER

10

Ashi was waiting for him, crouched down in the thick undergrowth that grew among the trees. Geth squatted beside her and took a glance back onto the road. Singe didn't look especially pleased, but he seldom did. Sometimes, Geth thought, the wizard was too busy being clever to know when he needed to act.

At least Orshok and Natrac were doing something—they'd dismounted and were holding their horses on short reins close to his and Ashi's, trying to disguise that there were now two horses on the road without riders. Geth twisted back to Ashi and murmured, "Follow me."

Before plunging into the woods, he'd looked back and fixed in his mind the spot where he had seen the mysterious figure. He didn't head that way immediately, though. Instead, he rose and slid deeper into the woods. He was counting on their stalker keeping his eyes on the column and holding his distance from the ogres. The dark-clad figure might be well-hidden from the road, but Geth was fairly certain he'd be much easier to spot from behind.

The shifter dodged from tree to tree and bush to bush, staying low and moving quickly. Ashi's passage through the woods was smoother and more flowing—the hunter slid from one patch of cover to the next with the lethal grace of a snake. Neither of them made any sound, though if they had, Geth thought the woods might simply have swallowed it up. The silent, ancient eeriness of the land didn't diminish away from the road. If anything, it seemed to have an even greater presence. The chaotic thrashing of the ogres seemed like little more than a distant rustling, even though Geth could still see the creatures if he looked. He gestured for Ashi to stop before they got too far into the woods. He had a feeling in his gut that he didn't want to lose sight of the road.

"Grandmother Wolf," he said under his breath. "I *really* don't like this place."

"*Che bo gri lanano ani teith*," Ashi murmured in response. "This land remembers its blood." Her eyes swept the trees and brush around them, then came back to him for a moment. "Geth," she said, "tell me why House Deneith should be so worried at someone spreading its training."

Geth growled softly. "This isn't the time, Ashi! Ask Singe when we're back—he understands the lords of Deneith better than I do."

"But you give honest answers," said Ashi. She eased a little closer. "I want to understand my new clan. Deneith carries the Mark of Sentinel. The Mark of Sentinel defends. Deneith must have greater concerns than one man teaching commands to anyone—even ogres."

He clenched his teeth. "The dragonmarked houses are more than clans. They've turned their marks into a source of power and wealth. They have special knowledge in their area of skill. If other people start giving away those secrets, the houses lose power and wealth." Ashi stared at him with a look of confusion on her face. Geth grimaced, trying to find a way to describe the vast power of the great house in a way the hunter would recognize. "They do it for honor," he said finally.

Ashi's eyes narrowed and her faced darkened. "There is no honor in wealth!"

"Talk to the lords and ministers of the dragonmarked houses and you talk to people who see something else. I wish you could have met Robrand, Ashi. I think you would have gotten along with the old man." Geth jerked his head in the direction of their stalker. "Enough talk. Come on—we have someone waiting for us."

They were deep enough into the eerie woods. Geth turned aside and began moving back parallel to the road. The tree that their stalker had vanished behind had a distinctive broken branch just beneath the level of the forest canopy. It didn't take long for him to spot it—and their stalker, pressed up against the tree and still intent on the column in the road. Geth paused again and bared his teeth as he studied the figure.

Big as a man and dressed in dark, close-fitting leather armor, just as he'd glimpsed. But he'd made a mistake in assuming the figure was a man or even human.

Their stalker was the hobgoblin woman from the Barrel in Vralkek, her orange-brown hair pulled back so severely that at a glance her head seemed shaved.

Geth stifled a growl. Between her presence in the tavern and her presence here, it seemed fairly clear that the hobgoblin's interest was in their little group and not Tzaryan Rrac's ogres. He gestured for Ashi to move around to the hobgoblin's other side. They would come at her from two directions. Ashi nodded and slipped away through the trees. Geth waited a few moments, flexing his fingers and his arm within the great gauntlet, then closed in.

He was within half a dozen paces before the hobgoblin woman, alerted by some sense that something was amiss, turned to glance behind her, her wolf-like ears standing up straight. Her dark eyes met Geth's for a fraction of a heartbeat and her ears pressed back flat—then she lunged away.

Ashi spun out from behind another tree, cutting off her escape with a naked blade. The hobgoblin reeled back. Her eyes darted between him and Ashi. Geth moved another step closer. "You're looking for us?" he asked in a snarl.

The hobgoblin bared teeth as sharp as his own. "You will not defile Taruuzh Kraat!"

Her words brought both Geth and Ashi up short. "How do you know about—?" Geth began, but the hobgoblin didn't give him a chance to finish the question. Her hands flicked the air and a low, musical word rippled from her lips.

For a moment, she seemed to shimmer and unfold as five exact duplicates stepped out of her body and spread out to surround her. Abruptly, six figures faced them. The hobgoblin drew a wide, heavy sword. So did her duplicates.

"Rond betch!" cursed Ashi. Raising her own sword, she leaped for the nearest of the duplicates.

Geth had seen this magic before. "Ashi, it's a trick!" he called. The warning came an instant too late, though. The duplicate swayed back before the first slash of Ashi's sword, but the hunter whirled and brought her blade around in another fast strike that cut across the hobgoblin's torso.

The duplicate flickered like a flame and vanished, nothing more than a fragile illusion. Ashi stumbled in surprise. The five remaining hobgoblins lifted their hands in arcane gestures and the chant of another song-like spell spun among the trees. Magic swirled around Ashi and froze her in place, muscles locked in the act of raising her sword.

Only one of the five had actually cast the spell, however. Geth roared and charged, slapping a powerful backhand blow from his gauntlet at the hobgoblin who had seemed to chant the words with the most vigor. In the instant of his charge, though, his target slipped back, passing through one of her duplicates as they rapidly rearranged themselves. It was like watching a nest of writhing snakes. Geth hesitated, then struck at random.

Another hobgoblin disappeared without a trace.

A sword darted at his side. Geth spun and blocked the attack with his gauntlet. Metal scraped on metal. His real enemy. His free hand lashed out in a punch.

This time he felt the impact and the hobgoblin staggered, a sudden trickle of blood running down the yellow skin of her chin. Her duplicates closed on her instantly, swapping places once again—and as soon as one passed through another, both bore the same trickle of blood. All of the hobgoblins turned back to him.

Geth snarled in frustration. He reached across his body with his free hand and ripped his sword from its sheath.

The ancient Dhakaani blade shimmered in the forest shadows. The four women facing him stiffened, eyes opening wide with sudden rage. *"Chaat'oor!"* they howled in a chorus. "Where did you—?"

Geth lunged, attacking on instinct alone. His sword tore through one duplicate and he jabbed a metal-clad fist at the belly of another. The illusions faded away instantly, leaving him facing only two hobgoblins. They seemed to swing at him in unison, both of them with teeth bared and ears back. Geth threw up his gauntlet and his sword, blocking both blows, then, with a roar, snapped out both arms.

The hobgoblin on his left parried desperately, thrusting her blade up to block his. The hobgoblin on his right caught the spiked forearm of his gauntlet across her face—and vanished.

Geth twisted his fist sharply, catching the real hobgoblin's weapon in the deep notches that scored one edge of his sword and forcing it high. Spinning under his own arm, he stepped in close and hammered his armored elbow into her gut. As the air rushed out of her lungs and she struggled to draw breath, he whirled again and kicked her legs out from under her. She hit the ground hard. Geth snatched the sword from her hand and stood over her, both swords poised to fall. He nodded toward Ashi, still standing in the grip of the hobgoblin's magic.

"Release her," he ordered. "And don't try anything else. I know a spell when I see it."

Angry eyes never shifting from Geth's face, the hobgoblin stretched out a hand and flicked her fingers at Ashi. The hunter staggered as the spell faded. Her face twisted in a scowl. "Magic is no way to fight!"

"Easy," Geth said. He looked back down at the hobgoblin. "Who are you?" he asked. "Why are you following us?" He remembered her curse when he had first approached. "What do you know about Taruuzh Kraat?"

Her ears twitched and drew back. Her lips twisted. "I'll tell you nothing, *chaat'oor!*"

Her eyes, however, went briefly to his sword. Geth glanced at the blades in his hands. Held side by side, it was apparent how little the basic design of hobgoblin weapons had changed over the millennia since the fall of Dhakaan. Both swords were heavy and wide with a forked tip, one edge sharp for cutting, and the other cruelly notched for ripping. Geth's sword, however, was clearly the better of the two. It was heavier than the other blade, yet still perfectly balanced. The notching was evenly formed, the cutting edge fine, and the metal smooth and clear; in spite of its age, it was free of the tiny scrapes and imperfections that marred the newer blade.

His sword had also injured a dragon, though neither Batul nor Singe could say why. When he had drawn it in Zarash'ak, a gang of goblins had fled from him. Again, no one could explain it. The sight of the weapon had inspired outrage in the hobgoblin woman before him, however. She recognized the sword. Geth extended it toward her. "You know something about this, don't you?" he said. "What?"

The hobgoblin's eyes flashed, but she stayed defiantly silent. Geth ground his teeth, then growled, "Fine." He gestured with his sword. "Ashi, get her on her feet. Maybe Chuut and the General can get answers out of her."

The hunter sheathed her word and hauled the hobgoblin woman up from the ground, then briskly searched her for hidden weapons. She found a knife, but nothing else. The woman's only gear was what she carried in a small satchel. Ashi scowled. "How could she have kept up with us all the way from Vralkek?"

The hobgoblin offered no response, but Geth glanced at her boots. They were finely tooled and decorated with Goblin script. "I imagine Singe could find something magical about those boots," he said.

The hobgoblin's eyes flickered with anger. "Thief!"

Geth snorted. "We don't want your boots. Ashi, keep hold of her." He turned back toward the road.

Singe, Orshok, and Natrac, along with Chuut and several other ogres, were waiting for them when they emerged from the woods. Singe stared at the hobgoblin with recognition on his face. "Her?" he said in surprise.

"She knows something about Taruuzh Kraat," said Geth. He slid his sword back into its scabbard and moved to help Ashi hold the woman.

"Who is she?"

"She won't say."

"Her name," rumbled Chuut, sounding displeased, "is Ekhaas."

Geth looked up at the ogre. "You know her?"

"She's a pest." He stepped forward and glared at the hobgoblin. "Tzaryan Rrac ordered your arrest if you were caught interfering in his affairs again."

Ekhaas glared back at Chuut fearlessly. "How was I interfering?" she asked. Now that she was calm, her voice was coarse but pleasant, like smoke from burning cedar. "I have no further quarrel with Tzaryan—only with would-be defilers of Dhakaan."

Singe's eyebrows rose and he shot a glance at Geth. The shifter nodded. Chuut, however, looked neither curious nor amused.

"Come with me," he said. "You're going to see the General."

An idea turned inside Geth's head. "Wait," he said quickly. He gripped Ekhaas's arm and met Chuut's gaze square-on. "She's my capture. If she's going to the General, I want to hand her over myself."

The challenge seemed to confuse Chuut. "The General said for you to stay in your place."

"Then she stays with me," said Geth. Chuut blinked and turned to Singe.

Geth was happy to see that the wizard wore a half-smile—he'd figured out what Geth was doing. "Tell your shifter to give her to me," Chuut ordered him.

Singe shook his head and crossed his arms. "No. He's right. We can either go to the General—both of us—or you can bring the General here, but until we see him the hobgoblin belongs to us." He raised an eyebrow. "If I were the General, I know what I'd want done."

Ekhaas turned her head to look at Geth. "I'm not a bone for dogs like you to fight over!" she hissed.

Geth glanced back at her. "You should have answered my questions," he told her. Ekhaas's ears stood up straight with indignation. Chuut groaned. His big finger pointed at Geth and Singe.

"You and you come with me," he said. "We'll take her to the General together."

"She comes too," said Geth, nodding to Ashi. "She helped with the capture."

Chuut's mouth drooped. "As you say," he agreed, "but the orc and half-orc stay. If you cause trouble, they'll be the ones to pay."

Orshok paled slightly at the threat, but Geth shook his head at him. "We won't cause trouble," he promised Chuut.

The ogre just grunted and turned to stride up alongside the resting column. Where he passed, lounging ogres leaped to their feet—and stared curiously at the smaller beings following in his wake.

Ashi returned their curiosity. "I still haven't had the chance to fight one," she commented.

"And I hope you never do," said Singe. The wizard looked over his shoulder at Geth. "Good idea, but let me do most of the talking. Remember, I'm the one who's supposed to be in charge."

Geth rolled his eyes and nodded. At his side, Ekhaas's ears perked up.

"You're up to something," she said.

"No, we're not," Singe replied blandly.

"I could tell the General what I've heard."

"From what *I've* heard, the General doesn't have too high an opinion of you," the wizard told her. "Is he going to believe anything you say?"

Ekhaas glared at him but fell silent.

As they drew close to the front of the column, Chuut tagged one of the leaner ogres and sent him running ahead. Geth spotted the General and Dandra, still on their horses, in the shade of the trees at the side of the road. Chuut's runner stopped a short distance from them and saluted the General. The shrouded man beckoned him closer and the ogre approached. As he spoke his message, Geth saw the General and Dandra both sit up straighter in the saddle and look back along the column toward them. The General leaned close to Dandra for a moment and she nodded, then turned her horse and urged it into a gallop, racing for them. Her face was sharp with concern. "Cover the hobgoblin's mouth!" she called. "The General says she's a spellcaster!"

"We know that already!" Geth shouted back. "She's under control!"

Chuut, however, obeyed the order without a moment's hesitation, shouldering Ashi aside to reach down and wrap a big hand across Ekhaas's face. The hobgoblin let out a muffled yell and struggled. Singe stared. "I don't think she can breathe."

The ogre grimaced in pain. "But she can bite!" His free hand fumbled at a pouch on his belt and emerged with a large rag. "Hold her," he commanded Geth. A moment later, Ekhaas wore a gag and a furious expression, and Chuut was cradling a bloody hand.

Dandra drew up in front of them and swung down from her horse. "Who is this?" she asked, staring at Ekhaas.

She hadn't seen the hobgoblin directly while they were in the tavern. Singe told her what they knew. Dandra's eyebrows rose. "What does she know about Taruuzh Kraat?"

"Nothing that she's telling us," said Singe. He looked Dandra over. "Is the General treating you well?"

"He doesn't say much, but otherwise yes." She nodded back to where the General was dismounting from his horses with the fumbling aid of two ogres, one of them kneeling like a stepstool. "The General wants a moment. He said we can approach when he's standing."

"He'll see us?" Geth asked.

"His words were, 'Your friends are stubborn.' "

"That's us," Singe said, but his eyes were on the General's struggles. "Dandra, does he go through this every time he gets on and off a horse?"

"Every time I've seen," Dandra said.

Geth watched the ogres trying to help the man almost knock him to the ground. "You'd think he'd have trained them in what to do!" he said.

Singe's lips pressed together for a moment. "Aye," he said.

It took a few moments longer before the General was standing—a little awkwardly—on his own two feet beneath the trees. He gestured them forward with his left arm, his right hanging as stiff as a piece of wood. Geth could feel Chuut's watchful gaze on all of them as they moved forward. Ekhaas seemed to pull back a little. Above the gag, her eyes were angry and confused. Geth growled and tugged her after him.

The General stopped them a few paces away from where he stood in the shifting, dappled sunlight that fell through the tree branches. "I don't want her any closer to me," he said. His voice was as harsh as Dandra had described. Maybe even harsher. Geth looked at his shrouded body and gave silent thanks that whatever else the Last War might have done, at least it hadn't left him crippled.

"General," said Singe, "I understand this woman has been causing Tzaryan Rrac trouble for some time. I place her into your custody with my compliments." He gave a formal bow.

The General nodded in return. "My master will thank you himself," he said. "Chuut, see that Ekhaas is kept under guard.

When the company returns to Tzaryan Keep, put her in the dungeon."

"Aye, General!" The ogre stepped up behind Ekhaas. Ashi and Geth released their grips on her, turning the hobgoblin over to him. For the first time, there was a flicker of fear in Ekhaas' eyes. She started to struggle, trying to shout through her gag, as Chuut took her away. She got one arm free of the ogre's grasp and thrust it out toward the general, but Chuut slapped it down again before Ekhaas could do more than point. Any spell she might have been trying to cast was ruined. The General didn't move, but just watched with icy calm. When she was gone, he turned his attention to back Geth, Singe, Ashi, and Dandra.

"You've been trying to meet me, Master Timin," he said. "Now you have. As Dandra can tell you, I'm not much for conversation. I prefer my own company. Does this satisfy you?"

"You're giving Deneith Blademarks training to Tzaryan's ogres," Singe said bluntly.

For a moment, the General said nothing. Between the scarves that covered the man's face and the changing patterns of light and shadow that made even his exposed eyes hard to see, Geth could read nothing of his expression, but when he spoke again his harsh voice had taken on a cold note. "It's unusual to find a scholar of Wynarn who also knows something of mercenary training—but I've found many surprises in Droaam. For your knowledge, I owe nothing to House Deneith."

To Geth's surprise, Singe made no response. He turned his head to look at the wizard.

Singe's face was tense with effort of holding back emotion. "No," he said finally, his voice cracking. "No, I suppose you don't—old man."

On Singe's other side, Dandra stiffened, her eyes going wide and darting to the General. Ashi looked confused, but Geth felt his gut clench like a knotted rope.

The General went stiff as well—then drew a deep breath of resignation and relaxed. His right arm and leg loosened. He straightened the fingers of his right hand and reached up to pull aside scarves revealing a face that was weathered and wrinkled with age, but not at all scarred.

"You're too clever, Lieutenant Bayard," he said "I knew I should have left you in Vralkek."

A smile spread across Singe's face and he leaped forward to embrace the man. "Robrand!"

"Robrand?" asked Ashi in amazement. "Robrand d'Deneith?"

"Robrand," whispered Geth.

They made camp for the night alongside the road. Robrand ordered his pavilion erected and invited Singe and the others to stay with him and to share his evening meal. Natrac and Orshok—pale with worry that something had gone wrong—were summoned up the column and were astounded to find the others settling down with an old friend. Robrand greeted them and Ashi with all the aristocratic charm that Singe remembered from years before. The old man even reintroduced himself to Dandra, apologizing for his deception.

Chuut and the other ogres, meanwhile, seemed more confused by the sudden change in the status of the General's guests than by Robrand's shedding of his disguise. Robrand chuckled when Singe pointed it out. "They knew I was disguising myself. Do you think I normally run around faking crippling injuries?" His wrinkled, weathered face twisted and he rubbed at the leg he had been holding stiff. "Because I wouldn't. It's not very comfortable."

Singe reached across the blanket on the ground that served as a dining table for their group—Robrand had a small folding table, but it would hardly seat seven people—and helped himself to an apple. The food eaten by the General was simple, but still significantly better than the rations they had been supplied with. Not that Singe wouldn't have eaten pig slop so long as it meant he was eating with Robrand again—except that they could have been eating together much sooner. He looked back to Robrand. "Then why disguise yourself at all, old man?" he asked. "You knew it was us."

Robrand grimaced again and eased back. "How long has it been since we saw each other, Etan?"

Natrac's eyebrows rose. "Etan?"

The wizard took a crunching bite out of his apple. "Singe,

Robrand," he mumbled, then swallowed and added, "And it's been almost five years since I even had a letter from you."

"Exactly," said Robrand. "Five years and a lot has happened in the world." He sighed. "The war changed people, Etan. People I thought I could trust."

His words had a bitter edge. Singe paused in the act of the biting into his apple again and looked up. Robrand's gaze had drifted to a far corner of the blanket. To Geth.

The shifter's eyes were down, his posture huddled. He did little more than pick uncomfortably at his food. Singe realized that he wasn't the only one to notice the tension between Geth and Robrand. Dandra and Natrac were both watching him and the old man as well. Since they had unmasked the General, Geth had been silent and withdrawn. If he could have, Singe guessed, he would have fled.

A part of the wizard wished that he would. Another part wanted him to stay and squirm before Robrand, the man whose life he had destroyed in Narath.

A third part reminded him of what he and Geth had accomplished since their ill-fated reunion in Bull Hollow. Until their argument in Bava's studio, he'd been close to forgiving the shifter. One look at Robrand's face, however, silenced any questions of forgiveness. His eyes were bleak. Singe could guess at what was in his head: he'd felt the same himself when he'd first faced Geth in Bull Hollow.

He felt a surge of admiration for Robrand. He had confronted Geth with fire and steel. The old man had greater self-control. He didn't deserve the ignominy that Narath had brought. Robrand hadn't been the one who'd failed the town.

Singe hardened his heart. "Robrand, I—"

His old commander waved him to silence and sipped from a cup of watered wine, When he spoke again, his voice was calm once more. "One of Tzaryan's ogres saw Ashi's confrontation in the street and reported it. He was taken by her strength and—and by Geth's gauntlet. When I heard him describe it, I recognized it myself. You don't come across a gauntlet like that worn by a shifter every day. I tracked you down at the Barrel and discovered 'Master Timin Shay.'" He glanced at Singe. "Didn't I say you should chose a new alias?"

"It does the job," Singe said.

"Either way," Robrand continued, "you're a distinctive pair. Although I'm surprised to see you together. I didn't think that was likely to happen."

Singe felt like Robrand had jabbed him with a knife. "There were . . . circumstances," he said. It was a clumsy excuse.

Robrand shook his head. "I have a contract with Tzaryan Rrac, Etan. I have a duty to him. You were trying to gain access to Tzaryan Keep under an assumed name. I had to find out more. I decided it would be best to keep you close until I knew exactly what was going on."

"And whether you could trust us?" Singe asked.

The old man's face tightened for a moment, then softened again. "It would have been less risk to have Chuut restrain you in Vralkek," he said, "but I decided to give you the benefit of the doubt. I didn't want to think you'd changed that much, Etan—that if you were trying to get to Tzaryan Keep, you had a good reason for it."

"And?"

"I haven't decided yet." Robrand took another sip of wine, then set his cup aside and sat back. "When did you know it was me?"

"I got suspicious this morning when Dandra described her meeting with you," Singe said. "There was a familiar pattern in how you manipulated her: implicating House Jorasco in your supposed scars so that we'd be too busy speculating about that to question whether you really had scars at all, telling her you distrusted kalashtar so she thought it was her own idea not to betray you with your powers—"

Dandra blinked. "But Chuut was supposed to bring Ashi from the tavern, not me."

Robrand's eyes flashed and his mouth turned up in a wry smile. "Another lie. I beg your pardon. I know something of the skills of kalashtar. You might have been able to draw the truth out of me and you could have relayed that information to Singe or Geth, so you were the one I had to convince with my story—but I couldn't let you realize it. Once I had you convinced, I knew that Singe and Geth would follow."

Singe found himself matching Robrand's smile. "If I need a new alias, you need new tricks. There were things through the day, too, like your note to us—written by Dandra so I wouldn't see your hand—or the way the ogres who supposedly helped you dismount all the time didn't look like they knew what they were doing."

He looked at Robrand sideways. "You didn't have Ekhaas gagged because she was a spellcaster—you had her gagged because she'd seen the General before. She could have given you away."

"A clever man is most vulnerable when he's trying to be clever," said Robrand with a shrug.

Singe nodded. "I didn't know for sure though until we actually met you. You were trying hard to hide your eyes in the shadows of the tree, but it was the hatred for House Deneith that gave you away." He spread his hands. "Why even meet with us? You might have been able to get away with it if you hadn't."

"It was a risk I had to take," Robrand confessed. "If I hadn't, you would have just kept pushing." He smiled. "Don't deny it. You would have. At least this way, it's out in the open and I have a chance to see you again, Etan."

Warmth spread through Singe's belly. "It's been too long, Robrand. The last letter I had from you reached me in Karrlakton. You haven't been in Droaam all this time, have you?"

"Tzaryan Rrac sought me out two years ago, just after the War ended." Robrand took up his cup again. His face creased with memory. "He found me in Shavalant in Breland."

"Shavalant's hardly a village!"

"I'd been living in Xandrar before a few heirs of Deneith realized who I was and started making my life miserable." He shrugged. "Shavalant wasn't so bad."

"You didn't fight them?" asked Ashi.

Robrand looked at her and shook his head. "It would just have exposed me. Fighting doesn't do much good when you're one of the most reviled men in a dragonmarked house. No, I ran. Like a coward."

Across the blanket, Geth stiffened.

Singe's fingers clenched on the core of his apple. He flung it away into the gathering darkness outside the pavilion and wrenched the conversation in another direction. "Robrand, who is Ekhaas? Do you know what she would want with us?"

The old man snorted. "She's just what Chuut said—a pest. A thorn in Tzaryan's side. Have you ever heard of the Kech Volaar?

They're a clan of hobgoblins in Darguun. They consider themselves the protectors of the glory of the lost Dhakaani Empire. Usually you don't find them much outside of Darguun, but Ekhaas has appointed herself as guardian of Dhakaani ruins in this part of Droaam." He nodded along the road in the direction of their destination. "That includes the ruins near Tzaryan Keep. Your interest in them probably attracted her attention."

"What's going to happen to her?" Dandra asked.

"It will likely depend on Tzaryan Rrac's mood when we arrive. What Chuut said was no idle threat—Tzaryan has warned her to stay away. The Kech Volaar carries no weight here." Robrand took another sip of wine. His dark eyes watched them over the rim of his goblet and when he lowered the vessel, he wasn't smiling. "But we're drifting from my problem," he said seriously. "Tzaryan is my master and you're approaching him under false pretenses."

Singe shifted uncomfortably under his former commander's sharp-eyed gaze. "Not all that false," he said. He glanced at Dandra, then back to Robrand. This was more than just a reunion. If he handled this right, they would have an unexpected ally in Tzaryan Keep. "If I tell you what's going on—the truth of it—will you help us?"

"You know better than to ask that, Etan. You're an old friend, but you'd be asking me to turn against a contract."

"You're not part of House Deneith anymore, old man," Singe reminded him. He gestured to the ogres outside the pavilion. "Do you think the lords of Deneith would have approved this?"

Robrand's eyes narrowed. "I didn't leave Deneith," he said. "Deneith abandoned me. Tzaryan gives me something like what I used to have. He respects me. He doesn't try to forget that I exist." He set his goblet down and frowned, then looked up again. "I can't promise to help you, but for the memory of the Frostbrand, I won't give you away either—so long as whatever you're doing poses no danger to Tzaryan Rrac or Tzaryan Keep."

"It doesn't. You have my word." He drew a breath and began their story with the one detail that the old man needed to know whether he was going to help them or not. He owed that much to a friend. "Robrand, your nephew Toller is dead. He died defending a hamlet called Bull Hollow in the Eldeen Reaches, but he's dead because of a man named Dah'mir."

Robrand listened just as Singe had known he would, saying nothing and absorbing everything. Singe considered leaving things out of the story—Robrand would understand that there were things he couldn't share—but found that he couldn't. He laid everything before his one-time commander. When he finished, the circle within Robrand's pavilion was silent. Robrand closed his eyes as he had after every battle Singe had fought at his side, committing the names and faces of the dead to memory. It was, the wizard knew, his way of mourning.

"Toller would have made a great commander, Robrand," he said after a long moment. "He died too soon."

Robrand drew a deep breath and opened his eyes again. "We die when it's our time. No sooner and no later. It's how we die that's important. Toller died well. I think he must have had a good teacher." He stood and offered Singe his hand. "I trust you, Etan. I'll help you however I can."

CHAPTER

II

Dandra could scarcely believe that Robrand d'Deneith was the same man she had ridden with the first day out of Vralkek. The man she had known as the General had been dour and tight with words. Robrand was charming, talkative, and pleasant. She knew that it had been an act intended to deceive Singe and Geth, but Robrand's self control was still remarkable. He was a joy to be around. Over the next three days, he spent most of his time talking with Singe, swapping shared reminiscences and stories of the things they had seen and done in the years since they had last been together, but he also opened up to all of them. He talked with her about her experiences, discussed business with Natrac, and made the most of what little common ground he shared with Orshok. He even attempted to address Tetkashtai—an attempt the presence answered with a terse response that earned her a laugh from Robrand but the mental equivalent of a glare from Dandra.

The old man was particularly interested, however, in Ashi. "I had a feeling that you were Deneith the moment I saw you," he told the hunter.

Singe's eyebrows rose in surprise. "How could you possibly have known?"

"The members of House Deneith may be spread wide across Khorvaire, Etan, but we still share ties of blood." Robrand took Ashi's chin between his fingers and tilted her face up. "She has a Deneith jaw, Deneith eyes."

185

Ashi flushed "Isn't a dragonmark the only way to know for certain?" she asked.

"It's one way, but not the only way. There are rites of divination that will confirm it, though I can tell you their results now: you *are* Deneith." He patted her shoulders in a fatherly gesture and Ashi's pierced lips stretched into a smile.

After that, she and Robrand spent a part of every day talking together as he told her something of life as part of the great house. In spite of an obvious distaste for Deneith, the old commander's eyes took on a wistful nostalgia when he spoke of past heroes and ancient glories. Dandra could tell that he still had pride in his house's history.

One night, as she and Singe watched, he even stripped off his shirt and showed Ashi his dragonmark. The Mark of Sentinel covered his age-softened chest, a colorful pattern like a tattoo but far more vivid and elaborate. Ashi stared at it in wonder. "It's bigger than I thought it might be," she said. "Did it hurt?"

"Hurt?" Robrand blinked in surprise. "Dol Dorn's fist, no. A dragonmark only looks like a tattoo. This is a part of me. When it first manifested, it was smaller—dragonmarks grow as bearers learn to channel their powers. My power is only middling." He slipped his shirt back on. "The most powerful dragonmarks—the Marks of Siberys—are supposed to cover their bearers from head to toe."

"The lords of the dragonmarked houses must be astounding to see," Ashi said in awe.

Singe hadn't been able to suppress a laugh at the hunter's wonder. Robrand gave him a disapproving glance—and Ashi a shake of his head. "The lords of the houses gain power through skill and guile, not the strength of their marks. The Marks of Siberys may be powerful, but they're rare. My mother used to tell stories of meeting an old gnome of House Sivis who carried the Siberys Mark of Scribing. He could draw a magical symbol of such power that it would kill anyone who looked on it but he was virtually a slave to his house."

Ashi looked confused. Robrand gave her a brittle, bitter smile. "You have a lot to learn about the dragonmarked houses, Ashi. You may wish you'd stayed in the Shadow Marches."

For all that the rest of them found companionship in Robrand, however, there was one person left out of the old man's pleasant circle. Geth took to riding apart from the rest of them, a little ahead of the column of ogres, silently but blatantly avoiding Robrand. As far as Dandra could tell, though, it was a mutual avoidance. Geth stayed away from Robrand and Robrand made no move to reach out to Geth.

Unfortunately, the shifter also took to keeping his distance from the rest of them, and the more withdrawn he became, the more tempting it was—in spite of what all of them had been through together—to spend time with Robrand instead, listening to his stories. Over three days, though, Dandra noticed something else as well. Among all the stories that Robrand and Singe swapped between themselves, they never mentioned Narath, and it seemed to her that if they ever got close to it, one or the other of them would glance toward Geth and quickly change the subject.

They traveled the last stretch of the road to Tzaryan Keep in the dark. Rather than make camp when they were almost within sight of their destination, Robrand pushed Tzaryan's troops onward as the sun sank below the horizon. Night or day made no difference to the ogres—they could see as well in the dark as shifters or orcs. Those few traveling with the column who couldn't rode together, laughing like revelers, in the pale glow of magical light called by Singe.

Geth rode alone beyond the light. Dandra watched him for a long while as Robrand spun out an account of how he had bested a squad of knights in Thrane as a young man on his first command. The others hung on the old man's words. When Dandra leaned over to Natrac and murmured, "I'm going to talk to Geth," the half-orc just nodded and grunted. Dandra urged her horse away and trotted ahead to join Geth.

He looked up at her approach, bared his teeth, and snarled. "Go away, Dandra."

"No," Dandra said. She pulled her horse around so that it walked beside his. "What's going to happen when we get to Tzaryan Keep?"

He blinked. "What?"

"What are you going to do when we get to Tzaryan Keep?" She nodded back toward the others, now well out of earshot. "You're supposed to be a guard. A guard's place is with his master."

The shifter growled under his breath. Inside Dandra's mind, Tetkashtai gave a derisive snort at his sullenness. *Pathetic. No concern for anyone but himself.*

You're not one to talk. Dandra pushed the presence away "This is part of what's between you and Singe, isn't it?" Geth stiffened. She pressed him. "You need to get past this. We need to work together. All of us."

He glared at her. "Have you given Singe this lecture, too?"

"He's not the one riding alone." She paused, then added, "This isn't just between you and Singe anymore, Geth. You've barely talked to any of us since Robrand revealed himself. It's all part of what happened in Narath, isn't it?"

He looked away—then back again. "If I say yes, will you leave me alone?"

His voice was thick with emotion. Dandra hesitated. "No," she said after a moment. "I'm not going to leave you alone. When I said we need to work together, I meant it. You're going to have face Robrand and Singe." She reached out and laid her hand over the cold metal of his great gauntlet. "But I want you to know this: I'm not judging you. Whatever you did in Narath, you've proved yourself to me. The first time we met, you were coming to my rescue."

Geth looked down at her hand, then covered it with his. The shifter's palm and fingers were rough and calloused. He said nothing for a long moment, then lifted his hand and sat up straight, looking away from her and up into the night sky. "Robrand let you see Ekhaas today."

Dandra knew a change of subject when she heard one—but at least Geth was still talking to her instead of falling back into silence. She turned her eyes to the sky as well. The night was bright: six of the twelve moons were full or very close to it. Their combined light cast deep shadows across the hillsides. "He did," she told him. "We thought maybe we could persuade her to tell us what she knows about Taruuzh Kraat. If she's the self-appointed protector of the ruins, she must know something."

"Did she talk to you?"

"Only to tell us that she won't speak with defilers of Dhakaan. We tried asking her about the Hall of the Revered and the Spires of the Forge. She didn't even react." Dandra shrugged. "But neither Robrand nor Chuut had ever heard of them either, so at least we're not missing some other real place. Maybe they really are just names invented by Dah'mir to describe Taruuzh Kraat for the Bonetree."

Geth smiled slightly. "If they are, then Chain was actually right about something. They really didn't exist." He paused, then added. "I don't suppose you asked Ekhaas about . . . ?"

His hand drifted toward his ancient sword. Dandra shook her head. "Should we have?"

Geth pressed his lips together and twitched his head. "No," he said. "I suppose—"

His voice choked off suddenly as they came around the shoulder of a hill. Dandra knew that if she had been speaking, she would have done the same thing. Both of them reined their horses in and stared at the vista that spread out before them.

Below the hill, lay a wide, shallow valley. Moonlight shone on an irregular patchwork of fencerows and fields, on the meandering ribbon of a small river—and on the dark bulk of Tzaryan Keep.

The fortress crouched on hills of the far side of the valley like an animal waiting to pounce. It was massive in both size and presence, its lower levels all but featureless, a heavy plinth for the profusion of towers and halls that formed its upper levels. The keep reflected little of the moons' light and, unlike a human structure, showed no light at its scattered windows The only illumination that Tzaryan Rrac's stronghold cast into the night came from two bright fires that burned at ground level, presumably on either side of a deep gate, and a third, much dimmer, at the top of one high tower.

The others fall silent as they, too, came around the bend and caught sight of the keep. They stopped as well and Dandra turned her head just in time to see Robrand lean a little closer to Singe. "Are you ready, Etan?" she heard him ask softly.

"Yes."

Robrand's eyes flashed in the magical light. "You play a dangerous game. I hope you play it well." He looked over his shoulder and called out, "Signal our return!"

In the front ranks of the column, several ogres put big,

grotesquely curved horns to their lips and sounded a call like the dying groan of some massive predator. It was answered by an enthusiastic roar from the throats of the troops so loud that the ground seemed to shake. Off in the distance, a flock of startled birds rose, then settled again. The ogres' pace quickened.

Singe and the others caught up to her and Geth. Dandra glanced at the shifter and tilted her head toward the riders. He grimaced but nodded, and together they slipped into the pack. Robrand's expression remained studiously neutral, but Singe gave Dandra a narrow look. She reached out to him with the *kesh*. *Geth belongs with us,* she said stubbornly, *not riding alone.*

No one forced him away, the wizard pointed out.

Dandra felt a flash of irritation. She shaped it into a stinging barb and flung it through the *kesh*. *Can you see what the anger between you is doing?*

Singe flinched at the force in her mental voice. *You wouldn't understand, Dandra.*

She hissed out loud in spite of herself. *Only because neither of you have given me a chance to!* She wrenched the *kesh* away from him.

Dandra? asked Tetkashtai, her light trembling. *Are you—?*

Dandra forced herself to breathe slowly and steadily, releasing the fury that burned in her like pent-up whitefire. *I'm fine,* she said. She reached and brushed her mind through Tetkashtai's, soothing the presence—and herself.

By the time they reached the valley floor, she felt calm and a little bit ashamed for her outburst. At least Singe looked somewhat chastened as well. She was considering apologizing to him when Natrac, riding to one side of her, stiffened. Dandra looked up to see a huddle of huts at the side of the road. She supposed they belonged to the farmers who tended the fields they had seen from the hillside, but Natrac's face darkened in anger.

"Those are orc huts!" he said. Dandra raised an eyebrow curiously. "Orcs aren't farmers," he added. "They've never been farmers. The only way orcs would farm is if they were forced to."

"Slaves?" Dandra looked to Robrand.

The old man shook his head. "Serfs. One of Tzaryan's projects.

He had them clear the valley after he built his keep—it was nothing but a tangled mess before."

Dandra sat up straight. The Bonetree story had mentioned entering a door above a tangled valley. Natrac didn't seem to catch the implication though. He was still glaring at the huts. "Slaves," he spat in disgust. "Filthy wretches!"

The loathing in his voice was so strong that they all looked at him in surprise. "Easy," Singe told him. "It's not their fault, is it?"

"Do they try to escape?" Natrac asked Robrand.

"Almost never."

Natrac glared back at Singe. The wizard spread his hands in silent surrender, then, once Natrac had looked away again, glanced at Dandra in confusion. She shook her head and shrugged. She'd never heard Natrac sound so worked up before.

Orshok looked uncomfortable as well, though he kept it to himself until they were almost all the way across the valley and practically in the shadow of Tzaryan Keep. "Something doesn't feel right here," he said. "It's as if something is disturbing the spirit of the land."

"If the land seems disturbed here, maybe it's because it's actually being used," Dandra suggested. The sense of desolation that had pervaded the landscape during the journey seemed to have lifted with their descent into the valley. Dandra couldn't say she missed it.

"Maybe," Orshok admitted grudgingly. He tore his gaze away from the keep. "Where are the ruins?"

"The Empire of Dhakaan didn't build in valleys," said Robrand. "Hobgoblin structures then were built much as they are today: mostly underground with an eye to defense. The Dhakaani who built their stronghold here chose the best location in the region. Tzaryan Rrac chose to build his keep in the same location." He raised a hand to the hills around the keep. "The ruins are there—you'll see them best from the keep in the morning."

Dandra's gut twisted with a sudden fear that the evidence they sought might have been destroyed. "Did Tzaryan build right *over* Taruuzh Kraat?"

Robrand laughed. "He knew better than that! How many times

have lazy builders tried to take advantage of old ruins only to have something come up from underneath them? Tzaryan heard those stories, too. It's almost impossible in these hills to avoid ruins entirely, but he made sure that he built well away from the main structure. The ruins have barely been disturbed."

The final approach to Tzaryan Keep, the last section of the road from Vralkek, took them back and forth across the face of a steep bluff. The road was distinctly narrower—the ogre troops were forced to redistribute themselves so that fewer marched abreast than had before—and seemed carved from the bluff itself.

"The bed is Dhakaani," Robrand explained. "Only the stones are new. When Tzaryan came to the valley, he found the switch-backs still in such good condition that his workers only needed to clear the road and lay a new surface."

"I'm glad it's the horse climbing and not me," said Ashi. For the first time, she actually seemed to be pleased to be riding instead of walking.

"We should be glad no one is trying to stop us from climbing," Dandra said.

Each turn of the trail was vulnerable to attack from the section above. It struck her as very odd that a location named for a smithy should be so difficult to reach. The slow climb would have made commerce inconvenient at best. Maybe the smithy had once produced weapons for an army and been given the defenses due to a military center. Even so, shipping weapons away from Taruuzh Kraat—or raw materials to it—wouldn't have been easy.

They lost sight of Tzaryan Keep as they climbed. The last turn of the winding road, however, was guarded by a high wall pierced through with a simple archway—as soon as they stepped through the arch, the great keep rose up before them like a mountain that had been hidden behind a handkerchief. Even though she'd seen its daunting glory from across the valley, the sudden exposure forced Dandra to look at it again, craning her neck back in awe. It had seemed massive from a distance. Up close it was if an enormous stone block had been thrust up from the earth and a palace built on top. Dandra counted no fewer than four long and broad halls, two towers of medium height, and one exceptionally tall tower with a rounded dome on top, all joined and surrounded by a high wall. The tallest tower was the one where a dim light had burned earlier though it wasn't visible now. The slightly angled base of the keep was dark gray stone; the upper levels were dark wood with tiled roofs.

The fires she had seen from across the valley did indeed burn on either side of a gate, but they burned in huge copper bowls. The gate was as massive as the rest of Tzaryan Keep, tall, broad, and set deep in the thick stone walls. Two ogre guards, polearms at the ready, stood before it and were utterly dwarfed. One of them called out in the heavy, deep language of ogres—some formal ritual of recognition—and Robrand responded, his human voice high and squeaking by comparison. The guards snapped to attention, stamping the butts of their weapons into the ground.

Robrand's face, as he led them across the marshalling yard before the gate, resumed the neutral mask of the General. "Welcome to Tzaryan Keep, Master Timin."

"Thank you, General," Singe answered with the same cool detachment. "Your company has been most welcome during our journey." He looked around and Dandra wondered if she was the only one who noticed the nervous twitching of his left hand. "Do we need to alert Tzaryan Rrac to our presence?"

"I'm certain he already knows."

"The General is correct," called a voice as deep as stones. "In fact, I have watched your approach for some time." The voice came from somewhere above them, rolling and echoing down the walls of the keep. Dandra's head jerked up again.

There was a large figure descending through the darkness overhead, dropping slowly with an ease that Dandra couldn't have matched. Tzaryan Rrac stood upright, arms crossed, as if floating down through the air was second nature to him. The ogre mage stood no taller than his ogre troops—now filing up from the twisted road and falling into rank in the marshalling yard—but he seemed even more powerfully built, his shoulders and arms broad and thick with muscle. His skin shone a pale blue-green in the firelight, contrasting with the rich crimson robes that he wore. Dark hair was pulled back and tied in a knot, exposing short ivory horns that sprang from his forehead. His square teeth and the heavy nails on his hands were black. So were his eyes—not black in the manner of humans, but rather reversed, black where humans had white, with a pale pinprick at the iris.

They were striking and eerie at the same time.

For a moment, his gaze met hers and Dandra felt almost as if Tzaryan's weird eyes saw right through her. She clenched her jaw and sat up straight and bold, but his gaze had already moved on to sweep over the others.

Robrand dismounted calmly and bowed while Tzaryan was still in the air. "Lord Tzaryan," he said. "All's well in Vralkek. Your troops acted with excellent discipline."

"*Your* troops, General. A fine commander makes fine soldiers." Tzaryan's voice was entirely free of the heavy accent and carefully practiced words that marked Chuut's conversation. He spoken naturally, at ease with their language. His black eyes remained fixed on Dandra, Singe, and the others as his booted feet settled into the dust of the yard. "I would like to know more about those who have accompanied you. A rare occurrence, I think."

Singe dropped out of his saddle with an unseemly haste compared to Robrand. As the others quickly followed his example, the wizard bent low in a grand, sweeping bow. "Lord Tzaryan, Timin Shay of Wynarn University at your service. My assistant, Kirvakri." Dandra pressed her hands together and bent over them respectfully. Singe gestured to Geth, Ashi, Orshok, and Natrac. "Our guards. The General encountered us in Vralkek and, when he heard that it was my intention to seek out your keep, was kind enough to offer me an escort."

Tzaryan's gaze drifted briefly over the others before settling back on Singe and Dandra. "Master Timin," he said, nodding his head. Reading his black eyes was difficult. Dandra thought she caught a gleam of interest, but she couldn't be sure. "Wynarn, did you say?"

"Queen's College," Singe answered. "A lecturer in history and legend, a dabbler in other areas—enough to know that we must be interrupting your skywatching on such a fine night. My apologies." He bowed again and this time Dandra was certain she saw curiosity burn in Tzaryan's face.

"There are many nights," said the ogre mage. "Think nothing of it. But tell me—what brings a scholar of Wynarn to the wilds of Droaam?"

Singe had him hooked like a fish. Dandra was amazed that the wizard managed to keep a straight face as he spun out their carefully rehearsed story of investigating the ruins of Taruuzh Kraat as a means of tracing the legends of Ashi's clan. "Which is why we've come to you, Lord Tzaryan. I beg your permission to investigate the ruins in the name of scholarship. I pledge to take nothing away except knowledge."

For a moment, it seemed that Singe's hold on Tzaryan might slip. The ogre mage's face hardened. The wizard's eyebrows twitched.

"I expect that a major paper will come out of my research," he said. "Perhaps even a book. One that could change the study of Droaam's history significantly. Of course I would name you as my learned patron in any publication."

When he had first tested the argument on her, Dandra had expressed doubt. Tzaryan was supposed to be intelligent. Why would someone that smart fall to such blatant flattery? Singe's counter had been that even the most brilliant people had their weaknesses—the trick was just in figuring out what they wanted. They really weren't asking for very much and in exchange for granting them access to the ruins, Tzaryan Rrac had the opportunity to see his name spread around one of the most prestigious centers of learning in the Five Nations. To someone who considered himself a scholar and cultivated the trappings of civilization, Singe argued, what greater incentive could they offer?

Dandra still held her breath as Tzaryan straightened slightly, his square teeth grinding in thought. After a moment, he said, "It wouldn't be prudent for me to accept such a request without due consideration. I'll think on it and give you an answer in the morning. Will that suit you?"

"It suits me very well, my lord," said Singe graciously, but Dandra could hear relief in his voice.

A faint, smug smile crossed Tzaryan's face as if he had recognized it as well. "In the meantime, I hope you'll accept the hospitality of Tzaryan Keep for the night at least," he said. "I'd be honored to have you as my guest."

He spread his arms, the broad sleeves of his robes flashing. Behind him, the gates of the keep groaned and began to open, revealing a wide, dark staircase leading up into the keep's interior. For an instant, Dandra wondered if the ogre mage commanded the magical equivalent of *vayahatana*—until she caught the muffled grinding of some heavy, hidden mechanism. The flash of his sleeves had been a signal. She held back a smile of her own at Tzaryan's trickery and bowed along with Singe.

Robrand moved forward again. "Lord Tzaryan, there is something else. We encountered an old friend who had been attracted to Master Timin's inquiries." He gestured and Chuut, accompanied by a second ogre, stepped out of the ranks of Tzaryan's troops. Between them, they held Ekhaas, her hands bound and the gag still in her mouth. Her eyes were wild and frightened. Tzaryan sucked in a sharp breath.

"Again, hobgoblin?" he roared. "By the Shadow, what did I tell you? Chuut, your mace—"

"My lord," Robrand said before the ogre lieutenant could draw his weapon, "could I suggest something else? Imprisonment might be a better option. Ekhaas has knowledge of the ruins. She has refused to speak with our guests before now, but I suspect she could be . . . persuaded to share what she knows."

Dandra stiffened at what the old man's suggestion implied and she glanced at Singe. He looked uneasy as well, but said nothing. Tzaryan only nodded his heavy head in approval. "An excellent suggestion, General." He looked down at Dandra. "Or did I see disapproval on you face, Mistress Kirvakri?"

He asked the question lightly, but his eyes were sharp. Within her, Tetkashtai cringed. Dandra swallowed. Ekhaas almost certainly knew something about Taruuzh Kraat, but she didn't want to see the hobgoblin tortured. "Perhaps we could speak to her again," she said. "After she's had time to consider the alternative. "

Tzaryan bent closer. "And if she remains uncooperative?"

Dandra froze, staring into his black eyes.

Singe cleared his throat and answered for her. "This is your domain, Lord Tzaryan," he said. "We are but guests."

The ogre mage straightened and turned a smile on him. "I can see that you are a man who has learned lessons outside the library." Tzaryan's smile grew into a grin that left Dandra with no doubt that under his fine robes and well-spoken manners, he was as much a monster as any in Droaam. "Put any questions you choose to her tomorrow and we'll see what lessons Ekhaas has learned." He gestured sharply to Chuut and the ogre wrestled the hobgoblin on through the gate. Tzaryan nodded again to Singe. "Until the morning, Master Timin. General, I'll take your report on the training in Vralkek in the morning as well."

"Lord," said Robrand with another bow, but the ogre mage was already rising back into the air, moving faster than he had descended. Dandra watched his form, crimson robes flapping in the moonlight, arc through the darkness toward to the tall tower with the dome top.

Tetkashtai whimpered in her mind. *Dandra—*

Her light was stretched thin with fear and fretting. Dandra felt a hollow echo of it in her own stomach. *I know*, she said. *I think we need to watch our backs around Tzaryan Rrac.*

No, more than that!

Hush, Dandra ordered her. It took an effort but she forced herself to rise above Tetkashtai's fear. She wrapped the presence in calming thoughts, stifling her objections.

Singe waited until Robrand has dismissed the ogre troops before drawing him close. "Robrand—" he hissed.

The old man held up a finger, silencing him. "Careful," he said. "Tzaryan hears more than you think. Flight isn't his only gift." He gave Singe a cold, hard look. "Would you rather she was already dead? At least you have a chance to save her now. I told you, you're playing a dangerous game. Did you think you were the only one making the rules?"

Vennet watched Tzaryan Rrac soar through one of the open archways below the dome of his observatory, the wind of his passage rippling in his crimson robes, and decided that he wanted to learn to fly as well. To ride on Dah'mir's back or in a Lyrandar airship were fine things, but to fly on his own power with the voices of the wind in his ears—

Tzaryan was staring at him. Vennet stared back at the ogre mage, meeting his back-eyed gaze fearlessly. "Teach me that," he said hungrily. Across his back, his dragonmark itched as it hadn't since he'd been a youth. In the days since the daelkyr's voice had burned him clean, the mark had felt as though it was growing again, increasing in size and power, a gift from the lord of Khyber. He spoke to the wind and he'd never heard of any member of House Lyrandar manifesting such a power. What else was he capable of?

"Vennet, be silent," said Dah'mir in reprimand. The heron stood atop a table piled with books and charts. He cocked his head and his eyes flashed. "Tzaryan?"

"It appears my general found them in Vralkek and escorted them here to keep an eye on them," the warlord said. "They want access to the ruins. Just as you said they would."

"You'll grant it to them?"

"There's not much to see unless they're willing to dig."

"They'll dig. If they don't, I've overestimated them."

The ogre mage smiled, showing black teeth. "The human you named Singe tried to bribe me by offering to name me as his patron in a book."

"Promises are as poor a currency as lies," said Dah'mir. "Real knowledge is gold to those who value it." He tapped a book with his beak. "Open this one and I'll continue my payment for your services, Tzaryan. There is a secret written on the moons of Eberron if you know when and where to look."

"Dah'mir!" called Hruucan from the scorched corner where he had squatted for much of the last few days. Vennet turned to look at him. His voice was a weary rasp and the tentacles that lashed the air were dim. "I feel him! He's close. I want him!"

"In good time, Hruucan!"

"I hunger now."

Dah'mir clicked his beak in frustration, then looked at Tzaryan. "Could you spare another slave?"

The warlord smiled again. "Knowledge is gold and you've paid me well. Is one slave enough?"

"More than enough." The heron ruffled black feathers. "My enemies have proved clever. I'm sure they'll find what they came here to learn quickly enough—and after they do, they'll fall knowing the truth of how pathetic they are." His voice sank into a snarl deep into his scrawny chest. "We'll be your guests for another day, Tzaryan, no more."

Tzaryan bent his head. "Your presence in my home is an honor, Dah'mir."

Vennet turned away as the two lords resumed their discussion of moons and stars and secret knowledge and looked out of the observatory onto the night. Far below on the valley floor, a shadow moved against the pale stripe of the road. A lone rider was approaching Tzaryan Keep on a horse with muffled hooves. A breeze brushed against Vennet and murmured in his ear. *Now who do you think that is?*

"It doesn't matter," he whispered in reply. In his head, he was flying as Tzaryan had flown.

CHAPTER

12

Tzaryan Rrac's reply was waiting when Singe descended from his bed chamber to the dining hall below the next morning. An orc woman wearing the blue star of Tzaryan Keep hurried to meet him as soon as he appeared on the stairs. Without speaking or meeting his gaze, she extended a silver tray on which rested a folded note, then darted away as soon as he had taken the note from her.

Dandra was already up and sitting at one corner of a long, empty table. Her face was drawn and her eyes were dark. "Is something wrong?" he asked her.

"I didn't sleep well." She rubbed a hand across her face. "Tetkashtai doesn't like Tzaryan Keep. She was fretting all night. It kept me awake."

Singe unfolded the note and scanned it. He smiled in triumph. "I think I know something that will make you feel better," he said, then read aloud "Master Timin, your request is granted. You'll find the ruins to the northeast of Tzaryan Keep. You may explore them as you wish, so long as you and your party return to join me for dinner and share your discoveries. I will see you this evening—I regret that my stargazing has left me with a nocturnal schedule. Speak to the General if there's anything you require. With respect, Tzaryan." He looked up to find Dandra smiling as well, weariness washed away.

"We're in?" she said. "You've done it?"

"*We've* done it." He looked around the hall. "Which way is northeast?"

Dandra pointed down the length of a hall, directly toward a shuttered window. Tzaryan's note crumpled in one hand, Singe strode to the window and flung open the shutters.

Robrand must have placed them in these quarters deliberately. The view from the window looked across a short stretch of Tzaryan Keep's roofs—their tiles a glossy green by daylight—and over the outer wall. The landscape around the keep was dry, choked with thorny bushes and brittle grass, but a short distance away, the scrub growth broke around heaps of rock, weathered by time but still too squared and regular to be natural. One stretched out across the land in a straight, narrow line, like a toppled tree. Another looked to have crumbled inward not so very long ago. It didn't take much imagination to picture them reassembled and standing tall.

"The Spires of the Forge," he said.

"Taruuzh Kraat." Dandra stepped up beside him, hesitated, then added, "Singe, about what I said through the *kesh* last night—"

Singe felt the stinging shock of her rejection again, the sudden emptiness after her withdrawal of the *kesh*. It hurt almost as much as his anger toward Geth. Almost, but not quite. "Don't say anything," he said. He turned away from her. "If we're expected back for dinner, we should wake the others and try to get out to the ruins as soon as we can."

They were out of the keep by mid-morning. They saw no one on the way apart from orc slaves—lean, frightened-looking creatures much reduced from the proud tribes of the Shadow Marches—and a few ogre guards. The grand upper levels of the stronghold, all polished dark wood and shining green tiles, were mostly empty. Tzaryan had built a fine palace, but no one came to his court. Singe thought he could guess one reason why. While the keep was impressively majestic in design, it was just slightly too large. Everything had been designed around Tzaryan Rrac's towering frame. Doorways were intimidatingly tall and wide, chairs and tables oversized, stairs awkward in the strange height of each step. In a grand inn or a great house, the bed in which Singe had spent the night would have been luxuriously large. In the surroundings of Tzaryan Keep, it just made him feel like a child, weak and helpless. The effect was disconcerting.

And the upper levels of the keep were all that visitors normally saw. Robrand had described to him the chambers hidden behind the thick stone walls of the keep's lower portion. Tzaryan's ogre troops had their quarters there. The orc slaves, too. The dungeons of Tzaryan Keep were down in the dark as well. When he and the others wanted to talk to Ekhaas, they'd find her there. Singe had considered going to her before heading out to the ruins, but decided against it. Even with Tzaryan's threat of torture hanging over her head, getting the hobgoblin to talk could have taken a long time and he didn't want to spend any longer in Tzaryan Rrac's fortress than he needed to.

Walking down the broad stairs to the gates was like walking through a canyon—a deadly canyon. Invaders forcing their way up the stairs would be vulnerable to attacks both from above and through murder holes in the thick walls. A broad landing halfway along the length of the stairs might have seemed like a haven, but Robrand had confided that it was actually a trap. The entire landing could be collapsed, dropping anyone on it into a deep natural chasm that waited beneath. As they passed out of the gates and between the still smoking fire-bowls, Singe let out a soft breath of relief and glanced back over his shoulder. The dark maw of the keep seemed even more intimidating by day than it had by night.

They skirted the wall of the keep, circling around to the northeast, then striking out for the heaps of stone he and Dandra had seen from the window. Robrand had been right when he'd said it was almost impossible to avoid ruins in the hills. It seemed that for every few paces they walked, Singe's eyes fell on the broken line of an ancient wall or some buckle in the earth with weathered stones protruding. Maybe they had been the outbuildings of Taruuzh Kraat, Singe guessed, maybe protective walls. Maybe stables—he wondered if the Dhakaani had kept horses or other mounts? The hobgoblins of Darguun used huge muscular antelopes called tribex as beasts of burden. Maybe the Dhakaani had, too.

The long stretch of rubble from the first of the collapsed chimneys appeared among the long grass. The second pile of stones was close as well. So was a third, far more tangled with creeping vines and scrub trees than the others—it must have fallen even earlier. Maybe it had been overgrown when the Bonetree hunters had come on their quest. Singe called a halt. "Spread out," he said. "The Bonetree story mentions the door above the tangled valley. See if you can find an entrance into the underground ruins."

It look only a few minutes of searching, though, before Natrac called out, "Here!" The half-orc stood in a depression in the ground, a kind of wide trough. One end of the depression, Singe saw as he and the others joined Natrac, was smooth and relatively level—the remains, perhaps, of a shallow ramp cut into the earth. Wind and rain had softened its edges and corners, blending it back into the landscape.

What would have been the deeper end of the ramp, however, was now a rugged patch of ground several paces long and sunk down by a good half pace. Geth climbed over it and pulled up a knot of grass. Tangled roots lifted thin soil with them. Underneath lay a jumble of stone.

Geth looked up. "Whatever was under here, it's collapsed now. It might have been an entrance, though."

They were the first words the shifter had spoken to him for days and Singe ground his teeth against a surge of loathing. Seeing Robrand had opened up old wounds. The loss of the Frostbrand pulled at him in a way that it hadn't in years. Talking to Geth in any way was the last thing he wanted to do.

Fortunately, Dandra spoke before he was forced to. "I could try using *vayhatana* to shift the rubble."

The idea was enough to pull Singe out of his anger. "No," he said before she could attempt it. "There's more to excavating a collapse than digging out rubble. You have to shore it up to make sure it doesn't collapse again. I learned that from a company of sappers during the war." He walked the length of the depression, staring at the broken ground. "We also don't know how far the collapse goes. It could extend—"

"Singe," said Ashi sharply, "don't move."

He froze at her warning, an instant reaction learned—like his knowledge of excavating—during the war, then stepped back cautiously as Ashi hurried forward to crouch over the ground he had been about to walk on. Leaning over her shoulder, he saw a footprint preserved in dried mud.

"What about it?" he asked.

"Look at the grass," Ashi said, examining the footprint carefully. "It hasn't rained here recently. This footprint at least a couple of weeks old. Someone was among these ruins not too long ago."

The others came to cluster around them.

"Tzaryan?" suggested Natrac. "Ogres on patrol?"

"The footprint isn't that big."

"Robrand?"

Ashi shook her head, the beads in her hair clacking softly. "Robrand's boots are old and well worn. Whoever left this wears good boots with no signs of wear at all."

"Ekhaas wears good boots," said Geth, still standing down in the depression. "And they might be magical. Magical boots don't wear out, do they?"

His curiosity aroused, Singe answered without thinking. "Not usually, no." He bit back a curse at having spoken to the shifter, but he had to admit that Geth might have been onto something. Ekhaas could have made the footprint. If she had, what had the self-appointed protector of the ruins been up to? A patrol of the territory she claimed? "Ashi, do you think she left any other tracks?"

The hunter rose and moved carefully, her eyes on the ground, in the direction the footprint faced. Her hand hovered in the air, then pointed. "Here—the mark of a heel. Here—another footprint. All in a straight line." She stopped and held out her arm, marking the path.

The footprints led directly to a shallow hollow filled with thorn bushes. Orshok took one look at the bushes and said immediately, "Those are dead."

Singe considered the bushes. "Are you sure? They just look dry."

"I know dead plants when I see them." The druid went up to the bushes and bent down low, peering underneath the tangled branches. "There's something behind them. A big piece of leather." He stood up and reached in among the bushes with his hunda stick, hooking the crooked end of the staff around a branch and tugging the mass of dry wood to one side. Geth helped him, gripping the prickly wood with his gauntleted hand. The dead bushes moved in a single mass to reveal a large section of heavy hide that was very nearly the same color as the soil. Stones had been lashed to the edges of the hide to give it extra weight and anchor it against the side of the hollow. Geth grabbed one and pulled the hide away.

Underneath was a hole just large enough for a big person to squeeze through.

"Well, well," murmured Singe. "Not exactly a door, but I don't think we need to be fussy." Drawing his rapier, he laid a hand against the blade and spoke a word of magic. A warm glow spread along the metal, practically invisible in the sunlight but bright as a torch when he extended the sword into the dark hole. The sides of the hole were smooth earth, packed solid and held firm by old roots; just a short distance beyond the tip of his rapier, the hole passed through the stones of a broken wall and opened into shadows. Of the space beyond, he could see nothing. He cursed under his breath and pulled back the sword. There could be a short drop on the other side of the hole—or a long one. He looked around at the others. "Any volunteers to go in first?" Everyone glanced at everyone else. Singe grunted. "Fine. Ashi, Orshok, hold onto my legs."

Geth interrupted again. "I'm stronger than Orshok," he said. "Maybe I should—"

Singe sucked air between his teeth. Talking to Geth was one thing. Placing his safety in the shifter's hairy hands was another. "Don't touch me."

Geth stopped and dropped back, a flush on his face. The others fell silent for a moment as well. Singe felt blood burn in his face for a moment as well—at least until the memory of Treykin, dying horribly in the streets of Narath but refusing to let an Aundairian touch him, came back to him. He stood straight. "Orshok can do it," he said tightly. "You're no weakling, are you, Orshok?"

The young orc glanced from him to Geth, then shook his head slowly. "No?" asked Singe. "Good." He turned back to the hollow, putting Geth behind him.

His righteous anger lasted until he knelt before the hole and stretched his arms—sword hand first—into the hole, then his head, shoulders and torso. Suddenly he felt like a rodent. The space was cramped. Stray roots tickled his cheek and neck. Dirt sifted into his hair. When he felt strong hands locked around his shins and ankles, he took a deep breath and squirmed forward, pulling himself with his elbows and his free hand.

His body blocked daylight, leaving only the magical illumination of his rapier blade. He stretched the sword out ahead of him. Its light fell on the stones he had seen before, then passed on into the space beyond to flash against another wall not far away.

There was writing on the wall, stark black characters on gray stone.

"Singe," said Ashi, her voice muffled, "we're almost at your knees!"

"Keep going!" he called back softly. He wriggled a little more and pushed his arms past the broken wall and into open air beyond. Another push and his head was through as well. Arching his back and propping himself up with his free hand, he stared in amazement.

He had emerged in a corridor constructed of large stones, carefully smoothed and tightly fitted. Angular writing—some form of Goblin—covered both walls, scrawled across the stones in irregular patches as though a scribe had taken to graffiti. The strokes of the writing were sharp-edged, like a pen on paper, but there was no sign of ink or paint. Instead, it was as if the stone itself had been stained—a simple magic, but one applied on scale far larger than Singe had ever imagined. The light of his sword didn't reach far, but it looked like one end of the corridor headed back toward the collapsed entrance, while the other continued on into darkness. The writing marched into the shadows in an unending stream.

The floor was an easy drop beneath him, the stones that had been removed to open the hole stacked neatly to one side. He lowered his rapier and carefully flicked it to the far side of the corridor. It fell to the floor with a swirl of light and a quiet clatter that rang like chimes on the still air. Singe paused, watching the darkness and listening, before twisting around and hissing back up the hole, "Let go!"

Hands released his ankles. Singe spread his legs, pressing against the sides of the hole in an attempt to control his descent, but he still came sliding out like the pit from a ripe cherry. He tucked as he fell, rolling back to his feet and snatching up his rapier in a smooth motion. He held it the weapon high and ready, light splashing around him.

Nothing stirred in the shadows. His breath hissed between his teeth and he stepped back over beneath the hole. He could see Dandra peering down at him. He gestured for her to join him. "Come down! Twelve moons, you have to see this!"

Geth was the last one down the hole. The slide into darkness was brief, the impact of his feet on the tunnel floor jarring, the cascade of dirt dislodged by his gauntlet extremely uncomfortable—it poured onto the top of his head and right down his back. "Rat!" he cursed, shaking himself and trying to dislodge it.

"Careful!" snapped Singe. The wizard was just lifting his hand from the head of Dandra's spear. Light shone from the weapon just as it shone from his rapier. Geth growled and bared his teeth at him, for a moment caught up in their old, familiar rivalry.

Except that the anger in Singe's eyes was real, just as it had been all the way along the road from Vralkek. Geth's growl died in his throat and the shame that had haunted him since seeing Robrand again returned like a punch in his gut. The instant that Singe's gaze left him, he pressed back into the shadows.

Why did it have to be Robrand working for Tzaryan? He could have happily lived his whole life without ever facing the old man again.

Orshok and Natrac came trotting along the tunnel. "You're right," Natrac said to Singe. "It ends at the collapse outside. Someone has been working down there—stones have been pulled out and pieced together on the floor like they were trying to match up fragments of writing."

"Ekhaas," Singe said. "I'd bet my hand on it." He raised his sword so that its light shone full on a patch of writing. "This is some variation of Goblin. I recognize the script."

"Can you read it?" asked Dandra.

Singe shook his head. "Not on my own. I can cast a spell that will let me, but the magic doesn't last long. We need to go deeper—try and find the heart of the writing."

"How? There doesn't seem to be any end to it." Dandra gestured with her spear, sending light dancing along the corridor.

The strange writing on the walls stretched as far as Geth could see.

Singe reached up and touched some of the black characters. "Dah'mir left us instructions," he said. "Look neither left nor right. The riches there are not for you. Hold to the path that leads to the Hall and find what waits in the shade of the grieving tree."

"If there were ever riches here, they're long gone," said Geth. Singe glanced at him coldly.

"They're not gone." He patted the wall. "They're here."

Understanding lit up Ashi's face. "The Bonetree hunters would have no use for writing—"

"—but Dah'mir would!" Dandra finished for her. She looked to Singe. "Do you think this writing is why he laired here?"

"I wouldn't rule it out." He lifted his rapier like a beacon and started down the corridor. "Follow me."

For a moment, Geth wondered if the wizard realized how much he resembled Robrand when he took command of a situation. The thought brought another twinge of shame—another flash of better times among the mercenaries of the Frostbrand company. He forced it out of his head. Dandra had said it best: they had to work together.

That would have been easier if Singe had been willing to give him something more than a sour frown. Geth drew a shallow breath. "One battle at a time," he muttered to himself, then winced. Another of Robrand's gems of wisdom. He reached across his body and drew his sword, taking what comfort he could in the simple, solid weight of the weapon.

Around his throat, the stones of Adolan's collar were a reassuring weight as well. He touched them. Grandmother Wolf, he thought, I wish you were here, Ado.

They crept down the dark hallway slowly, spreading themselves out so that they were close enough for comfort but far enough apart to swing their weapons if the need arose. The further they traveled along the script-lined corridor, however, the more Geth suspected that they had nothing to worry about. The shadows were still and silent. The dust of ages that lay on the floor had been disturbed by passage—Ekhaas, he presumed, since all the footprints looked the same—but there was no sign of struggle or violence. The air smelled of nothing but dust and rock . . . and maybe, if he breathed deep, old metal. He slid his sword back into its sheath.

At his side, Natrac leaned a little closer and whispered, "A different place from Jhegesh Dol."

Geth nodded silently. The ghostly daelkyr fortress that the two of them had passed through in the depths of the Shadow Marches had been lonely and eerie as well—but it had also born the horrendous touch of its otherworldly master and been haunted by the spirits of his tormented victims. The tomb-like quiet of Taruuzh Kraat was welcome by comparison.

"They're the same age, though, aren't they?" Geth said. "The Dhakaani Empire was destroyed in fighting the Daelkyr War. Taruuzh Kraat and Jhegesh Dol might have both been occupied at the same time."

"On opposite sides of the war, thank the Host." Natrac nodded to the blade in Geth's scabbard. "But your sword is that old, too."

Geth looked down at the heavy Dhakaani weapon. "I try not to think about that."

Natrac was silent for a moment, then added, "You really have Singe worked up. Him and Robrand both."

"I try not to think about that either," growled Geth. "Hold tight to your own secrets, Natrac." He moved away from the half-orc.

The corridor they followed curved gently and soon rooms began to open off of it, then intersecting hallways. All of them were lined with writing as well, some of the characters larger or smaller, some patches of text isolated, others running uninterrupted for paces. It was like walking through an enormous book. Aside from the writing, the rooms they passed were empty. Geth took a wary glance through each doorway and down each hall that they passed. The ruins might have been dry, but the passage of centuries had left behind only those things that could resist time's hunger. A fireplace, a counter crafted of stone and brick, scattered metal fittings amid the stains left by long decayed wood, a jumble of broken crockery fallen where some shelf or cupboard had crumbled.

And while Taruuzh Kraat might not have carried the terrible threat of Jhegesh Dol, the unending streams of text began to wear on him. Geth caught himself twitching and turning at half-glimpsed motion, only to realize that it was just another passage of writing on the wall. He bared his teeth and the hair on his neck and forearms bristled.

"When I was at Wynarn," Singe said abruptly, his voice brittle on the still air, "there was a researcher who specialized in planar cosmology. He usually wrote out his calculations in chalk on a slateboard, but sometimes when he was caught up in a problem that was larger than in his board, he would write on the walls of his classroom. One morning another researcher came in and found him backed into a corner, trapped by his own notes."

"A few years ago in Zarash'ak, one of the scions of House Tharashk went mad and wouldn't stop writing," said Natrac. "It was a scandal. She scribbled on anything she could reach with anything she could get her hands on. She had to be restrained or she would bite her fingers and try to write with her own blood."

Breath hissed through Dandra's teeth. "You're not helping!"

Geth glanced at her. Dandra's face was tight, her jaw tense, her eyes half-closed in concentration. The others saw it, too. "Dandra?" asked Orshok.

Dandra lifted her chin. "It's Tetkashtai," she said. "This place frightens her. Il-Yannah, it frightens me. There's madness here. You're lucky that you can only feel the edges of it."

"This was Dah'mir's lair," Singe pointed out. "Maybe something of his power is still here."

She shook her head. "No. This is different. It's—" She drew a rasping breath. "It's older. An echo of something that happened a long time ago."

"Can you tell what?"

"No," she said, shaking her head again. "But it's getting stronger." She raised her glowing spear to light the way ahead.

To her or Singe, Geth realized, it probably looked like the corridor just kept going on and on. Out beyond the edge of human or kalashtar sight, though, the shadows opened onto a deeper darkness, like the shallows at the edge of a lake. "There's something up there," he said sharply. "The hallway ends."

He felt an instant of bitter satisfaction as Singe's face wavered between disdain and the need to ask for help. The wizard's disdain won, though. He pushed forward, striding down the corridor. Everyone else followed hard on his heels. In only moments, the deeper darkness that Geth had glimpsed came into the light—a high archway with some kind of balcony beyond. Singe and Dandra stepped through the archway and out onto the balcony, their glowing weapons held high. Geth stopped just a pace behind them.

They looked down over a great chamber that still retained vestiges of the natural cavern it had once been. Vaulting arches of worked stone leaped across a high, rough ceiling. The lower walls had been smoothed and cut straight, but the chamber was still an irregular oval more than a score of paces wide and easily twice as long—even Geth's keen eyes couldn't make out its far end in the shadows. Broad stone stairs hugged the wall to one side of the balcony on which they stood, leading down to the floor ten paces below.

Spaced out along the walls and set into alcoves were the cold hearths of half a dozen ancient forges, soot staining the walls around them. Some still had the crumbling remains of huge bellows connected to them. Anvils, tools, and huge stone benches had been piled into the alcoves as well, all tumbled together as if they were nothing more than toys. Every smooth section of wall had been filled with more writing, though in this chamber the Goblin words were interspersed with strange sketches and diagrams.

In the center of the chamber, standing atop a broad platform, a strange sculpture of white stone reached up toward the ceiling. A thick base rose from the platform, narrowed, then spread and split into dozens of curved segments. The entire sculpture was cut with grooves across and along its surface. In places, sharp ridges and thorny spikes jutted out from it. The thing had an unpleasant, sinister look to it—so unpleasant and sinister that it actually took Geth a moment to realize what it was supposed to be.

"Grandmother Wolf," he breathed. "It's a tree."

"If this is the Hall of the Revered, it must be the grieving tree," said Singe. He looked at Orshok. "That's what kind of tree grows underground, I guess. A stone one."

Orshok just stared at the sculpted tree. "Why?" he asked. "What is it here for?" He glanced at Ashi, but she shook her head.

"Light of il-Yannah!" Dandra thrust out her arm. "Look there beside the tree."

Geth followed her pointing hand. Close beside the stone

tree—in its shadow—stood a strange heap of metal tubes and wires interspersed with pieces of glass or crystal. His eyes widened and his heart seemed to skip a beat. He'd seen something like it before, in memories Dandra had shown him through the *kesh* of her time as Dah'mir's prisoner. It was a near match for the device Dah'mir had used to trap Tetkashtai in the psicrystal and place Dandra in her body.

"I think we need to take a closer look." Singe grasped Dandra's hand and drew her after him down the stairs. Geth and the others followed, picking their way carefully. The same footsteps that they had followed in the dust along the corridor marked the dust of the stairs as well. Ekhaas had been this way. When they reached the floor of the of the chamber, however, he was surprised to find that there was no dust on the floor at all—it had all been swept away.

Ashi noticed as well. "Someone was trying to hide their presence, I think," the hunter said.

"Why here then and not in the corridor?" Geth asked.

Ashi shrugged.

The device beside the tree was considerably smaller than the one in the memory Dandra had shown Geth. In her memory, Dah'mir's device towered overhead. The device before them, on the other hand, was only a little taller than Ashi.

"This isn't the same size," Geth said.

"No," Dandra agreed, "it isn't." She circled the device and stopped before to a niche built inside it. To judge by the broken metal surrounding the niche, Geth guessed that something had been pulled out from inside the device. Something large—something the size of a crouching child.

"And find what waits in the shade of the Grieving Tree," he quoted. "That's where the Bonetree found Dah'mir's dragon-shard."

"He built a model of his device?" said Natrac.

"I don't think so." Singe stepped close to the device and pushed against a piece of age-corroded metal. It crumpled like paper, sending green flakes drifting to the ground. All of the bits of metal and wire that made up the device, Geth realized, were similarly corroded, the crystals among them clouded by time. "Dah'mir was here two hundred years ago. This is a *lot* older."

They were all quiet for a moment before Geth said. "The Dhakaani made this?"

Dandra stepped back and stared at the device. "That's impossible."

Singe spread his hands. "Maybe not. By all accounts, the Dhakaani were accomplished smiths. Their weapons helped fight off the daelkyr. I've never heard of Dhakaani artifacts that use dragonshards before, but—"

"No," said Dandra. "It's impossible that the Dhakaani could have made something to affect kalashtar." Her eyes were wide. "This device has to be thousands of years old, doesn't it?"

"I suppose so," said the wizard. "The Empire of Dhakaan fell after the Daelkyr War. I think historians agree it was dead by about five thousand years ago."

Dandra raised her hand and wrapped it around her psicrystal. "How much do you know about the history of the kalashtar?"

Orshok and Ashi looked at her blankly and shook their heads. Geth spoke up, repeating bits and pieces that he had heard during the Last War. "Kalashtar come from across the Dragonreach. From the continent of Sarlona."

"They come from farther away than that," Singe said. He frowned. "Kalashtar are the descendants of humans and spirits from Dal Quor, the plane of dreams. That's why you have psionic powers."

Dandra nodded. "We're not descendants as such—the Quori spirits that formed the first kalashtar were exiles from Dal Quor, and they were given refuge in Eberron by merging with a group of humans in the nation of Adara in Sarlona. As those first kalashtar married and had children, the original Quori spirits splintered among their lineages. The point is, we know exactly when kalashtar came into being. It was eighteen hundred years ago." She pointed her spear at the Dhakaani device. "How could an empire that was dead more than three thousand years before kalashtar even existed build something to affect us? Why would they?"

"Maybe they're not the same device," said Orshok. All eyes turned to him and the young druid shifted uncomfortably. "Dah'mir's device was bigger, wasn't it? A knife and a sword have a lot in common, but you don't use them for the same thing."

Singe's eyebrows rose. "But both devices were built around

the same Khyber shard. Once a shard is attuned to a particular magic, it can't be changed."

Geth was abruptly conscious of the weight of Adolan's stone collar around his neck. During the battle at the Bonetree mound, the Gatekeeper magic within the collar had protected him from the mental assault of a mind flayer. The Dhakaani sword at his waist had been forged to kill illithids and the other aberrant servants of the daelkyr; the ancient hobgoblins must have known about the tentacle-faced creatures' deadly abilities. "Dandra," he said, "are the powers of mind flayers psionic or magical?"

Her mouth opened, then closed as her eyes narrowed. After a moment, she said, "Psionic. They might come from the madness of Xoriat instead of the dreams of Dal Quor, but they're still psionic. It's like the difference between the magic of druids and the magic of wizards."

"The Dhakaani fought mind flayers during the Daelkyr War." Geth looked to Singe. "What if the binding stone traps things with psionic powers and all the wires and crystals around it are like . . . ?" He struggled to put the idea in his head into words. "Like a sieve that only lets certain things through. What if the Dhakaani built a device that let the shard capture mind flayers, but Dah'mir made a new device that captures kalashtar instead."

Singe drew a long, shallow breath and pulled on his whiskers as he turned back around to stare at the device. "Twelve moons," he muttered. He spun around sharply and walked to the nearest wall. Closing his eyes for a moment, he spoke a word of magic and laid a hand against the wall, then opened his eyes again and stepped back to scan the wall. His gaze seemed strangely unfocused but he clenched his teeth. "Twelve *bloody* moons."

"You can read it?" asked Dandra.

"Yes and no," Singe said. "No, because it's not all words. A lot of it is research notes, just like that researcher at Wynarn. And yes—" He blinked and turned around to face Geth. "—because *you* might be right."

Geth felt his gut tighten at the angry disgust in the wizard's voice, but no one else seemed to notice. Dandra was pushing forward. "It was meant to trap mind flayers?"

"I think so, but it's hard to tell." Singe turned and traced a hand across the wall, his eyes going unfocused once more. "These are mostly notes and calculations. They talk about illithids and arrangements of crystals that would attune the binding stone to their aura. I can only follow bits of it. They look more like the notes of an artificer than of a wizard. Other passages don't make any sense at all." He shifted his hand to another section of text. "This describes a sphere made of carved stone beetles linked together—it sounds like a child's puzzle." He touched other words. "This curses workers who fled the kraat. This tries to work breakfast into the equation for binding mind flayers. This—" He winced and lifted his hand away. "This just repeats over and over 'My name is Marg. My name is Marg. My name is Marg.' "

"I think someone lost themselves in their work," said Natrac. "You were right when you said you felt madness in the air, Dandra."

"Why would a Dhakaani have built something like this, though?" asked Ashi, still circling the ancient device. "Dah'mir had to tie Tetkashtai and the other kalashtar down to use his device on them. Wouldn't it be easier just to kill a mind flayer directly?"

"This might answer that," Singe said. He had paced further along the wall, trailing his hand over the writing. He read from another passage. "Too large! The first stones were so much smaller. The matrix can be made larger but focus will be a problem. How did he do it?"

Dandra paled. "There were other binding stones?"

"It sounds like there were—at one time, at least. Marg says *were* and it sounds like he was trying to re-create them rather than come up with something completely new." Singe looked up at the wall. "I wonder who this other 'he' was, though."

The wizard's pacing had drawn them past the strange stone sculpture of the grieving tree and the far end of the great chamber loomed in the shadows at the edge of Geth's vision. He squinted at it, took a few more paces, and let out a soft growl. "Maybe this was him."

Behind him, Singe and Dandra both turned and came forward. The soft glow of magical light spilled across the floor—then climbed over the legs of the statue that stood, tall as the sculpted tree, within the sharp point of the chamber's end. Dandra lifted her spear high, throwing light onto the statue's torso and head.

The statue depicted a Dhakaani hobgoblin, or so Geth guessed from its build and from the sword—very much like his own—that it gripped, point resting against the ground. The subject had been a man and muscular even for a hobgoblin, with massively thick arms and shoulders. He wore a smith's thick apron over a bare chest, with heavy gloves on his hands. Whether he had been fierce, benevolent, or wise, however, was impossible to tell. The statue's face had been ruined, hacked away leaving only deep scars in the stone.

The blade of the statue's sword, as wide as the shifter's own body, had also been gashed and as Geth moved closer, he saw that several characters had been crudely removed from the beginning of a longer inscription in Goblin. Writing identical to that on the walls throughout Taruuzh Kraat had been scrawled in its place.

Near the statue's feet, a few pitiful crumbled bones lay mixed with chips of stone, bits of metal ornament, an axe with a metal shaft, and a short black rod. One of the bones was a hobgoblin skull.

Singe slipped past Geth and laid his hand against the inscription on the stone sword. His eyes unfocused once more as he read the Goblin characters, then he lifted his hand and looked up at the statue's scarred face. "His name has been erased," he said. He pointed at the remaining text, moving his hand along as he read. "The rest of the inscription says, 'The Father of the Grieving Tree. The time will come again. Three great works stand together as allies: treasure, key, guardian, disciple, and lord.' "

The others fell silent, but Geth couldn't hold back a groan. "The Grieving Tree again. Grandfather Rat, another bloody riddle?"

"The spell lets me read a language," Singe snapped back irritably. "That doesn't mean I understand everything. The inscription might mean something in Goblin."

"What does the other writing say?" Natrac asked.

Singe looked up at again. " 'Keep your secrets, old master. Marg has surpassed you! I have created a new—' " He frowned. "It ends suddenly."

Ashi knelt beside the fragmentary remains at the statue's feet. "There's not much left of him," she said, "but I think Marg died in the moment of his triumph." She pointed at the skull and Geth saw that part of it was fractured. "I think he fell."

"An apprentice trying to outdo his master?" asked Orshok.

"I think you're right." Singe turned and walked away from the defaced statue to join them again. "Our nameless master created the first binding stones, but didn't share the secret. Marg went mad creating another stone, then died before he could do more than taunt a dead man." The wizard cursed. "But he still left a record of his research and thousands of years later, Dah'mir came along."

"But there's so much writing," said Dandra. "How long would it take to sort it out?"

Singe shrugged. "How much time does a dragon have? Decades? He spent two hundred years with the Bonetree clan before he tested his device on Tetkashtai, Medalashana, and Virikhad."

"Why leave Taruuzh Kraat then? Why did he create the Bonetree clan? Why not build a tribe of followers here?" Dandra pressed the tips of her fingers into her forehead in frustration. "We know where Dah'mir got the binding stone now, but we're no closer to understanding why he tried using it to turn kalashtar into servants of the Dragon Below."

Orshok took a breath and stepped forward. "No," he said. "We are. It's the sword and dagger again. Batul taught me that it was Gatekeeper magic and Dhakaani weapons that drove back the daelkyr and their servants and won the Daelkyr War." He touched the symbol of the Gatekeepers that he wore around his throat. "But Gatekeeper magic and Dhakaani weapons are meant to stop aberrations and the creatures of Xoriat."

Dandra's fingers slid down her face and she stared at the orc in amazement. Singe narrowed his eyes. "You don't use the same defense against a sword as you use against a dagger," he said.

Orshok nodded.

"What's that supposed to mean?" growled Geth.

"All of the ancient defenses against the great powers of the Dragon Below are focused against the madness of Xoriat," said Dandra slowly, as if she was working out the answer herself. She looked up sharply. "By subverting kalashtar to the service of Khyber, Dah'mir gives the daelkyr servants with the psionic abilities of mind flayers but without their vulnerabilities."

"And the ability to move about easily," Singe added. "Mind flayers are monsters, but kalashtar can pass unsuspected almost anywhere."

"Wait," Geth said. He pointed back at the Dhakaani device. "The binding stone was built to capture mind flayers, but *it* captured kalashtar as well."

"But it took a dragon at least two hundred years to figure out how to do that," replied Orshok. He looked frightened. His hands were clenched so tight around the shaft of his hunda stick that his knuckles were white. "We need to tell someone about this."

"Batul," said Geth. "The Gatekeepers need to know."

Singe nodded slowly. "I think you're right."

"What about Ekhaas?" asked Dandra. "Do you think she knows anything more about the history of Taruuzh Kraat? She might be able to tell us something that could help."

"We'll talk to her back at Tzaryan Keep." Singe led the way across the great chamber, past the pale stone of the grieving tree, and toward the stairs back up to the corridor. "We'll set out for Vralkek first thing in the morning—Robrand will help us. He might even know where we can find passage back to Zarash'ak and the Shadow Marches."

Out of the corner of his eye, Geth saw Dandra stiffen. Singe must have seen it as well because he muttered, "I'm sorry, Dandra. I don't think we have a choice."

"We'll be heading back toward Dah'mir," Dandra said.

Singe stared ahead grimly. "Maybe he's moved on by now."

The return trip up the long corridor was much faster. They didn't bother creeping along or trying to remain quiet. They didn't pause to look down side passages or into rooms. There was no point. Taruuzh Kraat was empty. They moved along the corridor quickly—Geth even caught Dandra with her feet off the ground, skimming the air as she did when she fought. No one said much. Geth suspected that they were all too caught up in what they had just uncovered.

The stream of sunlight that fell through the hole to the surface was a welcome sight. Singe paused beside it. "Geth," he said, pointing. "You first. You're the best climber and you're strong enough to help pull the rest of us out."

Geth growled under his breath, but there was no conviction to it. After hours in the ancient dimness of the ruins, open air and warm light would be a welcome change. Orshok and Ashi linked hands to help boost him up and into the hole. Geth kicked and wriggled, bracing himself with his elbows, then catching the stones of the broken wall with his feet and pushing. Below him, Ashi and Orshok coughed on the dirt he dislodged. He gritted his teeth and clawed his way up the sides of the hole until his head and shoulders popped out the other end of the hole. It was well on into the afternoon—the sun was low and bright in his eyes.

He was still blinking against the glare when something twisted in the dust around the hole. Geth looked down just in time to see the loop of a snare before it whisked closed and a heavy cord cinched tight around his chest.

"Don't try anything," rasped a deep voice. "I was hoping Singe might be the first out of the hole, but I don't think even the toughest shifter could shrug off a crossbow bolt in the eye."

Geth twisted his head around. Just out of his reach, Chain d'Tharashk crouched down with a loaded crossbow aimed straight at his head.

CHAPTER

13

His first instinct was to tuck in his feet, raise his arms, and let himself drop back down the hole. He didn't get far—the cord around his chest held him fast, the sudden weight jerking the snare even tighter and leaving him kicking desperately to hold himself up. Choking curses rose up from below. *"Rond betch!"* shouted Ashi. "Geth, what are you doing?"

Chain twitched the crossbow, the colors of his dragonmark flashing in the sunlight, as Geth managed to restore his purchase. "Go on," he said. "Tell them. And by the way, the cord is spiked in place, so pulling yourself up won't do any good either."

Geth bared his teeth at the bounty hunter, shock and anger fighting inside him, but he bent his head to shout back down the hole. "It's Chain! Chain's here!"

The cursing below ceased abruptly. Geth thought he caught a drift of murmured alarm, then Chain raised his voice. "No tricks!" he called. "I know Dandra can teleport, but if anything surprises me, a crossbow bolt is going to be last thing Geth ever sees."

"What are you doing here?" Geth growled. "You should be wandering Sharn!" His eyes narrowed. Chain's leather shirt was stained with salt as if it had been soaked in seawater. Orshok's insistence that he had seen someone fall from *Lightning on Water* just before the elemental galleon took her full speed came back to him. "Cousin Boar. You got free and swam to Vralkek?"

"A fishing boat picked me up, but *dagga*, I went overboard.

By the time I got to shore, you'd already fallen in with Tzaryan's ogres, but that gave me time to stock up. After that, all I had to do was stay back and follow until I had a chance to get the bunch of you alone. I told you—I'm the best." Chain held up his hand. The line of a deep scratch was just fading on it. "You thought I fell on the docks at Zarash'ak and scratched myself on a piece of wire. Not quite. A good bounty hunter never carries drugs or poisons if he doesn't have at least some resistance to them, he always has a back up stash of coin, and he's never without at least a makeshift lockpick. You never know when a piece of wire will come in handy."

"Bastard."

"Keep my mother out of this." He raised his voice again. "How are you doing down there, Singe?"

Singe's voice came drifting up past Geth's legs. "What do you want, Chain?"

"What Vennet paid me for," Chain shouted back. "I want Dandra."

"You can't have her."

Chain's crossbow drifted slightly. Geth heard the snap and creak of the bow at the same moment that pain shot through his unarmored left hand. He howled in agony and jerked his hand up, throwing himself off balance. He struggled to stay upright as he stared at the crossbow bolt that transfixed his palm. Someone below was shouting his name. Chain calmly dropped another bolt into his crossbow and recocked the weapon. When Geth's roar had died down, the big man raised his voice again. "This is what's going to happen. I'm going to keep putting holes in Geth until Dandra comes out. When she does—and when she's secure—I'll push this sorry shifter back down the hole."

Geth gritted his teeth and shifted. The feeling of invulnerability that surged through him eased some of his pain. The flow of blood from his hand slowed. He glared at the bounty hunter, then felt a cold fear push up his spine. Chain sat against a heap of rocks that Geth couldn't recall seeing before. The hole leading down into the ruins wasn't particularly wide. It wouldn't take much to block it. "Don't trust him, Singe!" he said quickly. "It's a trap."

"Twelve moons!" the wizard called back. "You don't say?"

Chain grinned at Geth. "You lot got on top of me in Zarash'ak," he said. "You're good. But when I say I'm the best, I mean it. You're not getting out of this."

"Chain!" shouted Dandra. "This isn't just a simple contract. You don't know who you're really working for."

Chain's crossbow drifted lazily. Geth stiffened and tried to get his gauntleted arm up, but the bolt through his left hand made it difficult to support himself. He clenched his teeth and put his weight on the injured hand. The gauntlet was a poor shield against a crossbow at close range, but it was all he had.

"And you don't know who you're dealing with!" Chain spat.

"I'm dealing with an idiot," said a strong, hard voice.

Chain and Geth both looked up at the same time. About ten away, Robrand d'Deneith was striding through the brittle grass of the ruins. "You must be Chain d'Tharashk."

Chain's eyes narrowed as they fell on the blue star of Tzaryan Keep pinned to the old man's coat. "This is a legitimate bounty," he said. "Leave us be."

"You're House Tharashk," answered Robrand. "You should know better than anyone what happens to trespassers in Tzaryan Rrac's territory."

"Tzaryan recognizes bounties."

"Not when they're his guests."

Chain stiffened. His crossbow steadied, pointed at Geth's head once more. "Stay where you are or he dies."

Robrand paused. Geth looked up at him. For the first time since Robrand had revealed himself on the road from Vralkek, their eyes met—and Robrand's gaze was cold.

Geth's arm sank slowly. His gut clenched. Nine years of running and hiding and it came down to this. Stuck in a hole with his life in Robrand's hands.

He didn't look away.

Robrand did.

The old man glanced back to Chain and started walking again. "You're within sight of the keep walls," he said. "Did you think you could get away with this? I have a company of ogres on their way. Surrender now."

It was a blatant lie, an outrageous bluff. If Robrand had been sitting at a table playing cross, Geth knew, half the other players would have raised the stakes immediately. He'd done it himself before he'd learned not to gamble with the old man. Chain didn't have that advantage. Geth saw his eyes flick briefly toward the looming bulk of Tzaryan Keep, then back to Robrand.

"You're lying. If Tzaryan's troops were coming, they'd be on top of us already."

"And if you kill Geth, you've got nothing left to bargain with," Robrand said smoothly.

"You're right," said Chain. He swung the crossbow toward Robrand.

Geth's old commander lunged forward even as Chain squeezed the trigger. The air seemed to spit light over Robrand's chest, then the bolt was simply rolling in the dust. Before Chain could reload or even grab for the sword at his side, Robrand had his sword out and at the bounty hunter's throat. Chain fell back and his leg lashed out in a brutal kick, but Robrand leaped up over it with a master's ease—and stomped down on Chain's outstretched hip as he tried to whirl to his feet. The big man writhed in pain and thrust himself back the other way.

Right into Geth's reach. The shifter roared and swung his right arm in a powerful backhand blow. He caught just a glimpse of Chain's eyes—open wide and white—before his gauntlet cracked hard against his face. Chain flipped over, rolled, and lay still, eyes closed, face bleeding from the impact of the studs and ridges on the gauntlet. Geth spat at him.

"Respect, Blademark!" snapped Robrand.

Geth stiffened instinctively and shouted back, "Commander! Yes, commander!" before he even thought about it, then jerked and caught himself. He looked up at Robrand in shock. The old man looked startled as well. A grimace of distaste crossed his face.

"Old habits don't die easily," he said.

"No," said Geth. "I guess they don't." His stomach roiled so intensely that he thought he might be sick.

To one side of them, the air seemed to fold and then part as Dandra stepped out of it, spear at the ready, the droning chorus of whitefire surrounding her. She blinked at the sight of Chain's unconcious form and the chorus faded. "We heard Robrand—" she began, then her eyes darted to Geth's hand, the crossbow bolt still piercing it. "Geth!"

The distaste on Robrand's face vanished and suddenly he

was once more the personable, pleasant old soldier he had been on the journey from Vralkek. "Get Geth out of the hole, Dandra," he ordered. "Singe! Send Orshok up first to tend Geth's wounds."

The next few minutes were a flurry of activity. Robrand cut the cord of Chain's snare, freeing Geth. Dandra took his free hand and hauled him free of the hole. A moment later, Orshok emerged, dusty and pale. As the others followed, the druid drew Geth away from the hole and examined his wounded hand, then took out a knife and carefully trimmed one end off the bolt so he could slide it free from the wound. Renewed pain burned through Geth's hand, but he clenched his teeth until Orshok spoke a healing prayer. Magic like a cool breeze closed the wound.

Geth let out a sigh and flexed his hand. "Twice tak," he said.

"There's probably going to be a scar," Orshok apologized. "The wound was almost too much for my magic. Batul or Krepis could have done more."

"I can live with another scar," said Geth. He jerked his head at Chain. The big man was groaning as Singe and Natrac tied his arms with his own cord. Blood and dirt had mixed to make a dark, patchy mess on the bounty hunter's face. "Especially if I've given him more than he gave me."

Singe finished tying Chain and stood up to face Robrand. "It's lucky you came along, old man, but somehow I don't think it's an accident you were out here. And I don't think Tzaryan knows you're here. If this was his business, you really would have ogres with you."

"I was looking for you, Etan," Robrand said bluntly. "It's Ekhaas. Tzaryan's getting impatient. I think he thought you would talk to her before you started exploring the ruins."

"There wasn't time."

"There's going to be even less time. Tzaryan's given orders to begin her interrogation." He contemplated the hole in the ground. "Is this Ekhaas's work, too? Tzaryan's not going to be pleased with that."

Singe let out a hiss. "He said he'd let me talk to Ekhaas before he tortured her—and you said he honored his word."

"He has limits." Robrand looked back toward the keep. "The ogres are waiting for my return—I was able to hold them back that long."

"Then your timing's good. We were going to talk to her when we got back anyway." He pressed his lips together, then added, "We found what we needed in the ruins, Robrand. We'll be leaving tomorrow. We have to get back to the Shadow Marches."

Robrand nodded. "You can take the horses you rode here on. I'll arrange for supplies—"

A loud groan from Chain interrupted them. The big man's eyes opened and fixed on his bound hands. His muscles tensed as he strained at the cord. Nothing happened. He looked up to stare at them all angrily. His gaze settled you on Robrand and his lips twisted. "How—? You were close! I couldn't have missed."

Singe picked up a pebble and flicked it at Robrand. There was a tiny flash of light and the pebble dropped to the ground without touching the old man. Chain scowled. "Deneith!" he spat in digust.

"Don't feel bad," Robrand told him. "I've been outwitting marksmen longer than you've been alive. If it means anything, you've got a steady hand."

Ashi gave the old man a puzzled look. "You used your dragonmark to protect yourself?"

Robrand nodded.

The hunter tilted her head. "Why not just use it to protect Geth?"

"He was safe enough." Robrand waved his hand dismissively. "It's exactly what I told Chain—if he killed Geth, he had nothing left to bargain with. But by using my mark on myself, I was able to surprise him and free all of you. Sometimes shielding yourself is the best way to shield someone else." He gestured for Ashi and Natrac to get Chain on his feet. "Bring him along. Tzaryan's going to want to have a word with him. I don't think he'll be bothering you again."

Dandra winced and Geth knew she was remembering Bava's story of the Tharashk prospectors who had run afoul of the lord of Tzaryan Keep. "Is that necessary? Maybe there's something less drastic."

Robrand shook his head. "Tzaryan takes his authority very seriously, Dandra. No one crosses him and gets away with it."

Chain went pale, struggling and cursing as Ashi and Natrac

hauled him to his feet. The hunter and the half-orc didn't look any happier at escorting him to an unpleasant fate. Geth saw Dandra glance at Singe with a beseeching look in her eyes, but Singe just gave her a slight shake of his head. Geth understood the wizard's dilemma: there wasn't much use arguing with Robrand once the old man had decided on something.

He was half-surprised himself that Robrand had bothered to rescue him from Chain at all.

At the gates of Tzaryan Keep, a call from Robrand brought ogres racing down the broad stairs to take charge of Chain. The ogres were far less gentle than Natrac and Ashi. They put an end to Chain's struggles with a quick slap to the back of his head and a couple of brutal twists on his arms. The big man looked small and maybe even forlorn in their grasp. Geth felt a twinge of pity for him. He wouldn't have wanted to be in his place.

They all followed up the canyon of the stairs to the upper levels of the keep, then through halls Geth didn't recognize until they came to the head of another flight of stairs plunging back down into the keep's innards. Unlike the broad stairs that led up from the gate, these were steep, plunging sharply down. The oversize steps—built for the feet of ogres—made navigating them difficult. Geth noticed that Dandra gave up trying to walk and let herself skim above the steps, sliding down them like a child on a smooth hill, supported by her psionic power.

There was no natural light at all in the depths of the keep. Orc slaves summoned by Robrand carried torches ahead and behind. The flickering light made the stairs especially treacherous, but without them, Geth knew, he would have been as night-blind as a human. Only Orshok and Natrac, with their orc-blood ability to see even in absolute darkness, seemed comfortable, though Natrac once again reacted with ill-concealed disgust to the presence of Tzaryan's slaves.

When the first flight of stairs ended, they passed along a hallway that was thick with the stench of ogre bodies and echoed with the sounds of rough leisure.

"The troops' barracks are that way," Robrand explained, gesturing off into the darkness. He turned in another direction, and they descended another steep flight of stairs before stopping in a second hallway that smelled even worse than the first. Geth's nose wrinkled at a mixture of hot coals, damp stone, and stale waste.

Robrand stopped at a thick wooden door and pulled it open. "This will do," he said. "Put him in here until Tzaryan decides his punishment."

The ogres brought Chain forward and muscled him through the door. The best bounty hunter in Zarash'ak looked substantially more frightened than he had chained in the hold of *Lightning on Water*. He ran at the door as the ogres forced it closed.

"Help me!" he shouted. "Don't let them—"

The door closed in his face and the ogres dropped a heavy bar into place across it. Singe looked to Robrand. "I don't like him, but do you think you can get Tzaryan to release him without doing anything too permanent?"

In the light of the torches, Robrand looked older than he was and even more harsh. "I'll try." He gestured and the two ogres retreated up the stairs.

Nearly a dozen paces farther along the corridor, a brazier full of hot coals stood beside another door. An older ogre with stringy gray hair tended it, stirring the coals with a heavy poker. The hilts of several knives protruded from the brazier, their blades buried inside it. A hobgoblin sword and other gear—Ekhaas's presumably—lay in the shadows nearby. The ogre looked up as Robrand and the others approached. His nose was missing, lending a strangely flat quality to his voice when he spoke. "As you orders, General. Waits for you."

"Well done, Lor. Leave us for now."

The ogre looked disappointed. "Leaves?"

"Tzaryan's guests will speak with the prisoner first. I'll summon you back when they're finished."

The old ogre's scarred face fell, but he pushed past Geth and the others and headed for the stairs. Geth choked and held his breath as the ogre passed—the smell of smoke and burned flesh clung to him. Dandra closed her eyes for a moment and looked away.

Robrand strode past the brazier and up to the door. "Singe," he said. "Help me." Between the two of them, they lifted the bar that lay across the door and dropped it to one side. Robrand stepped back. "She's all yours for as long as you need," he said. "She's gagged right now—you'll want to take that off, but be careful of her spells." He turned to go.

"You're not staying?" asked Dandra.

"You don't need me and I have to tell Tzaryan about Chain," he said. "Come find me in the upper levels when you're finished. You remember how to find your way back?"

Dandra and Singe both nodded. Robrand gestured for two of the orc slaves to leave their torches behind in brackets on the walls, then left with the other slaves lighting his way.

Singe drew a deep breath and turned to the door. "Let's see what Ekhaas can tell us about Taruuzh Kraat." He tugged the door open.

The cell beyond was possibly the first cramped space that Geth could remember seeing in Tzaryan Keep. A single ogre would have been squeezed tight in the cell; two creatures of human size could have stood close within it. Ekhaas crouched against one wall, chained to it by a collar around her neck. Her hands were bound and her mouth, as Robrand had said, gagged. She still wore her studded armor, though her hair was no longer so severely drawn back. Singe glanced at Dandra, then stepped into the cell alone while the rest of them watched from the doorway.

Above the gag, Ekhaas's eyes were bright and hard. Her wolf-like ears stood straight. "I'm going to take the gag off," Singe told her. "Bite me or try to cast a spell and it goes back on." He reached behind the hobgoblin's head. The gag fell.

Ekhaas didn't move except to lick her lips, working saliva around her mouth. There was a bucket of water close to the brazier Lor had left behind. Geth grabbed it and cautiously scooped some liquid into his mouth. It was stale, but clean. "Singe," he said, passing the bucket into the cell. The wizard took it and offered it to Ekhaas. She only regarded it with disdain.

"I won't take water from someone who intends to defile Taruuzh Kraat," she said, the cedar-smoke voice that Geth remembered rough and cracking.

"You might as well," said Singe. "We've already been inside. We found your hole—that's how we got in."

Ekhaas's ears twitched back. Her lips drew away from sharp teeth. Singe held the bucket closer, tipping it so that she could drink.

"Drink," he said. Ekhaas stared at the water, then stretched out her neck and sipped, her eyes rolled up to watch Singe. The sip turned into a gulp, the gulp into a greedy guzzle. Singe let her drink her fill, then took the bucket away as she sat back.

"Now," he said, "let's make sure we all understand the situation. Tzaryan Rrac is going to have you tortured. We may be able to persuade him to set you free. All you need to do is answer some questions for us and we'll talk to Tzaryan." He waited but Ekhaas made no response. He set the bucket aside and crossed his arms, looking down at the hobgoblin. "The General said you were a member of the Kech Volaar and that you knew something about the ruins."

"I am a *duur'kala*, a dirge-singer, of the Kech Volaar," Ekhaas said haughtily. "I know tales of glory from times before your ignorant kind set foot on this land, human."

Geth saw Singe stiffen, but the wizard kept his voice neutral. "Share some of them with us then. We've come a long way to learn about Taruuzh Kraat. We've been inside. We've seen the writing. We've seen the great hall and the grieving tree." Ekhaas's eyes narrowed and her ears sank low. "We didn't touch anything," Singe told her. "We're not treasure hunters. We just need to know about something. It's important."

He crouched down before her, putting himself at eye level with her. "Tell us about Marg and the stones," he said. "Tell us about the father of the grieving tree. Who was he?"

Ekhaas's ears flicked sharply. Her lips twisted and she gave a bitter laugh. "*Khaavolaar!* You ask the things that lull a child to sleep. You know nothing, human." She sat back against the wall. "Go away. Leave me to my fate."

Singe stood up again. "I know where there's another device like Marg's," he said. "I know what became of the stone that he made."

Ekhaas sat forward sharply. "You're lying."

"I'm not." He glared at her. "I'd wager that you've found signs that someone—or something—lived in Taruuzh Kraat for a long time about two centuries ago. His name is Dah'mir and he's a dragon. We believe that he came to Taruuzh Kraat to study the writing on the walls and to learn how to create his own version of

Marg's device for trapping mind flayers. We know that his servants took Marg's stone." He bent low to stare into her face. "Dah'mir follows the Dragon Below and we think that he was trying to use the stone to create servants with the power of mind flayers and a resistance to Gatekeeper magic. And if it takes a child's tale for us to understand more, then you're going to tuck us in and sing us a lullaby."

He stood straight once more and turned away from Ekhaas. His face was flushed. Behind him, Ekhaas was still, her ears standing straight, her dark eyes intent. Geth held his breath—just as Dandra did on one side of him and Orshok on the other—waiting to see what would happen.

Ekhaas drew a breath. "Mothers of the dirge, forgive me," she said softly, then sat as straight as her bonds would allow. "You've seen Taruuzh Kraat backward, human. Marg was nothing but a jealous madman. The device he built, the stone he created, were flawed reflections—poor attempts to emulate the genius of his master."

Singe turned back to face her. "We know. We saw the statue. Who was Marg's master?"

"Taruuzh." Ekhaas's voice swelled with pride. "What did you think 'Taruuzh Kraat' meant, *chaat'oor?* It is the smithy of Taruuzh, a stronghold of genius against the armies of the daelkyr. Taruuzh was the greatest *daashor* of his time—the crafter of marvels, the inventor of wondrous weapons."

"A *daashor* is an artificer?"

Ekhaas bared her teeth. "A *daashor* would make one of your artificers look like a wandering tinker."

"The inscription on the statue in Taruuzh Kraat called him the father of the Grieving Tree," said Dandra.

"The true Grieving Tree was his greatest creation. The one that stands in Taruuzh Kraat was said to be the first, but before Taruuzh died, a grieving tree stood in every city of the empire. The secret of their making was lost in the Desperate Times, but even today, hobgoblins of all clans emulate their use."

"What was so great about them?" Geth growled. "What did they do?"

Ekhaas's eyes darted to him. They burned with a zealous intensity that left him wishing he hadn't said anything. "The

Grieving Trees kill people, shifter. A criminal to be executed is hung upon a Grieving Tree. Today, the criminal must be broken and left to die, but in the time of the Empire, the tree drew his life out of him."

A chill ran up Geth's spine. Singe blinked, the color draining from his face. "Taruuzh's greatest creation was a way to execute people?" the wizard asked.

"What have your greatest artificers done recently, human?" Ekhaas demanded. "Built machines of slaughter for the battle-fields of the Last War? Will they stand and take pride in their work?"

None of them said anything. None of them could meet her gaze. After a moment, Geth swallowed. "What about the stones? Why would Marg try to re-create them instead of the Grieving Tree?"

"Because *daashor* across the empire knew how to create grieving trees. Taruuzh shared the secret freely. But the secret of his second greatest creation he kept to himself." Ekhaas eased herself back. "When the daelkyr and their armies poured forth from Xoriat into Eberron, the *daashor* and master smiths of Dhakaan rose to the defense of the empire. They mastered the twilight metal byeshk. They forged armor to defend against the strange powers of the aberrations and weapons to kill them."

For an instant, Geth thought the hobgoblin stared directly at him and his sword, but her gaze drifted to his side to rest on Orshok. "They allied themselves with the Gatekeepers and between orcs and Dhakaani drove back the daelkyr. But their triumph didn't come easily or all at once." Her ears flicked. "Gatekeeper! Have you heard of the Battle of Moths?"

Orshok started and stammered. "I don't—I don't think so." He shook his head. "No." Ekhaas frowned.

"No," she repeated tightly and sighed. "Once again, it is only the Dhakaani who remember." Her voice rose in the measured cadence of a storyteller. "Of all the servants and the living weapons of the daelkyr lords, the illithids were the most terrible, killing with their minds alone and weaving horrors with their thoughts. They were the generals of the hordes of Xoriat, and it was a blessing that their ranks were few. But upon the Marches, in a place where the land rose above the swamps, the illithids came together in numbers with other creatures of like abilities—lunanaes, psaretti, and kagges—to pay homage to the daelkyr known only as the Master of Silence. And from them, the Master formed a legion of generals."

"When the elders of the Gatekeepers learned of the danger, they knew that it was greater than their magic alone could contain. They dispatched one of their number, a seeress named Aryd who had foreseen the devastation that the legion would cause if left unchallenged, to appeal to Taruuzh for aid. At his forge in the shade of the Grieving Tree, Taruuzh listened to Aryd's appeal and agreed to help the Gatekeepers. He banished all of his apprentices from the forge while he worked with Aryd at his side through two seasons."

"When the seasons turned again, they were ready. Taruuzh and Aryd set forth from Taruuzh Kraat, gathering an army as they traveled—and just in time, for the legion of the Master of Silence had grown into its strength. On a night of eight moons, in the place where the land rose above the swamps, the legion of the Master of Silence and the army of Taruuzh and Aryd faced each other."

Ekhaas's words seemed to weave images in Geth's mind. In his imagination, he saw a dark plain lit by moonlight. On one side of the plain massed the ordered ranks of Dhakaani hobgoblins in heavy armor with swords and spears of purple byeshk, with milling crowds of orcs on either flank wielding only axes and armored only in their faith. At the head of the army, a hobgoblin man in a smith's apron and heavy gauntlets and an orc woman in rough leather robes. On the other side of the plain, waited a shadowy horde, all writhing tentacles and dead white eyes. There were dolgrims among them, and dolgaunts. Dark silhouettes took the place of lunanaes and psaretti and kagges—creatures he had never heard of, but whose names struck a strange primal fear into his soul.

"Madness was a tide that rolled before the legion of the Master," said Ekhaas, "but Aryd and the Gatekeepers raised their voices in prayer. Nature answered them and from the night, white moths poured forth in unending numbers. At the same time, Taruuzh spread forth the weapon on which he had labored for two seasons: a thousand blue-black stones, each no large than a finger, each wrapped in a filigree of gold. Like snow falling on mountain tops, Aryd's moths settled on Taruuzh's stones, a dozen or more to each, and bore them toward the Master's legion. Because they were small creatures without minds, the dread powers of the legion could find no hold on them, but as the moths passed among the legion, the stones of Taruuzh inflicted a deadly toll. Whenever a stone touched the flesh of an illithid or a lunanae or a psarett or a kagge, that creature's mind—the seat of its powers—was drawn into the crystal and bound there. With mind and body separated, they were helpless."

Geth felt Dandra stiffen at his side. One of her hands was wrapped tight around her psicrystal. "Light of il-Yannah," she breathed. "Binding stones. A thousand binding stones that worked by contact alone."

Ekhaas continued as if she hadn't heard. "The legion was broken. The scattered survivors were run down by the army of Taruuzh and Aryd. When the sun rose, the legion was gone—dead or fled into the court of the Master of Silence—and the battlefield glittered with Taruuzh's stones. The Gatekeepers gathered them, each and every one, and ground them into dust. With that dust, they made a mortar, and with that mortar built a seal, weaving their magics to bind the Master of Silence and all his court into the depths of Khyber. In the place where the land rose above the swamps, they raised a circle of stones to mark the site of the battle. And Taruuzh looked at his stones as they were ground into dust and said, 'Of all my works, this was second only to the Grieving Tree.' "

She looked up at them, her face calm and almost shining. *"Raat shan gath'kal dor,"* she said. "The story stops but never ends." Her ears twitched. "Does that answer your questions, human?"

Singe swallowed. "Yes," he said. "I think it does." His voice was strained. Geth dragged his gaze away from Ekhaas to look at him—and growled in surprise. The wizard's face was pale and dotted with a light sheen of sweat.

"Singe!" said Dandra. She started forward, but Singe raised a hand and stopped her. He looked at Ashi. "The first time I saw the Bonetree mound, you told me that a Gatekeeper circle stood there before Dah'mir shattered it to build the mound."

Ashi nodded slowly and a look of fear passed over her eyes.

Geth felt it, too. "Tiger, Wolf, and Rat," he said softly. "The Bonetree clan's territory is dry, a place where the land rises above the swamp. Do you think that when Dah'mir talked about his master he meant . . . ?"

He left the thought unfinished.

"Land can change in nine thousand years," Natrac said into the silence. "And the ancient Gatekeepers built circles all over the Shadow Marches." He sounded like he was trying to reassure himself.

Orshok shook his head. "But they never built them without a reason."

"Twelve bloody moons." Singe took a deep breath. "We wondered why Dah'mir would leave Taruuzh Kraat for the Shadow Marches, didn't we? I think maybe we know now."

Ekhaas's eyes were darting between them. "What is this?" she demanded. "What are you talking about?"

"A story to repay yours when we have the time," said Singe. He stepped backward out of the cell and bowed to the chained hobgoblin. "Thank you. You kept your end of the bargain. We'll keep ours and talk to Tzaryan." He straightened up and glanced at the rest of them. "Someone should stay here to make sure Lor doesn't come down and start before we get back."

Geth's hand dropped to his sword. There was another story he wanted to hear from Ekhaas, and if Singe convinced Tzaryan to free her, he might never have another chance. "I'll stay," he said.

Singe looked him over with narrow eyes. "No," he said tightly. The others paused.

"Singe!" Dandra said. She stepped between the two men, staring at the wizard with a harsh expression. "Why not?"

"I don't trust him."

Dandra's eyebrows rose high. "You don't trust him? You've fought beside him! He rescued both of us." She twisted around to look over her shoulder. Geth dropped his gaze to the floor rather than meet her eyes. Dandra let out a hiss of frustration. "Il-Yannah, I've had it with this feud of yours!" He saw her shift as she turned back to Singe. "What did Geth do that was so terrible you can still hold it over him nine years later?"

Geth's head snapped up, his heart leaping into his throat.

"Dandra, don't—"

It was too late. Singe's eyes flashed. "He abandoned his post," the wizard seethed. "The coward abandoned his post at Narath and because he did, the Aundairians got into the town behind our lines." Singe looked past Dandra to glare at him. "The massacre at Narath is his fault. More than a thousand people died because of what he did. Geth killed the Frostbrand. Geth killed Narath."

Silence. Geth could feel the weight of Natrac's gaze, of Ashi's and Orshok's as well. In the cell, Ekhaas watched, her ears pricked forward.

Dandra turned slowly. "Geth, is that true?"

He ground his teeth together.

Dandra stood fast, her dark eyes wide. "Is it true?" she asked again.

Geth looked at her—at all of the people he'd called friends—and the secret that he had only ever spoken before to Adolan slipped between his lips. "Yes."

CHAPTER

14

"Bastard." Singe's voice was cold. He picked up one of the torches Robrand had left behind. "You know what? If you want to stay here, you can stay. I don't want to look at you." He threw a glance into the cell. "Ekhaas, we'll be back."

The hobgoblin said nothing and Singe didn't wait for a reply. He turned to the others. "Come on." He started down the dark hallway toward the stairs without looking back.

Ashi and Orshok looked confused but they followed him. So did Natrac, though he turned to glance back with a strangely bleak expression in his eyes. Geth twitched his head away.

Dandra lingered. "Geth, I—"

He bared his teeth and snapped at her. She flinched back, then turned and darted after Singe and the others.

After a long moment, Geth turned to look at Ekhaas, still sitting silently in the cell. The hobgoblin's eyes glittered as she watched him. "Truth tears its way out of the belly."

"Shut your mouth," Geth snarled, but Ekhaas just sat back.

"I owe you no kindness, shifter. I'm here because of you." She looked at him with cold anger—and nodded toward his sword. "I know why you asked to stay and I'm pleased that your curiosity stung you."

Rage swept over him and he strode into the cell, ripping the Dhakaani sword from his scabbard. "Tiger's blood, if I'm going to suffer for curiosity, then I want an answer!" He held the naked blade in front of her, the torchlight from the hallway casting dark gleams into the twilight-purple byeshk. "I drew this in Zarash'ak and a gang of goblins scattered. I drew it against you and you tried to take my head off." He twisted the sword. "What is it?"

Ekhaas's eyes narrowed. "It's a *lhesh shaarat*, a warlord's blade. Goblin, hobgoblin, or bugbear, any descendant of Dhakaan recognizes a *lhesh shaarat*. They're the weapons of kings and heroes. Anyone who dares draw one proclaims his power. The goblins you faced in Zarash'ak probably fled in fear at the mere sight of you holding it."

"You didn't flee."

"I know that the weapons of heroes can be stolen by cowards, shifter."

His lips drew back. "My name is Geth," he spat. "Use it." He lifted the blade and light ran along it. "And I didn't steal this. I fought for it. Do the Dhakaani remember a ghost fortress called Jhegesh Dol?"

"Jhegesh Dol?" Ekhaas's ears lay back. "What do you know about Jhegesh Dol?"

"More than I want to." Geth drew a breath between his teeth, then looked down at Ekhaas again. "I found this sword there. A Gatekeeper told me it was the sword of the hobgoblin who killed the daelkyr master of Jhegesh Dol. Do you know anything more about it?"

"Nothing I can recall." A hungry expression crept across Ekhaas's face. "Why?"

Geth showed her his teeth. "Because I took a good chunk out of Dah'mir with it."

Ekhaas blinked and surprise broke through her hostility for the first time. "*Khaavolaar.* The dragon? You injured him with the sword?"

Geth nodded and Ekhaas's ears flicked forward—then lay back sharply.

"But you didn't kill him?"

"If I'd killed him, I'd be back in the Eldeen instead of talking to you and we wouldn't have anything to worry about," Geth said. He turned the sword and slammed it back into its sheath.

Ekhaas watched him with something like amazement in her eyes.

"What?" he growled at her. "Suddenly I'm worth talking to?" He turned away from her and stared back out into the corridor.

There was light coming down the stairs into the dungeon—the light of a torch, but accompanied by the sound of only one pair of feet.

Unease stirred in him. The footsteps that echoed down the stairs were quick and lively, but also heavy. A man's footsteps. A half dozen possibilities for who might be making those footsteps flicked through his head. The steps were too heavy to be Dandra and surely Singe wouldn't be coming back to face him. They were too loud for Ashi—the hunter moved in near-silence. Neither Orshok nor Natrac would have need for a torch. Tzaryan's orc slaves wouldn't have needed a torch either, and Geth hadn't seen any of the slaves move in anything more lively than a worn shuffle. The steps were definitely too light to belong to an ogre.

Robrand had come for him.

He swallowed. He shrank back into Ekhaas's cell. The hobgoblin's ears twitched. Geth motioned her to silence and closed his eyes for a moment, preparing himself for the confrontation he had been dreading for nearly a decade.

But the footsteps stopped well before the cell and a voice called, "Chain?"

There was a muffled reply, but Geth's eyes sprang open as horror knotted his gut. He knew that voice. Slowly, cautiously, he peered around the edge of the doorframe and down the hallway.

Vennet d'Lyrandar stood with a torch in one hand, wrestling the bar from across the door of Chain's cell with the other. Geth stifled a curse.

Behind him, Ekhaas shifted. "What?" she said, her voice pitched lower than a whisper. "What is it?"

He glanced back, put a finger across his lips, and gave her a shake of his head, then glanced back out into the hall. Vennet looked like a nightmare. His clothes were dirty and stiff with dried blood, his eyes fever bright, his long blond hair tangled and wild, yet at the same time the half-elf stood tall and proud, as if utterly unaware of how he looked. As Geth watched, he hauled the bar away from the cell door and let it fall with a thud that echoed along the hallway, then swung the door wide. "I'll expect the return of a portion of your fee, Chain," he said. "I didn't think you would need rescuing."

Chain emerged from the cell, squinting against the light of the torch while at the same time trying to stare at the sight of Vennet. The bounty hunter looked as shocked as Geth felt. "Vennet, what are you—?" he began, then caught himself and stood up straight. "I'm working on your contract," he said in a tone more like his usual gruffness. "I've followed your target here and come close to capturing her."

Vennet's hand snapped out and slapped the big man. "Don't whistle and call it wind." He gestured to the bar. "Close the door and put that back, then come with me. There might be a use for you yet."

Chain stared at Vennet as if ready to punch him back, but Vennet glared back at him without fear. After a moment, Chain swallowed and looked away, pushing the cell door closed with one hand and reaching for the bar with the other. Geth eased back into the darkness of Ekhaas's cell and listened as he laid it back into place. Two sets of footsteps climbed the stairs. The light of Vennet's torch faded from the hall.

"You look frightened," said Ekhaas.

Geth shook his head. "You have no idea." Horror gnawed at his stomach. What was Vennet doing here?

And if Vennet was here, where was Dah'mir?

The half-elf had moved with some stealth. It didn't sound as if he'd revealed himself to any of the others. Dandra and Singe probably didn't know he was there yet—but Vennet had to know they were in Tzaryan Keep.

Geth pushed himself away from the wall. "I have to go, Ekhaas. I have to find Dandra and Singe."

"Wait! Don't leave me here." Ekhaas leaned forward, rattling the chain that bound her to the wall. Her eyes were frightened, but also piercing. "You don't look like someone who expects to come back."

He hesitated, then growled. He stuck his head out of the cell and glanced at the equipment Lor had left waiting. Hung on the wall beside the ogre's brazier was a black iron key. He snatched it and stepped back to fumble with the collar around Ekhaas's neck.

The key fit into a heavy lock. Geth gave it a twist and the collar snapped open. "There," he said. "Make the most of it."

Leaping out of the cell, he grabbed the torch that had been left behind and raced down the hall. At the bottom of the stairs, he paused, looking up and searching the shadows for any sign of Vennet's torch. There was none. Either the half-elf was far ahead of him or had turned aside. Geth went bounding up the stairs as fast as he could, taking two tall steps at a time.

Just as he reached the upper corridor that led to the ogre barracks, however, a bulky figure stepped out of the shadows and into his path. Geth bared his teeth and raised his gauntlet before he recognized Chuut. He staggered to a stop on the last step below the corridor. "Chuut," he said, "have you seen Singe—I mean, Master Timin?"

Chuut looked down at him, his chin resting against his chest, and shook his head solemnly. "No," he said, shaping the word as carefully as always.

Desperation put an idea in Geth's head. "What about the General?" he asked. "Have you seen him? Do you know where I can find him?" Normally he wouldn't have even considered going to Robrand for help, especially now that his secret was out in the open. Even if Robrand had no love for him, though, the old man would try to stay the moons for Singe.

And this time, Chuut nodded. "Go that way," he said, pointing. He stepped back out of Geth's way.

"Tak!" Geth climbed up the last step and turned.

Just down the corridor, Robrand waited with his arms crossed and his eyes hard. Geth stopped still, startled.

Something moved in the corner of his eye. He started to turn, to lift his gauntlet, but Chuut's mace was faster. The heavy weapon slammed into his head just behind his left ear and sent him reeling into a wall. His torch fell out of his hands and rolled across the floor. Geth tried to clutch at the stones, to keep himself on his feet, but they slid away from him. Shadows swirled in the corridor. Ogre hands seized his arms and legs—Chuut to his right and Lor to his left. He shook his head and roared. Or tried to. With a coordinated precision, Chuut and Lor swung him head-first into the wall. Shadows collapsed down onto him.

He heard footsteps, heard a cold voice say, "Follow me," and felt movement. His body tilted—the ogres were taking him back down the stairs. He raised his head and blinked. Shadows gave way to hazy shapes of light and dark. He saw two of everything. Two of Chuut. Two of Lor. Two of the back of Robrand's head. Two of the torch the old man had picked up.

Two of Ekhaas as she crouched against a wall, her sword in her hands, scraps of frayed rope at her feet. Robrand and the ogres stopped. "Well," said Robrand. "Geth, you were busy." He gestured to Ekhaas. "If you can get out of Tzaryan Keep without being seen, you're free. You're of more use to me if you're not here."

"We could just kill her," said Chuut. Ekhaas stiffened.

"It's not worth the fight." Robrand flicked his hand sharply. "Go, Ekhaas!"

The hobgoblin's ears drew back in suspicion, but she slid around to one side of the old man. Geth tried to focus on her, to beg for her help as she eased past Lor, but neither his eyes nor his voice seemed to work so well. Ekhaas paused though and glanced back at Robrand.

"Give me his sword," she said.

"Take it," said Robrand. He turned his back on her, fixing the torch in a bracket, and stepped into the cell where she had been imprisoned. Geth felt Ekhaas reach forward and draw the ancient Dhakaani sword from his scabbard—then heard her dash away into the shadows and up the stairs.

"Bring him!" Robrand called.

Chuut and Lor heaved Geth in Ekhaas's cell. His throbbing head lolled but Chuut held it upright as Lor locked the collar around his neck.

"Look at me, Geth," ordered Robrand.

Geth's eyes rolled up and he looked at his old commander from under his eyebrows. Robrand stood as stiff as he had on parade or at memorial services. His face was like ice. All of the cold words, all of the harsh glances Geth had felt from him on the road to Tzaryan Keep—none of them could match the expression Robrand wore at that moment.

Geth tried to look away. Ogre fingers twined through his thick hair and wrenched his head up again. Robrand's lips twisted. "You were going to disappear, Geth," he said. "I was going to tell Etan that you'd run away. He would have believed that. But this—this is better. It's legitimate." He tugged on the hem of his coat, straightening the garment. "Tzaryan doesn't like people who release his prisoners. Didn't I tell you not to cross him?"

He didn't take his eyes of Geth, but he raised his voice in command. "Lor, you can soften him up—he's tough—but don't do anything serious." His eyes bored into Geth's. "I have a list of names I've been holding onto for nine years and I want to be sure he hears every one of them."

Robrand turned away.

"Dah'mir!" Geth tried to croak after him. "Tell Singe Dah'mir—"

The old man didn't look back. Strong hands bashed Geth's head back against the wall once more and this time the shadows swallowed him entirely.

CHAPTER

15

Dandra didn't need psionic skills to read Singe's emotions. He wore his anger and hatred openly. Red blotches colored his face, stark against the pale skin of his cheeks, forehead, and neck.

None of them said anything as they climbed up the stairs from the dungeon, heading to the upper levels of Tzaryan Keep. Even once they'd reached the light, they kept their silence. Natrac's face was hard. Orshok and Ashi looked like they didn't know what to say or how to react. Dandra didn't think she could blame them. She wasn't sure herself. Only the night before she'd told Geth that whatever he'd done in Narath, he'd proved himself to her. She wanted to think that nothing had changed, that she still trusted the man who had come to her aid more than once.

Except that something had changed. Singe's words haunted her. "More than a thousand people died because of what he did. Geth killed the Frostbrand. Geth killed Narath."

And Geth confirmed it

More than a thousand people.

I remember reading about Narath, said Tetkashtai. *Even in the depths of the War it was horrible. Karrnath was usually tightlipped about its defeats, but I think King Kaius wanted all of Khorvaire to know what Aundair had done.*

Her voice was brittle. Tzaryan Keep had worn her down. Dandra could feel it too now. Singe's revelation couldn't have come at a worse time. Hard on the heels of their discoveries in Taruuzh Kraat and of the terrible dangers Ekhaas's story had revealed, it was almost too much. She felt as though she was a knife blade that had been ground too fine and might snap if struck too hard.

The halls and courtyards of Tzaryan Keep seemed even more discomforting and quiet than they had before. Singe led them from one passage to another, looking for Tzaryan. The best he managed was to get them back to the top of the broad stairs down to the keep's gates. As the wizard glared at the stairs and cursed—the color in his cheeks rising even higher—Dandra clenched her teeth and stepped up to him.

"Singe," she said, "maybe you need to—"

"Maybe I need to what?" He whirled on her. "Give him another chance? Forgive him?"

Dandra stared at him, shocked by the sudden outburst. She took a step back. A cold anger ran along her back. "Maybe you need," she said, "to ask for directions."

The others stared at them both. Singe stiffened. Dandra thought she saw a flicker of shame in his eyes, but he didn't back down. "Ask who?" he demanded. He turned away to look around with angry eyes. "Twelve moons, this place is a tomb."

Natrac was looking around as well. "You're right," he said. "Where is everyone?"

"Twilight," said a deep voice from above them, "is a shift change here at Tzaryan Keep. Those who walked the day take their beds; those who will patrol the night are rising."

Dandra twisted around and looked up to see Tzaryan Rrac drifting down from an upper window as easily as a human might walk down a flight of stairs. The ogre mage's expression was calm, but curious. "You're still armed, Master Timin," he said as his boots touched the stones of the floor. "You haven't forgotten our agreement? You're to join me for dinner. I was just looking for you."

Singe wallowed his anger with a visible effort and bowed low. "Our apologies, Lord Tzaryan. We were looking for you as well when we lost our way."

"Then this is a fortunate meeting. Allow me to be your guide to the dining hall. Our meal will be ready very soon." Tzaryan bent his head and offered Dandra his hand. "Kirvakri?"

Dinner was perhaps the farthest thing from Dandra's mind, but it didn't seem that they had any choice but to accept Tzaryan's invitation. She shot a glance at Singe. He gave her a quick nod. She reached up and placed her hand in Tzaryan's.

The ogre mage's grip was surprisingly gentle, as though he was used to handling delicate things, but her fingers still disappeared between his. He turned, guiding them back the way they had come with Dandra on his right and Singe on his left. Ashi, Orshok, and Natrac fell in behind. "You're tense, lovely kalashtar," he said.

"We've had an . . . eventful day," Dandra answered.

Tzaryan nodded. "I apologize for the trespasser that troubled you in the ruins. Do you know him?"

She wondered briefly what report Robrand had given Tzaryan. She tried to exchange another glance with Singe, but with Tzaryan between them it was impossible. "One of our guards had things in his past we didn't know about," she said—then winced at the truth behind her own lie.

"I was in my observatory and saw what happened," he said. "Such things usually don't happen in my domain. I'm pleased the General was in a position to help you." He glanced over his shoulder and his black eyes narrowed. "The shifter isn't with you."

"No, my lord," said Singe. "We left him in your dungeon."

A gash of a smile opened on Tzaryan's face. "Were the things in his past that bad?"

Singe was silent. Dandra found she couldn't even manage a false smile. Tzaryan looked back and forth between them. "A joke," he said.

"I'm re-evaluating his service to me," Singe replied. "For now, he's standing guard over Ekhaas."

They stepped into a long room lined with tall wooden columns painted the same green as the tiles of the keep's roofs. Between some of the columns, corridors opened, leading deeper into the keep. Between others were mounted the trophies of a warlord: battered swords and shields, a suit of armor with a crest Dandra didn't recognize, another with a crest that she did—the emblem of the Church of the Silver Flame. She tried to ignore them, to pay attention to their ogre mage host. Tzaryan looked down at Singe as they walked. "That's unnecessary. If you were in my dungeon, you've seen that the cells are quite secure. I'll send one of my servants to fetch him for dinner."

Singe hesitated. When he spoke again, his voice was cautious.

"He's not trying to prevent her escape, Lord Tzaryan. He's watching over her. The General dismissed Lor, but we were concerned he might come back—"

Tzaryan's eyes narrowed and his grip on Dandra's hand tightened slightly. He cut Singe off. "Lor? What was Lor doing there?"

Dandra heard the wizard hesitate again and wished that she could escape Tzaryan's grasp.

Singe recovered himself quickly. "When the General took our attacker to the dungeons, we went along with the intent of speaking to Ekhaas as you and I had agreed, my lord. We found Lor getting ready to . . . ah . . ." He swallowed as pretty words failed him. "Torture her."

"Lor started without my permission?" The ogre mage's voice was like distant thunder. "I'll whip him for this!"

In Dandra's head, Tetkashtai stirred uneasily. *Something's wrong,* she said. Her yellow-green glow arced and snapped like captured lightning. *Dandra, something's wrong!*

Suspicion sank into Dandra as well. *I think you're right,* she told Tetkashtai. Robrand had said that Tzaryan had ordered Lor to begin torturing Ekhaas. But if Tzaryan hadn't known that Lor was in the dungeon . . .

"Perhaps I misunderstood what he was doing, my lord," said Singe. "I'm sure the General had a better explanation for what we saw when we—"

"I'll be certain to ask him," Tzaryan said. He quickened his pace, releasing Dandra's hand. She snatched it away as the implications of the ogre mage's words settled into her. Robrand had left them in the dungeon with Ekhaas to go and report to Tzaryan—but it almost sounded as if Tzaryan hadn't seen him.

Robrand had lied to them. Twice. Why?

Dandra, Tetkashtai said urgently, *listen to me! Do you feel—*

Not now, Tetkashtai! Dandra took a step back, moving a little closer to Ashi and Orshok as Singe hurried to keep pace with Tzaryan.

"My lord," the wizard said, "the point is that we spoke with Ekhaas and she co-operated with us. She told us what we wanted to know about the ruins. We agreed that if she spoke, you wouldn't have her tortured."

"I recall our agreement." Tzaryan nodded. "Very well. She won't be tortured. You have my word."

Singe relaxed, but only slightly. "My lord, what she had to say was extremely helpful to us. Her attempt to follow us from Vralkek was nothing by comparison—it's forgiven. Would you consider letting her go free?"

Tzaryan stopped and turned to look down at Singe. His lips drew back from his square black teeth. Dandra caught her breath. Holding back Tetkashtai's frightened ravings, she reached out to brush her mind against Ashi's and Orshok's. *Stay alert!* she warned them. *Something is going on here!*

Tetkashtai lunged for the mental opening of the *kesh*. *It's not Tzaryan!* she shrieked. *Listen to me—*

Ashi flinched at the presence's sudden outburst. Orshok's hand tightened around his hunda stick. Dandra cursed and hauled back on Tetkashtai, reining her in like a runaway horse. *Tetkashtai, be quiet!*

The warning and Tetkashtai's outburst had taken scant heartbeats. Tzaryan still stared down at Singe while the wizard did his best to look strong yet optimistic. Tzaryan's eyes flickered. "After dinner," he said finally. "Let us discuss the matter after dinner like civilized folk." He stood straight.

Singe took a long breath and stood straight as well. He nodded slowly. "Certainly, my lord." Tzaryan held out his hand, gesturing for Singe to continue along the hall. The wizard bent his head and the pair resumed their progress. The need to reach out to Singe with the *kesh* and offer him her warning as well burned in Dandra, but she didn't dare. Tetkashtai's ravings had become a desperate, mad struggle that took all of her concentration to maintain. She shouted at the presence, but Tetkashtai seemed beyond hearing.

The long hall ended in a pair of tall doors as green as the columns. Two orcs stood ready beside the doors. Tzaryan beckoned one forward. "Go to the dungeon," he told him. "Tell the shifter that Ekhaas is safe and that he is summoned to dinner. Guide him here." He frowned. "If you see the General, tell him that he is summoned to dinner as well."

"There's no need." Robrand came striding out of one of the corridors that opened onto the hall. Chuut was close behind him. Robrand's face was set in a stony mask. He marched up to Tzaryan and dropped down on one knee. "Lord Tzaryan, I've just come from the dungeon. Ekhaas and the shifter are both gone. He helped her escape." He glanced sideways at Singe and added, "Whatever trust you had in him, he broke it."

Singe's body stiffened as if someone were holding his feet and his neck and stretching them apart. His eyes opened wide, staring at Robrand with an angry intensity. His lip curled. He trembled. "No," he breathed—then he flung his head back and screamed, "Twelve bloody moons! Geth, you hairy traitor!"

Abruptly, everyone was talking at once. Robrand was on his feet, explaining to Tzaryan how he'd gone down to the dungeon only to find Ekhaas's cell empty and that a preliminary search of the keep had turned up nothing. "I doubt they're even here any longer," he said. "Ekhaas probably used magic to get them past the guards at the gate. I'm organizing patrols now. We'll find them."

Singe was ranting, stomping back and forth in the hall, his hand clenched around the hilt of his rapier. "I'll kill him!" he spat, his voice seething. "This time I *will* kill him. Devourer take him, I knew I couldn't trust him."

Orshok and Natrac leaped forward, trying to calm Singe down and defending Geth. "Why would he do it?" Orshok asked. "If he ran, it was because you drove him away!" shouted Natrac. Nothing they said had any effect beyond, however, making the din in the hall even louder. Singe thrust them aside and stormed up to Robrand and Tzaryan, demanding a place in any hunt. Tetkashtai was still wailing and pleading in Dandra's head, adding her penetrating voice to the chaos.

Dandra pressed her hands over her ears and clenched her teeth. A hand touched her shoulder. Dandra whirled to find Ashi standing at her side, her pierced lips drawn tight in concern.

"What's wrong? the hunter asked.

"It's too much," Dandra choked. "I can't think. Tetkashtai's gone—"

"Enough!" roared Tzaryan. His bellow rolled through the hall, silencing Singe and Robrand, sending Natrac and Orshok flinching back, bringing Chuut to stiff alertness, and tearing a frightened shriek out of one of the orc slaves. Even Tetkashtai

seemed shocked into a quiet whimper. Tzaryan's black-eyed gaze raked them all. His fingers stabbed out, pointing at the orcs. "You," he said, "leave us." The orcs fled as if pursued by hounds. Tzaryan turned to Chuut. "You—find a patrol and join it." The ogre nodded and turned for one of the other side corridors.

Tzaryan looked to Robrand and Singe, standing together with near identical expressions of cold anger on their faces, then to the others. "All of you—" He tugged on his robes, straightening them. "—will join me for dinner."

"With respect, Lord Tzaryan," Singe said, "unless you're serving roast of shifter, I've lost my appetite."

"Silence!" Tzaryan's hands jerked as he shouted into Singe's face. The crimson fabric of his robes tore under his grip, leaving everyone staring at wide rips through which blue-green showed like bone through a bloody injury. Tzaryan's teeth ground down. Slowly and deliberately, he pulled the ruined garment back together. "Dinner," he said with a horrible calm. "Now."

He stepped up to one of the doors at the end of the hall and gestured for the General to take the other, then stared at Singe. The wizard drew a harsh breath, then bent his head in grudging submission. Tzaryan glanced at Robrand and the old man nodded obediently. Tzaryan's grip tightened on the handle—

—just as Tetkashtai's voice rose in a howl above the silence of the moment. *Open yourself, Dandra, you stupid dahr! Think like a kalashtar for once and listen to me!* Her light coalesced, then burst across Dandra's mind like a slap in the face.

Dandra jerked, startled, and for an instant the walls she had erected in her mind to blot out Tetkashtai shivered and thinned—and Dandra felt the questing touch of another presence against her mind. It wasn't an active, probing touch like that of Medala or a mind flayer, but rather something passive, like the pull of waves on an ocean. She wanted to go to it, to enter the waves even though they could be her doom.

She knew the feel of that presence. She knew what had kept Tetkashtai on edge in Tzaryan Keep. She understood what Tetkashtai had been trying to warn her about—and why Tzaryan was so insistent they accompany him. Dandra gasped and grabbed Ashi's arm with a desperate strength. "Ashi, run! It's—"

The warning came too late. The green doors were moving,

swinging wide, to reveal a courtyard entirely open along one long side to the fiery sky of evening. In the courtyard sat Dah'mir, the setting sun turning his scales copper and gleaming on the Khyber dragonshard—now restored—that was embedded in the center of his chest. There was nothing of the weakness that Geth had described seeing in Zarash'ak about him. He looked strong and fit. Along the wall of the courtyard, black herons perched like a crowd gathered to watch an execution.

"Finally," said Dah'mir, "I thought you'd never come."

Tetkashtai's wails rose into a piercing scream as the power of the dragon's presence enveloped them. Dimly Dandra saw Orshok raise his hunda stick, saw Singe rip his rapier from his scabbard. She strained, fighting against the fascination that dug into her mind, straining to find some thought or power that would shield her, but Dah'mir's presence was overwhelming—

Strong, lean arms wrapped around her, snatching her off the floor, throwing her over a tanned shoulder. Long hair woven with wooden beads whirled around her, and feet pounded the floor in long strides as Ashi seized on her warning and ran.

Dah'mir's howl of startled rage followed them.

CHAPTER

16

A grunt and rapid footsteps were all the warning that Singe had. Dah'mir's gaze focused past him and the dragon roared in frustration. Herons rose into the sky in a flurry of black wings. Up so close, the sound was deafening. Singe staggered against it, but managed to twist around in time to see Ashi dart down one of the side corridors that opened off the long hall, carrying Dandra—dazed from even the brief exposure to Dah'mir's awe-inspiring presence—over her shoulder. The hunter had the right idea. Singe's rapier felt like a toy in his hand, the most powerful spell at his disposal a candleflame.

"Run!" he shouted at Natrac and Orshok.

But it was already too late for them. Dah'mir's roar fell silent and even over the ringing in his ears, Singe heard the rasp of the dragon's inhaled breath. Dread pierced him. Dah'mir's head whipped forward and his mouth opened. Singe whirled, trying to cover his face as if that would protect him from the dragon's acid venom. Except that no acid came—instead of searing liquid, Dah'mir's breath billowed around them, warm and wet. The taste of copper seeped into Singe's mouth and nostrils and across his tongue. Abruptly the air seemed thick. It dragged on him, impeding his every sluggish move. He turned back, looked up.

Orshok and Natrac had been caught in the dragon's strange breath as well. They moved with such agonizing slowness that it looked almost as if they were swimming. By comparison, Dah'mir's movements were fluid and lightning fast. Even his voice crackled in

Singe's ears, bellowing frustration turned sharp and staccato.

Further down the hall, Chuut and half a dozen other ogres burst out from one of the side corridors, weapons drawn and alarm on their faces—alarm that only grew deeper at the sight of Dah'mir in the courtyard. One of the ogres gave a yelp of terror and staggered back, but Tzaryan was already shouting terse orders in the ogres' deep language. Chuut recovered himself with the discipline of House Deneith training. Slapping at his squad, he drove them on across the hall and toward the corridor down which Ashi had turned.

Herons were settling back onto the walls of the courtyard. Robrand was still standing frozen against the door he had opened, staring at Dah'mir in shock. His mouth worked in silent motion before he managed to force out words. "Dol Dorn's mighty fist—!"

"Collect yourself, General!" said Tzaryan. "Dah'mir is our guest." The ogre mage turned to the dragon. "My ogres will bring them back. They won't escape."

"See that they don't." Dah'mir's head turned. "Don't just stand there. This lethargy won't last long. Seize them!"

To Dah'mir's left, two figures emerged from the shadows to reach for Natrac and Orshok. One was Vennet, though the half-elf's bloodstained clothes and bright, mad eyes scarcely matched Singe's last glimpse of him. Behind him was Chain, freed from his cell in the dungeon. And to Dah'mir's right . . .

A cold sweat broke out on Singe's skin. At first all he saw were licking, flickering flames and glowing embers, stark against the night, then he saw past the brightness. He stared at a burning corpse, risen from ashes. And not just any corpse. Tongues of flame took the place of tendrils and tentacles. Charred flesh marked hollows in an eyeless face. Below them, a thin mouth twisted in hate.

"No," Singe croaked. "You're dead."

Hruucan lunged forward, fiery shoulder tentacles lashing through the air. Singe tried to raise his rapier. He could feel the sluggishness inflicted by Dah'mir's breath already starting to pass, but Hruucan had been faster than him before and now he seemed to move like the wind. One extended tentacle whirled past Singe's face. The wizard lifted his rapier higher—and the other tentacle slammed across his belly.

The ring that he wore on his left hand glittered greedily, devouring the heat of the flame before it could burn him, just as it had protected him from the fiery spell he had used to kill the dolgaunt. There was more than fire in Hruucan's blow, though. The tentacle punched into his gut and seemed to wrench something out of him. A sudden flash of weakness that he felt in his very core sent him staggering back. Hruucan's tentacles whirled up for another strike.

"Hruucan!" snapped Dah'mir. The dragon's wings flapped and furled, sending a gust of wind across the courtyard. His herons stirred in an echo of his irritation. "I said seize, not attack!"

The dolgaunt froze like a serpent. "I've waited, Dah'mir! Give me my revenge!"

"Wait a little longer," Dah'mir said.

Singe saw Robrand swallow, then dart forward. With swift efficiency, he grabbed Singe's arm before anyone else could. Still reeling from the dolgaunt's attack, Singe couldn't put up any resistance. Robrand seized his arm and twisted it in a lock—for a moment bringing his lips close to Singe's ear.

"I didn't know about this!" he whispered quickly. "Dol Arrah's oath, Etan, I swear it!"

Singe forced himself to suck in breath. "Help us!" he answered in a soft gasp. When Robrand reached for his rapier to disarm him, he let him take it.

"I have this one, my lord," the old man said out loud. Tzaryan nodded his approval. Hruucan hissed, but backed down.

Chain had Orshok in his grasp and the druid's hunda stick was on the ground. Vennet held Natrac at the end of his cutlass. His eyes flashed merrily. "Like old times, Natrac," he said. "I like the knife. Very ingenious."

"*Da ga shek erat,*" Orshok snarled.

Vennet's face hardened. "Watch your tongue. I'd be happy to set you up for a matching set of cutlery."

He fell silent as a rumble grew out of Dah'mir's belly. The dragon rose and paced forward. Singe could feel every footfall through the stone floor. Dah'mir looked down on them. "There's one unaccounted for," he said. "Where's Geth?"

Tzaryan repeated Robrand's news of Geth's flight with Ekhaas. The rumble deepened. "Find him for me, Tzaryan," said Dah'mir.

"I owe him a special debt." He lowered his head until his eyes stared into Singe's. "It was a mistake coming here, Singe. Once I learned where you were going, I knew exactly what you were trying to do."

Singe shivered as Dah'mir's acrid breath whispered across his face. From the corner of his eye, he saw Orshok turn pale. "How did you know we were coming here?" the young orc asked. There was fear in his face. Singe felt an echo of it. Who knew they had been headed to Tzaryan Keep—or even that they were looking for the Spires of the Forge? Had Dah'mir found Bava after all? Had he somehow tracked down Batul and Krepis?

Vennet answered for the dragon. "A good sailor obeys his captain," he said. His lips twitched slightly. "Karth was a good sailor in the end."

The crusted blood that stained Vennet's clothes. *"Lightning on Water . . ."* Singe breathed.

Vennet turned his smile on him. ". . . never made it to Sharn," he finished for him. "Although I'm sure Marolis still had her on course right up until I split him open."

Dread and disgust squeezed Singe's chest. "Twelve moons, Vennet, your own crew? Your ship?"

"A ship?" Vennet's voice rose and broke. "What need do I have of a ship when soon I'll have command of the wind itself?" He shrugged with his free arm and his open shirt slipped down to expose part of his shoulders and back. "Do you see the power of the Dragon Below? My dragonmark grows. By the blessing of the master of my master, I will bear the Siberys Mark of Storm!"

Singe felt Robrand stiffen and mutter a curse of disgust. Orshok looked away. The bright pattern of Vennet's dragonmark was red and inflamed, as if he had been scratching at it. Patches were crusted with scabs. An open sore over his shoulder blade oozed thin liquid and pus. If the mark had actually grown, though, Singe couldn't see it.

Dah'mir's blunt muzzle opened in something like a grin. "I hope you found what you were looking for in Taruuzh Kraat. Do you think it was worth the price?"

A spark of anger rekindled itself in Singe's gut. He clenched his jaw and met the dragon's gaze with grim determination. "We found Marg's device and his ravings. We know Taruuzh's story."

He narrowed his eyes and added, "We know that the magic of the binding stone is the same magic that defeated the Master of Silence. Your master."

Less than an armslength from his face, teeth larger than knives clashed together. "Ironic," Dah'mir said, "isn't it? My master's servants will be born from his defeat."

Singe forced himself to stand tall when every instinct urged him to cower. "The binding stone that Marg made is broken. Dandra smashed it."

"So I have found." Dah'mir's eyes shone. "But I studied the great stone for two hundred years. I understand the magic better than Marg ever did and I have centuries more to perfect it. I will create another."

"If you could," said Singe, "you would have already."

Dah'mir reared back with a furious roar. Hruucan looked enraged at Singe's defiance. His fiery tentacles struck the air like angry serpents and he lunged forward, but one of Dah'mir's thick legs slammed down between him and Singe with such force that the stones underfoot cracked. Hruucan reeled away. Singe staggered, falling back against Robrand. Dah'mir glared down at him. "I didn't have Dandra and Tektashtai to study before."

Singe swallowed and staggered back to his feet. "You still don't!"

"Be glad of that," Dah'mir said, grinding the words between his teeth, "or I would already have given you to Hruucan."

The sound of heavy running echoed from the side corridor down which Chuut and his squad had pursued Ashi and Dandra. Moments later, the ogres burst into the long hall. Dandra and Ashi weren't with them. Chuut slid to a stop and dropped to one knee before Tzaryan. "My lord, they tricked us. We lost them."

For a moment, Singe felt a surge of hope. Dah'mir's growl rumbled on the air. Tzaryan looked furious—and embarassed. "General, take command. I'll take charge of your prisoner," the ogre mage said, striding forward. Singe's heart froze as he reached for him. "Turn the patrols you have looking for Ekhaas and Geth and set them after Dandra and Ashi. I want the keep searched—"

"No," said Dah'mir.

Tzaryan paused in midstride. "Dah'mir?"

"Searching will take too much time. I want Dandra found now."
The dragon eased himself back. His eyes flashed. "Chain!"

The big man flinched. Dah'mir glared at him. "Earn your
rescue. You carry the Mark of Finding—find me Dandra!"

Dandra was dimly aware of the corridor that Ashi ran down,
twisting and turning around corners, flashing from torchlight to
shadow and back to torchlight. She was somewhat more aware of the
discomfort as the hunter's shoulder dug into her belly with each
swift pace. She also knew that Singe and the others weren't with
them—that while Ashi's quick reactions might have saved the two
of them, the others had been left behind to face Dah'mir's wrath,
caught by Tzaryan's treachery. There wasn't anything she could do
about it, though. The farther they fled from Dah'mir, the more her
head cleared, sloughing off the shroud of the dragon's influence.
Unfortunately, her release was Tetkashtai's release as well.

She felt like a tiny vessel on the middle of an ocean storm as
her creator raged around her. *Tetkashtai!* Dandra shouted, trying
to calm her down. *Tetkashtai!*

Her thoughts were butterflies to the hurricane of Tetkashtai's
terror and Dandra felt a flash of fear herself. Back in Zarash'ak,
she'd told Singe that every episode of panic seemed to take the
presence closer to the brink of true madness. Abandoning
any effort to soothe Tetkashtai, she wrenched herself away. Or
attempted to. It was like trying to rip a limb from between the
teeth of a beast. Tetkashtai shrieked, dragging her back. In
desperation, Dandra drew up a memory of Dah'mir—acid-green
eyes shining—and flung it at her.

Tetkashtai's screams rose and she flinched back. Dandra
slammed the gates of her mind, trapping the presence outside
them. Echoes of Tetkashtai's terror rang in her ears. Dandra threw
her will against them and blocked them out. For a moment, her
thoughts were her own.

And she realized that Ashi's footsteps weren't the only ones
she could hear.

Dandra raised her head and tried to look behind them. Far
back, a squad of ogres swung around a corner. One—Chuut, she
realized—saw them and let out a deep shout.

"Il-Yannah," Dandra cursed. She twisted around in Ashi's grip. "Ashi! Let me down!"

"Wait." Dandra whirled in the air as Ashi slid around another corner—

—and came to a sharp stop. *"Rond betch!"* she spat and swung Dandra off her shoulder. Dandra turned around and stared.

The passage continued on but the torches they had followed were gone. The corridor ahead was pitch dark. To their right, stairs plunged down into darkness as well. To their left, a stout door stood closed. Ashi snarled and whirled, staring at their options with wild eyes. "We can't go on. Even if we had a torch, the ogres would see the light!"

Dandra spun to the door, reaching for the handle. There was no way of knowing what lay beyond it, but at least it was a hiding place—but if the ogres *didn't* see a light retreating down either the darkened hallway or the stairs, wouldn't the door be the first place they'd look? Her hand dropped. She turned back to Ashi. A glance at the hunter's face told her that she had realized the same thing.

Ashi had her spear clutched in her hand. She thrust it at her and Dandra took it, raising her chin in determination. Ashi bared her teeth and drew her sword, the bright blade shining in the dim light. Neither of them said anything. The pounding footsteps of their pursuers closed in. Dandra moved to face the turn in the corridor, stepping up onto the air and skimming the ground, ready to fight. Raising a hand, she reached into herself to call up the fierce energy of whitefire. The first ogre around the corner was going to burn.

Instead of whitefire's droning chorus, all that filled her was Tetkashtai's mad terror. It lanced through her, tearing a gasp from her throat as she fought it back. She stumbled, her feet dropping hard to the ground. Ashi's hand whipped out and caught her before she could fall.

"Dandra!"

Dandra shook her head, struggling to clear her mind. "It's Tetkashtai!" She tried to summon the concentration to lift herself off the ground once more, but the presence was like a drowning person, dragging on her mind. Dandra beat her back, but yellow-green light seemed to force itself into the corners of her eyes. Through the glare, she saw Ashi swing toward the sound of the approaching ogres like a cornered animal.

To their side, the door that they had seen and rejected as a hiding place swung open. Ekhaas leaned out through the door frame, gesturing for them. "Inside! Quickly!"

Ashi snarled, but Dandra shoved her toward the door. She felt no trust for the hobgoblin, but Ekhaas was no friend to the treacherous Tzaryan Rrac—and if Robrand was right, at least Geth had found some reason to set her free. "In!"

"The ogres will look in here!" the hunter said.

"No, they won't." Ekhaas reached out and grabbed her arm, hauling her through the door. Dandra slipped through on her heels. The hobgoblin held the door open for a moment longer. Her free hand gestured and Dandra caught a snatch of deep, swelling song. Two flickering lights flared over her palm. With a quick motion, Ekhaas hurled them into the darkness of the hallway, then pulled the door almost shut, leaving it open just enough to peer out. Through that thin crack, Dandra could just see Ekhaas's lights receding down the dark passage—exactly like torches carried by running fugitives.

The sound of heavy footsteps and ogre voices filled the corridor outside. Dandra heard Chuut give another shout and order the ogres onward. In moments, their pursuers had hurtled past them.

"Quickly," said Ekhaas. "We don't have much time. The lights won't last long. Down the stairs. Take my hand and I'll guide you." She pushed the door wide, then reached back and grabbed something from the shadows. The dim light in the hallway struck flashes of purple from a heavy byeshk sword. Geth's sword.

Fear and anger rose in Dandra's throat. Her spear darted forward, point quivering a finger's width from Ekhaas's side. "What's going on here?" Dandra hissed. "Where's Geth? The General said he and you fled together!"

Ekhaas didn't move, though her yellow eyes narrowed and her ears twitched back. "The General lies. Geth is in Tzaryan's dungeon—with Lor."

Dandra blinked. Ekhaas's breath hissed. She pushed Dandra's spear away, then stretched out her hand. Out of sight down the corridor, ogre voices rose in confusion. Ekhaas's ears flicked.

"Decide! Geth is in danger. You have my word on that."

Dandra glanced at Ashi. The hunter's eyes were hard and suspicious, but she nodded. Dandra clenched her teeth and took Ekhaas's hand. "We're all in danger."

"Be silent until I tell you it's safe." Ekhaas led them—Dandra's hand in hers, Ashi's hand on the shaft of Dandra's spear—across the corridor and down the stairs. The light of the hallway vanished. In the dark, the oversized steps of the stairs were even more treacherous, but Ekhaas descended with rapid urgency. They reached the bottom just as the sound of Chuut and his ogres echoed again along the corridor above. Ekhaas shoved Dandra and Ashi back against a wall and let go off Dandra's hand. Once again, the hobgoblin sang and two more tongues of flame, identical to the first two, appeared above her palm. This time, however, the flick of Ekhaas's hand left them hanging in the air at the bottom of the stairs. Dandra choked back a curse. Ekhaas was going to draw the ogres right to them!

Up above, harsh words became excited at the sight of the flames below. Footsteps started down the stairs—only to stop at a command from Chuut. An argument erupted, then ended with the sound of a closed fist on a thick skull. Chuut growled another command and heavy footsteps charged away, back along the corridor in the direction they had all first come.

In the lights of the flames, Dandra could see Ekhaas's face. Her ears stood high and she looked pleased with herself. From behind Dandra, Ashi said softly, "Are you mad? You almost brought them right after us!"

Ekhaas gave a disdainful snort. "You don't speak their language, do you? For an ogre, Chuut is smart—but not that smart. I knew he'd think the lights were just another distraction. We're safe for now."

"If we're safe," Dandra said, "I want an explanation now. What's going on?"

"Listen while we move." Ekhaas moved away from the wall and started along the lower hallway. The dancing lights she had brought into being moved with her, forcing Dandra and Ashi to stay with her as well or be left behind in the dark.

By the smell in the air, Dandra could tell that they were back in the hallway that led to the ogre barracks. She tried to keep her eyes and ears on the shadows ahead, but as Ekhaas swiftly told them what had happened in the dungeon—of Vennet's sudden appearance and Geth's attempt to warn them, of Robrand's treachery—she found all of her attention on the hobgoblin. Ekhaas's story left her with a sickening hollow in her stomach.

"He was going to torture Geth?" she asked finally.

"By the six kings, I swear it. It sounded like the General wanted revenge on him for something. Maybe the same thing you argued with him about."

"Why did you take his sword?" asked Ashi.

"It's a relic of Dhakaan. I would die rather than let it fall into Tzaryan's hands." She raised at the sword, studying it by the light of dancing flames. "It belongs in the vaults of the Kech Volaar. I should have fled with it."

"But you didn't," Dandra said. "Why? And why help us?"

Ekhaas was silent for a moment, then replied, "Geth told me he brought this sword out of Jhegesh Dol and used it to fight the dragon servant of the Master of Silence. Is that true?"

Dandra frowned, trying to guess why the hobgoblin was asking. "It's true," she said.

"Then your blond friend was wrong to call Geth a coward. No coward could wield this blade—and heroes shouldn't die in chains. Geth won the sword. It belongs to him now." Ekhaas's voice tightened with disgust. "If I took it, I would be a thief. It *must* be returned to him." She looked over her shoulder. "Finding help to free Geth just made going back easier. I know a way out of the keep, but I didn't relish fighting Lor on my own."

"You only rescued us so we could help you rescue Geth?" asked Ashi.

Ekhaas's lips curled. "You are less important than what you can do, *chaat'oor*." Her ears twitched. "Although I would enjoying knowing what you did to offend Tzaryan Rrac."

"Nothing." Dandra ground her teeth together. "Tzaryan betrayed us. Dah'mir is here."

Ekhaas's pace faltered for a moment. "*Khaavolaar.* The dragon? And the rest of you . . . ?"

"Dead? Captives? I don't know." Dandra drew a breath. "This way out of Tzaryan Keep—can you get us all out? Geth, me, and Ashi?"

The words hurt her, left her feeling cold and sick. Fleeing the keep meant leaving Singe, Natrac, and Orshok behind—if they were still alive—but they didn't have much choice. She had no defense against Dah'mir's power, especially with Tetkastai still pounding at her mind as well. Even Ashi and Geth had little hope against the dragon. They needed to regroup, to find out what was going on, before they could come up with a way to rescue the others.

Ekhaas's ears flicked back. "My price is your story. Tell me how Dah'mir stole Marg's stone and what he did with it."

"Done." Dandra felt like a coward.

Just ahead, the glow of torchlight marked the head of another flight of stairs—the stairs down to the dungeon. Ekhaas gestured and her lights vanished. The hobgoblin switched Geth's sword to her left hand and drew her own sword with her right, then crept softly down the stairs. Dandra could hear sounds drifting up from the dungeon: labored breathing, the slow grinding of a blade. She tightened her hand around the shaft of her spear and followed with Ashi at her side.

The door of the cell that had held Ekhaas was open and though a torch in one of the brackets on the wall outside cast the interior into shadow, Dandra recognized Lor's broad back as he crouched over his victim.

The sound of the grinding blade slowed, then stopped. Lor bent down. Ekhaas moved to the open doorway, her sword raised.

With unexpected speed, Lor ducked his head and reared up on his hands like a kicking horse. His thick legs shot back and slammed into Ekhaas's chest in a powerful kick that sent the hobgoblin staggering back. Lor twisted and rolled to his feet, a gleaming knife clutched in one hand, a whetstone in the other giving weight to his fist. He leaped out of the cramped space of the cell and charged, knife slashing, fist swinging.

Ashi pushed past Dandra and surged forward to meet him, her pierced lips twisted in a snarl. Lor punched at her with his left fist, but the hunter just spun inside the reach of his outstretched arm and thrust—once—hard with her sword.

Lor blinked, looked down at the hilt of the blade jammed between his ribs and up into his heart, and toppled over. Ashi grabbed his arm and pulled, twisting him around so that he fell back against a wall instead of face down on the floor. His incredulous expression ended up fixed on the ceiling. Beyond them, Ekhaas rose, one hand clutching her side, her face almost as astounded.

Ashi stared into Lor's unblinking eyes. "So that was fighting an ogre," she said—then snorted. "I was expecting something more."

There was a cry from the cell. "Ashi?" Chains scraped and rattled. "Ashi, help."

Geth's voice, but tight and strained. Dandra shoved Ashi to one side and sprinted for the cell, then caught herself on the doorframe. "Light of il-Yannah!"

Geth sat on the floor of the cell, chained by the neck just as Ekhaas had been when they'd found her, but with his arms chained and stretched up over his head as well. His legs had been tied down to keep him from kicking. He was barechested, his great-gauntlet, coat and shirt stripped off and tossed in a corner. The thick hair on the shifter's torso made it difficult to see the full extent of his injuries, but it didn't look like Lor had started to use his knife on him. Geth held himself awkwardly, though, and his breathing sounded painful. Blood matted the hair on his head and turned his face into a sticky mask. One eye was swollen shut. The other, hazy with pain, fixed on her and cleared sharply.

Geth drew a shuddering breath. "Dandra! Run! Vennet's here. Dah'mir can't be—"

Dandra pressed her lips together and stepped all the way into the cell. "We know," she said. "He's here. Tzaryan betrayed us. Ashi and I barely escaped. Dah'mir's strong again, Geth. That shard you shattered in his chest—it's been replaced."

Geth sagged a little. "What about Orshok? Natrac?" His voice seemed to catch. "Singe?"

She shook her head. "We're going to have to try and come back for them."

The shifter groaned. His head fell forward. "I tried to warn you, but Robrand. He and Chuut ambushed me."

"We know that, too."

Geth raised his head to look at her, then his eye went past her and opened wide. Dandra looked over her shoulder.

Ekhaas stood in the door. Geth bared his teeth and snarled like a wounded animal, but Ekhaas ignored him and held out a key of black iron. "Lor had this. You'll need it."

Dandra took the key and the hobgoblin retreated. Geth stared after her. "What's she doing here?"

"She helped us so that we could help you. She's got your sword." Dandra knelt at Geth's side and looked him in the eye. The shifter stared back at her with an expression that was halfway between defiance and fear.

After a moment, the defiance fell away, replaced by a bleak loss that left Dandra more shaken that rage or hatred could have. "Dandra," Geth said before she could speak, "I—"

"You snapped at me."

"I'm sorry." He turned his face away.

The motion left the lock on the collar exposed. Dandra reached forward and shoved the key inside, giving it a hard turn. Geth stiffened as if she had prodded him. The lock sprang open and she pulled the collar away. Geth stared at her. Dandra pressed her brow to his bloody, sticky forehead. "I didn't know you nine years ago, Geth. But I know you now and I'd trust you with my life."

He didn't say anything and his body didn't relax, but when she sat back, she could see that the bleakness was gone from his wide eyes. He looked at her in astonishment. Dandra gave him a smile and turned to the manacle that held his right arm—the same key fit the lock on it. "I think there's something you're not saying," she said.

The astonishment in his eyes hardened. He bared his teeth again. "You heard what Singe said."

"I heard what Singe said, but all I heard from you was 'yes.' I don't know the whole story." She looked at him. "Did Adolan know? Did he know everything?"

Geth's hand slid free from the manacle—and went to the collar of black stones at his throat. He nodded. Dandra smiled. "Then for now, that's good enough for me."

Freeing his other arm and then his legs was the work of moments. Getting him on his feet was more difficult. He was unsteady and his legs were weak. When he sat forward, Dandra saw that the blood that covered his face was nothing compared to what had gushed from his scalp at the back of his head. His hairy back was streaked with red like an artist's canvas. "Ashi!" Dandra called. "We need your help."

The hunter squeezed into the cell. Between the two of them, they got Geth up and out of the cramped space. Ekhaas's ears drew back, however, when she saw the shifter, and she uttered a curse in Goblin. Dandra knew how she felt—Geth's injuries weren't going to make it any easier to get out of Tzaryan Keep. "We could use Orshok's healing prayers right now," she said.

Ekhaas's ears flicked. "I can help a little." She put a hand against Geth's chest, narrowed her eyes in concentration, and chanted a few sonorous words. The snatch of song tugged on Dandra, something utterly different than Orshok's prayers. When the druid worked magic, nature seemed to stir in response, its power flowing through him. Something stirred in response to Ekhaas's song as well, but somehow it felt much more energetic, old yet active, an echo of the primal song of the world. Geth's eyes—both of them—opened wide and he drew a sharp, deep breath. He stiffened, all but jumping out of Ashi's and Dandra's grip.

"Grandmother Wolf!" the shifter said. He still looked horrendous, but he moved with something much more like his normal strength and ease.

"Better?" asked Ekhaas. Geth nodded. "Good. We need get out of here." She thrust his sword at him. He blinked then accepted it back, shoving it into the sheath that still hung from his belt. Ekhaas looked to Ashi. "Bring the torch."

Ashi had scooped up Geth's shirt and gauntlet in the cell. She handed them to him, then pulled the torch down from the wall. "What now?" Dandra asked Ekhaas. "Tzaryan's troops are sure to be watching the gate. We're not getting out that way and I didn't see a back door."

"Tzaryan Keep doesn't have back door," the hobgoblin told her. "But Taruuzh Kraat did."

She turned away before Dandra could demand an explanation, and once more they were forced to follow or be left behind.

At the top of the dungeon stairs, Ekhaas turned, heading toward the ogre barracks. "Try to keep the torch low," she told Ashi.

The hunter nodded. Dandra held her breath. Although the darkness ahead seemed quiet—she could only imagine that Tzaryan's ogres had been turned out to search for them—the idea of venturing right into their lair was still daunting. Just when it felt like the stench of the monsters alone would choke them, though, Ekhaas turned aside and led them down a short passage to a long but strangely narrow room. A closed hatch that would have been a tight squeeze for an ogre pierced one wall. On either side of it stood complex arrangements of winches and pulleys threaded with heavy chains. Ekhaas walked over to the hatch and lifted the simple latch that kept it closed. Stale, cold air puffed out as she pulled the hatch open.

"The back door of Taruuzh Kraat," she said. She stepped aside to let them approach the hatch.

Dandra stepped up and eased her head through. The space beyond was a dark and echoing shaft that smelled of cold stone. She could see almost nothing. "Ashi, give me the torch."

The hunter passed it to her and Dandra held it out into the shaft. The flame illuminated smooth walls that quickly became the unworked rock of a natural chasm. Just below the hatch was a ledge; from the ledge, a dark rope with knots along its length for easy climbing dangled down into the shadows. If Dandra strained her eyes, she could just make out the bottom of the chasm, a narrow rocky wedge in the shadows.

Overhead, the ceiling of the shaft was much closer. The chains and winches from the narrow room passed through the wall and connected to an array of beams holding up the underside of a stone floor. Dandra traced the chains and beams with a glance. If the winches were tightened, key pieces of beams would be pulled away. The floor would collapse. She narrowed her eyes and turned to look at Ekhaas. "We're under the landing in the great stairs. Robrand told Singe that the floor could be collapsed to drop invaders into a chasm."

Ekhaas nodded. "A chasm that has creased this land since the Age of Dhakaan. Tzaryan thought he could build away from the ruins of Taruuzh Kraat, but in deciding to use this chasm for his trap, he missed a passage. There's a door at the bottom so cunningly hidden no one could have found it from the outside. It opens into a network of ancient caves. There's another door in the hall of Taruuzh—I found it while exploring. It must have been intended as an escape route." The hobgoblin's ears stood straight with pride. "This hatch is here so Tzaryan's slaves can maintain the collapsing mechanism. I don't think Tzaryan ever expected anyone to come and go this way. I've been in and out of the keep under his nose for two years."

"I thought it seemed like you knew this place a little too well," said Geth. He had his gauntlet on his arm and with Ashi's help had fastened the straps that held the armored sleeve in place. He gave it a critical shake, then stepped up to the hatch as well, glancing down the chasm before looking to Ekhaas. "You're sure this will get us away from Dah'mir?"

"No one knows about the door," Ekhaas said. "Tzaryan Rrac probably doesn't even suspect the caves exist. We can take shelter in Taruuzh Kraat until we have the chance to escape."

"Until we can come back for the others," Geth corrected her. He turned and looked at Dandra. "We may be retreating but we're not abandoning them."

She gave him a tight smile, then watched as the shifter climbed through the hatch. He balanced for a moment on the ledge beyond before taking hold of the knotted rope and lowering himself down into the shaft. Ekhaas gestured for her to follow him. "You next," she said. "Then your tall friend. I'll come last and close the hatch."

Dandra drew a deep breath and leaned through the hatch once more. Geth was already a shadow on the edge of her vision. Her stomach tensed as she stared down into the darkness. With her powers, she wouldn't have worried about the drop at all. She might not even have bothered with the rope. Unfortunately, she couldn't be sure her powers would be there for her.

Tetkashtai? she asked.

The presence screamed back at her with a wail that made her stumble, though she caught herself against the edge of the hatch. Ashi stepped forward with concern on her face.

Ekhaas bared her teeth. "Move, kalashtar. As long we stand here, we're in danger!"

Dandra nodded grimly. She could remove the psicrystal and break the link to Tetkashtai, but that would do no good unless she gave the crystal to someone else to carry—and in her terror-maddened state Tetkashtai was sure to attempt to seize control of anyone carrying her prison. Geth had carried it once in a pouch, but a mere pouch might not be enough to block the presence's influence anymore. Tetkashtai's frenzy gave her a frightening strength. The strength of madness.

A sour taste rose in Dandra's mouth as something else occurred to her. Madness was what Dah'mir had been trying to provoke in his kalashtar victims all along. Medala had found that strength and murdered her psicrystal to reclaim her body. Virikhad had eventually succumbed to madness as well and his fight for Medala's body had destroyed both of them. If Tetkashtai fell, too . . .

Dandra lifted her chin, slid her spear into the harness across her back, and eased herself through the shaft onto the ledge beyond. The empty space of the chasm hung below her. For a moment, she wondered if giving in to Dah'mir's power would be such a bad thing.

She choked that thought off. She'd held Tetkashtai back so far.

She turned slowly to face the hatch, then bent down, took the knotted rope between her hands, and slid backward off the edge. She could feel the rope jump and shudder as Geth continued his descent below her. Gut churning, she focused on moving her grasp from one knot to the next, sliding down into the cold dark.

With one arm outstretched and his eyes closed, Chain spun like child playing a game. Vennet couldn't stop himself from laughing and chanting out the nursery rhyme that went with the game. *"Warding, warning, breeding, keeping, making, healing, storm and shade. Striding, scribing, always guarding, all as dark an end they made!"*

Chain's face, already pale with fear, tensed at the mocking—but his spinning still stopped exactly when the rhyme ended. His eyes snapped open and he stared at his arm, the Mark of Finding seeming to shimmer on it, in surprise. It pointed down toward the floor. The big man swallowed and forced his eyes up to Dah'mir. "There," he said. "She's about a hundred paces away—and moving."

Beyond Chain, Singe struggled to conceal an expression of dismay. Hruucan's burned face was inscrutable, though the movement of his tentacles betrayed pleasure and anticipation—the closer they were to capturing Dandra, Vennet knew, the closer Hruucan was to being given his chance for revenge on Singe. Tzaryan Rrac, however, just looked confused. "That's impossible!" said the ogre mage. "She'd have to be *under* the keep!"

Dah'mir's eyes shone in the darkness. "She's in the caves," he said. His voice made eddies in the air, tiny whispers of wind that murmured the praises of the Dragon Below in Vennet's ears.

Tzaryan's confusion only seemed to grow deeper. "Caves?" he asked. "There are no caves—"

"There are caves, Tzaryan," said Dah'mir impatiently. "I knew this area before you were a squalling infant. Chain, what direction is Dandra moving?"

The bounty hunter's muscular arm traced an arc toward the northeast. Toward Taruuzh Kraat. Dah'mir's breath hissed between his teeth and his thin lips pulled into a tight smile. "How fitting. This will end where it all began. Tzaryan, gather your ogres and get them into the ruins. There's only one exit from the caves into Taruuzh Kraat. I want to greet our fugitives when they emerge in Taruuzh's hall. Vennet, Hruucan—bring the prisoners."

He thrust off from the courtyard, great talons gouging furrows in the stone, herons scattering around him, and leaped into the sky. Huge wings snapped out and caught the air. They beat twice, then stretched wide in a glide. Vennet's heart thundered at the glory of the sight. He shoved Natrac toward Chain, and rushed to the edge of the courtyard to peer after the dragon. Tzaryan stepped up at his side—and let out a curse of amazement.

Under the light of the risen moons, with his herons circling overhead, Dah'mir landed and began to dig like a huge, scaly dog, reopening a passage into the ancient ruins.

Vennet whirled to sneer at Singe in triumph. "I told you once that you were too smart for your own good. Are you feeling smart now?"

The wizard's face was pale. Vennet laughed.

CHAPTER

17

Every movement that Geth made seemed to pull on something. Ekhaas's raw magic had healed the worst of his wounds, but there was still pain. His head still ached and Lor hadn't been gentle in stripping and binding him—it was a miracle the ogre hadn't damaged his gauntlet. Probably the worst, though, were the tiny tugs and sharp pricks of hair and skin trapped in crusted blood. It was as if a swarm of gnats had found its way into the dim chasm beneath Tzaryan Keep. Every hand-under-hand motion as he climbed down Ekhaas's rope brought on a new rash of torturous pinching. His head, his arms, his neck, shoulders, and chest—he craved water, not to drink but simply to wash.

Strangely, the pain that not so long ago had felt like it would consume him was easiest of all to bear. He'd finally faced Robrand. Narath had passed between them—not in words and not in a good way, but it had passed. Robrand's threats of violence and torture were utterly unlike the man that he had known and deep in his gut Geth knew he was responsible for the change in his old commander. At the same time, though, he felt . . . open. Narath, or at least as much of it as anyone needed to know, had been laid bare. His past wasn't something to suffer under anymore—it was something to fight against. He felt alive again.

Geth bared his teeth. Tiger's blood, he thought, this fight might not last long, but it's going to be a good one.

The floor of the chasm was under his feet. He let go of the rope and dropped the last short distance, landing in an easy crouch. The light of the torch high above gave him just enough light to see. He looked around the narrow space—if there was a door hidden down here, he couldn't see it—then reached up to guide Dandra as she approached the end of the knotted rope. To his surprise, her arms and legs were knotted with tension as much as exertion. "Easy," he said. "I'm here. Cousin Boar, why didn't you just float down?"

Dandra grimaced as she stepped away from the rope. "Tetkashtai's fear is blocking my powers."

The hair on Geth's arms and the back of his neck rose. His own brush with Tetkashtai had left him with a fearful respect for the presence's strength. "She can do that?"

"I don't think she's doing it deliberately—but she's more terrified than I've ever felt her." In the dimness, the worry on Dandra's face was undisguised. "The confrontation with Dah'mir might have been too much. I don't know if I can calm her down this time."

"Grandfather Rat." A new chill struck Geth. "When Medala went mad, she had the strength to take back—"

Dandra cut him off. "I've thought of that." She lifted her chin. "I've held her back so far."

Ashi joined them on the floor of the chasm, her feet hitting the stone with a quiet thump. Overhead, Ekhaas pulled the hatch leading back into Tzaryan Keep closed behind herself, then leaned out over the chasm. "Geth!" she called softly. "Catch!"

He barely had time to react before she let the torch go. It plummeted down through the darkness in a streak of guttering flame. Geth lunged forward with a curse and snatched it out of the air, scorching his fingers in the process. He looked up to glare at Ekhaas, but the hobgoblin was already on the rope and making her descent. He turned back to Ashi and Dandra.

"Twice tak for standing with me," he said simply.

Ashi's pierced lips pressed tight. "I know something of being forgiven for past deeds, Geth. Who am I judge you?" She held out her hand and Geth took it, returning her grasp hand to forearm in a warrior's grip. Ashi smiled. "I told Singe once that you were good enemy, Geth, but you're a better friend. *Do tai rond e reis*—you have fierceness and strength. I'm proud to stand with you."

"I think we all would have stood with you sooner if you hadn't driven us away," said Dandra. "Ashi, me, Natrac, Orshok—we were surprised, but we would have stayed to listen if you'd let us. I think the only one who's really angry with you is Singe."

Geth bared his teeth as he released Ashi's hand. "And Robrand."

Ashi spat on the ground. "I'm ashamed to share his blood. How much of his friendship was just a play until he had a chance to take his revenge on you?"

"Forget him," Geth growled. "How are we going to rescue Singe, Natrac, and Orshok?"

"If you want my advice," Ekhaas said grimly from above, "you'll forget about your friends. If they're not dead yet, they will be soon." She dropped to the chasm floor, landed in a crouch, and rose to face them. "I don't know much about Dah'mir, but I know Tzaryan Rrac. There's a reason his dungeons are small. He doesn't keep prisoners for long."

"Robrand—the General—is a friend," said Dandra. "He'll try to keep them alive."

"The same way he tried to keep Geth alive?" The hobgoblin stepped up to a large, angled rock that protruded from the rough face of the chasm. "You have no friends in Tzaryan Keep. You can't stay here—you should flee while you can. The hills to the north open onto the Watching Wood—"

"Blood in your mouth!" snapped Ashi. "We won't abandon them!"

Ekhaas's ears just twitched. She turned back to the angled rock and thrust her fingers into what looked like nothing more than a large crack.

With the faintest of scrapes, the entire protrusion swung forward and up on a heavy metal arm to expose a dark, cramped tunnel. "Come," said Ekhaas, and disappeared inside. Her voice echoed out. "There's a handle on the inside of the door. Last one in pull it closed."

Ashi scowled. "I don't like her."

"Neither do I," agreed Geth. "But she's right about one thing. We can't stay here. I'll go first. "

He handed the torch to Dandra, crouched down and went into the tunnel after Ekhaas. The floor had a gentle but persistent slope to it that made keeping his balance awkward. Knees pressed up, backside hanging low, his hands brushing the rock wall for balance, he felt like a waddling duck. Light flooded the tunnel and his shadow stretched out before him as Dandra followed with the torch. A moment later, he heard Ashi grunt. There was another faint scrape, then the sharp sound of a latch catching as the hidden door closed.

Tzaryan Keep was behind them.

By the time the prisoners, their captors, and a squad of a dozen ogres reached the ruins, the smell of fresh-turned soil was heavy on the night air. In the light of a pair of torches carried by an orc slave, Singe could see that the ruins seemed almost transformed. The ancient mounds and foundations that marked the location of Taruuzh Kraat on the surface were covered with a new layer of dirt. Here and there, large rocks and big sections of brick still joined by millennia-old mortar lay strewn like pebbles. Where Singe and the others had located the collapsed entrance to the underground complex that morning, a deep, ragged trench made a scar in the moonlight. The way to Taruuzh Kraat was open.

There was no sign of Dah'mir except for the herons that circled overhead. Tzaryan Rrac stood beside the trench, watching their approach.

Singe stumbled on a stone hidden by the torches' flickering. His arms bound behind his back, he staggered, trying to keep his balance. He might have gone down anyway if Robrand hadn't caught him and given him the moment of support he needed. The old man's face betrayed nothing. Singe kept his silence.

Vennet stalked just ahead, Chain following at his heels like a frightened dog. On Singe's right, Hruucan kept pace with them, too. Their enemies surrounded them. There'd been no chance to speak with Robrand, no chance to stage an escape.

Singe risked a glance over his shoulder, checking on Orshok and Natrac. The orc and half-orc were just behind him and Robrand, bound as he was and each with an ogre guard watching over them. Orshok looked terrified, but Natrac met his eyes with a grim determination. Singe gave him a curt nod of encouragement—false encouragement—and turned back to watch the trench drawing closer.

As frightened as he felt at his own prospects, the real fear that gnawed at him was for Dandra and Ashi. However they'd managed to find their way into the caves beneath Tzaryan Keep, their refuge in Taruuzh Kraat was going to become a trap.

He had to do something.

He drew a breath and risked raising his voice as they stopped at the mouth of the trench. "Tzaryan!" he shouted. "Where's Dah'mir? I'm surprised he left you behind—I wouldn't turn my back on you!"

Tzaryan's black-eyed gaze settled on him briefly, then went to Robrand. "General, keep the prisoners quiet!"

"Aye." Singe's ear stung as Robrand swatted him sharply, but the wizard had to hold back a smile as the old man picked up on his trick and repeated the question. "Where *is* the dragon, my lord?"

"Gone ahead," said Tzaryan. Singe glanced at the trench and the dark passage beyond. Dah'mir couldn't have fit down it. He must have transformed. The wizard tried to picture the great chamber dominated by the grieving tree. If they were lucky, Dah'mir's dragon form wouldn't be able to fit in it either. Singe doubted that they would be so lucky.

He swallowed and thrust himself forward. Robrand leaped after him, but the old man was just a little too slow. "What did Dah'mir promise you, Tzaryan?" Singe shouted, charging toward the ogre mage. "Is it worth surrendering yourself to him? Do you think he's just going to leave after—"

Vennet whirled around. His arm caught Singe right across the throat and swept the wizard off his feet. Singe slammed down onto his back, gasping for breath. "Are you trying something smart again, Singe?" Vennet asked. He lunged forward, punctuating his words with kicks to Singe's belly. "Give . . . it . . . up!"

Singe curled up around Vennet's boot and bright pain sparked in his vision, but he still saw Robrand storm up to them. "You! D'Lyrandar! Get back! This man is in my custody!"

Vennet took a swaggering step back. "Really? I thought he was *my* master's prisoner."

Robrand stopped, leaving Singe between him and the half-elf like a bone between two dogs. Singe twisted around and looked up at his former commander, catching his eye and mouthing a single word. *Chain.*

The old man's mouth tightened in almost imperceptible acknowledgment and his gaze flicked back to Vennet. His voice rose in sharp command. "Tzaryan company, alert!"

All around them, the small noises of moving ogres were drowned out in a rush of creaking leather and sliding feet as Robrand's squad snapped to readiness and turned to face him. Singe managed to sit up in time to see Vennet's eyes narrow with unpleasant surprise. Off to one side, Hruucan whirled around, surveying the nervous ogres—including Chuut—that surrounded him. His tentacles rose and he dropped into a crouch, ready to fight.

"General!" Tzaryan roared. "What are you doing? Company, stand down!"

The ogres relaxed again, but Robrand faced Tzaryan without flinching. "My lord, I think the prisoner has a point." He glanced at a nearby ogre—possibly the dumbest-looking brute Singe had ever seen—and pointed at Singe. "Watch him," he ordered, then marched to Tzaryan. "How much can we trust a dragon?"

"Mutiny!" shouted Vennet. "This is mutiny!" He started to turn his back on Singe, hesitated for instant, then grabbed Chain and shoved him toward the wizard. "You watch him, too!" He darted after Robrand, shouting protests. The ogre Robrand had pressed into guard service just looked utterly confused by the rush of events. Singe twisted around to face Chain. The bounty hunter looked almost as confused as the ogre—and, more importantly, frightened out of his wits, his arrogance crushed.

"Not exactly the job you thought, is it?" Singe asked him.

Chain's lips drew back from his teeth. "Don't mock me!"

"I'm not. Just listen to me." He nodded toward Vennet as the ragged half-elf cursed and railed at Robrand and Tzaryan. "Once Vennet and Dah'mir have Dandra, they're not going to need you and your dragonmark anymore. Here's my offer: help us and we'll take you when we escape."

"You're trying to trick me." Chain clenched his teeth. "I could escape on my own."

Singe bit back the desire to point out what a good job the big man had done of that so far. "Dol Arrah witness, this is no trick," he said instead. "You're as dead as we are."

His ogre guard finally seemed to realize that something

was going on. "You talks!" he said. "Tzaryan says prisoners no talks!" He strode forward and slapped at Singe with a hand as big as a ham.

When Robrand had swatted him, he'd pulled his punch. The ogre made no such effort. The blow spun Singe around and laid him back out on the ground, his ears ringing. Dazed, the wizard heard Natrac and Orshok yell out and saw them strain forward against the grasps of their own guards.

Tzaryan's voice rose over the ruins. "General, return to your place and see to the prisoners! Your suspicions are noted, but I trust Dah'mir to honor the agreement I have with him. Vennet, leave me alone and close your mouth before I have to apologize to Dah'mir for breaking your jaw. All of you get into the ruins with the prisoners! Dah'mir is waiting!"

Singe sat up as Vennet and Robrand both came back to them. Vennet looked ready to kill something. "Chain!" he snapped. "Hruucan! Into the tunnel!"

Robrand gestured for the ogre to get Singe on his feet, then sent him back to his place in the ranks. The old man took up a position beside Singe and pushed him forward toward the dark passage to Taruuzh Kraat. The orc torchbearer ran ahead of them to light their way; Natrac and Orshok and their guards followed behind. They passed beneath Tzaryan Rrac's gaze in silence, then the ceiling of the passage rose above them and cut out the night sky. Tzaryan began ordering the squad of ogres forward in their wake. Singe heard a whisper of frightened prayer from Orshok.

"I hope you got what you wanted," Robrand murmured. "I half-expected you to make a break for it before we got down here."

"Can't," Singe said, working his tongue around his mouth. "We need to warn Dandra." He spat out blood. "Twelve moons, I wish Geth was here."

Robrand's face twisted. "You can't mean that."

"If he was here, he'd be the one getting hit. He doesn't mind taking punishment," said Singe. He snorted and smiled. "And he can give it back. If there's going to be a fight, Geth's a good man to have beside—"

Something inside him lurched at the words coming out of his mouth. Words of respect. Words, Singe realized, that he truly meant. He *did* wish Geth was there and not just to take blows instead of him.

He missed having the shifter at his back. The last week with Robrand had brought back so many old memories—good and bad—that he'd ignored new ones. The battle at the Bonetree mound. The defense of Bull Hollow. And what he'd chosen to remember of the old days, of the Frostbrand before Narath, hadn't been exactly fair to Geth. For all that both he and Robrand had ignored it, the shifter had been in the background of virtually every reminiscence they'd shared. A bad, bad thing had happened at Narath—but there had been so many good things before and since.

Maybe Geth didn't walk to talk about Narath, but abruptly Singe wasn't so certain that—had he been in Geth's place—he would want to talk either. And it wasn't as if Geth felt nothing for his fallen comrades and the people of Narath. The look on his face when Singe had confronted him Bull Hollow, when he tried to talk to him in Bava's studio, when he'd exposed his dark secret to Dandra and the others . . . Geth had been afraid. Geth had been ashamed.

Singe felt a pit open in his gut that was as black and cold as the tunnel around them. "Lords of the Host, Robrand, I've made a mistake. We've a mistake. Geth—"

The old man hissed. "Don't tell me you're defending him, Etan! He ran away! Tonight, just like in Narath. He ran and left you to hang!"

"He didn't know Dah'mir was here any more than you did," Singe said. His jaw tightened. "And I don't know that he so much ran away as ran from us." He looked at Robrand. "Neither of us have been exactly—"

Robrand punched him across the face, sending him staggering across the tunnel and into Orshok. The ogre holding the druid grabbed him as well, but all Singe could do was stare at his old commander in shock. Robrand's face was flushed red with anger and he was breathing hard. "Don't you defend him!" he said. "Don't you *dare* defend him. He's a coward. You know it as well as I do. Whatever Geth gets, he brought down on himself!"

Singe couldn't even find the words to respond. Ahead of them, Vennet, Chain, and Hruucan turned to stare. Behind, ogres stumbled to a confused stop. Robrand glared at all of them. "What are you stopping for?" he said, his voice echoing down the long passage. "Tzaryan company, eyes forward! Double march!" He strode forward, away from Singe and past Vennet. Even the half-elf looked startled, but he was swept along and carried away by the moving ogres before he could say anything.

Orshok's ogre guard grumbled a curse at being left with two prisoners, but that didn't stop him from marching along at a pace that left Singe stumbling. The orc torchbearer had hastened after Robrand, plunging the tunnel into a darkness broken only by the eerie flames and embers of Hruucan's body. Orshok managed to lean close for a moment. "Singe, what was that?" he asked, his voice desperate. "Is this some plan?"

Stunned, Singe shook his head. If it was a plan, it wasn't one of his! Had he just driven away their only solid ally? Twelve bloody moons, he thought, how can this get any worse?

CHAPTER

18

It was difficult to tell how far or how long they traveled in the tunnel—their waddling pace made the distance seem to stretch on for leagues. Eventually, however, Ekhaas paused, blocking the passage. Beyond her, Geth could see an end to the stone walls of the tunnel. "What are you waiting for?" he growled. "Keep going!"

The hobgoblin bared her own sharp teeth back at him. "Have patience!" She twisted around in the tight space to look at them. "You enter a part of my people's history," she said. "What you see, only a few *chaat'oor* have seen anywhere. You will be the first to see it here. Respect it."

She didn't wait for a response, but just turned back and crawled forward out of the tunnel. Geth followed her, peering out cautiously, uncertain of what waited for them. The light that shone past him only made the shadows seem deeper. Even when he stepped out of the tunnel and stood up—gratefully stretching cramped limbs—the aisle of light revealed nothing more than an expanse of rocky floor. He looked for Ekhaas, a silent figure in the dark. "What's so special about this?" he asked.

Torchlight blossomed as Dandra crawled out of the tunnel and stood up. Geth's voice died in his throat and he stared around in amazement. Dandra let out a gasp. Ashi, emerging a moment later, swore out loud.

They stood on the edge of a long, tall cavern. Stone walls soared up over their heads, all of them covered with painted figures.

Crude but instantly recognizable, herds of animals raced

around the cavern, pursued by goblinoid figures. Hobgoblins and bugbears chased tribex, bison, and even mammoths, while goblins stalked smaller prey. Other scenes showed feasts, dancing, battles. Some showed rituals. Some showed monsters preying on the goblinoids: a dragon red as blood laid waste to a hobgoblin encampment with claw and fire.

A shadow loomed in the corner of Geth's eye. With a shout that rang through the cavern, he drew his sword and whirled around. He froze at the sight of another painting—larger-than-life hobgoblins, bugbears, and goblins, their heads thrown back in song as they worked at crafting stone implements and woven baskets.

"What is this place?" asked Ashi in awe.

"Taruuzh wasn't the first to find power in this region," said Ekhaas. Even her arrogance seemed a little humbled among the ancient paintings. "In times long before Jhazaal Dhakaan united the six kings, long before the clans even existed, caves like this were the refuge of shamans and wonder workers." Her ears stood straight and she spread her arms before the singers on the wall. "The early *duur'kala*. The predecessors of the *daashor*."

"I wouldn't have dreamed such places existed," Dandra said.

"Do you think we tell all of our secrets to *chaat'oor*? Be honored by what you have seen." Ekhaas lowered her arms. "We shouldn't linger. The power hasn't left these caves."

They moved through the cavern in silence, the figures on the walls flickering and almost seeming to move with the torchlight. Geth felt as if the painted goblinoids were following him through the cavern, hunting him as they had hunted their ancient prey. The hair on his arms and the back of his neck rose and a chill took hold of him. He had to fight to keep a growl from rising up his throat. Ashi looked uncomfortable as well—her hand was on her sword, though she didn't draw it. Dandra kept glancing over her shoulder.

Ekhaas wore a look of smug condescension—although Geth noticed that even her eyes darted occasionally to the deeper shadows of the cave.

"How far are we from Taruuzh Kraat?" he asked her.

"Not far. There are four caves. The last one holds stairs that lead up to the great chamber." The hobgoblin tried to keep her voice light, but didn't quite succeed.

The first cavern wasn't the only one that was painted. A deep crack angled upward through the stone wall to open onto a cavern decorated with scenes of children and childbirth. A third cavern had bare walls but its low ceiling had been spattered with a thousand dots of white. Stars, Geth realized. Twelve larger colored dots were moons. A heavy spray of white was the Ring of Siberys. The ancient hobgoblins had duplicated the night sky in their dark caves. He shivered again.

"Are you cold, too?" Dandra asked. Geth glanced at her. She exhaled and her breath made a stream of mist on the air. Geth flexed his arms, trying to warm himself. He turned and looked at Ekhaas. The hobgoblin shrugged.

"It's a cave," she said, her voice echoing slightly. "There are drafts." She led the way to a steep passage that had been cut with grooves for traction—grooves that must have been old when the Dhakaani Empire was young.

"The air is still," said Ashi. "There's no draft."

"What do you know about caves, March hunter?" Ekhaas asked without looking back. "Keep to your swamps and—"

Her voice died away as a long sigh rippled along the passage. The chill that had clung to Geth changed with the sound, seeming to seep right through his flesh and into his sprit. He bared his teeth and his sword snapped up. "That wasn't a draft! Ekhaas, what's down here?"

"Nothing!" The hobgoblin's ears stood high and alert. For the first time, her hand hovered near her sword as well. "I've been through these caves a dozen times and there's nothing—"

The sigh came again, rising and falling. This time, though, it was more than just a sound. It was words.

Wrath . . . returns. Has the time Aryd foresaw come so soon?

Geth's hair bristled and the nightmare passage through Jhegesh Dol that he and Natrac had survived came back to him—a passage that had been haunted by the moaning, pleading spirits of ancient orcs and hobgoblins. "That's not nothing! Wolf and Rat, that's a ghost!"

The torchlight grew brighter as Dandra and Ashi edged closer to him. Both women held their weapons at the ready. "I heard words," said Dandra. "What did it say, Ekhaas?"

Geth answered for the hobgoblin without thinking. "It said

'Wrath returns' and asked if the time Aryd had foreseen had come."

Ekhaas froze and turned to stare back at him. Ashi and Dandra stared at him to, but in astonishment. "Geth," Dandra asked sharply, "you understood what it said?"

"Yes, I—" Geth blinked. "You didn't?"

Dandra shook her head. So did Ashi. Ekhaas's ears twitched. "I barely understood it," she said. "It was an archaic form of Goblin, a hold-over from the time of the Empire."

Geth's eyes opened wide. His heart beat fast. "That's not possible," he said. "I don't speak Goblin at all!"

"Rond betch!" Ashi exclaimed. "Look at his sword!"

Geth glanced down at the ancient weapon—and caught his breath. The purple byeshk of the blade was coated with frost.

The sigh came a third time. *Wrath . . .*

Dandra looked up at Ekhaas. "You," she said. "Start talking. What's going on? You said these caves were safe!"

"They are safe!" Ekhaas said, then winced. "They should be safe."

"I know the name Aryd," Ashi said. "She was the Gatekeeper seer in the story of the Battle of Moths, the one who helped Taruuzh." She stiffened. "That voice. Is that Taruuzh?"

Ekhaas's mouth opened, then closed. She spread her hands. "When a *daashor* died, it was tradition to bury him beneath his *kraat.*"

"Grandfather Rat's naked tail!" Geth cursed in disbelief. "These caves are tombs, too?"

"No!" said Ekhaas. Her ears flicked and she pointed ahead into the darkness. "Only the last chamber is. That's where Taruuzh was laid to rest—but I've never seen a ghost here before! I've never felt anything like this!"

"Well, you're feeling it now," Geth told her. "What do you think raised him? What's this wrath he's talking about?"

She hesitated, then said, "I think they're the same thing." She pointed at the sword in Geth's hand. "That's Wrath."

"What?"

"Until you said how you found the sword, I didn't know, but then . . ." Ekhaas drew a breath and her cedar-smoke voice turned formal as she spoke a passage from a story. "And Rakari Kuun emerged from Jhegesh Dol, even in his triumph weeping for what he had seen—and what he had lost. The death of the daelkyr lord had claimed a high price and Aaram, the sword that would not accept the grasp of a coward, the *lhesh shaarat* that had been given to Duulan—first of the name Kuun—by Taruuzh, had passed from the world."

Geth shuddered as another ghostly sigh brushed over them. Ekhaas looked at him again. *"Aaram* is the Goblin word for righteous anger or wrath," she said. "What you brought out of Jhegesh Dol wasn't just any *lhesh shaarat*. It was a weapon forged by Taruuzh himself." She raised her hands toward the ceiling of the cavern and Taruuzh Kraat somewhere above. "You've brought Wrath home."

"And woken up Taruuzh," growled Geth. "Rat!"

Ekhaas's eyes flashed. "I didn't know that would happen!"

"It did!"

"Enough!" snapped Dandra. She pushed forward, stepping between them. "Light of il-Yannah, we can't just argue about this. We need to do something. Unless you can cast that spell of floating flames again, Ekhaas, we at least need to get up into Taruuzh Kraat before this burns out. I *don't* want to be down here in the dark!"

She gestured with the torch and Geth saw that it was burning much less brightly than it had before. A soft growl crept out of his throat. He looked to Ekhaas. "Can you?"

"If I need to," the hobgoblin said. "But that torch will last longer than the spell would."

"Rat," Geth said again. He drew himself up straight. "I guess we don't have much of a choice, do we?" He flicked his sword—Wrath—toward the top of the passage. "Let's see what we're dealing with."

Every step that they advanced up the steep slope seemed to bring a drop in the temperature. By the time they reached the top, Geth's sword wasn't the only thing coated in frost. The cold silvered Dandra's dark hair and brought a flush to Ashi's face. Ekhaas was shivering as she paused beside a gap in the rock. "Through there," she said. "You can see the tomb. The stairs up to Taruuzh Kraat are beyond it."

Geth squeezed past her to peer through the gap. The wintry air stirred at his approach and Taruuzh's ghostly voice tugged at him once more. *Wrath—my beautiful blade.* The words turned wistful and some of the longing in them gripped Geth as well. *They call me daashor, but I was first a smith. I made wonders, but your pure perfection brought the most pride of all to my heart.* Geth clenched his teeth and tried to ignore the voice.

The final cavern was small, no larger than a big room. Even if the eerie cold hadn't stopped them, they wouldn't have missed the tomb of Taruuzh. It dominated the chamber, a massive stone monument that would have rivaled some of the grand tombs Geth remembered from Sharn or Metrol. It stood upright, its tall sides carved with goblins and hobgoblins laboring at forges and over anvils—dozens of smiths at work, all depicted in flawless detail, an echo of the paintings in the deep caves. The stone figure of a hobgoblin stood out from the front of the tomb. Dressed in a smith's apron with thick gauntlets and holding a heavy sword, it was a smaller version of the great statue in the hall of Taruuzh Kraat except that this carving hadn't been defaced. Taruuzh's effigy stared into the ages with an expression that was stern but alert.

Frost, however, had touched the statue as well, softening its features and rendering the effigy as tired and lonely as the haunting voice. A coincidence? Geth couldn't imagine that it was.

Dandra pressed close, looking over his shoulder. "I don't see anything," she said.

"Not all ghosts are something you can see," Ashi said from behind her. Geth didn't look back at either of them, but just studied the chamber. Nothing moved. There were no more sighs, though the cold air seemed heavy, like a slow wind before a blizzard.

"At least Taruuzh doesn't seem like an unfriendly sort," he said after a long moment. Across the cavern, he could see an archway carved out of the rock, the foot of a worn stone staircase visible within its shadows. "There's where we're going," he said, pointing. "Do you think the ghost would follow us up the stairs, Ekhaas?"

"The power that drew the early *duur'kala* here belongs to the caves, not to Taruuzh Kraat," said the hobgoblin.

"And we didn't encounter the ghost when we were in Taruuzh Kraat before," Dandra pointed out.

"Good," said Geth. "Then let's hope Taruuzh is as pleased to see his old sword as he sounded. " He took a long breath, released it—and stepped out into the chamber.

Nothing happened. Geth raised his voice experimentally. "Taruuzh?" He stepped a little further into the cavern and called again. "Taruuzh!" His heart beating like thunder, he raised the sword over his head. "We have your sword, your beautiful blade. We have Wrath!"

The air tensed and rippled with another quiet sigh, but nothing else. Geth lowered Wrath and looked back to the others. "Hurry," he said. None of them needed urging. As they spilled out from the steep passage and hastened after him, Geth turned and strode for the archway and the stairs beyond.

Between one stride and the next, the tension in the air broke. The temperature changed in an instant, so quick it was like plunging into icy water, so sharp it took his breath away. He stopped short, choking on air that stung his lungs. Behind him, Dandra stumbled and cried out. The light from her torch grew suddenly dim. Geth spun around. Ashi had Dandra and was holding her up, but both women were staring at Taruuzh's tomb. So was Ekhaas as she pressed back against one stone wall. Geth stared, too.

The frost on the stone had spread and grown thick. In the wavering light of the failing torch. features that had been soft were now hard. Hard and angry.

Xoriat! Taruuzh's voice rose in a sudden howl. *I smell Xoriat! I know you, servants of the daelkyr! Wrath wakes me! I know you and I know what you seek! You may hold Wrath, but you shall not have the stones! They are saved up against the day that Aryd foresaw!*

Cold unlike anything he had ever felt, more intense than the fiercest winter gale in northern Karrnath blasted Geth. It scoured his skin and bit into his very soul. He tried to turn to face Taruuzh's tomb. "We're not servants of Xoriat!" he shouted back at it. "We fight the daelkyr—we fight the servant of the Master of Silence, just like you did!"

It didn't do any good. The air moved, churning into wind, whipping through the chamber and making the cold seem even more intense. Ashi flung a hand toward him, her other arm wrapped around Dandra. "Geth!"

He reached deep into himself and shifted, feeling the rush of his own ancient heritage flow through him, driving back some of the cold. He pushed forward against the wind and grabbed Ashi's hand. The hunter's fingers were like icicles.

"The stairs!" he yelled at her. "We have to try and get to the stairs!"

She nodded and pulled herself and Dandra toward him. Dandra looked the worst of all of them. She was breathing in shallow gasps, there were thick ice crystals on her eyelashes and the soft yellow-green glow of the psicrystal around her neck was brighter than the torch she cradled.

Geth's breath hissed between frozen teeth. If Dandra failed, Tetkashtai might have her chance to break through and seize her body. He wrapped his arms around both women as best he could, trying to will his body to generate warmth, and pushed them toward the stairs up to Taruuzh Kraat. How far up the stairs might Taruuzh's reach extended? He swallowed icy saliva and looked around for Ekhaas.

The hobgoblin was still huddled against the wall of the cavern, though as he watched she pushed herself away and stood upright, her eyes fixed on the tomb. "Ekhaas!" he called to her. "This way!"

She shook her head and drew herself up. "Ekhaas!" Ashi screamed, adding her appeal to Geth's.

Ekhaas didn't move except to draw a breath, open her mouth—and sing.

If the song with which she had healed him had seemed raw and energetic, the power behind her voice now was primal. Whatever magic had allowed him to understand Taruuzh's sighs and wails let him comprehend the words Ekhaas sang as well. It was no spell that poured forth from her throat, but a martial anthem, a song of honor and glory. The power wasn't in the words, but in Ekhaas's voice. Her song touched him, setting his blood pounding and giving him strength. He could feel Ashi stand a little straighter, a little stronger, as well. Dandra, too.

More importantly, the song seemed to settle Taruuzh. The phantom wind in the chamber slowed. The sharp edge of the cold grew dull. Even Taruuzh's wailing eased, then ceased, as if the unseen ghost was listening, caught up in the music.

Ekhaas's gaze darted from the tomb to Geth and she stabbed a hand toward the stairs in an urgent gesture. The shifter blinked and tore himself away from the power of the hobgoblin's song. "The stairs!" he said. "Quickly!"

The women nodded and stumbled forward. Geth glanced over his shoulder. Ekhaas was following at a slow and stately pace, timing her footfalls to her song. She gestured again for him to go. Geth swallowed and ran after Ashi and Dandra.

The cold faded even more the moment he was through the archway. Dandra and Ashi were already on the stairs and climbing fast. Geth heard Dandra gasp with relief. "Il-Yannah, it feels like summer!"

"Keep going!" he said. Ekhaas wasn't out of the cavern yet. As the light of Dandra's torch receded and the chamber fell into darkness, Geth realized that the tomb of Taruuzh was glowing with a pale, silver-white light. Against that light, Ekhaas looked almost spectral herself.

The mask of frost on Taruuzh's effigy had changed again. The stone hobgoblin's face was at peace, as if dreaming of ancient glories. Ekhaas, still singing, stepped past him. Geth fell in behind her, guarding her retreat more out of habit and respect than actual effectiveness—if Taruuzh's anger had reached after them, he knew there wouldn't be a cursed thing he could do about it.

But the ghost didn't come after them and the temperature rose swiftly as they climbed. Dandra had been right—the cave air couldn't have been more than cool, but it felt warm like summer. Geth let out a sigh of relief.

The stairs were steep, but not long; they opened into a short, unadorned hallway that ended in a wall rigged with a heavy iron arm much like the one that opened the hidden door in the chasm beneath Tzaryan Rrac. From this side, the door, with its latches and handles, was obvious. Dandra and Ashi were waiting for them. As Ekhaas stepped off the stairs and set foot on level ground, she finally stopped singing, took a deep breath and stretched. *"Khaavolaar!"* she groaned.

"Ekhaas, that was amazing!" said Dandra.

"I wouldn't be much of a *duur'kala* if I couldn't bring courage and calm when they were needed." The hobgoblin's old arrogance was back, but also a hint of well-deserved pride. Geth could tell from her face and the set of her ears that she knew she had done something extraordinary.

Something in the wails of Taruuzh's ghost gnawed at him, though, and left a sick feeling in his throat. "Ekhaas, did Taruuzh say what I thought he said? That his stones—" He tried to recall the spirit's words. " '—are saved up against the day that Aryd foresaw.' "

Ekhaas started, pride and arrogance vanishing into the shock of someone caught in a lie. Dandra blinked and stiffened. "Taruuzh's stones?" she asked. "The original binding stones? Light of il-Yannah, they can't still exist, can they?" She turned to face Ekhaas. "But your story of the Battle of Moths—you said they were all destroyed to create the Gatekeeper seal that imprisoned the Master of Silence."

The hobgoblin's ears twitched back. "I didn't tell you everything. But what I didn't tell you . . . it didn't seem important. There's an old legend—almost forgotten now—that Aryd convinced Taruuzh to set aside a small box of his stones before the battle, that she'd foreseen a second invasion of Eberron and that the stones would be needed again."

Dandra's eyes opened wide. Her mouth clenched tight in silent horror. Geth growled at Ekhaas. "How could you think that wasn't important?" he demanded.

"Because no one believes it's anything more than a legend!" Ekhaas said. "The Kech Volaar hold tight to our history, but even we know not everything is the whole truth. The tale says Taruuzh hid the stones before his death. Marg himself searched for them and found nothing. That's why he tried recreating the stones on his own. Generations of *duur'kala* hunted for them, too. They were never found. The riddle that was supposed to be the clue to their location couldn't be solved." She spread her hands. "The legend was set aside as a wild treasure hunt."

"No one listened to the ghost?"

Ekhaas bared her teeth. "Did you listen to me when I said I didn't know about the ghost? This might be the first time anyone has ever encountered it!"

Dandra spoke suddenly, her voice hollow and frightened. " 'The time will come again. Three great works stand together as allies: treasure, key, guardian, disciple, and lord.' Singe read that on the statue in the great chamber of Taruuzh Kraat. Is that the riddle?"

"Yes," said Ekhaas. "What drove those who hunted for the hidden stones is that the riddle of Taruuzh sounds so easily solved. 'The time will come again' refers to Aryd's prophecy. The riddle says 'three great works,' wonders crafted by Taruuzh, but mentions five things, so two things aren't works, but something else. The treasure is the stones, Taruuzh's second greatest work after the grieving tree. The first grieving tree stands in Taruuzh Kraat and was thought to be the guardian. 'Disciple and lord' was believed to refer to Dhakaani lords and Gatekeeper druids, sometimes called the disciples of Vvaraak—the allies that put an end to the daelkyr invasion. The searchers believed that Taruuzh was saying that the Dhakaani and the orcs would need to 'stand together as allies' to find the stones, just as they'd need to ally to stop a second invasion."

"So the riddle seems to tell where to find the treasure and who can find it," said Dandra. "What about the key? Was that Taruuzh's third great work?"

"It seems like it should have been." Ekhaas shook her head. "But the problem was that no one knew what Taruuzh's third great work was. *Duur'kala* compiled lists of the greatest wonders he created, trying to find a clue—but there was nothing. The riddle had no answer."

The sick feeling that had gnawed at Geth turned into a terrible ache. "It has an answer," he said slowly. "The *duur'kala* were just too caught up in legends to see it."

Ekhaas's ears laid back. "Are you joking?"

"No." Geth swallowed. He lifted Wrath and repeated the wistful words that Taruuzh's ghost had spoken. "They call me *daashor*, but I was first a smith. I made wonders, but your pure perfection brought the most pride of all to my heart."

As if in confirmation, a long, ghostly sigh drifted up the stairs from the cave below.

"Khaavolaar," Ekhaas whispered in wonder.

Dandra, however, staggered back against Ashi, her eyes full of terror. "Il-Yannah's perfect light illuminate us. If Dah'mir were to find out about this . . ."

"He may not know about the riddle," said Ashi. "This may mean nothing to him."

"The Riddle of Taruuzh isn't well-known, but it's no secret," Ekhaas pointed out.

"Maybe he doesn't understand the clues," the hunter said hopefully

Dandra's face drew tight. "Dah'mir laired in Taruuzh Kraat. He studied Marg's writings. He spent two hundred years working with the binding stone. He's a *dragon*. How can he not understand the clues?" She stood up and paced across the width of the hallway. "Il-Yannah, we know what he was able to do with Marg's imperfect re-creation of the binding stones. Imagine what he could do with Taruuzh's originals!"

"He doesn't have the answer yet," Greth growled. He thrust Wrath back into its sheath. "All we have to do is make sure he never finds out about this sword—"

Terrible, deep laughter cut him off. Words rumbled through the hallway. "Too late, Geth."

With a horrible crash, something huge slammed against the other side of the hidden door. The force of the impact shook the floor, sending them staggering. Great talons punched through the cracks that opened around the door, clenched on the rock, and heaved. A deafening bellow of exertion broke the air. The door ripped away, its iron arm twisting and snapping with an agonized squeal.

Acid-green eyes peered through the ruined opening. "Far too late!" roared Dah'mir.

CHAPTER

19

The overwhelming strength of Dah'mir's presence gripped Dandra. She was drowning, swallowed by the dragon's irresistible personality. Her world dimmed. All she could do was stare in awe at the eyes that stared through a door too narrow for the dragon's head.

There'd been no warning this time from Tetkashtai. Her creator's terror had gone beyond rising and falling. The borders of Dandra's mind were battered by a constant storm of yellow-green light and wailing screams. The eerie silence of the caves, the ghost's frigid attack, Dah'mir's sudden appearance—they were all the same to Tetkashtai.

And yet . . .

Dandra could see. She could hear. For the first time, it seemed that Dah'mir's power hadn't taken her completely. She couldn't move, couldn't lower the guttering torch still held above her head, could barely summon the focus to think, but she was at least aware of what was happening.

Ekhaas's voice rose in a scream of horror as she faced Dah'mir for the first time. Geth shouted, a wordless mingling of shock and fear, and ripped Wrath back out of its sheath, raising sword and gauntlet in a barrier of cold metal. Ashi had her sword out, too. Dandra felt the hunter grab her shoulder and the short corridor whirled briefly as she was pulled back to safety, to the very edge of the stairs back down into the caves. At the top step, however, Ashi stiffened and Dandra knew why.

Bone-chilling cold swept up from below, carrying with it a seething, grasping anger. The effect of Ekhaas's song on Taruuzh's ghost had worn off—or had been shattered by Dah'mir's appearance. Taruuzh's terrible moans drifted up the stairs. There would be no easy escape back into the caverns!

Dandra stared at a wall, caught between the stairs on her left and unseen combat on her right. She could see nothing, but she could hear. Ashi's hand left Dandra's shoulder and there was the sharp sound of flesh slapping flesh. Ekhaas's scream fell silent. Geth snarled. Dah'mir's scales made a fast, dry hiss as the dragon turned, shifted, moved—

No! Dandra yelled. *What's happening?* She tried to reach out with *kesh*, to touch Ashi, but all she found was Tetkashtai's storm of madness.

Let me in, Dandra! Let me in! Words emerged from the storm for a moment and Tetkashtai thrust herself along the *kesh*, trying to breach the defenses Dandra had thrown up to hold her back. Apparently Dah'mir's power had found no hold on the presence, either. Dandra hurled her back again, desperately pinching off the tentative connection of *kesh* for her own safety.

In spite of her efforts, her head turned anyway as if some primitive part of her unconscious sought out Dah'mir instinctively. It was a strange feeling to find her head moving without her control. The short length of the tunnel swung back into view—just in time for her to see Dah'mir thrust a foreleg through the ruined doorway and rake blindly at those inside. As the others cried out and pressed back, Dandra could only watch. It seemed that she could see every scale on the dragon's leg. Embedded in his thick hide, dragonshards—two bright, one dulled like a soot-darkened lantern—made glittering streaks in the shadows.

Geth darted forward and slashed at the flailing foreleg. Wrath bit deep. Dah'mir roared and dark blood sprayed Geth. He slammed his leg against the wall, trying to crush the flea that had bitten him, but Geth leaped away. The dragon snatched back his leg.

"What's he doing here?" Ashi gasped. "How did he find us?"

Dah'mir's eyes returned to the shattered door. They shone with anger. "A dragon knows the value of a dragonmark!" he hissed.

Chain, Dandra realized. The bounty hunter must have located them for Dah'mir. She cursed silently, then felt a burst of fear as Dah'mir's lips curled back and the sour, stinging smell of this breath gusted through the hall. They were an easy target for the devastating spray of his acid!

Geth stepped in front of all of them, Wrath's twilight blade held across his body. "Use your acid and you destroy the sword," he said. His gauntleted hand pointed back behind him. "The sword and Dandra."

Dah'mir's eyes narrowed and his lips twisted. "Do you think you'd still be alive if I hadn't thought of that? Dark lords of Khyber, the unsolvable Riddle of Taruuzh—answered by a shifter! I thought I knew all the secrets of Taruuzh Kraat, but you've surprised me. I should have known there was some power about that sword the first time I felt its bite." His eyes flashed. "Give the sword to me!"

The air itself seemed to darken with the intensity of his presence. His will engulfed her—engulfed all of them. It dragged Dandra's gaze to Wrath and she felt an urge to take the ancient sword away from the shifter and present it to Dah'mir. On the edge of her vision, she saw both Ekhaas and Ashi struggling against the same urge.

In her gut, she knew that she shouldn't have been able to resist the command any more than she should have been able to resist the dominating fascination of the dragon's presence. And yet she did. Her arms and legs tried to move, but didn't. Dah'mir's power seemed to break before it reached the core of her being, like waves dashing against rocks, like a storm surge driven into a swamp—

Like a song lost in screaming. Like a focused will broken by insanity.

Tetkashtai, she said in amazement. Her creator answered only with another wail, but in her mind's eye, Dandra could see Tetkashtai's light churning as it absorbed Dah'mir's power. Tetkashtai's madness was protecting her. Madness, she guessed as well, must have also been what allowed Medala to stand at her new master's side without succumbing to him. She felt a kind of awe rising inside her. Madness, the power of Xoriat, drew kalashtar in and trapped them. Once they had themselves succumbed to madness, they were Xoriat's servants. It was simple. It was brilliant.

She stood on the threshold, struggling to hold back Tetkashtai's terrified madness, protected by it, yet powerless. Dandra felt a rising terror of her own. *Light of il-Yannah, give me strength!* she whispered.

With a low cry, Ekhaas lost her struggle. She staggered forward, reaching for Geth. The shifter's eyes never left Dah'mir, though. His face twisted and the Gatekeeper collar around his neck seemed sharp and distinct in the torchlight, as if it was more real than anything else amid the nightmare of Dah'mir's power. "You'll *never* have this sword!" Geth snarled.

The intensity of Dah'mir's presence snapped. Ekhaas stumbled, then looked up, stunned. Dah'mir's displeasure rumbled out of his belly—and was cut short by a cold, echoing moan from the depths of the caves. The dragon's eyes opened wide, then narrowed. "What have you woken in the caves?" he asked. "No wonder you don't retreat!"

At Dandra's side, Ashi bared her teeth and spat at him. Dah'mir's lips twitched. "A defiant gesture, Ashi. I'll tell the Bonetree clan about it so they can add it to their stories of your treachery!" His gaze fixed on the sword. "That sword is a *lhesh shaarat*, isn't it?"

Geth kept his mouth closed. So did Ekhaas.

Somewhere out on the great chamber beyond Dah'mir, there was a rush of heavy, running footsteps, and voices called out "Master!" and "Dah'mir!"

"Vennet! Tzaryan!" Dah'mir sat back a little bit. "Come forward and bring the prisoners. I'm sure they'd like to say hello their friends." Cruel playfulness flickered in his eyes as he glanced back into the tunnel. "Let's see just how strong your will is, Geth."

Dah'mir's first roar had come while they were still in the tunnel approaching the great chamber. Vennet had let out a cry of "Master!" and Robrand had called out an order for a faster pace. The ogres surrounding them had broken into a shambling run, the guards watching over the prisoners simply scooping up their charges and carrying them along. With the dragon's second roar,

Singe's stomach had risen in fear, any hopes of finding a way to warn Dandra crushed.

They burst into the great chamber hard on the heels of Vennet and Robrand, Hruucan and Chain. The bounty hunter and Singe's old commander paused for a moment, struck by the size of the chamber that spread out below them, by its vaulted ceiling and abandoned forges, by the weird sculpture of the grieving tree. Vennet and Hruucan didn't stop, though. Hruucan hurtled off the balcony in an acrobatic swirl of flame to land lightly on the floor below. Vennet seized one of the torches from the orc slave who had accompanied them and raced down the stairs, calling for Dah'mir. An instant later, a gust of wind ruffled Singe's hair and Tzaryan's flying form soared overhead. "Dah'mir!" he shouted.

"Vennet! Tzaryan! Come forward and bring the prisoners." So large that he took up half the space at the great chamber's end, Dah'mir was a silhouette against a feeble light. The dragon crouched before the narrow mouth of a passage like a cat before a mouse hole. "I'm sure they'd like to say hello their friends."

Tzaryan settled to the ground and turned around. "General!" he bellowed. "Troops forward! Bring down the prisoners!"

Robrand stiffened and turned back to look at Singe. The anger that had been in his face before had faded; he wore the expression of someone caught between two hard decisions. Singe's stomach managed to rise again. For the first time since they'd been captured, their enemies had left them—only the ogres remained and they listened to their General. Once they were free, they still faced daunting odds, but they'd have a chance. They might still be able to rescue Ashi and Dandra and escape together. "Now, Robrand!" he hissed. "Help us now!"

The old man hesitated a moment too long.

With a look of desperation on his face, Chain stepped up behind him. Singe saw the flash of a dagger, then Chain had one arm around Robrand's neck and the other at his back. "Let them go!" he ordered.

Robrand looked startled. The nearest ogres stood straight, their weapons snapping up. Chain wrenched Robrand around so that they could all see the dagger he held. "I can kill him with a thrust," he said. "I haven't seen a Deneith dragonmark that could stop a dagger that's already tasting blood." He jerked his head at the ogres holding Singe, Natrac, and Orshok. "Let them go now and get out of my way!"

"Chain?" called Vennet. The half-elf froze on the stairs and turned back to stare back up at them. "Storm at dawn, Chain, what do you think you're doing?"

"Leaving, you bloody lunatic!" Chain snapped. He glared at the ogres. "I said let them go and get out of your way."

"Chain, no!" Singe choked. "This isn't what I meant—"

The ogres behind him stirred and parted. Chuut stepped out and faced Chain and his captive. "What do you want us to do, General?" he asked.

Robrand's gaze darted to Singe, his eyes hard and flat. Singe's stomach clenched. If Robrand chose, he could order them released. They would be free and his duty to Tzaryan would remain uncompromised. But there would be a price, Singe knew. "No," he whispered. "Ashi . . . Dandra . . ."

Robrand looked back to Chuut. His mouth opened. He drew breath—

He never had the chance to speak. Over the edge of the balcony, a fiery glow like dawn appeared. Tentacles of flame rose up out of the darkness and struck with the speed of serpents, one wrapping Chain's throat, the other around the arm that held the dagger. They wrenched on Chain, tearing him back away from Robrand. The old man fell forward. Chain stumbled backward and into Hruucan's arms as the fiery dolgaunt climbed over the edge of the balcony. More tendrils enfolded the bounty hunter. Chain's eyes opened in pain and a high, thin cry whistled from his constricted throat—then he burst into flames, writhing and struggling in Hruucan's embrace.

His struggles ceased in only moments and the dolgaunt let him go. Chain's burned corpse hit the ground in a spray of glowing embers.

Ogres stared in shock. Robrand sat frozen on the ground. Natrac's face was pale. Orshok was shaking. Singe's heart simply felt like a lump of stone. He lifted his head and stared at Hruucan. The dolgaunt's inscrutable, eyeless face stared back at him.

"What was that?" roared Dah'mir from below.

"Mutiny," Vennet called back. "It's been dealt with." He strode across the balcony and hauled Robrand to his feet. "I know you weren't going to do anything stupid, were you, General? Get your crew moving!"

Robrand tore his eyes away from Chain. "Company forward," he said, his voice strained.

If Singe had felt subdued before, he felt wretched now. They descended the stairs and crossed the great chamber. As they drew closer to Dah'mir, Singe could see that the passage beside which the dragon crouched opened through the tall statue of Taruuzh. The statue's legs and the blade of the sword it held had been a cleverly hidden door, though now that door seemed to have been torn off and thrown aside. The ancient bones that had been Marg had been crushed and scattered. Singe couldn't see more than a few feet into the passage, though; the light that shone out of it came from further inside. Heart beating wildly, he shouted out, "Dandra? Ashi?"

The ogre holding him grunted and gave him a jaw-rattling shake, but there was an answer from inside the passage—though not one he expected. "Singe!" Geth called back. "We're here!"

"Enough of this," said Dah'mir. He lifted one foreleg—Singe saw that it bore the long gash of a fresh wound—and pointed at the Grieving Tree. "Bring the prisoners around to face the passage and put them up on the platform."

The ogres obeyed the dragon without further orders from Robrand. Singe found himself dumped on the broad platform on which the grieving tree stood, Natrac on one side of him, Orshok on the other. The ogres stepped back, leaving only Robrand standing below them like a grim honor guard. Dah'mir moved aside and Singe stared down the passage. Near its end, Dandra stood, one hand holding her spear, the other a fading torch. Her face was slack, her eyes on Dah'mir and Singe choked back a curse. He should have realized that she would have been caught by Dah'mir's presence.

She had protectors, though. Around her stood Ashi, Ekhaas, and Geth. For just a moment, Singe actually felt buoyed up by the sight of the shifter. "Geth! Twelve bloody moons, you didn't run!" He glanced down at Robrand—and felt a twist of confusion.

Their old commander's face was flushed red with rage as he stared into the passage. "Impossible!" he spat. "Impossible!"

Vennet, meanwhile, sauntered up to the mouth of the passage

and peered inside. "Well, there you are, Geth!" he said. "We were wondering what had happened to you."

The shifter only growled at him. Vennet laughed and turned back around. "Tzaryan, what are you waiting for? Get your ogres in there!"

Alarm crossed Tzaryan's face and he swung around to Dah'mir. "My ogres would be at a disadvantage!" he protested. "The space is too tight. Dah'mir, you can't make them—"

"At ease, Tzaryan," said Dah'mir. "No one is going in. Geth is going to come out and give me what I want."

In the passage, Ekhaas started and leaned over to murmur something to Geth and Ashi. Singe saw Geth's eyes go wide. "Tiger's blood!" the shifter cursed.

Dah'mir gave an indulgent chuckle. "The hobgoblin has guessed what will happen. Tzaryan, who is she?"

"Her name is Ekhaas. She's a *duur'kala.*"

"Ah." Dah'mir peered into the tunnel. "Watch closely, *duur'kala*, and you'll see something out of your legends." He sat back and looked to the prisoners on the platform. "Do you know what it is you sit beneath?"

A chill spread through Singe. Ekhaas wasn't the only one who could guess what would happen. "It's a Grieving Tree," he said to Dah'mir. "It's a Dhakaani execution device."

"Not just *a* Grieving Tree, Singe," Dah'mir said. *"The* Grieving Tree. The very first one, created by Taruuzh. It's also more than just a device. The original Grieving Trees were alive in their own way. They grew—that's one reason why this one is so big. And like any living thing, they needed to be fed." His acid-green eyes flashed. "This tree hasn't been fed in a very long time." He spoke a word that sounded like Goblin.

Singe felt a stirring at his back and twisted around.

The Grieving Tree was moving, the strangely curved stone segments that made up its trunk and limbs grinding as they rotated against each other. They shuddered and dipped as the tree flexed. Singe's blood ran cold. Natrac choked and tried to squirm away. Dah'mir spoke another word.

A thick branch bent down and curved stone curled around the half-orc, whisking him up into the air and passing him from limb to limb until he hung in the shadows high above the ground.

Sharp ridges and thorny spikes rippled—and dug into his flesh. Natrac flung back his head and screamed.

Wherever a branch embraced him, the grooves carved into the stone turned dark and red, catching and channeling his blood. A shudder like an unseen, unfelt breeze shook the tree. Natrac's scream fell into a deep moan.

Dah'mir's voice was light. "Death on a Grieving Tree is slow. The tree takes only a little blood at a time. A strong person could linger on the tree for days. I recall a legend of a fallen Dhakaani hero who hung on the tree for two weeks before she died."

Natrac shifted—or tried to. The effort only dragged a new scream out of him. Dah'mir spoke the Goblin word a second time. Another branch twisted, reaching for Orshok. The druid saw it coming and shouted in fear. "No!" Singe yelled. He threw himself on top of the young orc, trying hold him down, to keep the tree from dragging him up. It was no good. Carved stone slid underneath Orshok and lifted both of them. His hands still tied, Singe couldn't grasp him. He slid and fell, landing flat on his back. The impact drove the air out of his lungs. Stunned, he could only stare up into the branches and watch Orshok thrash in agony as spikes dug into his flesh and the tree released his blood.

"No," he choked. He wrenched his neck around, trying to look for Geth, for Dah'mir. His eyes found Robrand. "Do something!"

The old man looked frightened and shockingly frail. He didn't move. Beyond him, Tzaryan wore an expression of cold curiosity, studying the tree as if calculating how he could make use of it. Vennet's face was alight with horrid, mad fascination.

In the passage, Geth's face was pale and tormented—but hard. His lips were pressed tight together.

Dah'mir began to speak the word that commanded the tree a third time . . .

"No."

Dah'mir stopped, the word of command poised on his tongue. Singe twisted around.

Hruucan stood over him, the fire of his body casting a bloody light up into the branches of the tree. His face was turned to Dah'mir. "No," he said again. "The tree can't have him. He's mine. I claim him."

The dragon's mouth curved into a frown. "Your kills end too quickly, Hruucan."

"This one won't." A tentacle of flame reached down. Singe tried to roll aside but Hruucan was quicker. The tentacle writhed after him, catching his leg and hauling him back. Once again, the ring that Singe wore devoured the flame before it burned him, but just as before, there was more to Hruucan's fiery touch than heat. His leg twitched, curled, and seemed to go numb. When the tentacle tore away, it ripped something out of his very soul. Singe jerked and cried out. Patches of darkness blotted his vision.

Dah'mir's voice came out of one of those patches. He sounded amused. "Take him with my blessing then," he said. "Enjoy your revenge."

Hruucan reached down with a charred hand and grasped the front of Singe's shirt, hauling him to his feet. The wizard stared in the black pits of the dolgaunt's empty eye sockets as he bared sharp teeth. "I will," Hruucan said.

His free hand rose and clamped across Singe's face.

Geth's stomach was filled with stones. His head had been packed with broken glass. His ears hurt. His eyes burned. His fists were clenched so tight that his fingers ached. He didn't look at Ashi or at Ekhaas, though he could hear them. Ashi's breath came in harsh rasps. Ekhaas was singing something softly, her voice near to cracking.

Out in the great chamber, Singe shrieked and came near to collapsing under the touch of the fiery undead thing that Hruucan had become. On the Grieving Tree, Orshok's voice rose in a babble of pain and Natrac moaned like an echo of Taruuzh in the caves below.

His friends were dying and there was nothing he could do.

Giving Wrath to Dah'mir would be giving the dragon Taruuzh's stones. He couldn't do that. He'd thought about breaking the sword—but that would only slow Dah'mir down. He could still take Dandra and Tetkashtai and kill the rest of them. Geth couldn't accept that either. There had to be something else he could do, something clever. Something that Singe or Dandra would have thought of. They were the clever ones. All he could do was fight.

Another voice rose in agony. Robrand whirled around and stared into the passage. "Dol Arrah's mercy, Geth—give him what he wants! End this! For Etan's sake, end it!"

Dah'mir's eyes stirred with interest and Geth could see the looks of surprise that Tzaryan and Vennet gave the old man.

"General! You know these two?" Tzaryan asked.

"They were under my command in the Frostbrand, my lord." Robrand's voice shook. "Etan was . . . *is* a friend. I promise you, I've given them no information or aid since they've been here that would dishonor the contract between us, but this—" He took a step toward the tunnel and raised his hands to Geth. "You can stop this, Geth. Whatever the dragon wants, give it to him!"

Geth's throat felt raw. "I can't," he croaked.

Robrand's face seemed to collapse. "You . . ." he said. He raised a trembling arm and pointed it at Geth. "You are a coward. You always have been. You always will be. Even when you can't run away, you're too much of a coward to act!"

The words were like blows. Only a few hours before, Geth would have curled up under them like the coward Robrand accused him of being, frightened of his old commander's rage, ashamed of his own past.

Not now. Fury replaced shame and fear. Geth took the blows and hit back. "You don't know what you're talking about, old man! You don't know what's at stake here—and you don't know what was at stake in Narath! Why don't you close your mouth and look at who you're standing with before you call me a coward again!"

Robrand staggered, then stood straight. He turned to Tzaryan. "My lord, your assessment of the risk in storming the passage does no credit to your troops. They can take the enemy position without undue loss."

A part of Geth flinched at being referred to as the enemy. He bit it back, though. He and Robrand had chosen sides. His rage already roused, he snarled out at Robrand, "Send them in! Let's see just how well you've trained them!"

Ekhaas twitched. "You're as mad as the half-elf!" she hissed. Geth ignored her and glanced at Ashi. The hunter nodded grimly, her hand tightening on the grip of her bright Deneith honor blade.

Beyond the passage, Tzaryan looked up at Dah'mir. The

dragon's eyes narrowed to shining slits as if he was contemplating his options. On the platform under the Grieving Tree, Hruucan released his grasp on Singe. The wizard gave a low cry and dropped to his knees. Hruucan turned away, only to snap around in a whirling kick that cracked into Singe's side and sent him sliding across the platform. Singe hit the trunk of the Grieving Tree hard—hard enough to shake the carved stone—and lay still. Hung on the branches above, though, the shock of his impact brought new screams from both Natrac and Orshok.

Tears threatened to cloud Geth's vision. A howl of anguish built in his throat.

"Hruucan," Dah'mir said sharply, "hold." The dolgaunt paused in midstride. Dah'mir lowered his head to peer into the passage. "Geth, I have a proposal for you."

"I'm not going to deal with you," Geth said. "All you want is the sword!"

"Not exactly. I also want to make you suffer for the injury you inflicted on me at the Bonetree mound. I want to punish Ashi for abandoning me." The dragon's voice was hard. "But I am capable of compromise. You're strong enough to let your friends die in a vain attempt to keep the sword safe, but I will have it eventually. I may not be able to reach you, but we both know that you can't escape. I can wait, you'll starve in that hole, and the sword will be mine."

Geth bared his teeth. "You'll be waiting a long time!"

"Exactly." Dah'mir blinked slowly, acid-green eyes closing then opening again like a double eclipse. "The Bonetree hunters would say that you've shown yourself to be a good enemy, Geth. You've survived everything I've thrown at you. That's why I'll offer you the warrior's choice. You can hold the sword and I'll claim it after you and all of your friends are dead—or you can surrender the sword to me now and I'll let all of you go free to try and win the sword back another day." His muzzle curved in a smile. "I like a challenge."

All of the tension inside Geth came together in a single knot. "You'd use the sword to claim Taruuzh's stones."

"Of course, I would. But I don't have all the pieces to the puzzle, do I? I don't have a hobgoblin lord. There's a little time for you to try to stop me."

Something tugged at Geth, something out of place in what the dragon had said, but he couldn't quite identify it. He thrust it aside. "What's to stop you from attacking us as soon as we leave the passage?"

"Geth!" hissed Ashi. "You're not going to take his deal, are you?"

"Take it!" Ekhaas said from his other side. "*Khaavolaar*, I don't want to die here!"

Geth swallowed. "I . . . I don't . . ."

"Not an easy decision, is it?" asked Dah'mir. "But I'll make it easier for you: keep the sword until you're out of this place. You've said yourself that I don't risk attacking you for fear of destroying the sword. So long as I need the sword, you're safe. Once you're out of Taruuzh Kraat, leave the sword and I pledge not to attack you or yours until we meet again." He bent his head. "*Majak wux aridarastrixszaka*—I give you the word of a dragon."

Suspicion rose immediately in Geth. "How can I trust your word?" he asked. "You've tried to kill us. You're our enemy. Grandfather Rat, you serve a daelkyr!"

Dah'mir smiled again. "You stand between a *duur'kala* of the Kech Volaar and a hunter of the Bonetree clan. Ask Ekhaas about the pledge of a dragon. Ask Ashi if I've ever failed to keep my word once it was given."

Geth glanced at the two women. Ashi's brow furrowed. "Bonetree legends say that when the Revered promised something, it was always carried out."

Ekhaas nodded. "Among the Kech Volaar, it's said that a dragon doesn't give his word lightly, but once given it's always honored." Her ears bent forward, though, and her voice dropped. "But it's also said that the word of a dragon can have many meanings."

Geth's jaw clenched. "He's trying to trick us." He looked back up—and focused on Tzaryan standing at Dah'mir's side. "Tzaryan, too. And Hruucan and Vennet. Your pledge extends to them."

Dah'mir's smile faded slightly, but his voice betrayed nothing. "Done," he said. "I expect you to honor the pledge as well. Leave the sword outside Taruuzh Kraat or you'll face a fury such as you've never seen."

"You'll have the sword," said Geth.

"You're going to do it." Ashi stared at him in disbelief. *"Rond betch,* you're going to give it to him."

"We'll get it back." Geth said. He glared at Dah'mir. "You have my word on that."

Dah'mir chuckled faintly. "I said that I like a challenge." He straightened up and turned toward Hruucan as he hovered over Singe's unmoving form. "Away from him," Dah'mir said.

The dolgaunt's tentacles whipped at the air. "He still lives!" he said, his voice an angry rasp. "My revenge—"

"—can wait. I need him alive. *Back away!"*

Dah'mir's presence poured through the command. Hruucan, poised on the edge of lunging for Singe, instead staggered and thrust himself back violently, tumbling off the platform and darting across the great chamber. Only when he could run no farther did he stop and turn back to bare his teeth at Dah'mir.

The wash of the dragon's power also seemed to bring Singe starting back to consciousness. His eyes twitched between Dah'mir and Hruucan in confusion. "What—?" he gasped.

"Don't ask questions, Singe," said Geth. He glanced at Ekhaas and Ashi. "Ekhaas," he said, "come with me. Ashi, bring Dandra to the mouth of the passage. Be ready to leave." He tightened his grip on the sword and strode forward with Ekhaas behind him. At the end of the passage, he hesitated for a moment, then stepped out into the cavern.

No one moved. Hruucan crouched against the far wall of the cavern, Chuut and the ogres of Tzaryan Keep arrayed in the shadows, Vennet to the right of the passage, Tzaryan Rrac and Dah'mir to the left, Robrand still standing near the base of the Grieving Tree—none of them moved. Every eye was on him, though.

He fixed his gaze on the grieving tree and walked. He passed Robrand. Neither of them said anything. Geth leaped up onto the platform and looked at Singe. "Do you think you can walk?" he asked.

The wizard grimaced and climbed unsteadily to his feet. "With help," he said.

"You may have to do it on your own." Geth glanced up into the branches, then turned and faced Dah'mir. "Get them down," he said.

Dah'mir growled a word and the branches of the Grieving Tree shivered. Natrac groaned as the carved stone passed him toward the ground. The tree released him with surprising gentleness, lowering him to crouch on the platform in a shuddering, shaking heap. "See to him," Geth told Ekhaas. "Carry him if you need to." He looked back up to Dah'mir. "Orshok!" he demanded.

Dah'mir's voice growled and once again the tree moved. This time though, there was little gentleness. As if reluctant to give up its prey, the Grieving Tree thrashed rather than shivered. Orshok screamed, then twisted among the branches. His drop was sharp and hard; he hit the ground with a cracking of bones.

"Orshok!" Geth threw himself toward the young druid's twisted body. One of Orshok's arms was bent at a hard angle underneath his body. His breath whistled in his throat. One of his legs shook in an uncontrolled spasm. Geth hesitated, then reached for him with his free hand. "Orshok."

The orc's eyes fluttered. "Geth . . ." He lifted the arm that wasn't trapped and groped for Geth's hand.

The instant that their fingers met, Wrath's blade flared with a purple radiance that seared Geth's eyes. There was a sharp crack like lightning striking close and the sword bucked in his hand. The branches of the Grieving Tree stiffened, its truck split—and, like an echo through the ages, Geth heard Taruuzh's voice cry out.

Three great works stand together as allies: treasure, key, guardian, disciple, and lord. The time has come again!

The grinding of sliding stone rumbled over a chorus of shouts and fell apart into the deafening clatter of rock against rock. Geth blinked, fighting to clear the radiance of Wrath's flare from his eyes, but all he saw were shadows as the Grieving Tree split and fell away from him. Orshok clung to him. He tore his hand away and staggered blindly to his feet.

The broken stump of the Grieving Tree stood before him like pedestal. Resting on it was a box of dull gray metal.

"*Yes!*" roared Dah'mir. "*Yes!* Vennet, seize that box and get it open! Tzaryan, forward! Secure your prisoners!"

Geth stared at the box. It couldn't be . . . there was no way . . . He stared down at Wrath, the blade once more dull as twilight in his hand. The key, the guardian, the disciple. "But I'm not a hobgoblin," he whispered. "I'm not a warlord—"

And in the same instant, he saw in his mind a gang of goblins running from his drawn blade in Zarash'ak and heard Ekhaas's words in the dungeon beneath Tzaryan Keep. A *lhesh shaarat* was a warlord's blade, she'd said, the weapon of kings and heroes. Anyone who drew one proclaimed his power.

Anyone who drew one. Not necessarily a hobgoblin.

Dah'mir had guessed it. The dragon's words had tugged at Geth because he'd only mentioned his lack of a hobgoblin warlord—he'd known that he had a Gatekeeper in his possession. He'd known that he only needed to bring Geth and Orshok together under the Grieving Tree.

A lithe body leaped up onto the platform and lunged for the box. Vennet. Geth howled and swung Wrath at the half-elf in a powerful arc.

The blade cracked against the heavy shaft of an out-flung mace. An ogre's strength thrust him back. Chuut stepped up between Geth and Vennet, mace raised to strike again—and abruptly Geth was aware once more of the chaos around him. He and Orshok were surrounded. At the mouth of the passage, Ashi tried to shield Dandra, her sword outstretched as she attempted to menace three ogres and Tzaryan himself simultaneously. Ekhaas, Natrac slumped against her, and Singe stood back to back, more ogres on one side of them and Hruucan's fiery form on the other. Robrand stood with his sword drawn, but not moving, just turning around and around as if overcome by the rush. He looked older than Geth could have imagined.

"Dah'mir!" Ekhaas's voice rose out of the confusion. "Your pledge! You gave the word of a dragon that you'd let us leave!"

Dah'mir stood tall in the shadows, his eyes bright and intense. "So long as I needed the sword!" he said with a triumphant hiss. "And now I don't need the sword anymore. Didn't I say that Geth would come out and give me what I want?" He looked down at Geth. "I'm certain," he added, "that when Taruuzh made that *lhesh shaarat*, he had no idea that anyone other than a goblinoid or maybe an orc would ever wield it. The Dhakaani had a high opinion of themselves."

"So do dragons," Geth growled.

Immense teeth flashed as Dah'mir's jaws snapped together. "In our case, it's the truth."

"Master!" Vennet had the box. It was no longer or wider than the length of Geth's forearm and no deeper than a hand span, but the half-elf hefted it as though it was heavy. An ogre reached out to help him but Vennet grimaced and twisted away. "Get back!" he snapped. He dragged the box off of the platform by himself and hauled it over to Dah'mir.

"Open it," said the dragon. Vennet set the box down, fumbled with the latch, then threw open the lid.

Blue-black dragonshards, each no bigger than a finger, each wrapped in a filigree of gold, shone against rich red fabric. There were fewer than Geth would have guessed—twenty maybe, no more—but the sight of them brought an ache to his heart. He'd failed. He'd made the wrong choice. Somewhere below the great chamber, Taruuzh's ghost let out a soft, fading wail.

"Take one out," Dah'mir told Vennet. "They won't harm you. Hold it up for me."

The ancient fabric cradling the stones crumbled at Vennet's touch, but the half-elf plucked out a stone and held it high. "They're beautiful," he said.

"They're more than beautiful." The dark shard reflected the acid-green of Dah'mir's eyes as the dragon bent close to examine it. "They're seeds. From them will spring my master's new servants." He glanced up at Geth—and smiled. "Perhaps we should plant the first seed now." His long neck twisted toward the passage. "Dandra," he said, "come here."

Unblinking, her face expressionless, Dandra took a step forward.

"No!" Ashi tried to push her back, but in the moment that she was distracted, the ogres facing her surged forward. Ashi's voice rose in a scream of rage. Her sword thrust and darted, caught one ogre in the knee cap and another in the belly, then Tzaryan Rrac stepped close and snatched the sword from her, wrapping his hand around the blade itself. For an instant, black blood flowed, but when the ogre mage flung the sword away, his hand bore no injury. Tzaryan and his ogres lunged at the unarmed hunter in unison, dragging her down. Ashi twisted, punched, and kicked, still trying to grab for Dandra. Geth cried out and would have leaped to Ashi's side, but Chuut swung his mace and he was forced to stumble back.

"Dandra!" shouted Singe. "Twelve moons—*Dandra!"*

Unmindful of anything that was happening around her, Dandra kept walking toward Dah'mir and the binding stone. Ashi squirmed out from among the writhing tangle of ogres that tried to hold her and grabbed at the kalashtar. "You won't have her!" she spat. *"You will not have her!"*

Tzaryan caught the hunter's leg. Ashi's grasp fell short. Her fingertips only brushed at Dandra's back.

But the air seemed to shimmer at that brief contact—and Dandra froze. For a heartbeat, her eyes opened wide, then she flung back her head and screamed. Against her chest, her psicrystal pulsed with a yellow-green glow. Her feet left the ground and she rose to hover an armslength above it, still screaming. Behind her, Tzaryan and his ogres sprang away from Ashi as if in shock at Dandra's cry but Geth realized immediately that they were springing away from Ashi herself.

Lines of radiant color were drawing themselves across the hunter's exposed skin, curling up from the hand with which she had reached for Dandra and racing across her arms, her legs, her face—

"By the houses," choked Robrand.

"A Siberys mark," Singe said. "The Siberys Mark of Sentinel!"

"No!" howled Vennet, the binding stone slipping from his fingers to fall to the ground. "She can't have a Siberys mark! *I* have a Siberys mark!"

Ashi just knelt on the ground, staring at her arms.

Then Dandra stopped screaming.

CHAPTER

20

She saw and heard everything. Taruuzh's howls from below at the wash of Dah'mir's mad power. Natrac and Orshok's torture on the Grieving Tree. Singe's torment by Hruucan. Robrand's cursing of Geth and Geth's rejection of the old man's anger. She saw the terrible decision that Dah'mir had forced on the shifter. She saw Orshok's fall from the tree, Geth's rush to the young druid, and the shocking consequences of his compassion. She watched Dah'mir roar in triumph as his allies surrounded her friends. Surrounded her, even as Ashi tried to hold them back.

She saw everything—and could do nothing, not even turn away. Her gaze was fixed on Dah'mir and everything that happened around the dragon.

Her mind's eye saw nothing better. With each moment that Dah'mir's power held her, the storm of Tetkashtai's terror only grew stronger. *Let me in, Dandra! Il-Yannah, let me in—I can't take this anymore!*

No! Dandra thrust back against Tetkashtai with all of her will. It barely moved the presence. Once she'd been able to contain her creator, to hold her in the prison of her psicrystal. Now it seemed like the connection that bound them had burst open like a floodgate—it felt like she was try to hold back a raging river. *Tetkashtai, work with me!* she begged. *Dah'mir's power can't hold you—maybe we can find a way to beat him!*

Beat him? Tetkashtai swirled and surged, her light flashing bright with new fear and pressing even closer. *We can't beat him! We have to run and you're not running!*

We can beat him, Tetkashtai, but you need to—

Beyond the storm of light, Dandra saw Vennet open the ancient box that had been hidden in the Grieving Tree and lift out one of Taruuzh's binding stones. Even through the storm she could feel the stone on the edge of her awareness like a void in the fabric of the world. *Il-Yannah*, she whispered silently. For a moment, panic gripped her—

—and gave Tetkashtai a grip on her. Light lashed through her defenses and wrapped around her like one of Hruucan's flaming tentacles. Dandra grasped and writhed. Tetkashtai's voice rolled through her mind. *I will have my body back!* the presence howled.

But another voice spoke even louder. "Dandra," said Dah'mir, "come here."

His acid-green eyes shone like beacons, drawing her to him. Dandra felt her body respond with a step forward. Ashi's hand grasped her—then was torn away as Tzaryan and his ogres pulled her down. *Tetkashtai!* she shouted. *Tetkashtai, stop fighting me!*

No! You stop fighting me!

Another step. Fear surged within her—fear for Ashi as the hunter fell out of her field of vision, fear for herself as she walked closer to the blue-black void of Taruuzh's stone, fear driven by Tetkashtai's fear. More of her creator poured through her failing defenses. The floodwaters of terror rose around her.

"Dandra! Twelve moons—Dandra!" called Singe.

She could still see him, standing with Ekhaas as Hruucan and more ogres closed in on them. The wizard would never hear her but Dandra shouted back to him anyway. *Singe!* She struggled desperately, trying to keep Tetkashtai back, but she could already tell the battle was lost. It was only a question of what would take her first: Tetkashtai's terror or Taruuzh's stone.

Ashi's voice rose from behind her like a reminder of her own fading determination. "You won't have her! *You will not have her!*"

Something brushed against her back—and the flood within her grew calm. The storm eased. She could feel Dah'mir's grip on her vanish. Her will was hers again.

But not her body. Not yet.

Dandra stood on the featureless plain of her mind and faced . . . herself. For the first time, Tetkashtai was more than just amorphous light. She had Dandra's form—or rather, Dandra had hers.

"What's happening?" Tetkashtai asked. She seemed calm, but Dandra could see the fear inside of her. It leaked out through her eyes, making them look wide and wild.

"I don't know." Dandra wondered what she looked like. She felt focused and determined, but at the same time oddly uncertain. "Dah'mir's lost his power over us. Something's holding him back—I think it's holding us apart, too."

Tetkashtai's wild eyes hardened. "The hunter touched us just before this happened. The brute *dahr* has done something to us!"

"If she's done anything, it's save us!" Dandra's heart clenched. "And don't call her a *dahr*. She's my friend!"

"Your friend—not mine." Tetkashtai moved slowly to the side, walking around her. Dandra turned to stay with her. "I don't think she's saved us. I almost had you before this happened. I almost had my body back."

A shiver crawled up Dandra's spine. "Tetkashtai, you'd gone mad with fear. Whatever's going on, it's given you a second chance."

"I feel like I've been nothing but afraid since Dah'mir used his device on us!" Tetkashtai stopped sharply and swept her arms out, gesturing to the open space around them. "Do you know what this place is?"

"My mind," said Dandra, then hesitated. "Our mind."

"*My* mind," Tetkashtai said. "This is where I came to create you." She pointed.

Off in the distance, a memory took shape: Tetkashtai in meditation, pouring her determination into a yellow-green crystal, creating an aid to bolster her will. Dandra felt a strange chill. She was witnessing her own birth as a tiny fragment of Tetkashtai's personality.

"That's right," said Tetkashtai. "A fragment of me—and by il-Yannah's light, that's what you'll be again!"

A spear flashed, shimmering into being in Tetkashtai's grip as she lunged forward. Dandra spun aside but the spear's sharp edge grazed her side. Pain burned in a bright line. Somewhere in the distance, someone began screaming. Tetkashtai lunged again, but this time Dandra was ready. She twisted, then twisted again, staying just ahead of the spear—then twisted back with a spear of her own, and knocked Tetkashtai's weapon aside. The uncertainty that had been inside her resolved itself into a sharp point.

"Don't do this," she said.

"If I don't," hissed Tetkashtai, "what is there for me to go back to?" She stepped into the air and slid forward. Dandra matched her, gliding backward. They moved faster and faster with each exchange of blows until the wind of their momentum shrieked around them.

"We're stronger together!" Dandra shouted over it. "That's why you created me!"

"Would you go back to being a psicrystal? Would you go back to being all but powerless, a prisoner unable to do anything but wait for your doom to catch up with you?" Tetkashtai twisted suddenly, sweeping low with her spear. The shaft of the weapon caught the back of Dandra's knees and knocked her feet out from under her. Dandra fell, momentum sending her tumbling across the flat earth. She caught a glimpse of Tetkashtai leaping high and flung herself to the side just as her creator's spear stabbed down. It pierced the ground where her head had been an instant before. Tetkashtai yanked it free and whirled to face her again.

"Would you give up Singe?" she snarled through clenched teeth. Dandra's heart caught. Tetkashtai's lips drew back. "No? Then why should I give up my life, my body for someone—for *something* that isn't even really a kalashtar? That scarcely knows what being a kalashtar means? That would use one of us as a weapon against another?"

Dandra rose to a crouch, spear held low in one hand. "Virikhad and Medala?" she asked. "Tetkashtai, I've told you, I did what I had to! Medala would have killed Singe, Geth, Batul—everyone—and handed us to Dah'mir to become like her. Virikhad . . ." She took a breath, trying to calm herself, to find her focus. "I'm sorry I had to use Virikhad that way, but the situation was desperate."

"Then you'll understand how I feel right now!" Tetkashtai threw herself forward.

Dandra flung up her hand. Within her mind, her powers came freely. *Vayhatana* rippled through the air in a wave, caught Tetkashtai, and sent her sprawling backward. Dandra dropped her spear and stood, gesturing as she wove a web of force to hold her other self. Tetkashtai struggled, then looked up sharply. The droning chorus of whitefire rang in Dandra's ears. Pale flames burst around her and she gasped. Her web of *vayhatana* vanished. Tetkashtai rushed at her, fingers curled like talons. "This body *will* be mine again!"

Dandra caught her hands, twining her fingers against Tetkashtai's. Whitefire leaped from her to Tetkashtai. Dandra met her creator's eyes and the mad terror that burned in them. "Please," she said one last time.

Tetkashtai's answer was a scream.

Dandra raised her chin. "I'm sorry," she said. "I have to do this."

She seized the fire and drew it into herself. All of it.

The screaming stopped. The only thoughts in Dandra's head were her own. The yellow-green crystal that hung around her neck was a prison no longer. She opened her eyes and glared at Dah'mir. There was shock on his face but he hadn't moved at all—her confrontation with Tetkashtai had taken place at the speed of thought. She was aware of everyone around, paused in amazement, but all of her attention was on Dah'mir. Dandra's lips curled in disgust and anger at the dragon. "You *dahr*," she whispered.

"This isn't possible," said Dah'mir. His shock flared into rage and he roared, "This isn't possible!" He reared back and his head almost brushed the ceiling of the great chamber. "You are mine! Submit to me!"

She should have felt the tidal rush of his presence, but she didn't feel anything at all. It was as if something stood between her and Dah'mir, shielding her completely from his terrible power. Dandra looked into Dah'mir's acid-green eyes and felt only rage at what he had done to her, to Tetkashtai, to Medalashana and Virikhad—at what he would do to other kalashtar if he had the chance.

If he had the chance.

For the first time since Dah'mir had torn her and Tetkashtai apart, powers that had been sundered were hers to command. With a thought, the chorus of whitefire swelled and throbbed on the air. Dandra heard ogres shout in fear. Dah'mir's acid-green eyes flared. His powerful body tensed and his growl was like thunder. *"You think you can destroy me?"*

"I don't need to destroy you," Dandra said. She wrenched her eyes from Dah'mir and down to Vennet at his side. To the ancient box at Vennet's feet.

Her arm snapped around and flung the torch she had gripped for so long. As it left her hand, it exploded with whitefire, psionic flames consuming the wood in an instant. She channeled all of her rage, fear, and hatred into the blast of flame and the whitefire roared with a focused heat hot enough to burn stone as it streaked toward Taruuzh's deadly treasure. Vennet shrieked and flung up his arms—

Faster than she would have thought possible, Dah'mir lunged and twisted around, trying to shield the binding stones.

Fire spattered like water against dark scales, filling the air with a burning spray and the stink of charred flesh. Dah'mir's howl of pain was like a living thing. It shook the air and seemed to shake the cavern itself.

But the dragon wasn't the only one to howl. In instant, Geth had seized the confusion—with a bellow of rage, the shifter threw himself at Chuut, byeshk sword whirling, steel gauntlet punching. The ogre lieutenant fell back before him, bashing away with his mace, but Geth was fast. He rolled under the ogre's blow and came up swinging, forcing Chuut back even further.

All around Dandra, Tzaryan's other ogres had forgotten their discipline entirely. Two . . . three . . . half a dozen . . . abruptly all the ogres were fleeing from the fire and the howls, and Robrand was turning around and around, shouting at them to return to their positions. He might as well have shouted at the wind. The ogres fled for the stairs out of the great chamber and the long passage back to the surface, their big feet pounding the stone in desperate flight. Even the orc slave who had been carrying Robrand's torches dropped the fiery brands and fled. The already dim light in the chamber flashed crazily as the torches rolled and skipped across the ground.

The screaming battle cry of the Bonetree hunters rose behind her. Dandra swung around to see Ashi—her body strangely striped in the feeble, flickering light—leap for Tzaryan Rrac, snatching her sword from the ground as she moved. The blade made a bright arc in the air. Forced to dance away from the hunter's attack, the arm that the ogre mage had pointed at Dandra's back instead swung wildly. Frost sprayed from his fingertips and one of the few ogres who had stood his ground cried out and fell, ice coating his shoulders and chest. Just a pace away, Robrand stared and threw himself back. Tzaryan cursed—and Ashi struck, her sword plunging into his side. She jerked it free.

Blood spurted for a moment, then stopped as the wound in Tzaryan's side healed over. Dandra saw Ashi's eyes open in disbelief. Tzaryan bared black teeth in an evil grin and drew a heavy sword, returning Ashi's attack.

"Dah'mir!" Hruucan's voice was harsh rasp. Dandra swung about again. The fiery dolgaunt crouched by Ekhaas and Singe, tentacles whipping the air as if he was torn between loyalty to his master and his revenge on Singe. He lunged at Singe, and Dandra felt the wizard's name rise to her lips—

—then Hruucan was past Singe and hurling himself at her, kicking off from the ground and spinning through the air. Dandra's cry turned into a gasp. Her hand came up, the chorus of whitefire pulsed, and pale flame washed over Hruucan.

It didn't even slow him down. If anything, it only made the fire that sprang from his burned body stronger. Hissing tentacles flailed at Dandra and she spun her spear desperately, catching them on the shaft. The wood charred and acrid smoke stung her nose and her eyes. Dandra skimmed backward on the air, but Hruucan was as fast as she was and followed close, hands and tentacles feinting and striking. Dandra blocked and slid aside, then released the whitefire and thrust out hard with *vayhatana*.

A rippling wave flung Hruucan halfway across the chamber, but he just twisted in midair, landed on his feet, and sprinted forward again.

Song so sharp it seemed to raise the dust from the floor burst around him and he stumbled to the side, clutching at his head. Ekhaas gave Dandra a fierce grin. At the hobgoblin's side, Singe shouted, "Ashi! Back!" His fingers traced a sign in the air and an arcane word hissed on his tongue.

Ashi flung herself away, leaving Tzaryan Rrac to turn to the wizard—and the gout of orange flame that burst from his hand.

Tzaryan yelled and staggered, his sword falling from a burned arm that showed no sign of healing.

For an instant, Dandra felt a moment of triumph.

Then Ekhaas shouted and flung up an arm. Dandra whirled around.

Dah'mir's twisted body was uncoiling. His wings rattled, his tail slapped the ground. His legs pushed. His body rose. His neck twisted and he turned his head and looked at her. The whitefire hadn't left him unmarked. One of his luminous acid-green eyes was dim and smoky and a long black wound had been seared down his neck, across his shoulder, and along his flank. His scales had been burned away along that stripe and his flesh still smoked. It was an injury that might have killed a lesser creature, but Dah'mir was still very much alive.

Dandra flung her spear away and raised both hands, reaching for the whitefire once more, trying to summon up the angry power that she had before.

"No," spat Vennet, ducking out from behind Dah'mir's rising bulk. "Not this time!" Eyes narrowed in a face smudged by ash.

Wind blasted at Dandra, pushing her floating body back through the air. Dandra tried to get her feet back on the ground, but she was too slow. The power of Vennet's dragonmark thrust her right into Ashi. For a moment, she and the hunter fought against each other to keep their balance, then both fell in the buffeting wind. The chorus of whitefire vanished and Dandra caught a glimpse of Vennet baring his teeth in fierce triumph.

On the ground beside him was Taruuzh's ancient box, utterly untouched. Dandra's heart seemed to stop and all she could do was stare at Dah'mir as he stretched up, wounded and angry and terrible.

Until a clashing of metal on metal that she had almost forgotten ended in the thud of a fallen body and a sharp cry cut short. On the platform where the grieving tree had stood, Geth ripped his sword from the ruin of Chuut's throat and stood tall over the ogre's corpse. His gauntleted arm hung limp and new blood soaked his already gore-matted hair, but he raised his face and lifted Wrath.

"Dah'mir!" he shouted.

The dragon swung around. Geth bared his teeth, flung himself across the platform and, at the very edge, leaped high, swinging Wrath as he hurtled straight for Dah'mir's broad chest and the Khyber shard embedded there.

Dah'mir's good eye opened wide in genuine fear—and his body abruptly seemed to fold in on itself and shrink. His hind legs shriveled, his tail vanished, and his forelegs shifted up and merged with wings that suddenly bore black feathers. When less than a moment before a dragon had stood, a heron beat wide wings and flapped high. Geth shouted and twisted around, struggling to swing his sword at this new target, but Dah'mir was already too high. As Geth slammed hard into the ground and rolled, the heron dipped its wings and circled. Dah'mir's oil-smooth voice emerged from the bird's beak. "Vennet, get the box! We have all we'll need. It's time to leave!"

Alarm rolled through Dandra even as Vennet snatched up the box and Dah'mir settled down on top of it. "No!" she shouted, thrusting herself to her feet—at the same moment as Tzaryan roared out, "You're leaving me?" and Hruucan rasped, "Dah'mir! My revenge!"

The heron only answered one of them. "Take your revenge, Hruucan, and my revenge as well." A green eye flashed and Dah'mir added something in a language Dandra didn't recognize, a language that seemed to sting her ears, then he spread his wings and spoke a word of magic. Among the feathers on one wing, a red dragonshard flared and went dim. Shadows wrapped around Dah'mir and Vennet—and they vanished.

Tzaryan lunged for the spot where they had stood, still roaring curses but Hruucan . . . Hruucan turned slowly, as if surveying the chamber and those who remained in it. Flames crawled across his body. His fiery tentacles drifted almost lazily in the air. His voice grated and crackled like flame itself. "Revenge . . ." he said. His gaze settled on Singe and his mouth split in a smile.

He burst into motion, tentacles snapping forward to seize Singe. The wizard, already weak, cried out, his cry dropping quickly into a horrible moan. Ekhaas, still burdened by Natrac, shrank away, but started to open her mouth in song. Without releasing Singe, Hruucan lashed out with a kick that knocked her back, sent Natrac tumbling out of her arms, and left a scorched mark on her leather armor. "You're next!" he promised her. His eyeless face sought out Dandra. "Then you!"

Fear stabbed through Dandra—not for herself, but for Singe. For all of them. Hruucan seemed unstoppable. Whitefire didn't affect the already burned dolgaunt. *Vayhatana* could throw him away, but he'd just come back. Hruucan was as fast as she was, faster than Ekhaas, and she had a terrible feeling that anyone without Singe's ring who came into the dolgaunt's grasp would not last as long as the wizard had. Dandra's eyes darted around the chamber. Orshok and Natrac were still down. Ashi was struggling back to her feet. Geth, stunned by his impact with the ground, was staggering as new blood rushed down his face.

Even Tzaryan looked frightened by Hruucan's intensity. The ogre mage met her gaze and thrust a hand at the ogre frozen by his misaimed spell. "If I hadn't wasted that on him, I might have been able to do something!"

A desperate idea formed in Dandra's mind. Light of il-Yannah, she thought, let me be right about this! Stepping into the air, she flung up a hand, spun out a web of *vayhatana*—and wrapped it around Singe's sagging body.

Hruucan must have recognized the touch of her power. His tentacles loosened instantly, leaving only wisps of flame to be devoured by Singe's ring, and leaped away with a frustrated shriek. He spun to face Dandra, but she already had what she wanted.

With all of her will, she wrenched on the invisible streams of *vayhatana*, pulling at Singe as hard as she had thrust at Hruucan earlier. Singe's body jerked into a blur of motion that ripped a startled cry out of him. Quick as thought, Dandra skimmed backward as fast as she could, flinging herself back into the passage that had been their refuge and dragging Singe—still hurtling through the air—with her.

Out in the chamber, Hruucan screamed. "He's mine!"

"Come get him!" Dandra shouted back. She caught a glimpse of the dolgaunt surging after her—then the floor fell away under her heels and in the instant that she tried to adjust to the uneven surface of the stairs, Singe's body hammered into hers.

The impact knocked her over and they both went crashing down the stairs. Dandra reached out with her mind, grabbing at the walls as they rushed past—and at Singe as he tumbled with her. Stones bashed her arms and legs, bruising her to the bone.

Singe yelled out once, then grunted and gasped, his limbs flailing. Solid ground hit Dandra hard in the chest. Singed slammed down beside and across her. The heel of a boot was like a fist in her back. For a second, it seemed that she couldn't breath, but she forced her arms to move, to push against the ground, to flip her over as fire flared above, the only light in the darkness.

Hruucan was on the stairs and rushing down at her like an explosion, his face a mask of hatred. Dandra grabbed for Singe and held on tight as she pushed hard against the base of the stairs with all of her fading mental strength.

The stone was unyielding. The rough floor scrapped at Dandra's legs as she and Singe shot backward—and into the chamber that held Taruuzh's tomb.

The howls of the ghost, stirred back to rage by Dah'mir's presence above, rose to a pitch. Frigid wind seized them instantly, dragging another gasp from Singe. His eyes snapped open in shock and he sucked in a choking breath. "Dandra! What—?"

He didn't have a chance to finish and Dandra didn't have a chance to reply. Caught up in his pursuit, Hruucan came plunging through the door and across the chamber. Dandra felt the heat of him flash across her face.

Taruuzh's howls broke—then reformed. Words emerged from the wind, harsh and unearthly. Dandra hadn't been able to understand what the ghost had said before and she still couldn't, but his voice held such anger that it seemed to freeze her spirit. She clung to Singe and he clung to her, both of them watching as the ghost recognized his true enemy.

Hruucan's voice rose in a scream as icy winds sucked the heat from his flames. It seemed to Dandra that he tried to fight back—one unliving thing struggling against another—but there was nothing for him to attack and nothing for him to burn. The fire of his tentacles swirled and streamed away. The light of his flames vanished, but a cold glow filled the air like moonlight on a winter night.

Hruucan staggered and turned like someone lost in a storm. The fluid motion of his limbs turned stiff and ungainly, until Dandra couldn't be certain whether he was still moving himself or if he was just a burned corpse held upright by the wind. Taruuzh's rage didn't stop, though. The rushing air scoured at Hruucan's charred flesh and a black blizzard of ash filled the chamber. Dandra choked and covered her mouth and eyes, pressing Singe's face against her body to shield him. Big pieces of something brittle and light fluttered across her like a storm of moths.

Then the howling wind was calm. The chamber was silent. The air that touched her was sharp in its chill, but not biting. Dandra opened her eyes and lifted her head. In her arms, Singe did the same.

Ashes lay in the crevices of the chamber and in the lee of their bodies like drifts of dark snow. The moonlight glow of the air caught on a slowly settling haze of fine dust. Hruucan had been torn apart.

In front of Taruuzh's tomb, a hobgoblin stood watching them, his body gray and translucent like old ice. His mouth moved and sighing words of Goblin stirred the ash. Dandra still couldn't understand them, though there no longer seemed to be anger in them. It didn't appear that the ghost cared whether she understood or not. His voice sighed once more, then he seemed to drift apart like warm breath on cold air.

The light faltered and faded with him. In the darkness, Singe found his voice. "Twelve moons," he croaked. "Are we still alive?"

Dandra kissed him.

CHAPTER

21

They left the chamber of Taruuzh's tomb and climbed back up the stairs by the glow of a light conjured by Singe, each of them leaning on the other for support. As Singe's light finally flashed on the roof and walls of the upper passage, Ashi's voice echoed down to them. *"Rond betch!* You're alive! What happened to Hruucan?"

"Taruuzh got in another battle against the servants of Xoriat," said Dandra.

She mounted the last few steps then gratefully reached for Ashi's hand as the hunter extended her arm. She couldn't hold back a gasp of surprise, though, at the sight of Ashi's skin. What she had glimpsed as shadowy stripes in the chaos of combat were actually bold and colorful lines that patterned her arms and her face.

"Il-Yannah, Ashi! That's a dragonmark!"

"It's a Siberys dragonmark," Singe said, accepting the support of Ashi's other arm. "The Siberys mark of Sentinel. I don't think there's going to be any question of whether you're part of House Deneith now, Ashi."

Ashi looked at Dandra. "It just happened," she said. "When Dah'mir called you to him, I tried to stop you but I couldn't quite reach you. I wanted to protect you more than anything else—and suddenly it was like something woke up inside me. It felt like I burned my fingers where I touched you, but instead . . ."

Dandra remembered the brush of the hunter's touch on her

back. She drew a long breath. "You did protect me, Ashi. Whatever power is in that dragonmark, it was enough to break Dah'mir's hold on me."

"And Tetkashtai's hold on your powers?"

The breath Dandra had drawn hissed out. "Not exactly," she said slowly.

Singe blinked. "Don't tell me it reversed what Dah'mir did to you?" He stiffened. "No—if it had, you'd be Tetkashtai."

Dandra raised her chin. "I'm not," she said, then touched the dead crystal around her neck. "Not much anyway. I started out as part of Tetkashtai—now she's part of me. I absorbed her."

"She's dead?"

"Only the worst of her."

"Twelve bloody moons."

They emerged into the great chamber of Taruuzh Kraat and Dandra stared at the scene revealed as Singe's magical light joined guttering torchlight. Tzaryan Rrac, his chest and arm still burned, and Robrand d'Deneith, his face pale and his eyes hard, had their backs against the platform where the grieving tree had stood, held at bay by Geth. Wrath's blade reflected only a dull purple gleam. Natrac, looking drained and weak, leaned against the platform as well, while on top of it, Ekhaas crouched over Orshok. As Dandra watched, she pressed a hand to the young orc's chest and lifted her head in song. Once again, Dandra felt the raw energy of the *duur'kala's* magic tug at her. Orshok spasmed and he cried out, but Ekhaas looked satisfied.

"He'll survive," she said.

Singe choked and cursed again. "Geth, what are you doing?"

"Holding prisoners," the shifter growled. Singe let go of Ashi's arm and staggered over to him.

"You're not holding anybody," he said. "First—that's Robrand." The wizard pulled Geth's sword arm down, then pointed at Tzaryan. "Second—he's an ogre mage. He can fly. Your sword's not stopping him."

Geth looked confused, then bared his teeth. "What's he still doing here then?"

"I didn't become a warlord of Droaam by not knowing when to talk instead of fight," said Tzaryan. He drew himself up straight and his black eyes glittered. "Dah'mir abandoned me. I can't forgive that. You're no friends to me, but it seems to me that the greatest revenge I can inflict on him is to let you go."

"Let *us* go?" asked Geth. He started to raise his sword, but Singe pushed it down again.

"Agreed," he said. He stepped aside and gestured for the ogre mage to leave. Tzaryan bent his head.

"I'll leave horses and your gear by the gates of my keep. Take them and ride. I don't want to see you again." He looked at Ekhaas and added, "You would be wise to go, too. My ogres are going to have orders to kill you on sight."

Ekhaas's ears stood up straight and her hand twitched toward her sword, but Tzaryan turned his back on her and strode toward the stairs out of the great chamber. After a few paces, though, he paused and glanced over his shoulder, frowning. "General, aren't you coming with me?"

Dandra saw surprise pass over Robrand's face. "My lord? I failed you."

"My ogres failed me, General," said Tzaryan. "They ran. You're still here."

Robrand stiffened and stood tall. "My feelings for Etan led me to conceal what I knew of his purpose here, my lord."

Tzaryan's eyes narrowed. "You said that you had given them no information or aid to dishonor our contract. Is that the truth?"

Robrand nodded tightly.

Tzaryan's wide mouth curved into a somber frown. "Knowledge is gold to those who value it," he said, "and I value what the lords of Deneith would cast aside. But your old command is gone, Robrand. I expect your full loyalty. Say your farewells."

Robrand gave him another curt nod and turned to Singe. To Dandra it seemed that the hard, cold man she had first met in Vralkek had returned—the warm friend who had shared stories with them on the road was gone once more. Singe seemed to see that change, too. For a moment, he looked lost. "Robrand," he said, "you don't have to stay. Come with us. I understand why you didn't think you could do anything—"

The old man's lined face tightened. "If you understood, Etan, you wouldn't speak of it. I have a contract to honor. And you—" His eyes darted past Singe to rest briefly on Geth. "—you have friends."

Singe's lips pressed together for a moment, then he stood respect and bent his head. "It was a pleasure to serve with you, commander," he said, his voice thick with emotion. "You are the most honorable man I've ever known."

An image of Geth, bound and bloodied in Tzaryan's dungeon, rose in Dandra's memory and anger made her catch her breath. Geth, though, glanced over his shoulder and shook his head sharply. *Don't say anything,* he mouthed silently. Dandra reached out and touched his mind with *kesh. Why not?* she demanded.

Because Singe doesn't need to know right now, Geth told her. *He's already saying good-bye to a hero.*

Dandra watched Robrand return Singe's nod—and turn away, falling in at Tzaryan's side and climbing out of the great chamber without saying anything more. Pain filled Singe's eyes as he watched his old commander go. Dandra's anger faded. She stepped forward and put her hand on Singe's shoulder. "We should leave, too," she said.

The night was cool when they stepped out of Taruuzh Kraat. Dandra, Geth, and Ekhaas stared in amazement at the open trench that the entrance to ancient ruins had become. "Dah'mir," Singe said wearily.

"*Khaavolaar,*" said Ekhaas.

Singe looked out into the night. Dah'mir's herons were gone, perhaps after their vanished master. Tzaryan and Robrand were already distant figures, well on their way back to the looming bulk of Tzaryan Keep. The old man and the ogre mage had made much better time through the long passage than their wounded group had. He looked back at the others and counted the toll that their confrontation had taken. He felt weak, his very spirit lashed by Hruucan's draining touch. Dandra was battered and bruised and looked utterly exhausted. Geth was as bloody as a surgeon and held his gauntlet arm gingerly. Natrac looked pale and drained. Thanks to Ekhaas's magic, Orshok was conscious again, but the druid would need more healing before he could walk—Ekhaas and Ashi carried him between them. Only the hunter and the hobgoblin had escaped injury.

And injuries weren't the highest price they had paid. Although they'd been strangely vague about how they'd come to join together and make their escape from Tzaryan Keep, Dandra and Geth had told him everything they'd discovered in the caves. Singe looked up at the moons and stars overhead, at the Ring of Siberys bright in the southern sky, and tried to hold back a grimace. He failed.

"What is it?" Dandra asked.

Singe's shoulders slumped and he looked back at her. "We're back where we were after the Bonetree mound," he said. "Dah'mir is gone and we're helpless."

"He probably thinks we're dead this time, though," said Natrac. "We don't have to worry about him looking for us—or for Dandra."

"I'd rather he was," Dandra said. She planted the charred shaft of her spear in the ground. "It would mean I was still his only link to raising a new line of servants for his master. Now he's got Taruuzh's stones."

A wave of exhaustion passed through Singe. A big chunk of mortared stones torn from Taruuzh Kraat's walls lay nearby. He sat down on it and rested his forehead on his palms. His fingers tangled in his hair. "We were so close. We found out so much and Dah'mir still beat us. Now we've lost him again. It's just like before. He's gone and we don't know where he is."

"We have a clue though," said Geth.

Singe raised his head sharply to look at the shifter. The others turned to look at him as well. Geth put his hand on the hilt of his Dhakaani sword. "It looks like Goblin isn't the only language Wrath understands. Whatever language that was that Dah'mir spoke to Hruucan in before he and Vennet vanished, Wrath put his words into my head. Dah'mir told Hruucan to meet him in the bright blade after we were dead."

"The bright blade?" Singe asked. "What's that?"

"Not what," said Ekhaas. "Where. Wrath translated Dah'mir's words too well." The hobgoblin raised her head proudly. "In Goblin, 'bright blade' is *ja'shaarat*—and Ja'shaarat was one of the greatest cities of the Empire of Dhakaan."

"Where is it?" asked Geth.

"Beneath a human city," Ekhaas said. "Ja'shaarat became the foundations of Sharn."

"Light of il-Yannah." Horror bloomed on Dandra's face. "Sharn holds the largest population of kalashtar in Khorvaire! That must be why Dah'mir's gone there." She stood straight. "We have to stop him. We have to warn the kalashtar."

"Kalashtar aren't the only ones in danger." Orshok struggled to sit up in Ekhaas's and Ashi's arms. His eyes were bright and sharp with lingering pain, but determined as well. "The Gatekeepers need to know that the Master of Silence is active!"

Singe sucked in his breath and looked at Dandra and Geth. "Which one?"

"Both," Geth said grimly. "We're going to have to split up." His eyes shifted between Singe and Dandra. "You two go to Sharn. I'll go to the Shadow Marches with Orshok and find Batul." He glanced at Ashi. "You know the Marches, too—"

The hunter shook her head. "I need to stay with Dandra," she said. She held up her free hand and the swirls of her dragonmark seemed to dance in the moonlight. "I'm the only one who can protect her from Dah'mir's power."

"I'll go to Sharn, too," said Natrac. The half-orc moved to stand beside Singe. "It's been a while, but I still know the city."

Singe nodded. Geth growled under his breath. "Two of us. I guess it doesn't take more than that to carry news—"

"Three," Ekhaas said abruptly. Geth started and Singe raised his eyebrows. Ekhaas's ears twitched back. "I know the stories," she said. "Someone needs to tell the Gatekeepers their history."

Geth spread his hands. "Three, then."

Singe felt a plan rising inside him, pushing back the despair he had felt only moments before. They weren't helpless anymore and Dah'mir hadn't gotten away from them after all—at least not entirely. They still had a task ahead of them. He pushed himself up from his seat. "We can take the road back to Vralkek," he said. "We'll be there in a few days and we should be able to find some kind of transport to Sharn and Zarash'ak."

Ekhaas shook her head. "Unless you find a Lyrandar elemental galleon again, a ship to Zarash'ak will take you almost as long as traveling overland." She pointed off to the northwest. "I know this part of Droaam. I can get us to the edge of the Shadow Marches."

"And I know the Marches," said Orshok. "We can travel fast.

Going back to Vralkek would be a waste of time for us."

Silence fell over the group as the druid's words sank into each of them. "So," said Dandra after a moment, "we part here."

"Aye," said Geth. "I suppose so. After we collect our gear from the keep." He rocked from foot to foot uncomfortably. "I'll send a message if I can. House Orien post from Zarash'ak to Sharn."

"Send it to the Deneith enclave in Deathsgate district. I know a Blademarks recruiter there." Singe looked at Geth—then swallowed his pride and stepped up to the shifter. "Geth, I'm sorry for what I said in Tzaryan's dungeon. I shouldn't have told everyone about Narath like that."

Geth stiffened and Singe hurried to force out everything he wanted to say. "You weren't ready to talk and I wasn't ready to listen. I think I am now. Whatever happened in Narath, I've realized something. I know you're no coward." He spread his arms and said again, "I'm sorry."

For a moment, Geth just stared at him with hard, flat eyes and Singe wondered if maybe he shouldn't have said anything at all.

Then Geth lunged forward, wrapping his arms around him, and squeezing him in a rib-cracking embrace. "Took you long enough, you bastard!" he said. Singe wheezed from the pressure and staggered when Geth let him go, but the shifter swung an arm around his shoulders and held him up, leaning close to murmur in his ear, "Tak."

"You're welcome." Singe straightened up painfully.

EPILOGUE

There had been no more trouble since the Revered had returned to the ancestor mound, then vanished again, taking his fiery Hand with him. Still, Breff had seen enough to be wary. For three days and nights after the Revered's brief appearance, he'd sat watch in a hidden place among the remains of the Bonetree camp, staring at the scorched battlefield before the mound, watching corpses fester and the scavengers come to call. Just before dawn after the third night, he'd risen, weak with hunger and delirious from lack of sleep, and made his way across the battlefield. Ravens and jackals had watched him pass, not even bothering to rise from their decaying feast.

At the mouth of the mound, he'd kindled a new honor fire and sat with it, half-dreading the reappearance of the dolgaunt with his flaming tentacles. Nothing happened though and as the sun rose, he had let loose one of the fluting calls of the Bonetree clan. The camp was safe again. The clan could return.

There hadn't been much to return to, but there wasn't much left of the clan, either. They'd moved into the charred remnants of the camp, buried their dead and scoured the battlefield, and begun to reclaim their lives.

As the moons soared overhead on the finest night for many weeks, Breff sat back beside a campfire, his favorite drinking bowl—recovered from the burned camp—in his hand, and looked up at the sky. He was the huntmaster now. The clan was his to command, to keep ready for the Revered's return. If the Revered returned . . .

He buried the thought. The Revered *would* return. He hadn't abandoned the Bonetree, no matter what some of the hunters who had fled after the fiery Hand's attacks might have said. "*Su Drumas*," he murmured to himself, "*Su Darasvhir*." For the Bonetree. For the Dragon Below.

He sipped from the bowl. It held only water flavored with rotto stem. His first command to the clan, he decided, would be to begin brewing beer again. His second would be to track down and bring back the cowards who had fled—

His eyes happened to be on the ancestor mound when silver-white light burst out of the air in front of it.

Breff jumped so sharply that water sprayed his face and ran down his chest, but he was on his feet in an instant. In the moonlight, he could see a dark figure staggering drunkenly before the mound. It fell, forced itself up, then fell again.

Others in the camp had seen the light, too. There were shouts of fear. The few surviving dogs that had stayed with the clan broke into mad howls. Those inside tents and makeshift huts threw themselves at thin walls; those outside fled into the night.

Breff watched the strange figure take another staggering step—then vanish into a second flare of light. The glare winked out but something lingered on the air for a moment longer, a wordless song like distant knife blades falling in a ringing, musical cascade.

A hunter barely old enough to have earned the name rushed up to him out of the shadows. "*Breff! Tokrii eche?*" she said in panic.

Cold fear spread through Breff's belly. Coming back to the camp and the mound had been a mistake. Maybe the hunters who had fled were right. Maybe the Revered had abandoned them. His eyes swept the night and he snatched up his drinking bowl.

"*Che bo gri lanano ani teith,*" he whispered.

They'd been wrong to come back here. The mound was cursed—he wouldn't keep the clan here to suffer another attack by the fiery Hand or something even worse. He turned and pushed past the young hunter, running through the recently restored camp and shouting orders for the last remnants of the Bonetree to gather their belongings and prepare to flee.

GLOSSARY

Adar: A small nation on the continent of Sarlona. Homeland of the kalashtar.

Adolan: A druid of the Gatekeeper sect, killed in the Bonetree clan's attack on Bull Hollow.

Ashi: A former hunter of the Bonetree, she has turned her back on the clan after discovering her descent from House Deneith. She wields a ceremonial honor blade granted to her ancestor by House Deneith.

ashi: A dark gold reed. The inhabitants of the Shadow Marches use its starchy pith to make a type of bread.

Aundair: One of the original Five Nations of Galifar, Aundair houses the seat of the Arcane Congress and the University of Wyrnarn. Currently under the rule of Queen Aurala ir'Wyrnarn.

Azhani: The language shared by the human clans of the Shadow Marches.

ban: A goblin expression of non-commital agreement, roughly equivalent to "yeah" or "your funeral."

Barrel, the: An inn and taproom in Vralkek.

Batul: An elder orc druid of the Gatekeeper sect and the spiritual leader of the Fat Tusk tribe. He is blind in one eye, but gifted with prophetic dreams.

Bear: A cultural hero figure among shifters based on one of the animal forms of their lycanthrope ancestors. Usually referred to as "Cousin," Bear embodies the attributes of strength and caution.

Bibahronaz, Bava: A human woman of Zarash'ak, originally of the Howling Rabbit clan. Under the name Bava Bahron, she is an artist known across the Five Nations for her paintings.

Bibahronaz, Diad: One of Bava's sons. A half-orc.

Bibahronaz, Mine: One of Bava's daughters. A half-orc and twin of Ose.

Bibahronaz, Ose: One of Bava's daughters. A half-orc and twin of Mine.

Blademarks: The mercenary's guild of House Deneith.

bo: Azhani for "a place, a piece of land or an area."

Boar: A cultural hero figure among shifters based on one of the animal forms of their lycanthrope ancestors. Usually referred to as "Cousin," Boar represents tremendous endurance, but also unrestrained and reckless enthusiasm.

Bonetree clan: A human barbarian clan of the Shadow Marches, worshipers of the Dragon Below. The heart of their territory is an enormous earthen mound built over generations. The Azhani term is *Drumasaz*.

Breff: Huntmaster of the Bonetree clan.

Bull Hollow A hamlet on the far western edge of the Eldeen Reaches, devastated in an attack by Bonetree hunters and dolgrims in pursuit of Dandra.

byeshk: A rare metal, hard and dense with a purple sheen. Weapons made of byeshk are capable of inflicting great injuries on daelkyr and their creations.

By the six kings!: A Dhakaani oath of sincerity.

chaat'or: Goblin for "defiler" in loose translation. In specific use, it refers to races not native to Khorvaire, especially humans. Elves, an ancient enemy of the Dhakaani Empire, are not considered *chaat'oor*.

Che bo gri lanano ani teith: An Azhani expression: "This place is haunted." Literally, "This land remembers its blood."

Che Haranait Koa shenio otoio ches Ponhansit Itanchi: An Azhani phrase from a legend of the Bonetree clan: "The Hall of the Revered is below the Spires of the Forge."

chuul: Monstrous creatures larger than a man, resembling huge crayfish with four powerful legs and enormous claws. The tentacles surrounding a chuul's mouth are capable of paralyzing its prey.

Chuut: An ogre among the troops of Tzaryan Keep, lieutenant to the General.

Cira: A beautiful woman with some skill in magic.

cross: A card game based on bluffing.

crysteel: An alloy created from iron and a rare crystalline substance. Crysteel is used to make weapons favored by those skilled in psionics.

d'Deneith, Robrand: A dragonmarked heir of House Deneith, once leader of the Frostbrand company of the Blademarks, disgraced after the Massacre at Narath.

d'Deneith, Toller: A dragonmarked heir of House Deneith, nephew to Robrand d'Deneith. Killed in the defense of Bull Hollow.

d'Lyrandar, Marolis: A dragonmarked half-elf of House Lyrandar. The junior officer on *Lightning on Water*.

d'Lyrandar, Vennet: A dragonmarked half-elf of House Lyrandar, captain of *Lightning on Water* and secretly a follower of the Cults of the Dragon Below.

daelkyr: Powerful lords of Xoriat, the daelkyr are madness and corruption personified. After the Daelkyr War, surviving daelkyr on Eberron were bound in the depths of Khyber by Gatekeeper druids.

Daelkyr War: An invasion of Eberron by creatures from Xoriat, led by the daelkyr, approximately nine thousand years before the present. Centered around the Shadow Marches, it ended with the defeat of the daelkyr by the united forces of the orcs of the Shadow Marches and the hobgoblins of the Empire of Dhakaan, but left both races decimated.

Da ga shek erat: An orc expression of rage, not fit for translation.

dagga: An orc expression of affirmation commonly used by folk of Zarash'ak. A more intense version, *Kuv dagga!* is akin to swearing a minor oath.

Dah'mir: A shapechanging dragon and a priest of the Dragon Below. Once leader of the Bonetree clan.

dahr: An Adaran expression for something or someone vile; pl. *dahri*.

Dal Quor: Another plane of existence, the Region of Dreams. Mortal spirits are said to journey to Dal Quor when they dream. Kalashtar are the descendants of refugee spirits from Dal Quor who bonded with human hosts in order to enter Eberron.

Dandra: Superficially a kalashtar, Dandra is actually the consciousness of a psicrystal inhabiting the body of her creator, Tetkashtai. She wears a yellow-green crystal containing Tetkashtai, wields a spear forged from crysteel, and specializes in whitefire, augmented by her skill with *vayhatana*.

Darguun: A nation of goblinoids, founded in 969 YK when a hobgoblin leader named Haruuc formed an alliance among the goblinoid mercenaries and annexed a section of southern Cyre. Breland recognized this new nation in exchange for a peaceful border and an ally against Cyre. Few people trust the people of Darguun, but their soldiers remain a force to be reckoned with.

dashoor: A goblinoid artificer, especially one from the time of the Empire of Dhakaan. The secret knowledge of the *dashoor* has largely vanished, but at one time they were capable of creating wonders. Most *dashoor* were male.

Deneith, House: A dragonmark house bearing the Mark of Sentinel. House Deneith operates services offering various forms of protection, including the mercenary companies of the Blademarks and the law enforcement services of the Sentinel Marshals.

Dhakaani Empire: *see Empire of Dhakaan.*

Do hiffi eche?: Azhani phrase: "Do you smell that?"

Dol Arrah turn away!: An expression of righteous violence.

dolgaunt: Horrid creatures created by the daelkyr from hobgoblins during the Daelkyr War, dolgaunts have long, powerful tentacles springing from their shoulders. They have no eyes but perceive their surroundings through sensitive cilia that cover their skin.

dolgrim: Foot soldiers in the armies of the daelkyr, dolgrims were created by the daelkyr from goblins. A dolgrim has four arms and two mouths and resembles two goblins crushed together.

Dragon Below, The: *see Khyber*

dragonmark: 1) A mystical mark that appears on the surface of the skin and grants mystical powers to its bearer. 2) A slang term for the bearer of a dragonmark.

dragonshard: A form of mineral with mystical properties, said to be a shard of one of the great progenitor dragons. There are three different types of shard, each with different properties. A shard has no abilities in and of itself, but an artificer or wizard can use a shard to create an object with useful effects. *Siberys shards* fall from the sky and have the potential to enhance the power of dragonmarks. *Eberron shards* are found in the soil and enhance traditional magic. *Khyber shards* are found deep below the surface of the world and are used as a focus binding mystical energy.

Droaam: A nation on the west coast of Khorvaire. Once claimed by Breland, this region was never settled by humans and was known as a wild land filled with all manner of monsters and creatures that had been pushed back by the spreading power of Galifar. In 986 YK there was a movement to organize the creatures of Droaam into a coherent nation. While this has met with some success, the new nation has yet to be recognized by any other country.

d'Tharashk, Chain: A dragonmarked bounty hunter of House Tharashk.

duur'kala: Among the goblinoid tribes that consider themselves heirs to the lost Empire of Dhakaan, *duur'kala* preserve the history and knowledge of past ages. Their music is the most common form of magic among the tribes. *Duur'kala* means "dirge singers." Because the magical power manifest mostly in females, *duur'kala* are sometimes refered to as "daughters of the dirge."

Eberron: 1) The world. 2) A mythical dragon said to have formed the world from her body in primordial times and to have given birth to natural life. Also known as "The Dragon Between." See *Khyber, Siberys*.

Ekhaas: A hobgoblin woman and a *duur'kala* of the Kech Volaar. Self-declared guardian of the Dhakaani ruins in the vicinity of Tzaryan Keep and Vralkek.

Eldeen Reaches: Once this term was used to describe the vast stretches of woodland found on the west coast of Khorvaire, inhabited mostly by nomadic shifter tribes and druidic sects. In 958 YK the people of western Aundair broke ties with the Audairian crown and joined their lands to the

Eldeen Reaches, vastly increasing the population of the nation and bringing it into the public eye. Inhabitants are known as Reachers. Among themselves, Reachers refer to their homeland as "the Eldeen."

Empire of Dhakaan: An ancient empire ruled by hobgoblins, the Empire of Dhakaan stretched across southern Khorvaire millennia before the arrival of humans. Dhakaan was weaked by the Daelkyr War and collapsed about six thousand years before the present.

Fat Tusk: A tribe of orcs living in the Shadow Marches.

Feita: A pompous gnome woman.

Frostbrand: A Blademarks company of House Deneith, commanded by Robrand d'Deneith, specializing in wilderness and winter operations. It was disbanded after the Massacre at Narath.

gaeth'ad: An orcish herbal tea that can be brewed with a variety of effects. Popular in the Shadow Marches and among members of House Tharashk. Generally brewed and served by the master of a *gaeth'ad* house.

Gatekeepers: A sect of druids, originators of the druidic tradition in the Shadow Marches and the Eldeen Reaches. Originally formed to defend Eberron from invasion by Xoriat during the Daelkyr War, they watch over the seals that bind the daelkyr in Khyber.

General, the: A myserious veteran of the Last War, hired by Tzaryan Rrac to train and command his ogre troops.

Geth: A shifter veteran of the Last War, he served with the Frostbrand until the Massacre at Narath. He wields a magewrought gauntlet that is both shield and weapon and an ancient Dhakaani byeshk blade recovered from Jhegesh Dol.

Ghaash'nena: A legendary orc spirit, the ghostly protector of lost children.

goblinoid: Common term for a member of one of the three goblin races—goblins, hobgoblins, and bugbears.

Graywall: A city in Droaam at the border with Breland, considered the gateway to the kingdom of monsters.

hiff: Azhani for "to smell."

Hruucan: A dolgaunt in the service of Dah'mir, he was killed by Singe's fire magic but has been reborn as a fiery undead creature driven by his need for revenge.

illithid: An abomination from Xoriat, the plane of madness. An illithid is roughly the same size and shape as a human but possesses a squidlike head with tentacles arrayed around a fanged maw. Illithids feed on the brains of sentient creatures and possess the ability to paralyze or manipulate the minds of lesser creatures. Illithids are more commonly known as mind flayers.

il-Yannah: A word from the Quor tongue, translating to "the Great Light." This mystical force is the focus of the religion of the kalashtar.

Itaa!: A goblin war-command equivalent to "Attack!"

itanchi: Azhani for a spire or other tall, narrow structure.

Jhegesh Dol: A stretch of haunted swamp in the Shadow Marches, once the site of a daelkyr stronghold during the Daelkyr War.

Jorasco, House: A dragonmarked house bearing the Mark of Healing. House Jorasco dominates the healing arts in Khorvaire.

Kagishi: A gnoll guide operating out of Vralkek.

kalashtar: The kalashtar are an offshoot of humanity. Stories say that the kalashtar are humans touched by spirits from another plane of existence and that they possess strange mental powers.

Karrlakton: A large city in Karrnath. Location of the headquarters of House Deneith.

Karrnath: One of the original Five Nations of Galifar. Karrnath is a cold, grim land whose people are renowned for their martial prowess. The current ruler of Karrnath is King Kaius ir'Wynarn III.

Karth: A sailor on *Lightning on Water*.

Kech Volar: A clan among the goblinoids of Darguun dedicated to the preservation of the lore of the Dhakaani Empire. Their name means "Wordbearers."

kesh: a kalashtar term for the telepathic mindlink all kalashtar can create with other beings.

Khorvaire: One of the continents of Eberron.

Khyber: 1) The underworld. 2) A mythical dragon, also known as "The Dragon Below." After killing Siberys, Khyber was imprisoned by Eberron and transformed into the underworld. Khyber is said to have given birth to a host of demons and other unnatural creatures. See *Eberron, Siberys.*

Kirvakri: An alias adopted by Dandra.

koa: Azhani for "a great place," especially a large, permanent structure but also a place of magical power.

Krepis: An orc of the Fat Tusk tribe and a druid of the Gatekeeper sect. A student of Batul.

kraat: Goblin for "a smithy."

Kuun, Duulan: A hero of the Dhakaani Empire, first warlord of the name Kuun and a friend of Taruuzh.

Kuun, Rakari: A hero of the Dhakaani Empire, slayer of the daelkyr lord of Jhegesh Dol.

lanan: Azhani for "to remember." An archaic form.

Last War, The: This conflict began in 894 YK with the death of King Jarot ir'Wynarn, the last king of Galifar. Following Jarot's death, three of his five children refused to follow the ancient traditions of succession, and the kingdom split. The war lasted over a hundred years, and it took the utter destruction of Cyre to bring the other nations to the negotiating table. No one has admitted defeat, but no one wants to risk being the next victim of the Mourning. The chronicles are calling the conflict "the Last War," hoping that the bloodshed might have finally slaked humanity's thirst for battle. Only time will tell if this hope is in vain.

lhesh: A Goblin term for a warlord.

Lhesh shaarat: Goblin expression for "a warlord's sword." *Lhesh shaarat* are swords of high quality and distinctive design and are often magical.

Lightning on Water: A House Lyrandar elemental galleon. Instead of sails, an elemental galleon uses a bound air elemental for propulsion.

long step: A kalashtar term for psionic teleportation.

Lor: An ogre torturer in the dungeon of Tzaryan Keep.

Lyrandar, House: A dragonmarked house bearing the Mark of Storm. House Lyrandar has economic control of shipping in Khorvaire.

APPENDIX

Marg: A goblin *daashor*, apprentice to Taruuzh.

Medalashana: A kalashtar. Once a companion of Tetkashtai and Virikhad, she was later driven mad by Dah'mir, turned to his service, and renamed Medala. She was destroyed in a psionic battle with Virikhad after Dandra forced his psicrystal into her hand. She specialized in the art of telepathy.

Metrol: The capital of Cyre. Metrol was destroyed by the Mourning.

mootu: Juicy, sweet bite-size morsels with a meaty texture. A delicacy among orcs. Possibly a breed of slugs.

Moza: A scarred goblin of Vralkek.

Narath: A river town in northern Karrnath, close to the coast of the Bitter Sea. Destroyed in 989 YK in the infamous Massacre at Narath.

Natrac: A half-orc of Zarash'ak who deals in indentured servants. Vennet kidnapped him and cut off his hand, using him as bait in a trap to capture Dandra for Dah'mir. He wears a prosthesis capped with a long knife.

nena: Orc for "mother."

Ner: A previous huntmaster of the Bonetree clan, killed by Medala. He was Ashi's father.

Orshok: A young orc druid of the Fat Tusk tribe, a student of Batul, and curious about the world beyond the Shadow Marches. He carries a hunda stick, a traditional orc weapon and tool resembling a staff with a hooked end.

otoio: Azhani for "below" or "beneath."

poli: Orc for "please."

pon: Azhani for "metal."

ponhan: Azhani for "forge."

Preesh: A goblin in the service of Chain d'Tharashk.

psicrystal: A sentient crystal created by psions as a tool and companion. Each psicrystal is a unique reflection of the psion who created it.

psion: Someone who is skilled in the art of psionics, the power of the mind. Kalashtar are natural psions, able to manifest the telepathic link they call the *kesh*. Many go on to master greater skills.

Raat shan gath'kal dor: A *duur'kala* expression meaning "The story stops but never ends." A formulaic ending to goblin legends.

Rat: A cultural hero figure among shifters based on one of the animal forms of their lycanthrope ancestors. Usually referred to as "Grandfather," he is depicted as a cunning and stealthy trickster. "Grandfather Rat!" is a common expression of frustration.

rohan: Azhani for "to make."

Rond betch!: Azhani expression of surprise or anger. Literally, "Fierce darkness!"

rotto: A plant of the Shadow Marches with a hard, woody stem used to make a cosmetic treatment. Quite rare and valuable.

Rrac, Tzaryan: An ogre mage warlord of Droaam, one of the first warlords to embrace the rule of the Daughters of Sora Kell when they seized power in 987 YK. He controls a large territory in southern Droaam, dominating local orc tribes with his ogre warriors. His symbol is a blue star.

run: Azhani for "true." Sometimes applied as a prefix to nouns to indicate authenticity or veracity, as in *runsheid*—a true hunter.

Ryl: An experienced half-orc guide operating out of Vralkek.

Sarlona: One of the continents of Eberron. Humanity arose in Sarlona, and colonists from Sarlona established human civilization on Khorvaire.

Sentinel Marshals: The dragonmarked House Deneith is the primary source for mercenary soldiers and bodyguards in Khorvaire. The Sentinel Marshals are a specialized form of mercenary—bounty hunters empowered to enforce the laws of Galifar across Khorvaire. This right was granted by the King of Galifar, but when Galifar collapsed the rulers of the Five Nations agreed to let the Sentinel Marshals pursue their prey across all nations, to maintain a neutral lawkeeping force that would be respected throughout Khorvaire. See *House Deneith*.

shaarat: Goblin for "a blade," especially a sword.

Shadow Marches: A region of desolate swamps on the southwestern coast of Khorvaire. The Shadow Marches have a strange connection to Xoriat and were at the center of the Daelkyr War many millennia ago.

Sharn: Also known as the City of Towers, Sharn is the largest city in Khorvaire.

Shay, Timin: An alias used by Singe. Taken from the name of a friend who died in childood.

shekot: An orc expression, roughly equivalent to "inconsiderate ass."

sheni: Azhani for "to be somewhere" or to be found at a location.

shifter: A humanoid race said to be descended from humans and lycanthropes. Shifters have a feral, bestial appearance and can briefly call on their lycanthropic heritage to draw animalistic characteristics to the fore.

Siberys: 1) The ring of stones that circle the world; seen as a shining band like clustered stars in the southern sky. 2) A mythical dragon, also called "The Dragon Above." Siberys is said to have been destroyed by Khyber. Some believe that the Ring of Siberys is the source of all magic.

Siberys mark: The most powerful form of a dragonmark. Extremely rare.

Singe: An Aundairian wizard specializing in both fire magic and swordsmanship. A lieutenant in the Blademarks, he served with the Frostbrand company until the Massacre at Narath. His real name is Etan Bayard, but he prefers his nickname.

Sovereign Host, the: a religion found across much of Khorvaire. The Lord of the Host are Arawai (god of agriculture), Aureon (god of law and knowledge), Balinor (god of beasts and the hunt), Boldrei (god of community and hearth), Dol Arrah (god of honor and sacrifice), Dol Dorn (god of strength at arms), Kol Korran (god of trade and wealth), Olladra (god of good fortune), and Onatar (god of artifice and the forge).

tak: a Reacher expression for "thank you"; "twice tak" is "thank you very much."

Taruuzh: A legendary Dhakaani *daashor.*

Tetkashtai: A kalashtar spirit imprisoned in a psicrystal by Dah'mir in an effort to drive her mad. While trapped in the psicrystal, she is virtually powerless. Dandra needs her help to use her psionic powers fully.

Tharashk, House: A dragonmarked house bearing the Mark of Finding. House Tharashk is known for its bounty hunters, inquisitives, and dragonshard prospectors.

Tiger: A cultural hero figure among shifters based on one of the animal forms of their lycanthrope ancestors. Tiger is noble being, a warrior of incomparable grace and speed. Unlike the other shifter culture-heroes, no relation is ever claimed to Tiger. "Tiger's blood!" is a common oath of anger.

tochit: Azhani for "without," meaning specifically lacking a quality.

Tomollan: A young Brelish man.

Treykin: A member of the Frostbrand company killed at Narath.

tribex: A heavily-muscled antelope-like creature with long, sharp horns. Used as a beast of burden in Darguun.

Tzaryan Keep: Stronghold of Tzaryan Rrac in Droaam.

Urthen: A servant in the employ of Natrac in Zarash'ak.

vayhatana: A kalashtar term for psionic telekinesis. Literally translated, it means "ghost breath."

Vralkek: A port town in Droaam, previously claimed by Breland. Ruins indicate that it was a settlement of the Empire of Dhakaan in the distant past.

Vvaraak: The black dragon who taught the first Gatekeepers and began the druidic tradition in western Khorvaire many thousands of years ago. She was also known as "the Scaled Apostate."

Webs, the: A network of platforms and rope bridges suspended among the pillars beneath Zarash'ak. It is the haunt of criminals and goblins.

whitefire: A kalashtar term for flame produced with psionics.

Wolf: A cultural hero figure among shifters based on one of the animal forms of their lycanthrope ancestors. Wolf is wise, honorable, and knowledgeable in the ways of magic. She is often referred to as "Grandmother" and "Grandmother Wolf!" is a common expression of awe.

Appendix

Xoriat: One of alternate planes, Xoriat is also known as the Realm of Madness. It is the home of the daelkyr and illithids, but has been held apart from Eberron since the end of the Daelkyr War thanks to the magic of the Gatekeepers.

Yrlag: A town on the Grithic River, the border between the Shadow Marches and the Eldeen Reaches. The westernmost port on southern Khorvaire, it is a barely civilized place and the trading center for much of this isolated region. Before humans arrived in Khorvaire, it was the westernmost outpost of the Empire of Dhakaan and the Dhakaani influence can still be seen in its oldest structure.

Zarash'ak: The capital of the Shadow Marches, often called the City of Stilts because of the architecture that raises it above the threat of floods.

ENTER THE NEW WORLD OF

THE
DREAMING DARK
TRILOGY

Written by Keith Baker
The winning voice of the DUNGEONS & DRAGONS® *setting search*

CITY OF TOWERS
Volume One

Hardened by the Last War, four soldiers have come to Sharn,
fabled City of Towers, capital of adventure. In a time of uneasy
peace, these hardened warriors must struggle to survive. And
then people start turning up dead. The heroes find themselves
in an adventure that will take them from the highest reaches of
power to the most sordid depths of the city of wonder, shadow,
and adventure.

THE SHATTERED LAND
Volume Two

The epic adventure continues as Daine and the remnants of
his company travel to the dark continent of Xen'drik on an
adventure that may kill them all.

ENTER THE EXCITING, NEW DUNGEONS AND DRAGONS® SETTING... THE WORLD OF

THE WAR~TORN TRILOGY

THE CRIMSON TALISMAN
Book 1

Adrian Cole

Erethindel, the fabled Crimson Talisman. Long sought by the forces of darkness. Long guarded in secret by one family. But now the secret has been revealed, and only one young man can keep it safe. As the talisman's powers awaken within him, Erethindel tears at his soul.

THE ORB OF XORIAT
Book 2

Edward Bolme

The Last War is over, and it took all that Teron ever had. A monk trained for war, he is the last of his Order. Now he is on a quest to find a powerful weapon that might set the world at war again.

TWO NEW SERIES EMERGE FROM THE RAVAGED WASTES OF... THE WORLD OF

THE
LOST MARK
TRILOGY

MARKED FOR DEATH
Book 1

Matt Forbeck

Twelve dragonmarks. Sigils of immense magical power. Born by scions of mighty Houses, used through the centuries to wield authority and shape wonders throughout the Eberron world. But there are only twelve marks. Until now. Matt Forbeck begins the terrifying saga of the thirteenth dragonmark . . . The Mark of Death.

THE
DRAGON BELOW
TRILOGY

THE BINDING STONE
Book 1

Don Bassingthwaite

A chance rescue brings old rivals together with a strange ally in a mission of vengeance against powers of ancient madness and corruption. But in the haunted forests of the Eldeen Reaches, even the most stalwart hero can soon find himself prey to the hidden horrors within the untamed wilderness.

ED GREENWOOD

THE CREATOR OF THE FORGOTTEN REALMS WORLD

BRINGS YOU THE STORY OF

SHANDRIL OF HIGHMOON

SHANDRIL'S SAGA

SPELLFIRE
Book I

Powerful enough to lay low a dragon or heal a wounded warrior, spellfire
is the most sought after power in all of Faerûn. And it is in the reluctant
hand of Shandril of Highmoon, a young, orphaned kitchen-lass.

CROWN OF FIRE
Book II

Shandril has grown to become one of the most powerful magic-users in
the land. The powerful Cult of the Dragon and the evil Zhentarim want
her spellfire, and they will kill whoever they must to possess it.

HAND OF FIRE
Book III

Shandril has spellfire, a weapon capable of destroying the world, and
now she's fleeing for her life across Faerûn, searching for somewhere to
hide. Her last desperate hope is to take refuge in the sheltered city of
Silverymoon. If she can make it.

www.wizards.com